ECHOES OF HOLLOW AND EMBER

TC JENSON

This is a work of fiction. Names, characters, places, and incidents are products of the author's imagination or are used fictitiously. Any resemblance to actual persons, living or dead, or actual events is purely coincidental.

ISBN: Paperback: 979-8-9926685-1-3 | Ebook: 979-8-9926685-0-6

Library of Congress Control Number: 1-14917193551

Published by TC Jenson

www.TCJenson.com

Cover design by J. N. Ignacio | sushify.artshop@gmail.com

Edited by Sara Unroe | Ink and Edit | inkandeditwithsara@gmail.com

Proofread by: Tranise Robinson | onyxoasisbookstore@gmail.com

Formatted by: Nicole Aisling | nicoleaisling.author@gmail.com

Printed in the United States of America

First Edition: June 2025

To the people who look for themselves in between the written pages, in the other realms, or at the tables that haven't set out your place setting yet, this one's for you. I hope you find a piece of yourself here.

- TCJ

ROSEBAY
R. 458

VAST
SEA

UNCHARTED

POPPYCAL
R. 146

PAPAVER
R. 626

SALEMFIR
R. 510

LAVIEGATA
R. 849

ROSWELL
CAMP

N

W   E

S

NEW STATES OF HERI

Drawn by Conscript Miravale

FAMILY TREE
RUNES

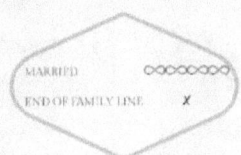

MARRIED ⚬⚬⚬⚬⚬⚬
END OF FAMILY LINE   X

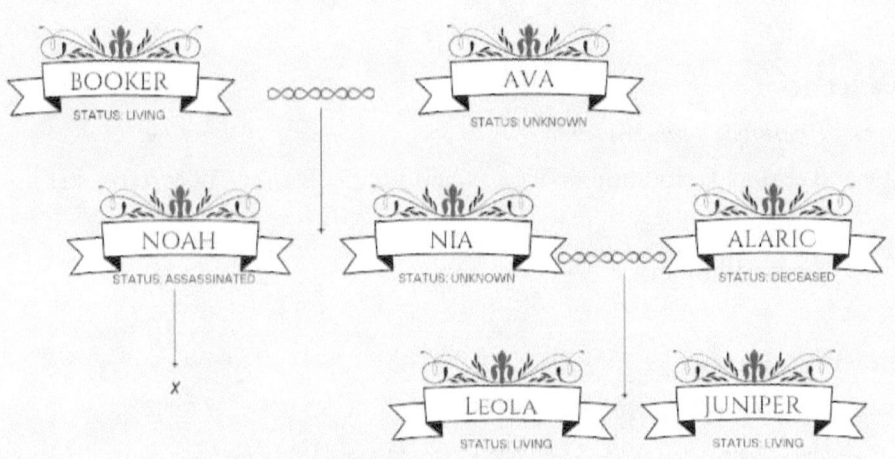

FAMILY TREE
WYNDMERE

MARRIED ⚬⚬⚬⚬⚬⚬
END OF FAMILY LINE   X

CHARACTER GLOSSARY

in alphabetical order

Ava Runes
- *Pronunciation: Ay-vah*
- Relation: Grandmother of Leola and Juniper Runes / Wife to Booker Runes
- Power: Illusionist

Asha Wyndmere
- *Pronunciation: Ahh-sha*
- Relation: Granddaughter of Sena Wyndmere / Daughter of Josephine Wyndmere / Sister to Bennjamin Wyndmere
- Power: Fa (serving the Underground)

Bennjamin (Benn) Wyndmere
- *Pronunciation: Benn-juh-min*
- Relation: Grandson of Sena Wyndmere / Son of Josephine Wyndmere / Brother to Asha Wyndmere
- Power: Time and Emotion

Booker Runes
- *Pronunciation: Book-er*
- Relation: Grandfather to Leola and Juniper Runes / Husband to Ava Runes
- Power: Earth

Daemon Zevaroth

- *Pronunciation: Day-mun*
- Immortal fallen founder of the Underground
- Founder of Opasteg
- Power: Illusionist

Josephine Wyndmere

- *Pronunciation: Jo-seph-een*
- Relation: Daughter to Sena Wyndmere / Mother to Asha and Bennjamin Wyndmere
- Power: Time

Juniper Runes

- *Pronunciation: Joo-nih-pur*
- Relation: Granddaughter of Ava and Booker Runes / Sister to Leola Runes
- Power: Earth

Leola Runes

- *Pronunciation: Lee-oh-la*
- Relation: Granddaughter of Ava and Booker Runes / Sister to Juniper Runes
- Power: Fire

Levi Miravale

- *Pronunciation: Lee-vy*
- Relation: No living family / Best friend of Bennjamin Wyndmere
- Power: Seer

Sena Wyndmere

- *Pronunciation: Say-nuh*
- Leader of the Underground
- Relation: Mother to Josephine Wyndmere / Grandmother of Asha and Bennjamin Wyndmere
- Power: Emotion

GLOSSARY

Academy of Powers and Poweresses
- Prestigious school for magical-wielders

Assignment
- Where spies from Underground or Opasteg will serve
  - Ex: 1855 Roswell Post
  - Format: Year / Site

Chattel(s)
- Name that refers to a person who is a prisoner of a Labor Camp

Conscript(ed)
- Spies who are taking their first Assignments from the Underground

Corruptor
- Spies who take Assignments from Opasteg
  - **regardless of rank or seniority

Darkbeing
- Magic-wielder whose soul has been corrupted by their practicing of dark magic

Demon
- Magic creature whose soul has been corrupted by their practicing of dark magic

Fa
- Members of the Underground or Opasteg that can speak and be spoken to by the Gods and Ancestors
  - Have the ability to deliver prophecies
  - Play a role in building Assignments

Gods

- While all forms of religion are recognized in Heri, the one that will be most prominent in this text will be the following:
    - Gaia: Goddess of the Earth
    - Mors: Death God

Labor Camps (Camps)

- Where enslaved Mundane beings live and are forced to partake in slave labor
    - Note: Abolished in 1865

Lesserbeing

- Another name for a 'Mundaner' that has now developed a negative connotation due to the mistreatment of the Mundaners from the new regime
    - 'Lesser': Shortened slang version that has an adapted derogatory connotation

Magic-wielder

- A person with magic in their veins. Synonym to power(ess/ex)

Maturity

- When a Mundaner or magic-wielder reaches adult age, usually at age 19
    - In most cases, this is when a magic-wielder's magic will manifest

Modern-Era

- Modern-day

Mundane(r)

- A human who does not possess magic-wielding abilities and has limited interaction with the magic-wielding world

Overseer

- Manage Chattels during their work and has the ability to punish them
- Overseers are Mundaners—however they are offered this paid role with the contingency that they will serve Opasteg

Opasteg

- *Pronunciation: Oh-pa-steg*
- Secret Society that strives to bring back Laborist Camps and a classist system where your worth is determined by your power or magic abilities
- Leader: Daemon Zevaroth

Power(ess/ex)

- A person with magic in their veins. Synonym to magic-wielder

Power Reserve

- The amount of power available to each magic-wielder in their arsenal
- Often referred to in percentages
  - Note: descending past 10% is NOT recommended and can result in death

Red Coup

- Significant historical event that unseated Heri's democracy
- Replaced the Democracy of Heri with the New Regime

Separatist Libata Laws

- Laws that separated Mundane people after abolishment of Labor Camps
  - Limited their resources, school choices, housing, and work opportunities, infirmary care rights, etc.
  - Abolished in 1978

The Underground
- Secret society that supports a world of goodness for all people, no matter the innate power they possess or do not possess
- Leader: Sena Wyndmere

CONTENT WARNING

This text takes place in a dystopian setting. Readers should be advised of the following:

Blood, gore, violence

Death

General Anxiety Disorder

Explicit language

Slavery (Graphic imagery)

Sexual assault (implied, off-page)

Imprisonment

Discrimination

Mistreatment of people

PROLOGUE

— LEOLA —

S TREAMS OF FIRE ERUPTED from her fingertips. Her flames soared above the treetops, lighting up the dusk lit sky. Her hair swung in a mass of rosewood-colored curls behind her, thick and curled like the flames that spurred from her power. Across the hilly meadow, Juniper, her younger sister, stood flexing her fingers as she gathered her power.

"Oops!" she gasped, peeking toward her grandparent's house to confirm nothing of importance was burning, before shouting, "Nevermind, we're good!"

Juniper shot tumbleweeds into the air that Leola's sparks sought out, engulfing the weeds in flame. The girls beamed and giggled as the weeds spun in the air like flaming pinwheels. This may seem like an abnormal activity for children at the young ages of seven and four years old, but actually, this magic—their power—was a part of their daily lives, and this happened to be their favorite game.

"More! More fireworks, Leo! More! More! More!" Juniper squealed as another one of her tumbleweeds incinerated, shooting more into the air, palms facing skyward. Her lips stretched over her toothless grin as her raven-colored, shoulder-length braids swung in the air.

1

The air quieted as if all of the fun evaporated, leaving only malice in its wake. As if they apparated, two dozen hooded figures surrounded them. Leola shoved her sister behind her back, shielding her from the view of the looming threat. She scanned the group, her nose wrinkling at the acetic, greasy stench oozing from their blood-red uniforms and the matching liquid that dripped from their weapons.

Juniper's whisper quivered. "These are the ones Papa warned us about, right, sis?"

As if confirming her question, the figures lifted their weapons in unison as flames ignited her palms. Panic seared through her bones.

"You thought you could hide." One of the figures leaned down until his rotten breath washed over her face. "He'll be so thrilled that we've captured you."

The ground split as vines erupted from the earth, binding the bodies of each of the hooded men. She retracted her flames as Juniper hopped forward, flashing her a beaming grin, as the men struggled and grunted against the binds.

"Woah, Bug, those are even stronger than the ones you trapped Papa in last week," Leola said. "Should we kill them? You know what Papa always says."

Juniper looked at her with wide eyes, repeating the words they'd heard many times, "Evil must die."

With a shrug and a twist of her hand, a ring of her fire surrounded the men, engulfing the vines that bound them. The putrid smell of burning flesh filled the air as she incinerated them all.

Papa appeared first, warping soundlessly from where he'd been in the house. He knelt to the girls' heights as he asked, "Are you injured?" His eyes warmed on hers as he took her face in one hand and Juniper's in the other.

Leola shook her head, loathing the tears that were forming at the realization that the figures—whoever they were—were burning from the innate power she'd treated as a toy.

She raised her shaking palms face-up as she explained, "I killed them, Papa."

His eyes were solemn. "You had no choice." He sighed, looking beyond her. "He found us."

Their grandmother appeared behind them. "Well, he's going to have to keep looking. Hide the bodies," she said.

Aromas of rain-soaked wood and freshly trimmed trees—the telltale sign of their grandfather's magic-scented the air, opening the earth with fresh dirt and burying the burnt bodies until any sight of the massacre was covered with the blooming meadow that had existed previously.

He picked two wildflowers, handing each girl a poppy, before saying, "It's time we tell them. Come, my girls."

Part I:

The Prophecy

CHAPTER 1

— LEOLA —

13 Years Later (Modern-Era)
1 July
Poppycal, Heri

ROARING JETS SOARED OVERHEAD, dropping messages as they did every morning since the Coup last year.

"Now I know this joker is out of his damn mind," Leola scoffed.

She snatched the leaflet out of the air, reading:

FELLOW HERIANS,

FROM HERE FORWARD, LESSERBEINGS WILL BE LIVING IN
SANCTIONED HOUSING PROVIDED BY THE REGIME.
PLEASE REPORT TO YOUR NEAREST CORRUPTOR
FOR YOUR ASSIGNED PLACEMENT.
ANYONE WHO DOES NOT COMPLY

WILL BE SENT OFFSHORE.

SIGNED AND ISSUED BY:
DAEMON ZEVAROTH
LEADER OF NEW HERI

Juniper shuddered as she grumbled, "I guess we're moving then."

She crushed the leaflet in her hand, grabbing Juniper's hand with the other. "Let's go get what Papa asked for. What was it again?" Leola questioned, squinting into the crowded street.

Juniper scanned the list in her free hand, answering, "An oil ration and a new pair of sneakers." Since Mundaners were no longer allowed to purchase new items, that could only mean one thing: "We get to go thrifting!" Leola let out a groan as her sister cheered.

They headed in the direction toward what had once been the Ashbury District, but the city name had been stripped, along with all of the names of Herian States, since the Red Coup happened. Now, they were ordered to call them by the assigned Region and Number.

Leola tensed as they passed the secondhand stores, still hearing the wails of the Lesserbeings as their property burned and Corruptors forced them to abandon their businesses; the next day, the same villains were owning and operating these stores as if those heinous crimes against Mundaners had never occurred. Today, these were the *only* stores that Lesserbeings were allowed to shop in. To her, the order was degrading, but her sister loved any excuse to thrift, so she would grin and bear it; besides, the dreamy glint that entered her sister's eyes in these old, mothball-essenced stores was enough to have her relenting. Also, Papa had a hole in his sneakers, and this was the best Mundaner sneaker store in their region.

A sign rattled on the door as they opened it, reading:

LESSERBEINGS PERMITTED BEFORE CURFEW

Leola gritted her teeth as she shoved passed the sign, holding the door open for her sister as the bell announced their arrival. Letting Juniper pass her, she sent one last look at the degrading sign.

'Lesserbeing.'

'Curfew.'

It's getting worse. She thought, her pulse spiking. *The sanctions... the rules—*

Her sister's sing-song tone pulled her from her thoughts.

"Blessed Day to you, sir," Juniper chirped to the store owner as she strode past him like she owned the place herself, not like her existence was barely tolerated by the guy.

He sneered at her sister, and Leola leveled a stare at him that promised a slow, tortuous death, wishing she could say, *How can you treat us like this? Just because we weren't blessed with magic means nothing.*

During the takeover, ownership of Mundane-owned stores was transferred to Corruptors, magic-wielders who'd served the dictator in secret prior to the Coup and now pledged their loyalty proudly to the corrupt regime.

She flipped her hair over her shoulder, pausing for one heartbeat to check for the exit point, in case the magic-wielder got any ideas.

"You can't buy anything with purple tags. Those items are new," the Corruptor reminded her, like she could forget.

Five years prior, leaders began to run for office in all of the major Herian regions that spouted hateful rhetoric toward Mundaners. They preached about wanting to bring back ways of life—heinous, ancient crimes against other beings—and Mundaners, now called Lesserbeings, were the scapegoat. Leola blinked and suddenly, the entire world hated her, her family, and her friends. Her sister had only been twelve years old at the start of the rise of the regime, so she did not remember life before it. Leola couldn't decide if that was a good thing or a bad thing.

"Leo, you promised that we could look at each shop, but your sighs are killing my mood," Juniper chided, picking up a milk glass ashtray and tracing the gold lining with her fingers.

Leola's nose wrinkled. "That may be true, but I didn't agree to spend an eternity in each store. You know the dust in these stores makes me antsy." Her voice loudened as she continued, "It's disgusting in here."

"Maybe it's the trash we let in," the store owner said, without looking up.

Leola rolled her eyes, saying in a quieter voice, "The discrimination never really left, but it used to be quieter. I don't like him. Let's hurry."

Juniper's hair was as dark as a moonless night sky, styled in new, waist-length box braids. She had dark eyes and eyebrows and a freckle-less face. The Runes sisters shared the same caramel-colored complexion. Leola had light eyes, auburn hair, and numerous freckles to match—each freckle its own unique shade of brown.

Their personalities couldn't differ more, yet they remained inseparable. While Juniper was easy-going, she was canny and clever. While she was observant, Juniper was extroverted. Both sisters were outspoken and bold; neither shied away from a challenge. They wore similar clothing and enjoyed the same hobbies—except thrifting, of course. Leola simply could not get behind this hobby, as Juniper affectionately called it, and now that this was the only way they could purchase clothing, she loathed it even more.

Her stomach twisted thinking about the lack of cleanliness in these old places. She could see several dust clusters in their vicinity, and these crowded racks were spiking her anxiety.

But, at least, she did not have to do Papa's shopping alone today; she hated shopping alone as much as she hated thrift stores. Almost as much as she hated the Coup and the new world they lived in. *Almost.*

— JUNIPER —

After hearing her sister sigh yet again, Juniper turned toward her, laughing at the aggressive scowl working across her face as she tried—and failed—to look interested in the secondhand clothes. Leola scowled at her, flipping her fresh silk press over her shoulders as she moved on to another rack.

The focused look on Leola's face clued Juniper in that her thoughts had wandered. Taking the moment as an opportunity to drift to another section of the shop, Juniper disappeared into the racks. Her sister's dwindling patience had a direct correlation to the time she would be allowed to explore the aisles. The store was cluttered, with long aisles and tall shelves. Despite being gifted in the height department and the added centimeters from the platform sneakers she wore on her feet, she had to push up on her tiptoes to see over the racks.

Snap. Snap. Leola snapped her fingers, catching her attention. In the same motion, she lifted a pair of sneakers for Papa and circled a single finger three times, mimicking what used to be their grandmother's signal for 'time-to-go.' Secretly, she wouldn't be too sad about skipping the remaining stores she'd talked Leola into venturing into today. Her growling stomach was determining how much longer she had before she turned into a hangry beast.

With that in mind, she scanned the surrounding aisles, spotting some intriguing trinkets along the wall in a glass case. Her curiosity flared, drawing her in, though the beautifully-adorned craftsmanship of the furniture would have caught her eye anyway. A layer of dust covered the pane of glass on the front.

Juniper's eyes moved across the items on the shelves, zeroing in on a gold pocket watch. Its pearlescent face boasted a unique design that mimicked botany. She squinted, not able to make out any more details through the dirty glass. What struck her the most was the lace-thin, emerald lining around the face—so thin that she found herself leaning in to see it. Her hand twitched at her side, yearning to touch it. Despite the fact that she had only two ration cards, she had no intention of leaving the store without it.

Juniper straightened, glancing at the store owner. Every time she'd visited this store since the Coup, the man had been grouchy, but she'd never had a question for him—until today.

She called out in her most polite voice, "Excuse me, sir, would you mind opening this case for me?"

Without looking up, he snapped, "Not for sale. Not for you."

Rude, she thought as her eyes narrowed, eyeing the crusty magazine he held in his withered grip. A makeover and an attitude check would do him well.

She flipped her braids over her shoulder. "Well, by that, did you mean that *nothing* in this case is for sale?"

"You a Lesserbeing?" he asked, again not sparing her a glance.

Emerging from the racks, Leola piped in, "You could have put a sign on the case. Why display something that is not for sale to Mundaners in a store that caters to us?" Her attitude was evident in her clipped tone.

He looked up—his answer was as frigid as his bloodshot eyes. "I do not cater to *your* kind. Not. For. Sale. I said it the first time. Now, you best make a purchase or move along, girl. I don't care for loitering Lessers. I shouldn't even allow your kind in my store."

'Lesser' was not technically a slur, but it sure as the Gods stung like one. Juniper tensed as she absorbed the sting like a brand. Leola shot her a knowing glance that she could instantly interpret: the man was intolerant—maybe hateful—toward Mundaners.

Juniper gave him a quick up-down, noting his graying hair and sun-damaged face. She was surprised to see that he was covered in expletive tattoos. She couldn't get a look at the details of each of them, but one stood out to her: a red flag with blue lines in the shape of an X across it. The universal symbol for Opasteg—a mythical terrorist organization that despised Mundaners. The marking made it more apparent why he'd gotten so cross with the sisters—why he had referred to them as 'loitering Lessers,' when they were regular customers.

She grimaced. *Just brand yourself with that symbol for life, huh? Asshole.*

Now she found herself wondering if the items in the case were not for sale or not for sale to *her,* a Mundane being.

"Well then," Juniper responded, flashing him a sweet smile that masked her annoyance. "Us *Lessers* will get out of your hair."

The man grumbled a curse under his breath that was interrupted by a telephone ringing in the back of the store; he stood, hobbling in the direction of the looping chime. She watched him wordlessly, but her mind was working.

In the months since the Coup, she'd developed and honed several useful skills that were vital to survival. Picking locks, fighting, running, and, the occasional, but most invigorating, stealing; she wasn't a kleptomaniac by any means, but when your agency for purchasing items is taken away by a corrupt regime, the rules *must* be bent. She'd worn her deep-pocketed cargo pants on purpose. Inside them was a pearl necklace for herself, an unused film canister for Papa, and a vintage matchbox for her sister's extensive collection.

Leola's voice grabbed her attention. "What a prick. I think that's enough thrifting for today. Let's use the ration card on these sneakers and get out of here. There's a sandwich place nearby that will serve us…"

Juniper tuned her out, eyes back on the case—specifically, on the pocket watch. The emerald details *glowed* like polished jewels. She stepped closer. It was a faint glow, but undeniable, nonetheless. She peeked over her shoulder to confirm that the man was still in the back of the store.

"Junebug. Hey, are you listening to me?"

"Yeah, great. Food. Sure," she responded, eyeing the lock on the case as her fingers stretched to graze it. One more glance over her shoulder showed her the man was nowhere to be seen.

Decision made.

"*What the hell are you doing?*" Leola hissed. "That man is *clearly* not a fan of Mundaners already. He called us trash and you're doing exactly what he assumed you would!"

She ignored her sister as she snagged a bobby pin out of her sling bag and pressed it into the lock. She leaned forward, shimmying it around until she heard the *click* she was listening for. The door to the case popped open, and she took the pocket watch into her hand.

"Juniper!" Leola snapped, voice low. "Put. It. Back."

"No way," she replied, shutting the case with a chuckle. "I'm taking this. Today, I'm the *trash* he thinks I am."

She slipped it in her jacket, ignoring the glare from her sister.

The man suddenly materialized next to them, his voice menacing. "I thought you were on your way out."

Juniper jumped back, until her shoulder brushed Leola's. Her protective grip on her wrist was as sharp as thorns.

"We were just leaving," her sister said as she pulled her toward the door. "Thank you, sir!" she called over her shoulder, not pausing to look back at him.

Juniper followed, tossing a look over her shoulder in the direction of the man. He was trailing them.

"I know you stole from me." His voice was icy as he grabbed onto her wrist. His touch was electric, sending a hot shock to her marrow. She pulled out of his grasp, stomping on his foot in the process.

"Do *not* touch her," Leola growled. Juniper was about to urge her sister to move faster, but the man stopped following.

His words were ice against her skin. "Not to worry. I'll be seeing y'all one way or another eventually. I felt your power. Bet you won't steal from a Corruptor again."

———

— LEOLA —

"Nope. Time to go." She'd had enough of the man's outdated ideologies and her sister's imbecilic shenanigans. "Let's put as much space between this liver-spotted creep, his dusty ass store, and us as possible."

The air was chilled, dewy, and relieving as they reached the exit that opened onto the crowded street. She broke into a jog, not releasing Juniper's hand until they reached the Mundane-serving deli. They ordered their usual, sitting down once they'd grabbed their sandwiches and drinks.

She eyed her sister as she pulled the paper wrapping off her sandwich. "You should *not* have done that, Bug. How the hell can you pick locks anyway?"

She shrugged, sipping her latte. "You are right—that was not my best idea. Stealing from a man with *that* tattoo. He's probably wishing we could go back to 1855."

Leola chuckled, dropping the topic while adding, "His hair looked like it hadn't been washed *since* 1855."

"You know, I don't think you paid for Papa's shoes," Juniper commented between bites. "Guess the five-finger discount is not just *my* thing."

Her mouth fell agape. "Great. Now we can never go back there, and that was the best sneaker store. Papa will be heated if we can't get shoes there anymore."

"Who cares? That man is a Corruptor. And he referred to us as 'your kind' and 'trash' and 'Lessers,' all in the same five minutes. Papa would call him mindless if we told him that happened," Juniper said with a tight smile, picking up their ration card

14

that had permitted them to shop today in the first place. "Screw him. Even if we're paying with a ration card—or were supposed to—we still deserve respect."

She catalogued the rare flicker of serious emotion that crossed her sister's features, making the reality of the dire state of their world even more bleak. As usual, as fast as it appeared, the hint of the emotion was gone, replaced with Juniper's witty jokes.

"Tell Papa you don't even need to take the gap year off of school now—we can be professional thieves, just as the Gods intended." The sarcasm in her words rang loud as a bell, but she smirked anyway.

"He would lose it if he heard you say that," Leola deadpanned. "Full blown, purple-vein-apparent, tantrum mode."

The sisters laughed as they ate their sandwiches, their conversation drifting to other things—concerts they wanted to go to, food vendors they'd one day try—assuming these activities would remain open to Mundaners, of course. That remained to be seen, as new missives arrived every day, and it seemed like with every new missive, they had less rights as citizens. Mundaners couldn't even travel between the regions. Despite the state of Heri, the conversation was easy, flowing like a stream between the sisters who doubled as best friends. Leola was talking about a new podcast she'd been listening to when Juniper interrupted.

"What was it like before?"

Leola tensed, the silliness from the conversation before evaporating, replaced with a heavy mist. She cleared her throat, glancing around the dated, empty deli. Lowering her voice anyway, she asked, "What was *what* like, Bug?"

"Life," she whispered, eyes pleading on hers. "As a Mundaner. Before the Coup."

"It was better—safer. Our rights were limited, of course, and we couldn't travel. But we could go to the schools we chose; we had the same opportunities as magic-wielders." She chose the whispered words with intention. "Corruptors are cruel—hateful—because the dictator encourages it. Magic-wielders aren't unkind to us, as

15

there are many who don't agree with the new regime. Papa says there's been whispers of a rebellion."

"But some believe we should go back to the past eras," Juniper said as she picked at the crumbs from her sandwich. "Someone at school said we should reopen the Camps. You know... the Laborist camps. That won't happen, though, right?"

She flinched. "No. They can't force people back into that kind of work— Mundaners or not. We would rebel."

"But it's getting worse," Juniper whispered as tears welled in her eyes. "The way they treat *us*?" Her voice cracked on the edge of that sentence.

Leola reached over and grabbed her sister's hand. "It will stop. But we will talk to Papa, and figure out what to do. In the meantime, stay away from any magic-wielders who repeat New Heri bullshit. They can't wield yet anyway, remember? That comes later, when they go to their academies. You can still take on anyone. You are just as strong as they are." She spoke the words to remind herself and Juniper.

Juniper's voice was hollow. "For now. I don't understand why they hate us. As soon as they reach Maturity, we're not a threat."

Leola's gaze drifted out the storefront window, focusing on the raindrops that raced down the glass panes. "It didn't happen overnight. The Gods chose to give some people magic and power, while others... did not get that gift." She sucked on her cheek. "Mundaners have always been the target of prejudices. That's not new. They got freed from the Camps, and then boom, they got hit with Separation and Libata Clauses. They were freed but not equal, and those clauses made integration polarized, leading to dangerous situations for Mundaners. They allowed those in power to limit the opportunities offered to Mundane beings, in the name of the law, hindering the prosperity of generations of people. Over time, kind magic-wielders took power, and as such, we got to experience more freedom—"

"And now we have new leaders who want to snatch that away," Juniper added to the end of the sentence.

"They have malintentions," said Leola, her voice low. "Poppycal is safer for us, so at least we're here and not somewhere else."

"Somewhere like Laviegata, or should I call it Region 849?" Juniper asked with a raised brow.

Words deserted her as she blinked at her sister, who she'd thought had been unaware of the rising conflict around them.

She rolled her eyes. "I know what's going on, Leo."

Leola recovered. "We don't use the Region names. And yeah, things are bad in Laviegata. Always have been."

"That's where the Camps were?" she pressed. "That's where the new regime would reopen them?"

"Nothing is confirmed." Silence befell them until she broke it, asking, "Bug, what was up with that clock you stole today?"

"Pocket watch," Juniper corrected with a grin, pulling it out of her jacket pocket. "Looks pretty old. Maybe from the early 1900s. Maybe even earlier." She held it over the table between them, letting her thumb run over the intricate design on the gold covering.

Leola opened her palm so she could get a closer look at it, feigning excitement, unsure what her sister loved so much about this old watch. She held it in her hands, careful not to damage it. It seemed fragile, though it held weight. A slight vibration ran through her hand from where her palm met the watch.

Wariness flooded her as she asked, "Is it magic?"

"It has to be. Open it, Leo," Juniper said, excitement becoming evident through her wide grin.

She thought it was silly, but obliged her sister anyway. She opened the gold covering to reveal a normal porcelain face with dark accents. There was something peculiar about the green lining around the face, though, almost like it was glowing.

Confirming her thoughts, Juniper whispered, "Do you see it? The glow?"

17

Okay, so it is glowing, Leola thought and then responded, "Yeah, I see it." Her eyes narrowed on the watch. "Maybe you should take this to a jeweler and get it inspected. It could be mercury causing the glow. You wouldn't want to get mercury poisoning. That shit is fatal. And if it's not Mercury, then it's magic, which could also be fatal to you."

With a roll of her eyes, Juniper asked, "Do you *ever* stop worrying?"

Though she *did* think her sister had a point, whatever it was, this pocket watch was *not* Mundane and that glow was suspicious. And no, she did not ever stop worrying.

The pair spent a few more minutes admiring the watch when someone approached their table—a tall, looming man, hovered next to their table, uninvited. He wore a denim jacket with patches on the sleeves and leather pants. He carried a black backpack and wore sneakers with white socks. Her eyes zeroed in on the right sock that was splattered with dark red splotches.

Is that...blood? Leola's stomach pitched. With another look at the man, she noticed blood dotting his sleeve as well; it was hard to see under his jacket, but the smell was unmistakable.

That's blood, she answered her own question, hating the metallic scent that overpowered her senses and twisted her stomach. This blood smelled old, like it had been on his clothing for a while. Not only that, it was red, which was magic-wielder blood—not the silver-toned Mundane blood. Either way, he was dangerous—or at least, violent. Her spine tingled with fear. She wanted to get as far away from him and away from that stench as possible.

"Hello," he greeted politely. "While I was sitting over there, I couldn't help but notice you two admiring that pocket watch. I've been looking for one just like it."

Liar. Leola's eyes narrowed. His smile was friendly enough, but there was something about his piercing blue eyes and inky hair that had her leaning back in her chair. She would have noticed his striking appearance when she'd scanned the other tables earlier, but they'd all been empty. Now, he claimed to have been sitting at one long enough to 'watch' them.

Juniper's reply was flat, a stark contrast to her usual sing-song tone she used with strangers. "Thank you, it's a beauty. I saw it in a store earlier today."

Double strange. Juniper's catching the same vibe I am, she thought. *She is not nearly as excited as she should be that someone is asking about the clock.*

The man leaned closer toward their high-top table, which caused both the sisters to lean away from him. They weren't keen on sharing their personal space. Under the table, she reached for Juniper's hand.

"What would it take for me to buy it from you?" he asked through a tight smile. "It can't have been too expensive, especially if you thrifted it."

"No thanks," Juniper said. "I'm going to hold onto it."

The man responded too fast, leaning closer still. "I insist. Name your price."

Juniper's smile dropped, her voice firm. "It's not for sale."

The man put his hands on their table, gripping the edge until his knuckles turned white. Preparing to request that he leave their table, Leola opened her mouth but stopped when she noticed his blue eyes were now fully black. No irises to be found, just a midnight-black swirl. She glanced across the table to see Juniper frozen in fear, her eyes on the man as she held onto the pocket watch in a tight fist.

The man spoke, his accent changing to a thick, menacing drawl, "Now, I'll say this one more time. My offer stands to purchase the relic." His Cheshire smile was frosty as he continued, "Decline my offer, and I won't be so nice."

Relic. Oh, right, because it's magic. Magic-wielders don't want us taking their treasures. Leola observed the exchange and thought it might be a good idea for her sister to just sell this damn thing, if only so they could be rid of this creep. Her knowledge of relics was limited, but the man wanted this item, that much was clear.

But Juniper wanted it, too, so instead of backing down, Leola threw the words back at the man, making sure to let venom leak into her tone. "Step away from us, or *I* won't be so nice."

The blackness of his eyes flickered as he sneered.

———

— JUNIPER —

The pocket watch heated in Juniper's palm and she looked down to see the face of the watch that was now an illustrious, sparkling emerald. It was beautiful and fascinating; she couldn't look away. The heat from the watch was not painful, but instead, mimicked the sensation of a pleasant, tingling sunlight. It warmed her arm, moving into her shoulders, filling her entire body with excitable energy.

This guy is after my enchanted pocket watch? No way am I selling this to him, Juniper decided as she glanced at her sister, who was locked in a staredown with the man. She squeezed her sister's hand to get her attention.

Leola's eyes met hers and, in the same breath, the man reached for Juniper, his hand grazing her jacket. As if in response, the heat in Juniper's body surged. A flash of green, blinding light filled their vision. Raging wind swept through the deli, whipping their faces and rattling the tables and walls.

Throwing her body across the table, she grabbed Juniper's other hand, as they were thrown into a viridescent cyclone. Suffocating, atmospheric pressure popped in her ears as she fought to hold onto her sister. Dust and debris were like needles on her face, so she squeezed her eyes shut to protect them from the mess. The icy, vibrating air charged all around them.

Her sister screamed over the roaring wind, "Don't let go of me!"

A resounding crack filled the air around them as the green mist cleared. Wood shattered around them, propelling them in two different directions until they, at last, landed on muddy earth.

CHAPTER 2

— LEOLA —

HER EYES OPENED TO A dusklit sky. She coughed, rolling onto her side as her limbs were met with muddy foliage. Thanks to a quick check of her feet and hands, she discovered she was unharmed, despite the soreness in her limbs. Her head throbbed and her mouth was as dry as the desert, leaving her to wonder if she'd hit her head during the chaos and made a note to check her eyes with a light as she'd done during the clinic seminar her school offered.

The area surrounding her was... unfamiliar. The sinking sun hardly broke through the dense treetops and the sticky air left her arms slick with sweat. She inhaled the warm, humid air with a grimace.

Since when is Poppycal this warm? And at dusk? What time did we leave Ashbury? She rolled her neck, her memories flooding back to her in a rush. *Shit. Where am I? Where's Juniper? Where's that man?*

She willed her pulse to calm, fighting her terror as she tried to orient herself. Her pulse quickened as she looked in all directions, recognizing nothing.

She was lost.

Horrified.

She peered through a gap in the trees to where the sound of hooves traveled from, squinting toward a group of men on horseback. They'd stopped walking, but it was difficult to see them in the dwindling light. She did not want to lose where she was, or where *they* were in the forest before she found Juniper.

I'll find Juniper and then flag them down for help.

A black coat lay on the ground, twenty yards from where she'd awoken. Her breath caught as she located her sister's motionless body. She tried to call her name, but a voice in the back of her mind cautioned her to stay quiet. Instead, she swallowed her words. Careful not to disturb any branches or gravel, she trembled with fear as she approached her sister's too-still body.

"Bug?" she whispered, crouching down toward her sister's restful face. No answer. She let out an urgent hiss, "*Juniper!*"

Nothing.

Her palms slickened as she touched her sister's neck and checked for her pulse. She was breathing and somewhat unharmed. *Thank the Gods.* She scanned the forest again, noting the men on horseback hadn't moved, and wondered idly where that man from the deli had slithered off to. *Is he with them?*

Her stomach dropped. She needed to weigh her options, and she wasn't even sure what they were.

This place is eerie. We can't stay here. With one more look at Juniper, she decided to leave her there and walk to the dirt road to get a closer look at the riders. Dusk was barreling toward night and she needed to act while they still had daylight. She started walking, frowning at the realization that all of her options were shit.

A thick wind ruffled her hair, strong enough to make her turn toward the breeze.

She paused. *Something is off about this forest. It feels like... no, it can't be.*

Her grandmother's words rushed into her mind. She could practically hear the eccentricity in her voice saying to her, '*You have magic in you, child. It will protect you, if you need it.*'

Enough, Leola thought as she straightened her chin, taking a few determined steps toward the men. She would not panic and certainly wouldn't be thinking of her grandmother's voice at this moment; that would help no one. *We haven't seen Grandmother in years.*

The ground rushed up to meet her as her foot caught on an overgrown root. Groaning, she rolled onto her back, trying to catch the wind that had been knocked from her lungs as she peeked at the treetops. Her eyes caught on a dangling mass.

What are those? The dwindling light made it impossible to see as she squinted to get a better look—whatever they were seemed to blend into the darkness. They looked like hanging sacks. She scrambled to her feet, her head rushing at the movement. She recognized the ropes before she noticed the pattern in which they swung. With the slight swinging, she assumed whatever was connected held some weight. She rose to her tiptoes. *Nests?*

NO. Her hands rushed to her mouth to muffle her scream. *What the fuck?*

A body. Hung. She did a slow turn, fighting the nauseous wave rising in her throat. Then, she saw it: bodies all around her—hung like the first one she'd seen— each in its own state of decay.

She lost her footing, shock sending tremors through her limbs.

Young bodies.

Old bodies.

Not just men, but women and children, too.

Her knees crashed into the hard ground as she vomited. Her hands pricked as she crawled to a nearby stream, cooling once she pooled water in her palms to splash her face and rinse her mouth. The familiar tightness in her chest threatened to swallow her until she remembered her sister was still in this nightmare forest, too. Exposed.

Leola's legs wobbled as she sprinted back to her sister, skidding to a halt.

A man leaned over Juniper, running a mahogany-toned hand across her face and chest. He looked to be the same age as her and appeared to be searching for signs of life. Although his concerned demeanor made her pause, she trusted *no one* here. Without thinking, she picked up a branch off the ground and swung it. He caught it before it could meet his skull and stood to his full height. He yanked the wood from her hands, splintering her palms in the process. A chill ran down her spine as he observed her. She considered picking up another branch, deciding to do so.

The branch rose to her hand so fast, her acute stress responses blocking out the thought, but she registered the wood biting at her palms.

He eyed the branch. "I wouldn't do that if I were you."

"You're not me." She swung.

He raised a hand and the branch froze as he caught it, annoyance deepening in his frown.

Magic-wielder. Her legs shook, but she kept her feet planted.

"Where have you come from?" His accent was Rosebayish. Proper and eloquent, oozing with poise and confidence.

She raised an eyebrow. *I'm not answering that.* Straightening her chin and trying to hide the tremble of her hands, she countered, "Where did *you* come from?"

"That way," he said as he pointed in the direction where the horsemen had stopped.

"Us too," she lied, shifting herself so she was in between him and Juniper. A lie was better than admitting that she had no idea how they got here.

His cheekbones were angled and sharp. He was a few inches taller than her and, from what she could see, lean muscles threaded his arms. He would likely overpower her, so it was best to stay calm, despite her trepidation. His tattered clothing caught her attention, as they were a stark contrast to the proper language he'd been using.

He gave her a once-over. "A lie," he sniffed. "Clever idea, though. That'll be useful later."

She looked up, averting her gaze, when she noticed more bodies in the trees beyond his head.

Her stomach roiled and her mind hung on his comment. "Sorry, useful for *what*?"

He looked toward the men and horses. They hadn't moved. "We need to go. Was she *lethargic* before you came here?" he asked, emphasizing the word like he was hesitant to say it.

She felt an instinct to defend her sister, especially in this moment of vulnerability.

They were both vulnerable. And alone.

She swallowed her fear, forcing it down until she could give a proper answer. "I woke up a few minutes ago... over there." She pointed in the direction of where she'd come from. "I found her over here. She doesn't seem injured... just unconscious." She kept her eyes trained on him and fought against the worry clouding her senses.

He glanced toward the unmoving men. His restless energy was palpable. She was apprehensive in giving her trust to the stranger—how could she not be? But he'd seen them both, so he knew they were here. Her branch attack was a spectacular failure, so it seemed the options she did have... were all still shit. Again.

She sighed. "It seems you're wanting to go—"

The stranger cut her off. "Yes, you're correct. And I'd like to get a move on, if we could stop dallying," he used a tone that was much less speculative now, one that erred on the side of arrogant and overbearing.

"Who's *dallying*?" she snapped. "I would like to get the hell out of this place, too, but I'm not leaving without my sister. You, on the other hand, are free to go." She shooed him with a wave of her hand that echoed her words.

His gaze flickered as he said, "Sisters. What are your names?"

"Leola," she answered, eyes widening at her foolish admission. "And this is my sister—" She prepared to make a name up, but his voice cut in.

"Juniper, right?" He gave her a knowing look that peered straight into her soul.

She didn't like *that* at all. She wanted to move back a step, but instead, she held her ground, knowing she was all that stood between this stranger and her sister. Her head swam again as she tried to get control of this situation.

The migraine plowing between her temples. The releasing of her stomach contents. The admission of vital information about herself. She had a concussion that was becoming more evident with every passing second.

Her eyes narrowed as she asked, "How did you—?"

He put a hand to her mouth, his focus drawn to the men in the distance. "We're wasting time. The spell will wear off any minute."

She dug her heels into the ground and ripped his hand off her mouth. "There is no *we. I'm* staying here."

Did he just say the spell? *This must be a nightmare. Now would be a great time to wake up, Leo.* She pinched the back of her leg and waited. Nothing changed. The pinching sensation was *real.* She ignored the heat rising to her neck as these vivid feelings didn't have a place in her nightmares. She would not be waking up from this horrible nightmare.

Though he was still occupied with watching the men on horseback, occasionally, his dark eyes flitted to her. She had the sinking instinct that he was paying close attention to her, whether he was watching her or not. With one last scrutinizing look at the man, she determined through his quick defensive reactions and the arrogant presumption that she would go anywhere with *him*, that he had access to magic or power of some kind—something she would be utterly defenseless against.

She willed bravery into her veins. *I just need to buy us time.*

Shaking her head, she bent down and shook Juniper, quietly begging for her to wake up. She was so peaceful and so... still.

The man leaned down, now eye level with her, as he brushed a large hand over Juniper's face. "Perhaps, when you traveled, she was impacted by the..." He trailed off.

Leola ignored him and her rising dread brought on by his closeness. She debated grabbing another branch to use as a weapon.

Be brave, Leo. Use your mind. She forced air in and out of her lungs. One breath, two breaths, three… just like her therapist taught her.

She stood, motioning toward the men on horseback. "I'm going to flag down those men and see if they can take her to the infirm—"

The stranger grabbed her, his desperation evident in his change of tone. "*NO!* Are you mad? Calling those men over here would surely end in our deaths."

She shoved him away from her and huffed a breath. "What do you suggest then?"

This was only getting weirder, and she had to accept that, whoever this guy was, he knew more about this place than she did. She weighed the odds of her overpowering the one man in front of her versus the group of men and dogs that lingered in the distance. Either way, she might lose, but as an all-state archer and fencer, she was swift on her feet. With Juniper awake and moving, which would be a best-case scenario, their odds of overpowering *anyone* looked better against the man in front of her.

Two-against-one or two-against-many. Those were her choices. The former held the better odds.

A horse neighed, pulling her back into the reality that had sweat trickling down her neck. He pulled her to the ground with him. The men had begun moving up the dirt road.

"Cover her with leaves. We leave at nightfall." The man spoke in a hushed tone, gathering leaves into a pile on the ground.

She started to protest but was stopped as he covered her mouth again. The calluses on his hands were rough, his palms smelling like the dirt surrounding them.

"You don't know me, but your only option is to *trust* me. If *we're discovered, we will hang in these trees.*" His frantic whisper turned her blood to ice, the images of the swinging bodies flashing into her mind. As if knowing she wouldn't respond, he lowered his hand from her face.

She picked up what she could to use to cover her sister, now praying she would stay unconscious long enough to go unnoticed. They covered her, leaving enough space, so she could breathe. She did the same with her sister's discarded coat, before stealing one last look at Juniper. The man threw Leola over his shoulder and sprinted deeper into the forest, her stomach leadening as she left her sister behind.

She picked at her broken nails and hand splinters, numb from this onslaught of lifelong trauma. They sat side by side, him calm and her still shaking as her teeth chattered.

He broke the silence."If your teeth chatter any louder, you'll give our hiding place away." He had the gall to sound annoyed.

She didn't acknowledge that, keeping her eyes on her sister.

"My name is Benn, by the way," he said, although he didn't look at her. His voice was barely audible over the stream sounding beyond the log they sat behind. "It's not me you need to be afraid of out here."

She highly doubted that, but again, said nothing. The group of men got closer to the area where Juniper lay. Lying a few yards off the dirt road was advantageous; they would have to know she was there to find her. The silence stretched on as they watched, his earlier question surfacing in her mind. She wondered if it would serve her to exchange a small amount of information.

"Poppycal. Sorry, Region 146." Tears filled her eyes, but she blinked them away, hiding them from the stranger sitting next to her. "That's where we came from."

"Rosebay." He did not elaborate, but it was clear what he meant.

What is this place? she wondered, fearing the answer.

Curiosity won out as she whispered, "Where are we?"

He stiffened, sending her a questioning look that dissolved into a calm, unreadable mask. "Roswell, Laviegata. Year: 1855."

Leola stilled as her emotions took over.

Confusion.

Panic.

Terror.

She started putting it together. The horsemen dressed in odd clothing. Not only *odd*, but clothing from a different *era*. Her mind flashed back to the bodies. Each one different in every way, except one trait that remained glaringly similar—their blood. *Silver*. Mundaners.

The only time that that level of atrocity would be tolerated against Mundaners was prior to the changing of the Camp laws in... 1865. Revulsion. Anger. Confusion.

All a storm whirling inside her. Undiluted fear swelling within.

Yet, each emotion came to a screeching halt the moment she saw her sister sit up.

— JUNIPER —

Juniper's eyes opened to the twinkle of a star-littered sky. Gasping, she flexed her fingers and toes and stretched her arms and legs. She tested her ability to sit up and found herself to be unharmed, aside from being buried in leaves and dirt. Fully. Head to toe.

Taking a look at her surroundings, she wondered how she'd ended up in the park.

She'd never seen these trees before but recognized them instantly. Poplar trees. Their scent was a sweet, earthy musk. Hot and sticky air had the leaves sticking to her face and body.

Ugh, she thought, still trying to catch her bearings. *This will curl my edges.*

She wrinkled her nose at the unfamiliar smells and strange weather. Then, she noticed an incessant buzzing.

Oh, hell no. No. No. No. Not bugs. She scrambled to her feet, not willing to spend a second longer in the dirt, when she could hear bugs of various kinds buzzing around her. There was only one solution—she needed bug repellent, now.

Her coat lay a few feet away from her and she stretched to reach for it. She didn't need the coat, as she was warm enough in this misplaced heat, so she draped it over her arm. Cracking her stiff neck, she tried to remember what she was doing before she woke up.

Corruptor, pocket watch, sandwiches... strange man. Juniper's mouth dried as she remembered. She spun around.

To the left, forest.

To the right, forest.

Behind her and in front of her—more forest.

Where the hell am I?! And where is Leo? Her hammering heart drowned out the buzzing. Her palms slickened with sweat; she needed to find her sister. *Don't panic. Don't panic. Think. Did that man drug us and bring us* here? *Does he have Leo? Is she hurt? Is* he *coming back?*

She tried to make sense of her surroundings that made no sense at all. The best option was to climb and get a better vantage point of the area. She eyed the nearest tree; it was ancient, but the branches looked sturdy enough to hold her weight, so she set her coat on the ground, reaching for the first branch.

Please don't let me fall.

Not that she had the opportunity to fall, because a man wrapped his arms around her, covered her face, muffled her screams, and carried her into the darkness beyond.

CHAPTER 3

— BENN —

Year: 1855
30 June (The day prior)
Laviegata, Heri

S *NAP.*

Benn caught the man's limp body in his arms, his neck lolling to the side at an unnatural angle. He was dead, but Benn confirmed that when he'd snapped his neck seconds ago.

Thirty seconds.

Thirty seconds until the Overseers noticed he was gone.

Peering around the house, he checked for witnesses. The Camp was empty, save for those working the land to the East. He paid them no mind; they weren't close enough to see him.

He cast a beam of power to the designated drop point. Wind whipped around his face as he warped, landing at the drop point, still carrying the man with him. Soundlessly, he set the man onto the ground, placing the kill card on top of his chest.

He murmured the summoning spell and a warpcraft shimmered into view. The warpcraft was gone as quickly as it had appeared, taking the man's body with it.

One down.

A branch snapped behind him. "*You*," a voice hissed.

Benn reached for his power, freezing time, as a dagger nearly collided with his neck. He turned, snatched it out of the air, and looked over the man standing across from him.

Opasteg uniform. Overseer leathers. Undercover, as Benn was, but this man was fighting for the wrong side. Benn flicked his wrist, using practiced binding power to bind the man's wrists and ankles together. This was small magic that could be used to restrain, a skill that Benn spent years perfecting. He sent another bind of magic to cover the man's mouth, silencing him, before releasing the freeze on time.

"You could have said hello first," Benn said, scanning the forest for any lingering threats. The man struggled against the binds, his voice muffled, but the rage in his eyes made it easy to guess what he was attempting to say. "Nice dagger by the way. It looks custom. I think I'll keep it." He flashed a smile at the grunting man as he continued, "Right. Wish I had time to chat, but I'm both on the clock and not interested in listening to you. I'll make this quick. You could've said nothing and let your dagger hit my throat. You could've observed me and taken the information back to whichever scum you serve. You could have lived today."

Benn lowered his shield, opening his power that would read the man and give him a glimpse into who this man was and what he intended to do.

Torturer. Spy. Egotistical personality, whose narcissistic confidence made him think I'd have been an easy kill. Benn almost chuckled.

The man screamed under his binds, which Benn answered with a bored stare.

"But you didn't do any of those things. So you'll meet the Gods today. I could do as you lot do. Kill innocents. Harm people in all eras. Wreak havoc on the Gods' creations. I could *torture* you. But no, that's not our way. So, a swift death for you it is, which is more than you deserve," he said as he snapped the man's neck with a twist of his hand, the pop of his vertebrae filling the silence of the forest. "You're welcome. Enjoy the Ancestral hell."

He summoned another warpcraft for this body—not having a kill card that would identify this man was a problem. The body was gone in seconds, so Benn left the area by warping, landing himself back in the field of the Camp.

He dropped the dagger he'd taken into his uniform. Chattels were issued tattered clothes upon arrival or birth. Over time, he'd sewn in secret pockets and hidden sheaths—for his daggers and a few other items—then spelled the pockets so they would conceal themselves in the threadbare clothes. He checked his watch and dropped it back into a different pocket.

He was an assassin—trained from a young age to be a lethal weapon in this war. Upon initiation, however, he expected to be tasked with more than that. So far, he'd been disappointed and tasked with menial, entry-level assassin runs.

Just like grandmother said, earning my place and all that. He picked up his pickaxe that he'd stashed in the cotton field he was working in today. *Here we go again.*

Three months.

Three months since Benn left Rosebay after being deployed to the 1855 Roswell Post.

Three months of pain. Three months of trauma. Three months of *silence* from the Underground, besides the kill cards delivered by Headquarters each morning. That left him time to do assassin runs before he began his work at the Camp. 88 kill cards received, and 89 kills sent to HQ via warpcraft—he refused to kill unless Headquarters required it, but today was an exception. The man's dagger had been a lover's kiss away from his throat, for Gods' sake.

Three months of preparing the land for seeding season, picking cotton until his fingers bled, building structures in the blinding heat, sleeping on a straw cot fit for an animal, and taking orders from individuals who saw him as nothing more than livestock. Three months of back-breaking, *soul-tearing* work. Work he was, of course, doing for free. In fact, all of the Chattels at Roswell were working for free. Chattel was a glorified word for a person doing slave labor in a Laborist Camp, but truthfully, he was not a Chattel.

He was a free man from the Modern-Era serving an Assignment as one, though he had received no vellums on whatever came next. No, he was in this Camp due to the need to conceal his identity. He had to give it to leadership; it was an ingenious spycover, as no one ever suspects the powerless.

Now that his kill cards were completed for the day, he was forced to work as a Chattel while doing reconnaissance for the Underground.

This work—torture—is not my purpose. This is the interim until my true mission begins. He chanted his daily mantra to himself so he wouldn't succumb to the insanity tugging at his mind. His time spent here was much longer than he had ever imagined it would be, and each day, the voice chanting the mantra lost a little steam, growing quieter and quieter.

His blistered hands brought him back to reality and he scanned the fields in search of a dreaded Overseer. He had been lost in his thoughts and had paused working. He sent up a silent prayer that an Overseer hadn't seen him pause because he did not want to get the whip today. He looked down at the Laviegata soil and swung his pick-ax.

He began counting.

One. Two. Three.

He lost count at 327 swings, as his mind drifted to a night three months prior, in Rosebay, in the Modern-Era.

He met up with Asha, his mentor and older sister. She was easily recognizable, with her voluminous, blonde afro and rich maple-toned skin that sparkled in the night. She smiled when she saw him, her brown eyes crinkling at the sides.

"Ready for tonight, little brother?" She clapped her hands and started walking, not checking to see if he was following.

He replied, "I think you mean to say *younger* brother. I'm loads taller than you now, Ash."

"You have been taller than me for years," she said as she fluffed her hair and scoffed. "Bet I can still beat you in the sparring ring, though."

She was right; Benn was an expert with a sword and a dagger, but Asha had taught him everything he knew and continued to train herself. He wasn't about to let her know that though. "Doubtful. Guess we will have to test that theory sometime."

He followed her to a large flat in West Rosebay. They reached a door and she fished a gold key from her orange palazzo pants. He chuckled.

She eyed him before turning the key. "Something funny?"

He smirked. "You insist we're to remain inconspicuous, yet your bright trousers could literally stop traffic?"

"No time for your sarcasm, brother," she snapped at his jab, but as she turned toward the door, he saw her smile. "Tonight is a special occasion."

He found himself smiling, too. He loved his sister and was grateful for their banter, especially now. His nerves were worsening by the second, and he could use the distraction of teasing her.

"You're ready for this. You trained. You did marvelous at the Academy. After last year, you are destined for a great Assignment. You will make the Ancestors proud, Bennjamin," Asha said as she turned the key, gesturing toward the door, now ajar. "In you go. To the center of the sitting room, please. Though, there won't be anywhere to sit."

He took a deep breath and stepped over the threshold. The spacious sitting room was empty of all furniture, save for a small table in the middle of the space. A large map had been spread across it. He looked up, letting his eyes adjust to the candle-lit room, noting the circle of magic-wielders standing around him. Every person made space for him to pass, each holding a little candle in hand, staying quiet but leaving their eyes on him. Asha remained in the shadows, and he desperately wanted to stay by her side. He looked down, tucking his shaking hands into his pockets.

He had anticipated this moment for most of his life; there was no going back to the life he previously led. The faces of his friends at the Academy, pleasures of his passions, and dreams of the future played through his mind. He wouldn't be able to contact anyone while he was on Assignment. His best friend had taken an advanced Assignment last year, and he hadn't spoken to him since. He didn't even know where he'd gone—or if he was alive.

He gave a slight shake of his head to bring him back to the moment. No, he was excited; he was ready. He was ready to take his Assignment and begin the path to earning his place in the Underground and saving the modern world.

Soft, steady footsteps sounded in front of him in a familiar rhythm.

He lifted his head, meeting the smiling eyes of his grandmother. They hardened quickly.

"Bennjamin." Her powerful voice broke the silence. "It is time."

His grandmother, Sena, had raised him and Asha. She was headstrong, ambitious, fierce, and formidable, and he absolutely adored her... behind closed doors. In front of his magic-wielding peers, it was different. She was a dedicated and decorated soldier, well-known for her contributions in both battle and strategy during her decades of service. It was not a surprise to him, nor anyone else, that she had been elected and then re-elected to lead the Underground.

He was not sure how to address her tonight, though, so he kept quiet, giving her a slight bow of his head as she approached.

"As your grandmother, it is my duty and honor to perform your initiation." She snapped her fingers, a weathered book appearing in her hands immediately. Clearing her throat, she spoke to the room. "Bennjamin, you have completed ten years of combat training."

Her eyes flashed to his, so he responded to her, "Yes, I have."

"You have completed thirteen years of education at the Academy. You are physically prepared for Assignment. You are intellectually prepared for Assignment."

She looked at him, so he said, "Yes, I am."

She paused, turning the page of the book. "Due to the ordinance of 2016, you have completed the required pre-Assignment behavioral therapy... and then some." She smiled. "You are more than prepared—physically, intellectually, and emotionally—for Assignment."

His chest swelled with pride. His grandmother was impressed with his devotion.

She continued, "Upon initiation, your power will be at its full use. As you know, your strengths shown in your adolescence are indicative of the magical abilities that will manifest today. Due to your accolades and achievements through your years of training, the Order anticipates no issues with your ability to harness or control your magic. Would you agree?"

This was the moment to elaborate on his skill and training, so he replied, "Yes. I excelled at the Academy, was active on leadership councils and extracurriculars." He inhaled to slow his jittered speech down. "I even showed evidence of power... an innate sense for emotions and intentions."

A flicker of pride crossed his grandmother's face. The others in the room let out sounds of agreement and celebration. His grandmother turned the page.

"There's one more thing," he said as his stomach knotted. "Under extreme duress, I've shown signs of another power," he admitted, something he had only said aloud to two people.

"Go on," Sena said as her eyebrow raised in the way it did when she was shocked, imperceptible to most that she encountered, but not to him. Benn had not told her, not out of distrust or malintent, but purely out of fear in having told her, then coming here tonight, only to have the valuable gift *not* show during his initiation. Emotion-wielding was the power he'd shown consistent signs of, or so he'd told his grandmother. The time-wielding showed itself only out of desperation. He could not have told Sena and trusted her to not expect something he might not deliver.

But here that decision was, catching up to him as Asha had said it would, as he surprised his grandmother in front of her colleagues. But he was an honest man, so he continued, "It is a timepower of some form. It's happened a few times in short bursts, but never stayed long enough for me to learn more about it."

Gasps filled the room. Sena raised a hand to quiet the crowd of magic-wielders. He yearned to look away from his grandmother's piercing gaze to find his sister's warm eyes, but now wasn't the time for weakness. At least he wasn't shocking *both* of the women in his life tonight.

I'll save the apology for later. He straightened his chin. *Besides, if the time-power doesn't show, I'll have worried for nothing.*

"Let us see what the Gods confirm on your behalf," Sena said. "Though you have been recognized for your combat skill, we encourage you to always stay sharp," she added with a tight smile as she opened her hand where a golden chalice appeared, replacing the log book.

She took his hand in hers, as her pointer finger transformed into a sharp blade, slicing into his palm. His blood trickled into the chalice. A sparkling, emerald smoke overflowed the chalice, spilling onto the floor and filling the room in thick, flickering clouds.

She spoke aloud, watching the chalice, "Based on your history, it is believed, Bennjamin, that you will possess emotion-wielding power—a warrior who can impact his surroundings by leveraging the emotions of others. The Gods have confirmed." Applause filled the room. A fleeting emotion flickered in her eyes. There was little time to wonder, because then, his grandmother was speaking again.

She held his gaze as she continued, "The Gods have spoken. Time-wielder. Confirmed."

Benn stopped breathing. Stopped seeing. He was a dual-power—extraordinarily rare gems in nature. He assumed he would be powerful, as his lineage was composed of legendary magic-wielders, but he'd never expected to be gifted two coveted abilities.

He and Asha had spent hours theorizing which power would be confirmed once he was initiated. Time was his mother's power, and while he was grateful, his heart pained; even though he had almost no memories of her, he would wield the power that became her posthumous legacy. She'd gone missing in his toddlerhood, and the siblings had wished to be nearer to her each day while being forced to endure her devastating absence instead.

His grandmother's voice broke through his thoughts. "Bennjamin Wyndmere, you're now aware of the depths of your magical abilities. Do you swear to use your magic to defend the defenseless?"

A sense of pride and belonging warmed his soul as he heard his name and the slogan of the Underground in the same sentence. He put his right hand over his heart, nodding.

"Yes," he pledged.

"Bennjamin, do you swear to carry out all Assignments, each with an equal amount of tenacity and desire to succeed?"

"Yes," he responded.

"Bennjamin, do you swear to never speak of the Underground to non-members, unless they have previously been vetted by the Order?" she asked.

"Yes," he swore.

"Bennjamin, do you swear to inspire, fight, and die for the Underground, if need be?" she asked.

"Yes," he vowed.

The golden chalice flashed until blinding white light filled the room. Tingling sensations filled his limbs to the point of discomfort. His limbs twitched, strengthening; his vision sharpened, and he sensed the new magic flowing through his veins. Benn wanted to squirm but resisted, not wanting to show weakness amongst his newfound peers.

"Bennjamin Wyndmere, welcome to the Underground," his grandmother said.

Sounds of excitement and cheers filled the room.

Sena hushed the group. "Let us determine Bennjamin's Assignment."

Once again, she opened her palms, one of which was filled with pebbles, the other holding an ink pen. The pebbles would determine where his Assignment would be, while the pen would determine when his Assignment would begin. His grandmother walked a slow circle around Benn, chanting an Ancestral spell. She paused at the small table and dropped the pebbles onto the map. She released the ink pen. It fluttered out of her hand, with a flight-like pattern of a butterfly, landing soundlessly on the map.

His eyes followed. The pebbles circled Laviegata. He watched each curve of the pen with anticipation.

"Location: Laviegata. Year: 1855," his grandmother announced to the room.

She flicked her wrists and lights filled the space. He squinted at the sudden brightness in the room, staying trained on the area of the map.

They can't mean to send me to the Camps. He blinked, wanting to ask, but knowing that was not permitted. There was no questioning where the Gods sent you on Assignment.

His grandmother's voice was cold and brief—which could be attributed to the fact that she was the unyielding Underground Leader Wyndmere in this room and not the loving and kind Grandmother Sena he preferred. She continued, "Meet with your mentor. Pack the essentials. You embark in two weeks' time, Conscript Wyndmere."

Asha accompanied him to the departure location. It was a different flat in Rosebay, in a different area than the one they'd been in for initiation just two weeks prior.

The walk was quiet. He sensed the swirl of emotions in his sister. Despair. Discomfort. Uncertainty.

He had not expected emotions to have tastes and scents when the emotion-wielding power fully manifested. The sticky, unpleasant emotions filled his mouth, twisting his features into a grimace.

"Asha," he called, slowing to a halt. "How do I—? Where am I—?" He tried to find the words, but they didn't exist. His throat tightened as the terror in his stomach seized his throat.

His sister was silent—brooding—beside him. He looked up to see quiet tears streaming down her cheeks. They both knew the dangers and horrors of entering Laviegata in 1855 with the spycover of a Mundaner. Mundaners were not treated well in the Modern-Era, but in the past, it'd been much, much worse for them. He would hardly be seen as chattel in the Camps.

They stopped walking, reaching their destination; it was time for the goodbye he'd been dreading for weeks. Asha's hand trembled as she held out a vellum. He took it, rolling the parchment around in his fingers.

"The vellum is enchanted. It will find you when there are messages from the Underground," Asha explained. "Don't be caught with it. Do not let it be confiscated, nor let it fall into the wrong hands."

He asked, "What is my mission?"

"Blend in with the Chattels at the Roswell Camp. Do recon. You'll receive your next vellum there."

His stomach roiled at the confirmation of his worst fear, at the vagueness of her answer. He responded, frustration lacing his voice, "I don't want to go to a Camp. What was the purpose of all of the training if I won't even be serving as a free man? I won't even have rights... won't even be seen as a human. I thought I'd be working to undermine Corruptors."

Her voice was solemn. "In time. You must be patient."

His composure broke, along with his voice. "Be *patient*? What for? What can be done as I'm 'blending in' with the Chattels?"

The look on her face remained unreadable as she responded, "Blend in, observe, and await further instructions." She pointed to the vellum in his hand.

Benn nodded, understanding that her giving him more information would go against protocol, violate Asha's oath, and endanger them both. Asha was a Fa, a being who could speak and be spoken to by the Gods and Ancestors. As a Fa, she used enchanted vellums; she could deliver prophecies and messages to maintain the confidentiality of communication between the Conscripted and the Order.

He embraced her to say goodbye. His chest tightened as his throat burned, his voice cracking as he said "I'll miss you, but I'll see you soon. I love you, Ash." Tears ran down his face, ones that mirrored the tears on Asha's face.

"Remember, I'm proud of you. Remember the Underground. Defend the defenseless. Be safe, brother. I love you, too." Asha's voice played in his head as he thought back to his last moments in the Modern-Era, letting the warmth of the memory soak into his mind.

CRACK.

An ear-splitting cracking sounded in his ear as he was met with the blinding pain of the whip connecting with his shoulder blade.

He hunched over, catching himself on the pickaxe stuck into the soil, which happened to be the only thing preventing him from falling.

"No time for *resting*, Lesser," the Overseer sneered, the burly horse he rode casting a shadow over Benn. "At Roswell, we hang the slow ones."

He kept his eyes down but straightened when the Overseer addressed him with the slur. He'd avoided talking to the Master's Overseers, hoping it would help him go unnoticed. After all, he was supposed to be blending in.

The venom in the Overseer's voice matched his words. "You hear me? Lazy Lesser."

Looking him in the eye, Benn replied, "Yes sir."

The Overseer spat on him before his response was out. He tried not to flinch, only letting a slight tremor run through his hands. He'd trained with battle-axes at the Academy and he had half a mind to turn his pickaxe on this asshole. Alas, he didn't feel like killing anyone else today.

Or being whipped a second time.

Or being hung.

So, the greasy Overseer would live to see another day.

He blinked as spit stuck on his cheek. He eyed the russet horse that stood in front of him as an idea sparked in his mind. His magic flared to life, the sensation buzzing in his fingertips. He looked into the horse's eyes, preparing to influence the horse by using the emotion of fear.

He's an enemy. He pushed the thought toward the horse, wondering if his plan would work. *Drop his ass.*

Neighing in answer, the horse bucked the Overseer off his back, careening him into the air, making him land flat on the soil.

Benn wiped the spit off his face with his tattered sleeve. He approached the Overseer, offering his free hand to the man, holding his pickaxe in the other.

"*Don't you touch me, Lesserboy,*" the Overseer hissed as he scrambled to his feet.

His hand dropped as he smirked at the slur that he'd grown used to hearing at Roswell Camp. Wordlessly, he returned to the area of the field he had been working.

He swung his pickaxe again.

Again. Again. Again. Again.

Two hours later, his hands were calloused, his skin blistered from the relentless sun exposure, and his joints weak from the lack of nutrition the Camp slaves were provided.

If he was not living in a state of denial, he would admit that his self-worth was diminishing to new lows every minute. But he could not, because that was what worried Benn the most.

How did anyone survive this? This—this worthlessness. He thought, reflecting on how nice the small use of power had felt when he influenced the horse. He'd use small magic during his daily assassin runs, but it was not the same as using his true power.

He found himself questioning why he was here, again. A pang of guilt twisted in his chest as he remembered the generations of people enduring this torture.

Right, that is why I'm here. He looked around, teeth gritting, as he swung his axe again. *In this hellscape. To prevent this shit from happening in the Modern-Era. To protect the Founders' mission. To assassinate Corruptors working for Opasteg.* He swung his axe again. *The ones who want to prevent the origins of the Underground.*

If he ever dropped his shield, the emotions of the Chattels around him would swallow him whole into a pit of misery and devastation. He could not endure that trauma, so he forced the shield to remain in place at all times. Shielding from emotions was simple magic and had little impact on his power reserve, but here, everything was different. The terrible conditions, scarcity of food, and traumatic happenings he witnessed had taken a toll on him, leaving him to operate at a low power reserve.

Chattel. Benn gritted his teeth as the word roared.

He despised the practice and wanted to throw out a colorful curse at the sky regarding his Assignment. His drive to succeed kept him going. He refused to let that go. He needed to focus on who *he* was, so he could make it to the next phase of Assignment—whatever that was.

He continued to rage in silence as he swung his pickaxe.

His thoughts turned dark. *67 Mundaners keep Roswell Camp running. Harvesting, planting, hunting, gardening, cooking. Preparing the land, building structures, cleaning the house, raising children, feeding babies. Being assaulted. Being bred for money. Being hung when they rebel or sold when they are no longer useful. Eaten by the dogs if they—*

He forced the memory of the Master sending his dogs on the escaped Chattels out of his mind. It had happened several times since his arrival, and he had vomited each time afterward.

Their screams haunted him, the mere thought of the sounds made bile rise in his throat. He refused to be sick in this field. He swung the axe again.

This is the best-case scenario, he reminded himself. *At least I haven't been bred or sold.* The nausea rose again. He took a deep breath to calm himself.

To him, each of the slaves looked different, but to the Master and Overseers, that was not the case. They did not seem to notice the differences between each of the Chattels who worked here. That was an unexpected blessing for him at this wretched place, allowing his arrival to go unnoticed by the Master and Overseers. He swung his pickaxe again, as his mind wandered to the past.

Three months earlier

He landed in the Laviegata wilderness and opened the vellum.

It read:

WHO: Conscript Bennjamin Wyndmere
WHERE: ROSWELL CAMP, LAVIEGATA, HERI, 1855
ROSWELL POST
WHEN: TODAY APRIL 1855
TASK: ARRIVE IN CHAINS, REMAIN INCONSPICUOUS,
AND AWAIT INSTRUCTIONS. TEAR THE VELLUM IN HALF
AFTER READING.
REMEMBER THE UNDERGROUND.
-U. H.Q.

Upon his arrival, he followed a group of Chattels walking behind the Overseers on a dirt path, using the forest to remain unseen. They were coming from a market, where Chattels were sold and purchased. He caught up to the group, following the sound of the chains dragging on the ground.

His magic flared as he paused time. Needing to conserve his power, he grabbed the chains and shackled his ankles and wrists quickly, before he released his hold on time.

Ah, I have reached the point of no return, he'd joked to himself.

———

Idiot. He swung the pickaxe once more, angry that he was still doing this miserable task and had yet to receive another vellum. *Working at a desk would have been better. But, no, you're the fool that had to have a fulfilling role in life. Now, look where we are.*

He wanted to yank at his hair in frustration, but his arms were too heavy to do so, and any additional energy expended would be wasted, so he resisted the urge.

This is my calling? he internally shouted, swinging his pickaxe with more force this time, dirt clouding his vision and filling his mouth.

He used his tattered shirt to wipe his eyes and dropped it with a huff. His eyes blinked the remnants of the dirt away. Centimeters from his axe, a small vellum lay atop the dirt.

Benn leashed his excitement so the Overseers wouldn't suspect anything amiss. His hand shook as he grabbed it, placing it in the secret pocket of his rag-patched trousers.

He looked around, his magic livening; he sent a wave of sympathy, which was meant to manipulate the Master into feeling bad for the Overseers. He watched the entrance of the Main House as the Master called out to the Overseers.

"Why don't y'all come enjoy some tea? Come out of that heat for a bit," the Master called to them, Laviegatian accent shaping his tenor voice.

He smirked at his handiwork. He did not know the Master, yet his magic could manipulate him from hundreds of yards away. He knelt in the field, out of sight of the Main House, as he unraveled the vellum.

It read:

WHO: LEOLA RUNES / JUNIPER RUNES / RELATION: SISTERS
WHERE: ROSWELL CAMP, LAVIEGATA, HERI, 1855 ROSWELL POST
WHEN: TOMORROW, DUSK.
TASK: RESCUE THE SISTERS. THEY MUST BLEND IN AS CAMPEES.
THEY DO NOT KNOW OF THE UNDERGROUND BUT HAVE BEEN VETTED. ESTABLISH TRUST. EDUCATE THEM.
AWAIT FURTHER INSTRUCTIONS.
REMEMBER THE UNDERGROUND.
-U.H.Q.

He wanted to rejoice. He wanted to frolic. He must have reread the vellum twenty times before tucking it back into the hidden pocket. Anxiety pricked at his mind—these mysterious sisters did not know of the Underground. Idly, he wondered how that was possible.

How does any magic-bearing being not know about the Underground? He pursed his lips, swinging his axe.

He finished his work in the field and returned to the barracks, entering the one-room shack where he slept every night.

He removed his working clothes, taking a look at his wound from the Overseer's whip. It was nearly healed. He was not immortal, but his body healed faster as a magic-wielder—he could thank the Ancestral magic in his blood for that.

He lay in his straw cot, attempting not to disturb Miss Ava, his roommate.

She was a friend to Benn—another unexpected blessing to him on this Assignment. She was an elderly, kind, plump, and slow-moving Mundaner. She wore a faded apron and rag-fashioned bonnet that pulled her inky curls into a bun. She worked in the kitchen, so they rarely crossed paths until nighttime.

Each night, Miss Ava taught him songs and gossiped about the Master and Overseers; he was grateful to have her company. She made him slippers and fixed his clothes anytime they were damaged. There was little to fix, but he appreciated the gesture nonetheless. He'd been reluctant to trust anyone here, but he sensed her *empathy* toward him from the moment they met. He knew immediately that he found a friend in her.

Miss Ava snuck in herbs and fruit from the garden that she graciously shared with him. Food at Roswell was scarce—especially for Chattels who worked in the fields. He reached under his cot, their predetermined hiding place for contraband food, and was relieved to find five apples, a cucumber, and mint leaves waiting for him.

Most nights, he would tell her jokes or recite poems he remembered. He could not decide if it was depressing or endearing that a woman the age of his grandmother had become his best friend. Probably depressing, but at least her presence had helped quell the loneliness that had plagued him during this time.

He stared at the wall, using one of his blades to slice one of the apples, until Ava's hushed whisper stopped him. "Bennjamin, you will tell me when you get the next vellum."

His head whirled toward her, mouth agape in shock.

She flashed him a knowing smile and rolled over in her cot, turning her back toward him, not saying another word.

Another Underground member? He looked at his roommate with fresh eyes. *How?*

He woke up today defeated and terrified that he would never receive another vellum—that he would be condemned to assassin duty for *years*. Now, sitting in his cot, he sent a smile to the Gods and went to sleep with an unexpected ally, his heart beating with anticipation rather than the dread he was so used to.

CHAPTER 4

— BENN —

Year: 1855
1 July
Laviegata, Heri

H E SAT UP WITH A START, having somehow slept longer than he planned, but not long enough to beat the exhaustion that had settled into his marrow. He looked toward Ava's cot, seeing she'd already left. He didn't know what time it was, but the watercolor sunrise was an indication that the day was beginning and that his kill cards would be arriving any minute.

He peeked outside the dusty window and began his usual morning routine. He reached into his stashed herbs, pulling out citronella and mint. He ground the former in his fingers, dabbing the crushed herb on his neck, wrists, and ankles. It was necessary to keep the bugs at bay. He stashed mint in his pockets for chewing later as he worked in the fields.

He reached under his bed aiming for his slippers when his fingers hit a familiar object. Another apple. A grin spread across his face. *Thank you, Miss Ava.*

A soft puff of air sounded, signaling the arrival of the kill cards that now lay on his cot—right on schedule.

"Only three today. Light work," he quipped to no one.

He flipped through each card, cataloging the travel time each task would require—and the power it would cost him. Each card gave the approximate coordinates for the person on it, making finding them easy. Every morning, he received the pack of cards and followed the same process: look over each headshot, memorize the name, read the description and, if provided, the discography of crimes. He liked to know the reason why before ending their life.

There hadn't been a single person who did not deserve to go back to Mors, but he didn't enjoy this part of his job. He preferred to strategize, not round up the scum and send them back to the Death God. Anyone on his list was serving the enemy, though. Every single one was a Corruptor, and if they were serving Opasteg, in 1855, they were there with one goal: undermine the Underground and prevent the Founders from starting the organization. While he hated to admit it, it was a genius move by Opasteg leadership, to send their assassins to pick off the Underground Founders. It almost succeeded—until Sena and the Order discovered their work and deployed two cohorts of Conscripted to this era in response. One cohort deployed three months prior, as Benn had, and the other deployed some months before that, disclosed to no one except Underground leadership, Fas for messaging, and the Conscripts who answered the mission calls.

He sliced the apple, eating it in the privacy of the barracks so no one would see him. Chattels were punished—or worse—for stealing food. He stashed the core in his secret pocket, planning to bury it in the orchard later in the day. He eyed the sky again, assuming he had six minutes before he needed to report to the orchard.

Three kill cards. Six minutes. He pulled his stopwatch out of his hidden pocket, tied the laces of his Modern-Era sneakers, and warped to the first location.

He landed in the forest, roughly a day's walk from where he lived and worked. The forest was easy. There were no witnesses to consider in the forest.

He spotted the man, eyes narrowing as he watched him knot two nooses for the Chattels standing next to him.

Two teenage boys, who both shook with fear. Benn's jaw ticked in anger.

Unnecessary loss of life was abhorrent; Benn never understood how Corruptors could be so careless with the lives of Mundaners—the population that made up the Camps. He didn't need to lower his shield to get a better understanding of the man's crimes, because here he was, committing one. With a flick of Benn's wrist, the man collapsed—neck snapped, life severed. He summoned the warpcraft that would take the body back to Headquarters.

He warped to the teens as he said, "Stay quiet. Take my hand."

Both of them reared back, startled and unsure as they had no reason to trust a man who had just landed in front of them. Their onset of emotions and intentions flared, triggering Benn's power.

Fear. Uncertainty. The one on the right weighed the odds of running away versus fighting Benn. The one on the left marveled at his sneakers. Neither took his outstretched hand.

He let a smile glance his usual stoic features, attempting to make them less fearful of him. In the Modern-Era, Mundaners and magic-wielders interacted in certain spaces, but in this era, that was not the case. In this era, magic was a new privilege gifted to a limited and specific group of humans, and in most instances, magic-wielders were not kind to humans. They were right to be afraid of him.

Five minutes, twenty-nine seconds. His mental clock was ticking.

He thrust his hand forward again. "Take it. There's no time."

They exchanged a look that gave him the impression they knew each other—or at least, trusted each other. With a slight nod, they interlocked hands, and both boys reached forward to grip his outstretched palms.

Wind whipped their cheeks as he landed a three-day walk northeast of where they'd been previously—to a safe house where he'd been numerous times before. The fire pit burned, confirming that it was safe to send Chattels to the back door.

They looked at him in question.

They were young—maybe a couple years younger than him.

"Head to the back door. Knock five times. Go inside. Tell them Medgar sent you. They'll help you get free."

Five minutes. Ten seconds.

Without another word, he warped to the next location. It was a risk to take the boys—not because it wasn't safe, but because he did not have the time to spare. He did not care; the risk was worth it every time he could spare a life. He killed an Overseer right in front of those teens, and they would have taken the blame for what he did. If he left them, they would have been in nooses by lunchtime.

He landed in a bathroom this time, which was not as easy as his preferred forest setting, but he was short on time, so it would have to work.

He looked around the bathroom, spotting the man at the same time the man saw him.

Fear. Rage. Disbelief that an enemy assassin found him. Benn smirked at the emotions running through the man's mind.

The man threw a dagger and Benn caught it, tsking his tongue before using his free hand to twist, cutting off the man's air supply. He sank to the floor in a heap of a bathrobe.

He approached, checking his pulse. *Dead.* He cracked a window, summoning another warpcraft.

He examined the dagger; it was nice, sharp, and new. He dropped into his hidden pocket—it never hurt to have a spare in the collection.

Three minutes, thirty-nine seconds until he needed to report.

He landed in the third location, a path that led to the trading markets. A carriage approached as Benn waited in the trees, looking for the man whose face was on the card. He saw him.

Silver hair. Silver beard. Green eyes. Olive-toned skin. Overseer leathers. Corruptor.

He lowered his shield to confirm it was him. It was, so he twisted his hand, hearing the snap of the man's vertebrae and the exclamation of his companion in response.

He summoned the warpcraft to himself and sent a message: "The man on my kill card is in that carriage and I need to report at my Camp. Subject is dead. Will need retrieval at a later time." He inputted the coordinates into the warpcraft, sending those and the message to whatever Fa monitored this channel of communication, knowing they would receive the message, but were not permitted to respond.

Thirty seconds. Shit. He warped, landing in his barrack, tearing off his sneakers and yanking on his work slippers. In seconds, he was starting the long walk toward the orchard, grabbing a pickaxe out of the supply shed on the way.

Every morning, the Overseers met the Chattels at the orchard, where they would assign tasks for the day. Each of the Chattels arrived early to avoid punishment. Benn liked this time because it was the only time all of the Chattels got to spend together each day. This time made him feel human again. It made him remember his mission. But today, he found himself wondering if there were more Conscripts here than himself and Miss Ava, though he would have no way of knowing that. He made a mental note to ask Miss Ava *how* she had known that he'd received a vellum and if she knew of any other Underground spies in the area.

The day passed slowly. Despite another day of brutal work, his mind was consumed by formulating a plan for his task tonight.

He needed to get into the forest that surrounded the Roswell Camp without being seen. The vellum indicated that the sisters would arrive at the Roswell Camp Drop Point, which was where he had arrived as well.

At least, I know where I'm supposed to be. Relief filled him for a brief second before it was replaced with dread.

His eyes drifted to the area where the Overseers were gathered across the field. The Chattels weren't permitted to leave their quarters after dusk, and the last thing he needed was to be caught in the forest by Camp Patrol.

Nope, you won't catch me today, demons. He swung his axe, letting his muscle memory guide his overused body.

Camp Patrol was like Neighborhood Watch—except they were armed, cruel, and bloodthirsty on their hunt for escaped Chattels.

A shudder ran through him as he imagined the treatment of those they caught. Patrollers got to serve the punishment of their choice to anyone they captured. It could range from something mild, like branding the runaways or cutting off one of their limbs, or depending on the gruesome nature of the captor, it could morph into a much worse fate, such as a hanging or... the use of the dogs.

His stomach twisted. Patrol was responsible for the bodies in the trees. *Yeah, that's a definite no. Never.*

He needed a plan that resulted in him and the sisters making it back to Roswell, *alive.* As more time passed, his anxiety rose. He had no suitable plan and dusk was approaching at breakneck speed.

The Chattels worked until midday when they were pulled back to the orchard for a short meeting with the Overseers—which was strange. Overseers never interrupted the work of the Chattels... unless it was for punishments.

Benn stood under the coveted shade of the orchard, seeking out his friend. He kept his shields intact, not needing to use his power to read the emotion written all over Miss Ava's face. The look she gave him indicated that her apprehension mirrored his.

The Overseers all matched—squeaky, black leather pants with a vest, an undershirt, and black shiny boots. A contrast to the ragged hand-me-downs he wore. Overseers were employees of Roswell and every other Camp in Laviegata. They were paid, unlike the Chattels. They lived in nicer quarters than the Chattels but were still trapped in the role of an Overseer. They were not as powerful as the Master, but they certainly were not as disposable as the Chattels. Most were lowborn, coming from families who were too poor to purchase land or people, so they could never achieve real power in this era. Unlike Corruptors, Overseers were Mundaners—powerless. So, they each carried a whip in hand, as if to remind the Chattels of their place here— like they could ever forget. Like the whip set them apart, simply because the Chattels and Overseers were all Mundaners, just born under different circumstances.

The Overseers were all present, though they looked stiff. Emotion-benders could sense emotions, traits, lies, and truths, but it wouldn't take one to know that something was *off*. Benn lowered his shields to let the essence of the emotions around him in. The air held a stench that was oily and thick, similar to tar or sulfur.

Is that... dread? He pondered over the new emotion he was finding in the Overseers.

A similar emotion flickered into his bones, anticipating whatever came next. His eyes caught sight of Master Roswell approaching the orchard with a man he did not recognize. This man was middle-aged with night-dark hair. He wore leather pants, work boots, and a denim jacket with Modern-Era patches. Benn's eyes zeroed in on the various patches, noting the obvious modernness of this man's attire.

A Corruptor. He seethed, almost baring his teeth. *A stupid one at that.*

A list of angry phrases filled his mind at this unexpected encounter, causing his magic to writhe under his skin, waking at the opportunity to protect himself.

In the ongoing battle for power between the Underground and Opasteg, Opasteg members consisted of magic-wielders, also called powers and poweresses, who were similar to Mundane humans in appearance, but were less fragile beings who were gifted magic abilities that awakened at birth and continued to manifest with age. They lived among the normal society, but they remained unnoticed by Mundane humans—unless they chose to reveal themselves.

The Conscripted, like Benn, were the spies who served the Underground; Corruptors held the equivalent role in Opasteg. The two societies have been at war for decades—a war that has withstood the test of time and, more often than not, caught Mundaners in the crossfire.

The Underground worked across the eras for justice and a free world. Its forces served as trained vigilantes in all areas of the world and in all eras where human society has ever thrived.

Opasteg rivaled the Underground in numbers and worldview. Opasteg fought for a world where rights are determined by class and wealth—putting Mundaners, or Lesserbeings as they call them, at ground-level of their classist totem pole. They did not stand for rights for all, and most abhorrent of all, they wished to bring back Separation, Libata clauses, and Camps for the Mundane.

The societies agreed on nothing else, other than the one fundamental law they both followed: to never, *ever* reveal the societies to Mundaners. The emotions and moods of the Mundane beings were unpredictable, making them dangerous and impulsive.

This asshole has on a denim jacket from the Modern-Era. With patches *that do not exist here.* His eyes sharpened in disgust at the Corruptor's carelessness to remain inconspicuous to the Mundaners surrounding them. He looked to Miss Ava again, shifting closer to his roommate, in case he needed to defend her.

"Everyone, listen up now. I don't want to take up too much time with this." A smile tightened Master Roswell's weathered skin as he addressed the Chattels. "After all, the fields won't work themselves."

Benn resisted the urge to roll his eyes and leaned back against a tree. Best to not appear as defensive, when he could freeze time if he needed to jump in front of Ava.

Master Roswell gestured to the Corruptor who stood beside him. "This nice fellow is looking for two of your friends... lost them in the woods last night. We need to enlist some of y'all to seek them out."

His stomach revolted at the thought of doing the Corruptor's dirty work but kept his face neutral.

Master Roswell continued, "I don't want this stopping your work, so the search will commence at sundown. And don't be getting any foolish notions, the Overseers—"

Slave Patrol, Benn corrected internally.

"--will be out there with ya, watching over the search party, and will escort you back once the two girls have been returned."

His blood chilled. *The girls?* His thoughts returned to his current mission. *The sisters I need to find? The girls know nothing of the Underground, so why would a Corruptor be hunting them? This can't be a coincidence—unless this sick twat is doing it for sport.*

"Any volunteers will get a spare grain ration, simply because I'm feeling generous today." Master Roswell chuckled, clearly waiting for someone to volunteer.

A few hands raised; Benn's did not. Instead, he sucked his cheek and began to devise a plan that would land him in the woods at dusk—unsupervised, obviously. He figured out one piece of the puzzle that was carrying out this mission. He *would* be at that drop point at dusk—he just needed to land there before the Overseers and their search party arrived.

I'll sneak into the forest and find the girls before these jokers have a chance. What could go wrong? He nearly laughed at the absurdity of this mission, which he would have, if it were funny. The first vellum he'd received in months had been missing *vital* details.

Locate the sisters, educate them on the Underground, and transport them safely to Roswell Camp. Sure, easy enough. He flexed his fingers. *Add an addendum that says:* 'By the way, Benn, the sisters are being hunted by a Corruptor, twelve Overseers, and some of your Chattel peers.'

Master Roswell's voice intercepted his thoughts. "Meet here just before dusk for orders. You'll go to the forest from here. And one more thing, don't make me look bad in front of my new friend." He gestured to the Corruptor. "You're dismissed."

Message received. Somehow, they know the sisters are landing here tonight, Ope spies are good—even if they dress like fools. The sisters must be important. But, if that were the case, why are they not educated? Who are they?

He straightened, grabbed his pickaxe, and started the walk back to the fields. The heat burned his face, but the anticipation of his task—of doing *something* other than working the Master's land—had him giddy.

This is going to be fun. A smile tugged at his lips. *We might be dead by the end of the night, but isn't that what I signed up for?*

CHAPTER 5

— BENN —

H E EYED THE SUN AS HE returned his pickaxe to the shed. His hands ached and bled from the work he had done in the fields all day, but they started healing the moment the pickaxe left his grip.

Judging by the remnants of light coloring the sky, dusk was twenty minutes out. He stalked toward his barrack, trying not to walk too fast; he would gain nothing from drawing unwanted, additional attention.

He rinsed off using the small tub outside the barracks and changed into a clean work shirt, one made of inky cloth that would blend well with the nightcover of the forest.

He'd just pulled on his pants when Miss Ava landed right in front of him. He stilled. *Did she just—?*

She interrupted his thoughts in a hushed voice. "Obviously I can warp, dear boy. Anyone with magic in their veins can." She waved her hand as she spoke, like that admission was old news, when, to him, that was quite the opposite. "Listen, we don't have much time," Ava said as she reached into the trunk under her bed—for what, he couldn't tell. "I'm a member of the Underground. That much, I hope you've figured out by now." She looked up at him, waiting for his answer, so he nodded. "I was deployed to Roswell a while ago to carry out a mission."

Vague. His eyes narrowed.

"Ah, here it is," she said, holding up an old, leather backpack. She rose to meet his gaze. "This is enchanted. I've been keeping it for you. It can hold anything and *everything* you need to have with you, and will conceal its contents, if that's what you wish." He nodded again. Her hands clapped together. "We'll need to hustle."

She turned toward his bed, the glow of her magic filling the air in waves of soft lavender, stunning him for a few heartbeats. It was as calm and familiar as the emotions he'd sensed on her since the day they'd met. He lowered his shields, reveling in the essence of her excitement. It was a rare emotion at Roswell. She manifested a cloth shirt and canvas pants, both dark as midnight and newer than his uniform. She handed the clothes to Benn as she said, "For you."

His eyes went wide as moons. *An illusionist.*

"Stop looking so shocked, young one; get dressed," she commanded, the glow of her magic illuminating the room again. Two more sets of dark work clothing and slippers manifested, landing on Ava's bed with a soft thud. "For Leola and Juniper," she explained as she put the clothes and slippers into the enchanted backpack, thrusting it into his hand.

He had so many questions. Ava was an illusionist—strong enough to manifest clothing out of thin air. She was seasoned, well-practiced. She was moving faster than he'd seen her move in the three months he'd known her.

Who is she? She can't be an Ope spy, or else I'd sense her lies. His eyebrows raised in question. *How does she know of my mission, if I never showed her the vellum? How does she know their names?*

All of these questions swirled in his mind as he looked down at the enchanted backpack. "Miss Ava, I—"

She shushed him, placing a weathered finger to his mouth. "Hush, Bennjamin. Focus on your mission. It's essential that you all make it back here safely. I'm sure

61

you have questions. They will, too. We shall chit-chat about the details later, I assure you."

There was no time to spare with questions, so he reluctantly agreed to save them for later. He headed toward the door, backpack in hand.

"One more thing," she said as she kissed both his cheeks. "Remember the Underground."

He chuckled, saluted his friend with a fist in the air and warped into the Laviegata woods.

CHAPTER 6

— BENN —

H E LANDED AT THE ROSWELL CAMP Drop Point right on schedule. Enough light remained, so he could still see his surroundings. He looked toward the dirt path, noting the search party had started heading toward the woods.

If all goes well, I'll pick them up and warp back to the barracks in ten minutes. He gazed at the gnarled branches of the trees as his eyes snagged on the bodies that he'd been trying to ignore. *Five minutes, max.*

'Educate them,' HQ said. Per usual, he was thinking ahead, leading him to wonder what the sisters knew of *magic. Their ages weren't listed on the vellum, but I would've crossed paths with them at the Academy if they were enrolled during my time there, so why don't I know them?*

He shook off his anxiety, hoping they possessed master-class knowledge of their abilities and that he was not responsible for *all* of their education. *No, that'd be ridiculous. There's no way they'd do that to me; Headquarters wouldn't pair me with untrained companions.* He exhaled, forcing calm to settle into his tight jaw. *There are smaller schools for magic-wielders—perhaps, they attended one of those. They'll be trained. They have to be. If not, I'll send a colorful complaint of curses with the next warpcraft I see.*

He scanned the area, eyes zeroing in on one girl. She had full features with a rounded face that led him to guess she was in her late teens—close to Maturity, but not quite. Her hair lay brushed over her shoulder in long, raven-colored braids. Her skin was coated in a thin sheen of sweat that brought a pallid look to her caramel-hued complexion. There hadn't been a photo of the sisters, so he had to assume she was one of them. She lay motionless on the ground as if she was under some sort of sleeping spell. Lethargy was a known side-effect of time travel, especially in circumstances where the body was not prepared for it. He warped to her, leaning down to where she lay on the ground. He held out a hand, relief flooding him as shallow breaths confirmed that she was alive.

Time magic was active in the area, but he could not identify the source. It was an emerald green fog in the air, difficult to see, but discoverable if one knew what to look for. He did. Since they'd never met, he wouldn't be able to identify if this magic belonged to either of the sisters. He did, however, see it as a win that they were using their own magic as a resource.

Another time-wielder as a companion? I'll take it. He grinned. *And no deaths. Not bad for the first mission, Benny.*

Elemental magics were present, too—fire and earth. One trail seemed to give off heat, leaving an orange mist in its wake. The earth magic appeared in the form of a sage vapor. The magic trails were hard to detect, but he could see them. He wondered if the girls had intentionally disguised their magic trails, in which case, he'd be impressed. His eyes followed the orange vapor, attempting to locate the source.

He locked eyes with a crazed-looking girl who he hadn't heard approach. She seemed to be around his age, looking similar to the girl on the ground aside from her masses of auburn hair and freckles that matched each other exquisitely. In a different world, Benn would have found her beauty striking, but in this world, he had little time to consider it, as the girl was swinging a branch directly at his head. He caught the branch before it could hit him, wincing as the wood bit into his calloused hands. He rose up onto his feet, dropping the branch to the ground.

Found the other sister, he thought, pleased that no time had been wasted looking for her.

His throat burned—a courtesy of the panic filling her mind as she recognized that the plan with the branch had not worked. The emotion flashing in her eyes was thick and tar-like in his mouth.

She's scared. Mentioning I'm here to retrieve her and her sister will only scare her more.

Another branch rose to her hand so fast, he was impressed by her use of small magic at play.

Eyes bouncing between her eyes and her grip around the branch, he said softly, "I wouldn't do that if I were you."

And she's going for it, he thought, preparing a bind of his own magic to defend.

"You're not me," she seethed.

The branch froze in the air as he caught it with the other hand and set it on the ground.

He pondered how to approach the auburn-haired girl—woman, actually. He considered how this looked: while he had come here to pick them up, she'd not been expecting him; that much was clear, and it looked bad. He needed to establish trust. Now.

The smell of her fear set his power ablaze—readying to defend and protect. He peered over his shoulder to locate the search party—still on the Roswell property, but he could see they'd moved closer.

We need to go. His palms slickened.

He asked the most unassuming question he could think of, "Where have you come from?"

The girl gave him a withering glare, confirming she didn't trust him. Even less so now.

He frowned at her. *We're pissing away our time to escape. We need to move.*

She tossed his question back, with an Eastern accent—louder and nothing like his. "Where did *you* come from?"

He didn't appreciate the sarcastic tone, especially because he was risking his life and spycover to retrieve them. Nonetheless, he gestured to the search party, replying, "That way."

As he motioned to the search party, he noticed their speed was increasing—and, worse, they were heading in their direction.

Can't have that. Benn thought as his magic flicked to his fingers, seeking out the men. He sent a strong wave of lackadaisicalness to hinder their urgency. He sighed in relief as he saw them pause, getting distracted by something on the path.

He barely heard her answer but sensed the lie anyway.

"Us too," she uttered. She wanted him to believe that she and her sister had come from the direction he had gestured toward.

She has no idea where she is, he discerned. *There's nothing but bloody Roswell land in that direction for miles. Clever attempt; only a rookie tells their whereabouts to a stranger.*

"A lie," he declared, trying to indicate to her that he could sense lies, so she would be more truthful with him and save them all time. After all, they were to be allies. "Clever idea, though. That will be useful later."

He regretted that admission the second it was out of his mouth. *I shouldn't have said that.* She'd been looking down at her sister, so he hoped she hadn't heard his mistake.

She gave him a look of shock, hands going to her hips, as she asked, "Sorry, useful for *what*?"

Well, shit. She's observant. He watched her instead of answering.

She scoffed; she was in disbelief at her surroundings. Her voice had gotten louder, so it was obvious she was unaware of how dangerous this forest or the slave patrol was.

Benn looked toward the men again; his magic was slowing their pace, but it wasn't going to be enough. They needed to get moving, but if he had learned anything about the unnamed sister standing in front of him, it was that she was going to challenge any and all of his ideas.

"We need to go. Was she... lethargic before you came here?" He kept his voice low, hoping to accelerate their conversation to a place that would move them one step closer to leaving these woods. At the question, he sensed her emotions shift from fear of him to an instinct to protect her sister, who was *still* lying on the ground. He couldn't warp her until he confirmed her body could withstand the travel.

He sensed her apprehension, but she replied anyway, "I woke up a few minutes ago—over there." She pointed in the direction of which she had come. Benn sensed that fact was true. "I found her over here. She doesn't seem injured, just unconscious."

He sensed worry plaguing her emotions, but there was something else present in her mind.

Compliance. Benn almost smiled as he identified the emotion. *She's starting to trust me. We're getting somewhere.*

He snuck a glance in the direction of the search party, hoping to not draw her attention to them. He did not want to scare the girl by letting her know that she and her sister were being *hunted*.

She noticed and prodded, "It seems you're wanting to go—"

He interrupted, "Yes, you're correct. And I'd like to get a move on, if we could stop dallying."

"Who's *dallying*?" she snapped, and he flinched. "I would like to get the hell out of this place, too—but I'm not leaving my sister. You, on the other hand, are free to go."

He ignored the rude shooing motion of her hand because she'd finally mentioned a detail that he could hold onto without showing her that he'd known about their arrival all along.

"Sisters?" He followed that question up by asking for their names. Once again, trying to make up for time lost—which happened to be their time to escape. Sweat was running down his neck, nervousness filling him with every passing second that they spent in this cursed forest. He must have been too quick with his question regarding their names because he got the sense that the girl was going to lie to him, *again*.

Leola, she'd answered, seconds before. But then, as she gestured to her sister, he sensed the lie forming in her mind. In tandem, he felt a sense of mistrust guiding her decisions.

"And this is my sister—"

The men had moved closer; the closer they got, the more danger they were in. His pulse quickened.

Enough, he thought. He answered his own question before Leola could lie to him. "Juniper—right?"

Her mouth fell open and her terror flooded his senses, heightening his anxiety even more, making it impossible for him to think. He threw up his shield, but it failed. His patience was dwindling, along with his power reserve and his semblance of control of this mission.

She tried to question him, but Benn put a hand to her mouth, keeping his eyes on the men in the distance. "We're wasting time. The spell will wear off any minute," he said, trying to urge her to move without scaring her.

She dug her heels into the ground and shoved him away from her. "There is no *we. I'm* staying here."

He contemplated his options, as the men moved faster. He couldn't pause time tonight. His power reserve had taken a hit due to the nature of life at Camp—that, combined with the extra power he'd used to move those two Chattels to the safe house that morning, he couldn't spare more power to freeze time, even though he needed to. He needed to conserve his power to warp them all to safety, or emotion-wield if the men got too close to either sister.

Why is the girl still unconscious? He leaned over to check her pulse, becoming eye level with the sister who was standing.

"Perhaps when you traveled, she was impacted by the—" He stopped himself. He didn't know how they'd arrived here and there was a possibility that she had not realized she wasn't in the Modern-Era yet. The auburn-haired sister leaned over the unconscious one, shaking her and begging her to wake up. Her emotions were changing too fast for him to interpret.

She was frantic.

She was panicking.

She was desperate.

She gestured, her words startling him. "I'm going to flag down those men and see if they can take her to the infirm—"

His nostrils flared in fear, and he grabbed her shoulders before even realizing what he was doing. "*NO!* Are you mad? Calling those men over here would *surely* end in our deaths."

How could she see them *as trustworthy? Where does she think we are? Hasn't she seen the forest we're in? The bodies?* His thoughts frenzied, he realized she didn't just not know of the Underground—she didn't seem to know anything at all.

"What do you suggest then?" She deflated, her *annoyance* shouting in his mind.

He'd been distracted by his worry. The search party caught his eye; they were less than 90 yards from them now.

Too fucking close. He pulled her to the ground with him. *We waited too long.*

There was no way for all of them to leave without being seen. The Overseers would string him up, especially if they saw him helping the sisters. They would do it even if he were simply *discovered* in the woods after sundown. They'd do it for fun. Worse was what they would do to the sisters if they found them. They needed to wait for the search party to pass, and leave once they had moved onto another area of the forest.

"Cover her with leaves. We leave at nightfall," he whispered.

She let out a sound of protest as Benn covered her mouth once again to prevent the men from hearing her voice.

"You don't know me, but your only option is to trust me. *If we're discovered, we will hang in these trees*," he whispered, tears pricking at his eyes at how poorly this mission was going.

Whatever she saw on his face had her scooping leaves and burying her sister with the same frantic urgency.

The men drew closer, *closer* still, until he could hear their words. He tensed, hearing them make crude jokes about what they would do to the girls once they found them, how they would violate them and send a message to other runaways with their bodies. He worked faster, knowing that if they were discovered by the search party, the torture they'd endure would make them wish they were dead anyway. And, while he was prepared to die for the Underground, he was not about to die at the hands of these assholes. Not today.

They finished covering the girl with leaves, leaving enough space around her face and mouth so she could breathe. The girl paused to take one last look at her sister, so Benn grabbed her, put her over his shoulder, and sprinted deep into the forest, out of sight of slave patrol.

He cursed this tortuous Assignment for how weak and out of shape he was, as he lowered her to the ground. He inhaled to catch his breath, trying not to reveal how winded he was. Weakness could not be his first impression.

They sat in silence behind a fallen tree, where he had a clear vantage point of the search party. He scanned the trees, letting his eyes fall onto the woman next to him. She kept her eyes trained on her sister, her posture strained, as if she would flee their hiding place if anything went awry. His eyes went back to the group. They were passing the other sister, who was not far away enough from the dirt road they walked on.

His hands shook. He needed a distraction from the anxiety that radiated off the woman next to him in waves. Her teeth chattering was driving him mad. He'd commented on that fact, and then Benn told her his name, noting he hadn't introduced himself before he'd snapped at her for her aggressive teeth chattering.

"Poppycal. Sorry, Region 146." Tears filled her eyes, but she blinked them away as she continued, "That's where we came from."

He was silent a moment longer, hating that she corrected her use of the state name, her words stinging him with the realization of just how far the world had fallen since the Red Coup. After a few quiet moments, he murmured, "Rosebay."

He did not bother saying the region name, but he didn't need to. He would *not* be using the new region title that Opasteg required they use. Rosebay was Rosebay. Not Region 458. More importantly, he served the Underground, and he would take a stance against the new regime at every opportunity.

Her sadness washed over him in strong currents, and he prayed to the Gods that his shields would work; they did not. She was crying now. He fought back tears of his own when he had mentioned his hometown of Rosebay. He wished he could warp there and abort this whole fucked-up mission. They fell into silence again. Tense and strenuous. Fragile.

Her voice was quiet in the darkness. "Where are we?"

He answered, "Laviegata." Then, feeling the need to mention the year in case she was not yet aware, he added, "Year 1855."

Her emotions of fear and shock confirmed his assumption.

The girls do not know where they are—in space or time. They don't know of the Underground. His jaw clenched. *Did they even mean to come here?*

He was willing to bet they did not, but he didn't have time to consider how that was possible, because the other girl shot straight up, right as the search party passed her.

He took off running, racing through the trees, attempting to reach her before she made *any* noise. He weaved through the trees, eyes darting between the men and her. She was preparing to climb a tree nearby. How they'd not noticed her was a blessing from a Luck God he'd thank later.

Get down! No. No. He picked up his pace, moving his feet faster and pumping his arms with more force. He needed to get to her *now*.

Better yet, two minutes ago. He hurdled over a decaying log, continuing to sprint.

Her grip on the tree branch caused it to rustle, the search party turning in her direction. They held their lanterns in the air, readying to release their dogs. Blood roared in his ears, and the horror of what was happening set in.

He was not going to make it.

He slid to a stop, grabbing a palm-sized rock. He gripped it, pulled his shoulder back, and threw it as hard as he could muster in the opposite direction of the girl.

As soon as the rock left his hand, he risked the power use and warped the rest of the way. The rock landed on the opposite side of the tree line, causing the search party to turn in the other direction, away from her.

She reached for the lowest branch as he landed soundlessly behind her. He grabbed her, pressed a hand over her mouth, and then pulled her deeper into the forest.

He kept watch while the auburn-haired one calmed her sister. A pang of guilt hit him. *Of course I need to eavesdrop. I'd be a shit spy if I didn't.*

The sisters sat a couple feet behind him. The dark-haired sister was adamant about not trusting him, and from what he could read on both of them, neither trusted him. However, they understood their options were limited and had identified him as their best option for survival. They also could take him two-on-one, as the younger of the two had reminded him.

Multiple times.

Given the fact that he'd yanked her from a tree and dragged her back here, he did not expect anything different. She'd fought like a rabid animal, kicking her feet, and clawing her nails into his face in an attempt to free herself from his grasp; he had defensive wounds to prove it. Once she'd seen the other one waiting, she had relaxed.

Slightly.

He could sense her wariness, both by using his emotion-wielding and the harsh looks she cast toward him as the other sister relayed the situation to her.

— **LEOLA** —

She hated the look in Juniper's eyes as she explained what she could about the situation. Her mind was reeling—her head pounding—so she regurgitated the facts she had figured out: they needed to focus on where they were. She nearly vomited again as she motioned to the bodies hanging in the trees. After a few deep breaths, she regained her composure, which was lost once more when she looked at Juniper's tear-ridden face. Dread pooled in her stomach as she prepared to explain that they were not just in an unfamiliar place, but in a different era. And on top of that, it was one where Mundaners were considered property.

She swallowed, holding her sister's hand in hers as she explained, "There is one last thing, Bug." She paused. "Where we are—well, the year is... is 1855." The blank look on her sister's face told Leola that she was not comprehending the words she'd said, so she tried again. "I think that weird guy in the deli—um—caused us to travel back in time," she said as she watched her sister, waiting for a response.

Eyes locked on the ground, Juniper let out a humorless laugh. "You mean, we had the opportunity to *travel through time*—" Her voice broke. "And *this* is where we ended up?"

Leola blinked twice at her sister's sarcastic remark until a bout of hysteria-induced laughter forced itself through her lips. Within seconds, both sisters were laughing, covering their mouths to keep quiet.

— BENN —

He learned a few key details while listening to the sisters. Neither of them had mentioned magic, so it was possible that they did not know they had access to magic, even if magic *was* in use when he had first found them. They hadn't come here on purpose. And he found himself wondering, who this *man* they kept referring to was.

He let his shields drop while the sisters were talking—a result of exhaustion, but mostly because the shields were ineffective against the auburn-haired sister, so using his power reserve with faulty shields was a waste. With his shields down, he tried to glance into their power or magic, but was met with a strange block. It was like nothing he'd ever seen before, but it was somehow familiar; he was too low on power to look further, and they needed to move.

The girls were still laughing in whispered breaths when Benn turned toward them. He tried to discern if the sisters were unwell from today's events or if they actually found this situation funny. He decided it was the former.

He interrupted their fit, saying, "The search party is giving up. We're safe to warp back to the barracks. Let's go."

He was starving and stressed; he needed to get them to safety—to Miss Ava, who might have ideas to offer. There was a short pause in the hushed laughter, until they looked at each other and started again.

The auburn-haired one spoke through her laughter. "You want us to do *what*?"

The dark-haired one smirked, wiping the corners of her eyes. "He said—" Her voice dropped to a lower octave; she was mimicking him. "*We're safe to warp.*"

Benn rolled his eyes at the inaccurate Rosebayish accent she'd used, but they just laughed harder.

He gave them a second to regain their composure, and they paused long enough to look at him. He raised a brow. He had little experience with Mundaners, and he did not have the time or energy to explain what warping meant tonight. For a reason he could not possibly understand, the Underground had sent him Mundaners—or at least people who were not close enough to magic culture to know what warping meant—to look after.

He cleared his throat and said, "Yes, that's exactly it."

Without another word, he grabbed each of their hands. Warm, summer air whipped around them as they warped, landing inside the small, candle-lit room.

He could taste their terror and confusion and felt a little guilty for the sudden change of scenery. At least they were all safe now. He raised his shield and was able to block one sister's emotions out; he grimaced as the other one's emotions seeped into his mind. "Welcome to my humble abode, also known as Roswell Camp," he muttered with a mock bow, trying to ignore the exhaustion that was cloaking him like a weighted vest.

He leaned his back against the mud wall, trying to quiet the emotions swarming his mind; they weren't even his own. For the first time since his arrival three months ago, he was relieved to be back at Roswell Camp.

CHAPTER 7

— JUNIPER —

J UNIPER EYED BENN AS HE lit a candle on the narrow windowsill while she
digested the small space he had *warped* them to—though she was unclear on what
that word meant. The room was shadowy and stank of stale air and old soil. She
attributed that to poor ventilation and the tiny window on the wall.

No one was talking. The silence may as well have been screaming the way that
it crept into her bones.

She was standing in a Mundaner Camp; as she turned in a slow circle, she half-
expected someone to jump out of the shadows and explain that this was some
distasteful prank gone wrong. Her fingers grazed one of the straw cots in the room.
While she was not expecting to find a high-end mattress here, she cringed at the use
of straw for a bed. The shack was built of weathered wood and caked mud, and it
was far more suitable for livestock to live in—not Mundaners. She swallowed the
thick lump that had formed in her throat at the realization that this was how her
ancestors had lived, for generations. Seeing a Chattel barrack with her own eyes left
her speechless—her soul crushed in ways she'd need to examine later.

— BENN —

He was more than comfortable in the silence that stretched between them; the immense stress of the last few hours was enough to traumatize him for days... no, weeks, if he was being honest.

As much as he hated to admit it, his mind had been so focused on getting the sisters away from the drop point that he hadn't thought about what would come afterward. He'd planned on meeting Miss Ava here, as they'd discussed, but she was not in the room when they arrived. She would have an idea on how they should proceed—once she returned.

Or is it possible that I could get another vellum with directions, perhaps? he prayed to the Gods. *If you can hear me, now would be a lovely time for a new vellum to appear.*

He held his breath, waiting, but as usual, there was no answer and no vellum.

Splendid. Benn scoffed, frustrated and a bit terrified.

He rubbed his hands together, channeling his restless energy. "We'll wait here for my friend. She has been helping me since I arrived here." He paused, wondering if they could hear the nervousness that riddled his tone. "We share this room, so she should be back anytime. She'll know what to do next."

He was trying to convince *himself* of that fact more than the two sisters in front of him. They said nothing, exchanging a look between themselves that he wouldn't interpret. They probably knew he was full of shit, but it wasn't like they had many options other than to trust him. Maybe that was a blessing.

'Establish trust. Educate them.' The message from the vellum played through his mind on a torturous loop. The vellum mentioned that they weren't aware of the Underground, so it was safe to assume that they were not privy to the mission either. He would start by informing them of the situation, then try to discern what kind of magic they possessed or what the reason was for the block shielding their power from emotion-wielders.

From him.

By the Gods, are these girls even soldiers? Benn schooled his face into a calm mask and sat on the cot, motioning for them to do the same. When they didn't, he rose to his feet.

"We're good standing... while we wait for your friend," the older sister said, her eyes unblinking on his.

"Hopefully we aren't here too long, but for the time being... you ladies need to fit in," he explained, pacing between the two cots, his fingers tugging at the ends of his curls. "Here is what I know. There was a man here, earlier today, looking for you both. That's why the Master sent a search party into the woods tonight. There's no doubt that he will keep up his search for you, especially now that tonight was unsuccessful."

The raven-haired sister had been leaning against the wall but straightened at his words. Her brows knit together as she crossed her arms in front of her. "What kind of man?" She stammered over the next sentence. "We—we met a strange man before we—uh, got here."

What is her name? Leola and Juniper—but which is which? He scolded himself. This Assignment had forced him out of battle training and now he had forgotten to mark their identities. He chose not to dwell on that mistake, figuring the answer would reveal itself.

"Blue eyes, dark hair. Jet-black. He was wearing typical clothes for this era... aside from a denim jacket, one that was not from this time period." His jaw tensed as he recalled the memory of the man standing in the orchard today. "Corruptor."

The raven-haired sister snapped her fingers in the air as she said, "The creep in the deli looked the same. That *must* be him. Nobody else would be looking for us. No one knows we're here. We don't even know how we got here."

She is observant, too. The thought relieved some tension in his shoulders.

"Most likely. Based on his clothing, he is not from this era. Which would mean he is working for Opasteg. So, when you two traveled through time, he followed. The things I can't figure out are *why* and *how*. It would be helpful to know how you two arrived here..." He trailed off, hoping to leave space for the girls to mention that they possessed magical capabilities.

Neither acknowledged the comment and he, again, questioned their knowledge of magic. His mouth tightened when both of them stayed quiet. In the silence, he snuck quick glances at each of them, trying to figure out their ages. As soon as Benn looked toward the auburn-haired sister, he regretted it. As distracting as her beauty was to him, her mind was the real issue.

Recognition. Familiarity. Wonder. Each emotion swirled in her thoughts, and he was hooked, leaning forward like her emotions were a magnet drawing him in; he needed food or rest or *something* so his shields would remain intact.

He forced his lips into a flat line to keep from frowning. *How in the Ancestral hell would a Mundaner—or whatever she is—have the power to get past* my *shield?*

His thoughts were interrupted, snagging entirely on the auburn-haired sister again—who was now chewing on her full lip, lost in thought.

That isn't helping. He averted his gaze, blinked a few times then spoke to her. "Tell me what you're thinking about."

"Our grandparents spoke of Opasteg..." She trailed off, her full brows drawing together. "They're a secret society, right? A terrorist organization. With the new regime ruling, there have been talks of it being led by Opasteg sympathizers. Papa stopped speaking of them once—" She stopped talking as another indistinguishable glance passed between the sisters.

Pain and grief accompanied the look, and he wondered idly what that glance exchanged between them signified. He and Asha could communicate with only a glance, so he had to assume these sisters could do the same.

Benn pondered what information he should tell them, considering they had been vetted by the Underground and he was to educate them. His mind recited teachings from his years at the Academy:

```
Mundane civilians are not aware of the works of
Opasteg or the Underground, but they often
```

encounter rumors that discuss the secret societies. The Underground has chosen not to involve them until necessary, to protect them as long as possible. Any information gleaned by Mundaners can offer grave danger to the Underground. For this reason, speaking of the Underground or Opasteg to any Mundane being is punishable by banishment, imprisonment or, if determined by jury, death.

Mundaner civilians possess no magic and have limited resources to protect themselves. They are easily manipulated and cannot be trusted. BEWARE: Opasteg is not above using Mundane civilians as weapons against others of their kind. Opasteg is known to use tragedy and terror to distract non-magic civilians from the actions they take against both magic-wielders and Mundaners. In some cases, this practice has led to them manipulating Mundane civilians to carry out Opasteg plans. These consisted of crimes against other magic and Mundaners, ranging from smaller crimes like petty theft to abhorrent crimes like domestic terror or political assassination.

- Rules of the Underground Ed. 5, Vol. 12, Pg. 167

Another look passed between the sisters, and Benn could sense that they'd gained some sort of understanding.

The younger sister said, "Our grandmother used to speak of Opasteg, but she is—" She cut off the end of her sentence.

"*Gone.*" His eyes snapped to the auburn-haired woman who had finished her sister's sentence. Her voice hardened into something akin to fury and her chin straightened when his gaze met hers. Her throat cleared as she elaborated, "She disappeared a few years ago. She and Papa raised us, then one day she leaves without a trace. Without telling us, or Papa, where she'd gone. We haven't seen her since."

Her anger was bitter on his tongue. He was surprised at her admission, especially because he was not using emotion-bending to coax it out of her. The trust building was crucial to their success in working together. Plus, he was really enjoying being a part of a conversation that was not focused on his duties as a Chattel, and instead focused on his true work. Even if the conversation had turned a bit sour, he still felt accomplished at the amount of information sharing that was occurring between him and the sisters.

Progress. He nearly smiled but instead sent a sympathetic glance to both of them.

He crossed the room and opened a bag to find the clothes Miss Ava had given him earlier. It was empty due to whatever enchantment was bestowed on the bag. He sent soft waves of a revealing spell to the enchanted bag, attempting to convince it to open. In his experience, these ancient, enchanted items could be stubborn.

Come on, I'm a friend. Nothing to fear from me. The bag wiggled, revealing the contents.

He pulled out two worn uniforms and slippers, presenting them with a grin. Both sisters were scowling and the contorted expressions made them look scarily alike; he needed to find out which sister was Leola and which was Juniper, fast.

"Back to fitting in..." Benn explained. "These are for you."

The dark-haired sister gagged audibly, shaking her head.

The other sister frowned, crossing her arms over her chest as she said, "Absolutely not. There is *no* way I'm wearing *those*." She sniffed the air. "They smell like death."

"You can smell death?" He contemplated where these items had come from and figured they were probably worn by Chattels who had passed onto the Gods.

"Obviously. Hard to ignore the scent of rotting flesh," she fired back.

Despite the twist in his stomach at the thought, he leaned toward the clothes, sniffing them, but not picking up the scent of death that she was referring to. These clothes had been washed, and the only scent Benn could detect was the smell of the washing powder that the Chattels used to clean clothes. He shrugged, but the fact was not lost on him that the older sister had the power to detect death. Anyone could smell the scent of decaying flesh, but it required a powerful magic to detect death that had been disguised, covered up, or washed away. It was not a power per se—like that of a magic-wielder. A person who could detect death needed to be born from a line of magical-beings in order to have the gift to do so.

They have magic in their blood. His hopes were confirmed. He handed the clothes to the auburn-haired one. *Gods, she's distracting. What's her name?*

The same sister watched him, mouth gaping as she said, "They *are* from dead people. You weren't even going to tell us, were you?" Her gaze was accusatory on him, but her emotions were reading as resigned.

He could work with that, but her focus was on the wrong thing, so he leveled a flat stare at her, deadpanning, "No sense in telling you what you've seemed to figure out yourself. As I'm sure you can guess, death is common around here and it's not like the Chattels are being given new clothes every day... so yes, these clothes likely belonged to someone else at one point. Either way, blending in is the only option." He gestured to her. "Your pink tennis outfit isn't going to do you any favors here. If you give them—whether it's the Master or the Overseers or that *Corruptor*—a reason to suspect you as trespassers—" He inhaled, willing his voice to soften; only, his words did not match his tone. "Well then, you'll find yourselves hanging in the Poplar trees. And I won't be there to save you."

The sisters stiffened and, as much as he preferred not to elicit fear in people, fear would keep them safe. Fear would sharpen their instincts and connect them to their power; what their power looked like remained to be seen, of course.

The other one snatched the clothes from him with a scowl. "Leo, I assume we're changing our clothes in here?"

The auburn-haired one looked down at the clothes, now gripped in her hand, as she responded, "Yes." Her vicious glare met him. "Now, close your eyes, or I swear I'll gut you, Benn."

"Gladly." He turned around, facing the window. Finally, he'd figured out their names. Did he feel pathetic for forgetting them in the first place? Absolutely. *Thank the Gods Asha isn't watching to chastise me for that blunder.*

For good measure, he reminded himself of their names a dozen times while the girls changed. *Juniper: dark hair. Leola: freckles.*

Leola gave him the all-clear once they were both dressed. He opened his eyes, noting that both sisters had taken seats on his roommate's bed, wearing clothes similar to the ones Miss Ava wore every day.

They'd folded their Modern-Era clothes into neat piles. A jacket sat on top of one of the stacks and his power caught on it. Something was inside the jacket—and it was calling to his magic. His gaze narrowed as his magic sparked under his skin.

Time magic.

Juniper fished her hand deep into a pocket within the jacket, saying, "So, that man in the denim jacket, I might have an idea of what he wants. It came to me while I was changing. In the deli, he offered to buy this from me. He told me to 'name my price.'" Juniper held up a pocket watch, causing him to stiffen.

"What are you doing with a relic?" he asked as the pieces fell into place—the time magic he had sensed in the forest was here now and she was holding the source.

Miss Ava landed in the room with a bright smile, speaking before she was fully visible. "I can confirm that is *exactly* what that demon was after. And maybe a couple of other things of importance." All three of them jumped at her sudden entrance into the room.

"Miss Ava," he greeted her, rising off the bed, pausing as he was overcome by the auburn-tinged shock that flooded his mind—courtesy of the woman sitting across from him.

"Grandmava?" The girls whispered the name in unison.

A tearful smile crossed Miss Ava's face. "Leo. Junebug. My girls. Welcome to the Underground."

CHAPTER 8

— BENN —

NGER SPARKED IN HIS MIND—his own, which was as irritating to him as it was surprising. He rarely gave into the emotion of anger, and now was not the time to do so. His grandmother, who was an emotion-bender herself, had raised him to be strong, telling him countless times, *"Anger makes you weak. Use your power to stir it in others, but never give into it yourself."*

His eyes darted between Miss Ava and the sisters, cursing the vagueness of the vellum, wondering why he hadn't been trusted with the information that he would, in fact, be retrieving *Ava's* granddaughters. For demons' sake, Miss Ava could have told him that herself.

He wilted at the idea that Miss Ava hadn't trusted him; she had been his only friend during this brutal, traumatic Assignment, yet she had not trusted him with vital information. He cursed the notion that if he had failed in bringing the girls back to Roswell, he would have had to face her, unbeknownst to the precious cargo he had been trusted to retrieve.

He inhaled, using his power to calm his nerves. Alas, this was the nature of the Underground, and it was what he'd signed up for. He'd dreamt of being in the position he was in as a Conscript, but the truth was, some days were hard.

Harder than *hard*. Today was one of those days.

He took another deep breath, flexing his fingers and relaxing his jaw that had been locked since seeing the trio's tearful reunion. He hoped that Miss Ava had not sensed his chaotic mood shift. After this stunning discovery, he couldn't bear the idea that—on top of everything that had occurred tonight—she might find him weak or unstable. Those were signs of emotion-benders who would weaken the Underground, and that was *not* the type of soldier Benn Wyndmere was meant to be.

Ava's voice was soothing. "Girls, I see you have met Mr. Bennjamin. I apologize I was not able to assist in your retrieval, but I had no doubts that you two would be in the *best* hands."

His chest swelled with pride and he offered a soft, gratuitous smile in her direction. Jealousy scalded his mind and his eyes met the source. He swore to the Gods that an orange glow flashed in Leola's narrowed eyes, whose voice was full of venom when she asked, "Where have you *been*, Grandmava?"

— LEOLA —

The gratefulness of seeing her grandmother wore off, leaving her raw with unsettled emotion.

"Who is Benn to you? Is this who you abandoned us for?" she whispered, anger searing through her like a heat-seeking missile.

She assumed her grandmother had *died* when she disappeared, and here she was living, breathing, and *smiling* at this stranger. Papa had given them no information when she left. In fact, he had acted like he knew nothing at all, denying Juniper and her the chance to go look for answers. The whole situation and what followed it had been bizarre. He'd carried on with life like nothing was different, when, in fact, everything had changed, shattering her heart in the process.

Her sister's excitement was palpable, and as much as she did not want to ruin this moment for Juniper, she needed to ask these questions—to get the answers that she and Juniper deserved. She needed to protect Juniper from another heartbreak. And maybe herself, too, though that was not at the forefront of her mind. Her grandmother sighed, clasping her hands together while guiding the sisters to sit on one cot, motioning for Benn to sit on the other.

"Answer me, please," she whispered, ignoring the feel of the stranger's eyes on her. Despite her rising temper, the emotion in her grandmother's gaze hit her right in the chest. She looked different than the last time she'd seen her; her caramel-hued eyes were riddled with exhaustion... like decades had passed since she had last seen her instead of just two years.

"Oh, my girls. I'll share my story, and I hope you both will understand why your Papa and I had to make the choices we did. We were forced to make a lot of decisions quickly." Her grandmother paused, fighting back the tears that threatened to spill over her eyes. "I can never ask for your forgiveness, but I'd like to ask for your understanding. As I bet you can imagine, we have a lot of catching up to do."

Grandmava addressed Benn, and Leola fought the urge to flinch at the familiarity between them. "First, Bennjamin, enough with that *Miss Ava* business. You'll call me Grandmava as the girls do. When the girls were younglings, they had a hard time with the pronunciation of Grandma and *Ava*. So, Grandmava I became."

And now the stranger from the forest is referring to her as we do. She hardly stopped herself from rolling her eyes.

Juniper's question cooled her internal rage. "Um, are we related to him somehow?"

"No, but his grandmother, Sena, and I go way back. We grew up together; we were inseparable, like sisters. Gods, I *miss* her. I haven't spoken to her since I was deployed to this place." Her grandmother's eyes took on a wistful sheen, as if the memories playing in her mind were unfolding before her like a movie. "Let's begin there. Sena and I grew up on the same block in Poppycal. Your great-grandparents, Moses and Lucille, descended from Chattels, as you know."

Leola raised a brow. "Yes," she said as she gestured to herself. "The traumatic history of the Chattels comes with the Mundane body." The stranger looked at her like she'd just sprouted a third arm. This time, she did roll her eyes.

Grandmava sighed. "For some, yes." Her eyes flickered in a way that made Leo's stomach plummet. "Papa and I... well, we left some things out. You see, we spent our young lives training to be members of a secret society that your great-grandparents served. Their lineage followed in their footsteps, as most do. Serving them in various ways—"

"*What?*" Leola's voice turned incredulous.

"You know, as messengers, leadership, professors, spies," her grandmother continued with a nonchalant shrug.

"No," Leola interrupted. "No, I do *not* know. You've never mentioned anything about this to us. And, again, what the hell does *he* have to do with any of this?" She pointed to the stranger.

"Bennjamin is a descendant of a Founder and followed that same path to gaining his membership—as we all did. He went through training and initiation. I believe his entire family has served the Underground, right?" She turned to the stranger, who nodded curtly. "Even when someone is a direct descendant of magic-wielders, new members *must* accept their membership in order to serve a role within the Underground. For example, during his initiation, he swore an oath; they pricked his finger, then used blood magic to awaken his powers and make his oath binding."

"So, you're a spy?" Juniper asked him.

"Somewhat. Though I spend most of my time as an assassin these days."

"That is... pretty cool," Juniper said as Leola shook her head at her, gawking. "So, Grandmava, that makes you a... what?"

"Well, I've served many roles. Started as an assassin, spent time as a spy, and worked in the Order for years."

Leola didn't buy it. "And what did you tell Papa while you were doing all this"—she gestured to the damp room they were crowded in—"Spywork?"

"He was doing the same," Grandmava said. "We worked together. I've never been a professor, though. That's his thing." She sent a soft smile toward her. "You don't believe me, Leo, I know. There's a reason for that. Not to worry dear, let me show you."

Scents of lavender, similar to a bubble bath, wafted into her nose. Her eyes were as wide as moons as a colorful, enchanting illusion filled the room. It evolved into varying scenes, illustrated by her grandmother's words.

"You see, before lowborn people were brought to these Camps, they lived in different parts of the world as free people. As populations increased, farming became essential to keep people fed. It was a growing industry—lucrative and profitable. Growing large amounts of crops required an astronomical amount of labor to cultivate, and, well, that is when greed took over."

With a sigh, Grandmava flexed her wrists, the illusion morphing from people living in harmony in distant lands to people being forced into vessels. The images were sickening, showing starved people—*dead* people—being transported against their will. Men, women, and children, too. Parts of the illusion even showed the nightmarish sight of women enduring childbirth on the vessels.

"Highborn people realized that they could import lowborns from faraway lands to use as a source of free labor, so they did; they captured them, separated families, loaded them onto cramped vessels where the food, water, space, and air was limited, so limited they usually could not stand or walk. The vessels brought them to Laviegata—a journey that lasted for 80 days, forfeiting many lives in the process." Grandmava's voice darkened as she continued, "If they did survive the journey here, they found themselves chained and sold at daytime markets. Auctioneers labeled them as Chattels, not humans, as a way to extinguish their humanity and make the maltreatment of these people stomachable. They limited their education, forcing them to work on their crops and lands, to raise their children, and to build their homes. In many cases, they bred them against their will—all to make sure they had enough people to sell as Chattels so they could keep the Camps operating and keep their crops profitable."

The illusion was ever-changing, showing images from different Camps, leaving a heavy, eerie weight in the air. It transformed again.

"The Chattels rebelled over and over but realized they didn't have enough power to make a real impact because they were outnumbered. If they wanted to level the playing field, they needed a *strategy*. They needed *allies*. Whispers carried from the houses to the fields about Chattels who supported the ideas of outlawing Laborist Camps and freeing the Chattels."

The illusion changed again—flashing scenes of people meeting in secret and passing messages through coded letters and symbols. It flashed to 1804, when the practice of Laborist Camps was abolished in the northern states of Heri.

"The movement took off in the northern region of Heri, where the Chattels were freed. This meant they could work and contribute to society on their own terms. They could meet other like-minded people to discuss ideas that would fuel their cultures. For the first time ever, they could have *influence*; they could have *power*. Former Chattels wanted to share this power and influence with their brothers and sisters in the southern parts, who still lived life in the Camps. So, they reached the hand back and chose to fight for a better world for everyone. Word of their endeavors spread, and they began to organize."

The image transformed in front of them, showing a table of twelve individuals—all Mundane.

"In 1808, the Underground was founded by its twelve Founders. Six of those Founders were freed Chattels, the other six were people of highbirth—people who had never been Chattels, but didn't support the practice of Laborist Camps. Each of them believed in the utopian idea of a better world, where all people would be free of slave work and oppression. They swore an oath to protect this idea, to live, breathe, and even die for it. They each pricked a finger and combined their blood into a gauntlet before the Gods." Grandmava chuckled, as the Mundane beings began to be surrounded by magic in her illusion. "As you all know, unity is power. Since these people joined together for a cause greater than themselves, the Gods answered and rewarded the Founders with a gift."

"Magic?" Juniper whispered.

"Yes. That gift granted these Founders with magical abilities that would eventually travel through their lineage *forever*, creating the first generation of magic-wielders of all kinds: illusionists, emotion-wielders, time-wielders, elemental powers like those of earth, fire, wind, and water. They all were granted the ability to warp across distances. Each of the Founders was granted immortality, which came accompanied with otherworldly strength and the ability to heal quickly, which translated across their lineage along with the warping. The Founders studied their gifts, learning everything they could about them. They learned how to replicate them, hoping to share the powers with those around them. However, magic has limits, and the powers couldn't be shared with everyone. So, they found a way to utilize blood magic during initiation into the Underground, so long as they maintained balance. Once someone swore the Sacred Oath during initiation, certain gifts—determined at random by the Gods—would spread to that person. They couldn't prioritize gifts for one person over another, nor could they grant immortality to anyone else. And the Gods allowed them to keep this up and pass on magic through their blood, creating generations of magic-wielding beings, on the contingency that they would serve others and be kind to Mundaners." Grandmava sighed. "This went well for a while, but then, one of the Founders, Daemon, became... misled."

"Daemon Zevaroth—the leader of the new regime?" Leola guessed, as the recognizable name of Heri's dictator weaved itself into her grandmother's illusion.

Though, like all of the missives and leaflets Daemon sent, his face wasn't shown; he never revealed his true identity, which remained obscure even in the illusion.

"Yes. Daemon succumbed to the evils of power and greed. He manipulated beings of all kinds, spewing hate-filled messages into their minds so they would worship him. This violated the laws of magic. He was called upon by the other eleven Founders, who attempted to take his power and stop him. However, he'd gotten too powerful and escaped before they could strip him of his power. He then used the masses of people he had manipulated, all magic-wielders, to create an entity that served dark purposes."

Familiar symbols surfaced in the illusion—flags and messaging that supported the corrupt regime that had overthrown Heri's government six months prior.

"Opasteg?" Leola thought she might choke as she muttered the name of the terrorist organization that had been a hellish myth—to be whispered about in the safety of the night—until about five seconds ago. "Are... are they real?"

"Yes, dear girl. Opasteg is very real and their leader rules Heri, as of last year," Grandmava explained.

"They performed the Red Coup," Leola breathed as shock burned through her as the illusion played out, showing events she'd experienced in real-time. Now, she saw them through a polished, informed lens. "But *why?*"

"Daemon's heart was blackened with rage and anguish at the thought of creating a better world for all. He believed in a better world for *some*—those who had power, wealth, and thought the same as he. He didn't believe in handouts for people who weren't born with those comforts—or so he claimed. He chose Mundaners as the scapegoat—a less powerful people who couldn't defend themselves from his rise to power. He used everything he'd learned alongside the Founders of the Underground to build his own organization," Grandmava said as the room filled with the sounds of terrorist attacks—in Poppycal, Rosebay, Papaver, and all the other states in Heri. Blood ran through the cobblestones as people in red hoods terrorized Herians—killing them, burning them, dragging them through the streets.

"Opasteg was born—an organization fueled by hate instead of goodness. He learned to extend his immortal magic to his descendants and to anyone who would use their blood to swear a Sacred Oath to Opasteg. He tied the blood magic to the leaders of anti-Mundane societies, fueling their magic from the hate living inside their hearts. He created a network of Corruptors to rival the great work of the Conscripts of the Underground. Today, the Underground is led by eleven of its original Founders, while Daemon controls Opasteg on his own, working closely with a few trusted members he refers to as his council."

"And now he controls Heri," Juniper said in a quiet tone.

"Correct. The tide shifted on the day of the Red Coup. Many people lost hope, fleeing Heri to other countries. But, years ago, there was a prophecy delivered by a Fa." Again, the illusion changed, outlining an intricate and vast messaging system. "Fas are able to communicate through different parts of time, so the Underground relies on Fas to send messages to the Conscripts, which arrive in the form of vellums. Opasteg does the same, of course. When Fas receive messages from the Ancestors or the Gods, the messages are delivered in the form of prophecies. While prophecies are ever-changing, they can be a useful tool. About nineteen years ago, a Fa received a prophecy, one that would change everything. The prophecy said:

'Two entities will go to war.
Hate will prevail, only to be undone by two powers, new to the world.
The strength of the elements will determine our fate. "

Scenes of thorny vines and sparkling embers erupted through the air, crackling and twisting around the illusions, causing both sisters to jump.

"They earned the nickname of the Prophesied Pair, though no one knew who they were quite yet. At the time, the Underground believed the 'two powers' referred to youngling men. The immortals trained cohorts of Conscripts so they would be ready to defend and save the free world of Heri, but they were wrong. Our Fas had received messages prophesying a battle in a remote area of Salemfir. The newest soldiers, all Conscripts, arrived first. They were ambushed. Daemon's numbers had grown with his use of Darkbeings and demons; they were overtaken by his army. They captured the living and left the dead for us to find. He captured 228 members that day. Daemon tortured all 228 people, hoping to gain information about who these two powers might be. None of the prisoners gave him information because none of them knew. No one knew. But he never returned the magic-wielders he captured that day in Salemfir—including both of your mothers."

Leola gasped as her mother's face appeared in the soft vapor of the illusion. Beside her was a beautiful woman whose dark eyes and sharp cheekbones looked identical to Benn's. Her eyes flitted to his for one heartbeat, just in time to see his hardening as they beheld the illusion in front of them. In the next blink, the expression was replaced by his seemingly usual, stoic mask.

"Months passed; no males were identified as the Pair. So, we asked ourselves: could the powers of the prophecy be *poweresses* instead? Again, no women were strong enough to be the source. They checked every combination of members— nothing—until Fas confirmed that the Pair had not reached Maturity. They were *children*." Her voice caught on the last word. "Daemon raged, sending his Corruptors to kidnap children of the Conscripts, Sentinels, and Generals—simply to kill them. Years passed and he never found them. Sena mandated we hide all infants and send younglings to the Academy at age six, which was six years earlier than they typically went to the school because that was the safest place for them."

A memory flashed into Leola's mind: a short burst of her splashing in a play pool, her grandmother standing over her with wide eyes, and, strangest of all, the water around her was... boiling.

Her grandmother's words cleared the haze of the memory. "At the time, I had no doubt you two girls would be powerful, as you come from a powerful line. But..." Grandmava chuckled. "You girls were showing your abilities before you could even walk. It is so rare for a youngling to access their magic prior to being initiated. Only the most powerful beings are able to do that... Yet, I can't tell you the amount of times Leola singed my hair off because she didn't want a bath... or Juniper trapped me in vines stronger than chains just so she could watch cartoons for a bit longer.

"I was in denial. I'd already lost *my* children to his evil and I couldn't fathom that my two precious granddaughters, my lights, might be the Prophesied Pair spoken of by the Gods. But your powers grew each day, matching the themes of the prophecy. Papa convinced me to go to Sena to discuss it, so I warped to her estate in Rosebay. There, I met Bennjamin, only a few months older than Leola. He'd been training, as you girls had been doing. He was so talented. Hope sparked in me that maybe *he* was one of the powers and maybe, just maybe, one of my granddaughters would be *spared*." She sent a sad smile toward Benn. "But then, Sena handed me a vellum, addressed to both of us. *A dual mission.* I opened it:

> *'Protect your young.*
> *Flames. Thorns. Time.*
> *Combine them to right the world.'*

"We knew that Daemon's Fa had received this same message. Bennjamin's mother is known for her unmatched time magic, so Sena made preparations to move him to the protected training school, even sooner than she had planned. I warped home with plans to do the same. But when I arrived home, I paused to watch you girls play in the meadow—unaware that your whole world was about to change. Devastated by the war, yet you both were so wondrously innocent."

Tears streamed down Grandmava's cheeks. "I wished for one more moment of normalcy for you. I wished to take that last moment in, to cherish it, before we sent you away—Juniper shooting tumbleweeds into the sky, and Leola using wind to spin them while also using her power to engulf them in flame. They exploded like fireworks over the meadow. It was thrilling to watch... sisters playing with, *learning* their magic. I couldn't deny how powerful you were then; you were just little girls and already had so much control, such a reserve of power." Her voice, steady at first, turned razor-sharp, each word cutting through the air like a blade.

"Then, I was met with the rotten stench of Opasteg, oily and slick as it permeated the air around me—their weapons already drawn, ready to take you. I spun an illusion so they wouldn't see you, but *you* saw them first." Her voice cracked. "I watched in horror and awe, two very different feelings, as Leola's flame incinerated all of their weapons, causing the hooded henchman to drop them, their flesh peeling off as flames melted the skin of their palms. One lunged toward Leola, but Juniper's vines erupted out of the ground, trapping them. They writhed in agony, trying to fight the thorny chains. I ran to you, but a henchman grabbed me, pressing a dagger to my throat. He stood in the shadows; neither of you girls had seen him. The blade sliced into my skin. My last thought was that my granddaughters would witness my death. I prayed to the Gods that they would spare you from seeing me like that, until he started to gurgle. I looked up to see vines slithering out of his mouth and nose, contorting his neck as they moved—*grew*—through his esophagus. He fell to the ground, dead. A fiery wave overtook the hooded Darkbeings, courtesy of Leo. I knew then that Daemon's men had witnessed too much, and since Daemon can read posthumous memories, well, he would know what you two had done—what you were capable of within minutes. We were left with *seconds* to decide."

There is something monumental about what happens to one's brain chemistry as they watch someone who they have only seen as strong and formidable *break*. And that is exactly what was occurring as Leola listened to her grandmother recount a memory she possessed... though in her mind, it played out differently.

She shook her head, disbelieving the words. "No. We played outside *everyday*, Grandmava. I'd remember this. If someone attacked you—*us*—I'd never forget that."

Grandmava let out a strangled sound, like each word she spoke caused her physical pain. "No, dear girl. The henchmen had *seen* me. They saw *both* of you. They were all dead, but their deaths could be tracked, so we fled. We moved to a different area—to Mundane housing—where I created an illusion that disguised our identities. The only person who knew who or where we were was Sena. Daemon would have tracked your magic, so instead of sending you away to the Academy as planned..." She released a sob, covering her face as if she could hold in the sound. "I—I took your memories. I used my power to enter your minds. I picked through them and manipulated them to show the life you'd lived but left no memories of any magic. I left the joys of your childhood, your mother, and your passions, so you would one day be able to find yourself. To find your *power*. To become the poweresses you were—*are*—meant to be. Leo, you are a child of the elements. Most little girls don't collect matchboxes or chase wildfires, but you did. It is why you're immune to flame and heat. Juniper, your love for gardening and botany is not by accident. Your strong sense of the climate is your power. The Earth responds to you. That is the magic in your veins, fighting the block I placed, revealing remnants at every opportunity."

"It cannot be; we're Mundaners," Leola choked out. "We've been living as second-class citizens since the Coup—and even years before that."

Her voice was as soft as her dark eyes as she continued to explain, "All to keep you both hidden. He is too repulsed by Mundaners to ever consider you would be living amongst them. The block prevented you from using your magic, which is a horrible violation, one that kept your identities hidden. We couldn't risk losing our most valuable assets in this war against Daemon."

"What do you mean '*most valuable assets*'?" Juniper whispered.

Benn finally spoke up, "The block—I sensed it in the woods. But now that you've realized it's there..." He trailed off. "You're... the Prophesied Pair."

CHAPTER 9

— LEOLA —

"SO, YOU DID ALL OF THIS to protect us and then... left anyway?" Leola shook her head.

Her grandmother gestured to Benn—who she'd been desperately trying to ignore. "Sena and I swore to protect each other's families years ago. Elders can learn of Assignments before they are given. When Sena learned of his Assignment, she asked that I take a similar one to accompany him—to protect him, if needed. Roswell is an Assignment that most don't survive. So, I landed at Roswell a few years ago, when I left you both with Papa, to be Benn's guide. Leaving you two was the hardest thing I'd ever done... but I knew you'd be in capable hands with Papa. Without me, Bennjamin would have had no one here. Three months ago, I received a vellum that said:

'One comes tomorrow. Two will follow.
Protect all three.
See the prophecy unfold.'

"The Gods were sending Bennjamin. I watched over him during his months here, never revealing my identity because I wanted him to discover himself on this mission without feeling like Sena had sent someone to coddle him. I apologize for the deceit, Benn. I could sense the change in him when he received his first vellum, so I gave him a small hint and waited for him to bring you to me." Grandmava stopped speaking, smiling at them all.

Leo kept her eyes trained on her hands that now lay locked in her lap. In a matter of minutes, her grandmother unraveled everything she knew to be true about her life, and she was barely grappling with the fact that her grandmother was *breathing* the same air as her after so long.

Her vision blurred—a result of the rage and confusion churning in her body. She refused to cry in front of Benn, a stranger whom she did not trust, but even worse, her grandmother, who was now a stranger to her, too.

I listened to Juniper's sobs every day for two years—mine too—as we mourned her... and now she is just here? Grandmava is alive, I have magic *in my veins, Mother might be* alive? Her thoughts were an angry, heartbroken mess; she began to nibble on her thumb, as she tended to do when lost in thought. *Juniper and I are some kind of*—Prophesied—*what?*

She looked up to see Benn's dark eyes cast toward her. She flashed a scowl in warning before turning her body to face the opposite way. After hearing her grandmother's admission and reasoning, she understood, but the pain of the knowledge was a burn across her heart.

She kept her eyes on her grandmother as she spoke. "I was seventeen when you left. You could have trusted me. You could've informed me—I would've chosen the right time to tell Juniper. You left us to think, what, that you'd *died?* Papa won't even speak of you, Grandmava." Her voice sounded like it had been raked across sand. "It was like we were expected to pretend you didn't exist. I understand why you left without telling us. I understand why you took our memories. I get it. It's the decisions that took place *after* you were gone that I can't seem to wrap my head around."

"I am sorry. It was too dangerous, Leo. We had no guidebook and no way of knowing how close Daemon was lurking. We couldn't risk it. We could not risk anything." She stepped closer to her and Juniper; Leola resisted the urge to flinch away as Grandmava said, "You are essential to the movement. You make up the legs of the stool of The Prophesied Pair—the Pair that Opasteg fears, Daemon loathes, and the Underground has been praying for. You needed to be protected."

Her gaze snapped back to Benn as he spoke. "Brilliant," he whispered. "I was beginning to think the Pair was something of a myth—like the Fa got it wrong." He shook his head, his eyes shooting an assessing gaze over her and Juniper, one that had Leola snarling in return. "But they didn't. That was brilliant to hide them, Ava—Grandmava. Absolutely *brilliant*."

She blanched at him and his gall to discuss her and Juniper like they were not present in the room—but she could not deny, much to her dismay, she was envious of the stranger. He knew more about Grandmava than she did. He knew more about this magical world, and worst of all, he seemed to know more about Leo than she did of herself.

She lifted her chin, eyes flitting between her grandmother and Benn. "I forgive you, Grandmava." She paused to choose her next words. "But, I need time—maybe just a few hours—to process what—"

Juniper's abrupt questions buzzed with excitement as she interrupted, "How can we get our magic back? Can you return the memories? Undo the block?"

Her grandmother raised a hand to calm her sister's questions. "I was waiting for you to ask that, child. I can return it all—the memories and the magic—but it will exhaust you. You'll need time to recover—for some, it takes weeks. We have no way of knowing how long you'll be affected, so we need to establish what's next. Then, I'll return what is yours," she explained. Grandmava looked to the stranger that Leola was back to ignoring. "Bennjamin, have you managed to learn any information about that dreadful Corruptor? I know you have not had much time for observing today."

She wanted to roll her eyes at his arrogant smirk as he responded, "I don't need time for basic recon. It's all I've been doing for the last few months."

"Thought you said you were an assassin," Juniper quipped.

"Sure." He nodded. "Only in the mornings." He crossed his arms over his chest, threaded muscles peeking out underneath the tattered shirt he wore. "The Corruptor wore Modern-Era denim and the mark of Opasteg. The Overseers were wound so tight in the orchard today that I assume the Corruptor is important. Though his identity is not confirmed—let's go with he's a man of influence. Even the Master called him his 'new friend.' I expect he'll be hanging around Roswell and the surrounding Camps for a while," he said, motioning to where the sisters sat. "From what they told me, they saw him before they traveled to the drop point, so he *followed* them across eras—and was willing to risk his spycover to ask the Chattels and Overseers here to assist in his search." He lifted a finger as he listed off the qualities. "He is either reckless, powerful, or difficult to kill. Maybe all three. Initially, I thought he was here for the time relic, but after hearing what you, Miss Ava— Grandmava—just shared, he..." His jaw ticked as he dropped his hand, meeting Leola's glare.

"The Corruptor is looking for us," Juniper finished the sentence, her eyes widening as if the horrifying memory of the man's soulless eyes had resurfaced. Leola reached out for her sister's hand, squeezing. "When he was trying to buy the pocket watch off of us, I said no, obviously. Then his eyes turned black. No pupils, no retinas, no nothing. Only black."

Benn growled, momentarily losing the stoicism that she'd been wary of, and he said, "An illusionist. Opasteg's members have powers that equate to those of the Underground. But, since their leader has foolishly delved into malevolent magic, their powers manifest differently." He started pacing in the small room as Leola tracked his movements. "It's why when Grandmava spins an illusion, she puts off a lavender-scented haze; it is called a magic trail, but all magic has trails. The scent and aroma will surround the person viewing the illusion, whether they are aware or not. Even if she is intending to defend or harm the person, they'll still pick up on the tranquil energy because her magic has never been used for malice; her magic is benevolent. An Opasteg's magic is inherited and drawn from an evil source, so it will manifest in the form that *feels* evil to the beholder—no matter how hard they try to disguise it. Magic-wielders will sense a magic trail; they might sense an oily or tar-like feeling, especially if it's malevolent. Mundaners will feel discomfort—a tingling against the back of their neck or chills across their arms. They may feel restricted in movement or experience sensations of bugs crawling on them. Their instincts will encourage them to run from this magic, to get away from the threat." He tapped his chin as he continued, "When you declined the Corruptor's offers to purchase the pocket watch, he must have started to spin an illusion, causing his eyes to turn black. You both have magic in your veins, so you were able to see the magic manifesting in the Corruptor's eyes."

"So, even when we were unaware of our magic, it still protected us?" Leola asked, hopeful that she may be able to access her magic someday. Maybe even sooner than she'd originally thought.

Grandmava's voice was gentle. "Yes, you are no Mundaner, girl. Try to reach out, envision the power, then search for it. The block is in your mind, but I never hid it from you—you just never knew to look for it. Find it. That'll make the restoration process more seamless."

She found solace with the decisions Grandmava and Papa had made on her and her sister's behalf, though it still grated on her as any violation would. She wanted those memories, the power her grandmother had spoken of back. She'd been powerless since they were transported from Modern-Era Poppycal. Warmth spread under her skin, traveling at a leisurely pace through her veins.

Is this my power? She tried to reach out to that warmth—tried to corral it—but she was met with a block that stopped all efforts. She tried to envision what it would look like—*a flame, heat, sun.*

Once again, she was met with that midnight dark block.

Wonderful. She let out a huffed breath.

"Your magic will *always* protect you." Leola glared at him as he spoke to her. "You are descendants of powerful magic-wielders; that kind of Ancestral power can't be extinguished." For the first time, she didn't recoil from his words.

— BENN —

His mindset had shifted since receiving the vellum the day before. It was a familiar internal battle—the constant conflict between his humanity and the cold, calculated focus that took over his mind when assessing a wartime situation. He tried to let humility drive the bus as he sat, considering his options in regard to the woman sitting across from him. At the Academy, his combat instructors had drilled into him the importance of thinking in a tactical manner and making decisions based on facts. So, of course, with no clue how to deal with this woman, he was clinging to that method with unyielding ferocity.

Fact: Leola confused him.

Fact: the woman was destined to be a weapon for the Underground.

Fact: she needed to be able to access her power to become that weapon.

Fact: the very power that he sensed was burning in her veins, humming just beneath her skin.

Fact: she absolutely, undeniably, *indisputably* hated him—emotion-wielding be damned, that was clearer than glass.

With the facts came the dreaded unknown. What he couldn't predict was how much damage pushing her would inflict on the fragile peace that hung on a knife's edge between them. He asked himself how she would react if he told her he could sense her power. Was whatever reaction that awaited him worth revealing that information?

Given how all of our encounters had gone so far, not well. He chewed on his cheek, answering his own question. *But, does it matter if I'm helping the Underground? The mission? This is the poweress who is supposed to be able to help us defeat Daemon— the poweress that's struggling to find her power after it was taken against her will. And why do I care about her feelings at all? The mission is always paramount.*

Her auburn-tinged power yanked him out of his thoughts—not that he minded the distraction. One of his favorite aspects of emotion-bending was the ability to detect the power source within the magic-wielders around him. This particular gift was unique—a result of how powerful his family line was, and he was grateful for it. From the beginning of his life, he knew he would have access to great power. His grandmother had trained him since he could walk, as Grandmava had described, preparing him to bear his gifts well. Like any skilled emotion-bender, he could shatter the shields designed to protect against powers like his and navigate the untrained or unshielded emotions of those around him. However, few emotion-benders in history could truly perceive the depth of the power or magic that lived within others, which made him gifted, unpredictable, and lethal. His grandmother would be thrilled to learn how his emotion-bending power had manifested—if only he could reach her to tell her.

He'd tuned out the conversation taking place across the room—or at least he attempted to. He caught on quickly that the sisters were attempting to get a sense of their power; out of the two, Juniper seemed to be having more luck.

"Try again, Leo." Grandmava's voice was soft as she spoke.

She said nothing in response, her face trained on her crossed hands. Her frustration was obvious to him, though the emotion all but screamed to him through her nonexistent mental shield.

Neither of the sisters has been trained to shield. That'll need to be remedied as soon as possible. Benn ticked his jaw so he wouldn't be caught grimacing.

Grandmava had summoned meals from the house—something she only did when food was abundant and no one would notice it was missing. He picked up one of the plates, carrying it to his cot. He checked the shields that he never lowered, the ones that protected him by preventing his access to other minds. They were intact, for Juniper and Grandmava, at least. He hadn't managed to produce a shield strong enough to block out Leola, but after eating a meal and letting his power reserve recharge, he was confident that—

Fuck. He gripped his fork in an iron fist, nearly cracking it in his hand. His shield against Leola failed again. He hid his frown with a sip of water, reaching for his power and strengthening the shield—until it slipped. Just like that, her emotions were playing in his head again. It was both as defeating as it was distracting. He gritted his teeth and tried again. He reached for his power, scoured his shield for weak spots and refortified them, then he hauled the shield up against the auburn-tinged presence that lingered at the edge of his mind.

Each time, it slipped.

Over, and over, and over again.

Shield. Reinforce. Slip.

Again. Three times.

Seven more times.

Shield. Reinforce. *Slip.*

As much as he tried to ignore her mind, it was like she was shouting at him, and he was being forced to listen. He knew he was only exhausting his power reserve the more times he attempted to raise the shield, and that power use was not worth it. He needed to be at full strength for this mission, and since she posed no threat to him, he let out a sigh and relented.

Maybe she has some kind of power that negates shields. I'm a dual-power, so I guess she could be, too. She is one of the Pair, after all. He stole a glance in her direction—her frustration felt slimy in his mouth, leaving an uncomfortable aftertaste. He watched her try and *fail,* but he sensed no power other than the elemental power within her, though that did not mean other power was not present. *Her other power must be dormant, but the fire is* there. *Does she even know that she passed my shields?*

He wondered idly how he could encourage her without violating her privacy. He was a combat expert and a trained assassin for the Underground. Despair triggered his senses, but he couldn't decide if it was hers or his own.

He winced as his mind continued to race. *The Academy and the Gods turned me into a dual-powered weapon. And she—she is learning this all for the first time. Completely unguarded. No shield. She is a victim of a prophecy—a whole world—she knew nothing about.*

Flexing his hands, Benn prepared himself for panic to sink its claws into her mind, knowing he would not be able to shield her out, which meant that he would be forced to feel it, too. Panic was ugly and distressing for emotion-benders, and he was apprehensive to have to sense *that* without a shield.

He waited, but it didn't hit.

Quick as a blink, a dart of determination flashed through her mind. He fought a smile at the unexpected shift in her mood.

Leola. Leo. A lioness waiting to be released. He admired her, taking another look at her auburn hair. Ringlets had begun to curl in the humid Laviegata air, replacing the blown out style she'd worn it in when he'd first found them in the forest... Her freckles were more pronounced in the soft glow of the candlelight—each unique marking a source of luminescence in the room. *A beam of light—lighting up the darkness of this shit place. What is that, poetry? You idiot—it's her power. It's like you have never seen a poweress before. Relax, mate. You're not a poet; you're a spy for demons' sake.*

Her eyes snapped to his. He cleared his throat, compelled to speak, and found himself blurting out his thoughts without considering them first. "I can feel it, you know... the fire. You are close."

She blinked. Discomfort flared to life across her face and in her mind, and he immediately regretted the words. Timidity followed as Benn stilled.

And... you blew it. There goes the trust, he scolded himself.

Juniper's eyebrows jumped, and Grandmava smirked; he ignored them both, knowing their attention would be counterproductive for Leola.

Her tone was harsh, but he'd expected that. "Well, I sure wish *I* could read everyone's mind. Maybe that would be more useful than the *'fire,'*" she said, her sarcasm obvious as she used finger quotes on the last word. "Next time you feel like dancing through my mind, try asking permission first, Benn."

His smile was tight, more from his own regret than from offense at her sharp reply. In fact, he somewhat *enjoyed* her fiery personality. She was unique—different—from the other girls he'd met at the Academy.

"Noted," he fired back. "It would make my life easier if you would learn to shield. I can teach you. In fact, you going about this mission with no shield will be the death of us all."

She scoffed, but the confusion that surfaced in her emotions confirmed what he'd guessed; she did not know anything about shields and was not attempting to negate his. He caught another glimpse of the rising power, as if it answered to her heightened frustration. He needed her trust, but they needed her power more. Magic was more accessible in times of surges of emotions, so he decided to take a risk and piss off the woman in front of him. This should be easy—she hated him, and he could sense her temper exceeding new depths, so truthfully, they were halfway there. He flashed a smirk and stretched his arms to appear relaxed—cocky, even—whatever it took to achieve the level of annoyance she needed to get past the block.

"I can teach you, you know," he said once more. "I've been shielding for years. It seems Juniper is on the right track already. You'll catch up eventually," he added with a wink, so he wouldn't wince at his own insult. "No need to worry, I have thick skin. I'm not fireproof, but your words aren't going to hurt me, Leo."

Intense, fiery anger burned through her—to the point where Benn wondered if he should prepare to get burned by her—until Juniper's laughter filled the room, snagging Leola's attention, quieting her mind, and blanketing the flames. Benn let out a chuckle, because even though the firepoweress across from him despised him, she'd just sensed her power for the first time.

CHAPTER 10

— LEOLA —

S HE LOOKED TOWARD THE MUD WALL in front of her, trying her best to tune out the laughter of her sister and Benn, who she hadn't decided if she trusted yet. Her frustration was a metal grate against her nerves—her body temperature soaring in tandem with her paroxysm. She crossed her arms over her chest, like that would do anything to protect her from the furious anxiety lapping at the edges of her mind. She was known to lash out at others when she felt cornered. Then again, he hadn't made her feel cornered; he'd made her feel *seen*. Her guilt at snapping at Benn churned her stomach uneasily—that was an emotion she was not ready to confront, considering he was a stranger who had been hanging out with her missing grandmother. Still, her eyes drifted back to the man sitting on the cot opposite her. He had been wanting to help her and she shrugged him off.

With the way he and Juniper were laughing, she didn't think she would need to apologize; he was clearly unaffected. She knew her quick responses could be withering, and she was digesting a lot—too much—right now. If she was being real with herself, anyone who crossed her now wouldn't be safe.

Not that his feelings matter to me. She focused back on her power and how Benn had mentioned that he could *sense* it. *If he can sense the fire, then the fire is there.* She pulled at her tattered shirt. *Gods, is that why it is so hot in here? That can't be me doing that, right? I can't heat a room.*

Juniper's giggles dissipated her focus as she said, "The tension is palpable in here." She was fanning her face as Leola gave her a sideways look that begged her to stop. "Grandmava, you mentioned a plan and I'm ready to get my memories back. Plus, I want to trap some bad guys in my *vine cages*." Her sister made a gesture similar to a martial arts move, continuing, "Give me my powers back. Let's fulfill this prophetic shit."

Grandmava rolled her eyes, chuckling. "Glad to see you're invested in the prophecy." She gave each of them an assessing once-over. "We need you two to fit in here. I see he gave you the clothes. But there is another problem. The Corruptor *saw* your faces, and since he is still actively looking for you, we can't risk him recognizing you, so we need to disguise your identities—glamour you. Which one of you wants to go first?" Grandmava looked between the girls, seeing their confusion, so she went on to explain, "A glamour is magic used to disguise—it can change your look for good or bad. I'm an illusionist who is particularly skilled in this kind of thing, but all powers and poweresses can do it, if they are taught. Now go on, you can choose any look you would like."

He asked, "Is there a performer you admire? Grandmava can use an image of them in her mind to mimic their features while she is glamouring you. It isn't necessary, but it makes it easier."

Juniper snapped her fingers. "That actress from that one alien movie. Timelessly beautiful and best cheekbones in the game."

Grandmava's shoulders straightened as she flicked her wrists, transforming Juniper right before her eyes. She knew that her sister loved her own skin, too, but the shimmery glow that overtook her features was magical. It was a rich, stunning dark brown.

Juniper's eyes were closed as she waited with an expectant grin. Her eyes opened a crack as her hands shot to her head. "Can I keep the braids? I just got them a few days ago. I didn't spend 8 hours in a chair for nothing."

"Yes, keep the braids," Grandmava said as the calming mist swirled in the room again.

"Good, my scalp *still* hurts," she whined as she finger-combed her waist-length hair.

Leola was gaping at Juniper's transformation, when her grandmother addressed her. "You're next, my honey."

She considered her options. She needed to pick from the shortlist of notable performers that her Grandmava would know—which limited the options to, maybe, twelve people. In addition, it would not make sense for her to choose someone who looked at all similar to who Juniper had chosen—they looked alike in their true appearances, and she didn't need to give the Corruptor or anyone else a reason to suspect they were related.

She hummed as she spoke. "That game show hostess. From before the Coup." She began smoothing her auburn ringlets that now twisted around her face. The humid air had obliterated her silk press, and given that she did not have any hair product to style her curls with, the best option was to opt for a protective style. She continued with her description of her future self. "Give me large cornrows and I want zigzag parts. Please."

Lavender mist enveloped the room, settling like dew on her skin once again. Grinning as she traced her hands over her fresh cornrows, her auburn hair was now a honey-brown color, similar to what the woman who inspired the glamour would wear. The best part was the cornrows didn't even hurt, and they were styled on her head within seconds.

Juniper asked the question that Leola was wondering, "Wait, does this mean you have been able to glamour my hairstyles this *entire* time? Why the hell have I been sitting in Miss Nani's chair for hours?"

Grandmava shrugged and smiled, giggling. "We were not using magic with you two. So, you had to learn the Mundane struggle."

"Cruel. That's just so cruel." Juniper flipped her hair over her shoulder as she asked, "So, can I glamour braids on myself?"

"Yes, it is easy magic. I'll teach you," Grandmava answered.

Juniper gasped. "Locs, twists, and silk presses too?"

Grandmava laughed. "Yes, child. But you still need to wash that hair. You can't glamour away *odors*."

"Hmm. Nice cornrows, sis. Might have to copy those in my next *glam* sesh." Juniper giggled toward Leola, but her mind was elsewhere, watching Benn as he glamoured twists into his hair. They rested above his eyebrows and they looked... nice. She squashed the thoughts and looked away, turning toward Juniper to laugh with her.

Grandmava clapped her hands. "Your clothes are time appropriate; your identities are disguised. You can work tomorrow without being recognized or standing out too much."

He cut in to ask, "Won't Master Roswell notice *two* new Chattels on his land? They are young and at the age of..." Grandmava's face darkened as he trailed off, his face becoming unreadable—Leola's laughter died at whatever wordless exchange she witnessed passing between them.

"The Overseers will check the barracks and find them anyway." Grandmava spoke in a lower voice. "Girls, we can't *hide* you while you're here, so you must be out in the open during working hours. You must *not* stand out. In fact, refrain from talking as much as possible. You are both outspoken, but here, you can't act that way. Any retorts will be met with a whip from the Overseer."

Her mouth snapped shut as Juniper flinched away from her words—the room falling into melancholic silence. No one was laughing anymore—only cringing at the weight of where they were, the Roswell Laborist Camp.

Her grandmother spoke first. "Bennjamin works in the field, and I work in the gardens and the main house. Today, I overheard that the Corruptor is giving the Master a new shipment tomorrow as a thank you." She rolled her chestnut eyes. "It'll be best if you both come in on that shipment. I doubt the Master has counted the numbers. Once you arrive, head to the garden and house. The Overseers usually assign roles to Chattels in the morning, but since the shipment will arrive midafternoon, they will assign you to tasks where people are needed. No matter what, you will go to the garden—where you will get a role assignment from me."

"Shipment?" Juniper whispered the word.

"People. It is a shipment of *people*, Juniper. More Chattels. Bought and sold at the markets," he murmured.

Leola fought the urge to vomit up the meal that Grandmava had summoned. She nodded, staring at the ground. She focused on the plan to distract herself as she asked, "How do we get in the shipment? How do we intercept it?"

Grandmava gestured toward him with one hand, casting an aerial map of Roswell onto the wall behind Benn with the other. "Luckily for us, our Bennjamin here, joined Roswell the exact same way. He can walk you through it."

Not our *anything,* she thought to herself.

— BENN —

He rose and pointed to the forest covering the southern border of the Camp as he said, "I waited in the forest here, where I landed; it's the same place you landed today. This long dirt road—where we saw the search party tonight—leads to the main entrance of Roswell. Any carriages bringing in shipments will enter through that entrance." His mind worked, identifying holes in their plan, as he continued, "I used my power to freeze time and jumped in the Chattel chain line. Not all of the shackles were full, so I took an extra place behind the others and shackled myself. Then, I unfroze time and walked the rest of the way into Roswell with them."

He had a different skill set in his arsenal than the sisters had, but that did not mean that the sisters would not succeed in joining the shipment undetected; they would just need to be creative. He crossed the room, reaching down to pick up the pocket watch from where it lay next to Juniper. Like all relics, its weight was heavy in his hands—the magic heavy on his soul.

You are a friend, the time relic spoke to him, calling to his own time magic. *We know each other well. You know time as well as I do.* The bone-chilling voice curled in his mind; he had years of experience with enchanted relics, but their voices never failed to send a shiver down his spine.

When a person encountered a relic of magic similar to their own, the relic could use the connection to communicate. A magical being of lesser power would hear whispers in an unfamiliar language when interacting with those enchanted relics. He inherited his time magic from his mother; it was no surprise that, like her, he could understand relics. The sisters did not possess time magic, but he'd used his power to pause time when he had joined the shipment months ago, and he needed to guarantee that the time relic would help the sisters do the same. He held the ancient relic in his hand, resisting the urge to grimace at the whispers in his ear.

Yes, I'm a friend. I have two new friends that need your help tomorrow. You've met them. Actually, you brought them here. He responded only to the relic; relics didn't prefer to communicate publicly. *Thank you for that, by the way.*

Oh yes, the powers of the prophecies. Hollow and Ember. I brought them for you, the relic whispered back, the eerie sounds slithering down his spine.

His thoughts snagged on the odd wording. Relics operated with self-preserving goals and weren't known to reveal their intentions. He chose his words with caution. *For me? Why would you want to help me?*

We are friends, aren't we? the watch answered. *You are the third piece of the Prophecy. I am on the side of the just world. Lend me to your friends, and I'll help them get where they need to, unnoticed. All I ask is that you let me accompany you on your journey so I will see that this prophecy is fulfilled. I want to exist in a just world.*

He'd never given much thought to his role in the prophecy. Grandmava had called him "necessary," but he hadn't considered what that meant—he hadn't had time to. Now, the idea of being essential filled his chest with pride. At least the pocket watch had requested something that he could deliver. *Sure, I'll take you with me. Take care of my friends tomorrow. Talk soon.*

He handed the pocket watch to Juniper as he said, "I spoke to him; he'll help you tomorrow."

"*Spoke* to it?" Juniper asked, eyes narrowing. "Explain, Benny."

"*Him,* more like. Relics will speak to magic-wielders of similar magic to their own. It takes the right amount of power to do it; my mom was powerful, so I inherited the ability to hear them," he said as his throat tightened in the familiar way it always did when he thought of her.

Recognition flickered to her eyes, but was contradicted by her joke. "Benn's got *all* the powers." She mimicked his voice in the same way she had in the woods. Her hands rested on her hips and she stood taller to copy his stance.

In the woods, it had irritated him, but now he realized the silly nature of the younger sister was consistent with her personality. It was opposite to her sister—whose personality was more serious—stoicism forced from the anti-Mundane world she'd been forced to live in. The sisters were matched in quick-witted jabs, but Juniper was the comedian out of the two.

He shook his head at her, fighting a laugh. "I sound nothing like that."

"You sound exactly like that," Leo commented, eyeing Benn with what looked suspiciously like a smirk.

Grandmava spoke, voice pensive as her brows drew together. "I overheard some talk while I was in the kitchen today. A friend of the Corruptor's will accompany the shipment. You'll need to be wary of him. If one of them is searching for you two... they all are." She waved her wrists as two additional cots appeared, crowding the room even further. "Now, time to restore the memories; you'll be tired—exhausted perhaps—as your body acclimates to the changes. The memories will return and the powers will follow. Don't be alarmed if it takes a few days for the power to manifest. Close your eyes and reach for the power," she said, her voice crisp and matter-of-fact, no sign of the emotion it had held in their previous conversation.

The sisters took their places on the new cots. His breath caught as Leola's skin emitted a deep orange glow. The room warmed like there was a fire present, and he fought the instinct to retreat from the heat prickling his skin. Juniper was next. Sage green replaced the topaz and whites of her eyes as they became a viridescent swirl. It was familiar—the same magic he'd sensed in the forest when Juniper had been unconscious, yet her power had been active in spite of that.

Grandmava mused, "Like it never left."

The room cooled. He marveled at what was happening as Leola smiled, pushing her rosewood hair over her shoulder. She shot a stream of white-hot flame in the direction of her sister. Juniper squealed, dodging it, snapping her fingers as Leola's limbs became bound by thick marine foliage.

Leola gawked and Juniper threw back her head, laughing. "How could I have possibly forgotten about this?"

"Sis, we are so back." Leola returned the laugh. "Now, untie me."

"The Prophesied Pair," he murmured, glancing between the two sisters, who now used their power with effortless craft. He was grateful to have the sisters as companions on this journey. He'd have doubted the prophecy if he'd known who the Pair was when he'd met them in the woods—seen how vulnerable and uneducated they were—but the two were much more capable than he could have ever dreamed. He could sense the magic thrumming beneath their veins, itching and clawing to be freed, yet here, it had only been partially released.

They all talked for hours after—Grandmava and Benn exchanging information gleaned during recon and sharing updates on his assassination runs. Grandmava walked the sisters through small magic lessons—straightforward binds and simple wards—reiterating that honing the craft would take time, a caution that both sisters objected to. Interest piqued, he observed the interactions between the sisters and their grandmother—his friend. A shift occurred as he began to view the Pair as both the tactical weapons that they were destined to be in this war and as two sisters who were raised as Mundaners—allowing them a harsh upbringing that brought a liberal perspective of the state of Heri and the worlds beyond. He fell into a dreamless, peaceful sleep—the first he'd had since his arrival at Roswell. He felt relieved—more capable of fulfilling the prophecy after meeting the sisters, the ones chosen by the Gods. Their presence gave him hope that the bleak state of their world could be undone.

Minutes before sunrise, he warped them to a safe spot in the woods, where the sisters would hide until they could intercept the shipment. Benn had kills to deliver, and since his absence in the Camp fields would be noticed if he wasn't prompt for his role assignment, he wouldn't be staying with them while they waited. He checked his watch, using the little time he had left to reinforce the lessons he'd taught them the night before.

"Try your shield again," he said to both of them.

"I've shown you ten times," Juniper chided. "You said they were flawless."

"Satisfactory," he corrected, his eyes flicking toward Leola. Juniper's shield was near impenetrable—not to Benn, but rather to any medium-grade emotion-wielder or illusionist. The shield would do well; he was impressed. Still, he said, "Again."

With Leola, he lied, telling her they were stronger than the night prior when really, he couldn't sense her shield at all. He justified the lie for two reasons: One, if it was his power failing, he would not be admitting that to someone he'd just met, and two, if she had no ability to shield at all, he needed to talk to an elder—someone who was an expert on shields to figure out why that was.

He watched the wheels of her mind turn as she exercised the power and then turned her gaze on him. A silent question as she waited for his feedback on how she was doing.

"Good," he lied.

He ran them through the basics of warping, which was easy enough, considering all magical beings possessed this skill in some capacity. He had not been remotely surprised when Leola excelled at warping; part of him wished that he could stay a few minutes longer—to see how far she could go—but they were running on a tight schedule today. The sky was lightening as daytime neared, and Benn had evil beings to kill before he reported to the orchard to meet the Overseers—a task he needed to complete before anyone realized he'd left. He picked through the four kill cards, determining the order of operating that would be most efficient.

Juniper materialized over his shoulder, causing him to jump. "Are those the people you're killing today?"

"It seems you've figured warping out." He sighed as he straightened. "Yes, evil beings—maybe even Darkbeings, if their soul is polluted enough."

"Darkbeings. Right. Grandmava mentioned those yesterday," Juniper said, cocking her head to the side as she tossed her braids over her shoulder. "Can I come with you? That sounds a million times more fun than sitting in this forest."

Leola appeared in front of him, soundlessly, like she'd been warping for years and not hours. "Agreed," she said as she glared toward the trees. "This forest reeks of death—and I'm not just talking about the bodies in the trees."

He stopped himself from glancing up at what he already knew was there; the Overseers and Patrol put so many Chattels to death that there was never a shortage of decaying bodies in the Poplars.

"I can't take you. It would be irresponsible to waste the power carrying you both. Plus, I travel faster alone." He shrugged, masking the apprehension knotting his stomach up at the thought of leaving them alone in this dreadful forest. "I trust you'll both stay hidden while you wait for the shipment."

"Oh, Benn, chill out." Juniper waved a relaxed hand in the air. "I mean... you *are* leaving us to be intentionally caught *and* shackled by the friend of the Corruptor who is hunting for us." Juniper smirked. "What could go wrong?"

That didn't ease his anxiety. He forced his face into a bored mask, concealing his perturbation.

"You seem nervous." Leola patted him on the shoulder, sending a gentle smile in his direction. "Don't be. We'll handle ourselves—we're not Mundaners anymore, remember?" A sphere of flame floated over her hand for emphasis.

This morning had been more peaceful between them—he wondered if her grandmother had something to do with their unspoken truce. He didn't care about the reason, but he was grateful for the quiet alliance between them—a metaphorical ceasefire, perhaps. A truce hedging on the fact that if *anything* went wrong today, they would all die. He tried not to acknowledge that that was the first time the auburn-haired poweress had sent a smile in his direction; he was way too happy about that. He blamed his traitorous heart for that idiocy.

Stay cool, Benn, he scolded himself for the untimely giddiness flaring to life in his chest.

He looked between the sisters. "Practice your shielding. Trust no one."

"Appreciate the warning, though it's unnecessary," Juniper said with a grin, now leaning against one of the Poplar trees. "We don't even trust you, Benny boy."

"The feeling is mutual," he said as he started to warp, disregarding the intense dread chilling his spine. Wind whipped across his cheeks as he landed at the coordinates of his first kill card, simultaneously praying to the Gods that their plan would work.

CHAPTER 11

— LEOLA —

Year: 1855
2 July
Laviegata, Heri

THE LAVIEGATA SUN WAS FIERCE, making the air around them as balmy as it was muggy. She stood against a tree fanning the bugs that swarmed her face. She was ready to leave this forest, even if that meant she would be in *chains*. As much as she despised the idea, there wasn't a better option here. As Benn had pointed out this morning, their choices were limited, and this was the 'least shitty of them,' as he'd so eloquently described it.

It was midday now, so the shipment would be arriving any time. She bobbed on the balls of her feet, eyes trained on the dirt path that led to Roswell.

She didn't enjoy standing or sitting still; she longed for a distraction. Her fire had returned to its full capacity during the night, now behaving as a living entity under her skin, refusing to be ignored.

Benn had mentioned a possibility of her being able to access *another* power, though she couldn't sense it. It was different from the fire; the fire seemed to exist within her soul, fueling it in a way that was so innate that she couldn't fathom how she'd ever lived without it. Closing her eyes, she found the familiar thrum that burned beneath her skin.

There you are. Having her power returned to her was salubrious—a missing piece of her soul reunited with the rest. She raised her hands, letting flames dance over her limbs, as she waited.

Incredible. The flames danced at her command and moved at her will. With her memories back, it was second nature to control the flames. She was eager to get to a larger space, to see just how much fire she could summon. And though she could use the flames without smoke, they couldn't risk drawing any attention to themselves, so she refrained.

— JUNIPER —

As her memories resurfaced last night, fond times she'd shared with her Papa melded together, as the magic returned to each memory. She'd inherited the Earthpower from her grandfather; he was marvelously strong. She wondered if she was stronger than him now.

Her lessons with him were limited, as were her years spent learning the power, but he was an expert. He trained Juniper to master her botany abilities before she could even form full sentences. But she'd never been given a chance to summon visions from the earth, as she knew her grandfather could.

"One day, Junebug. Be patient. You need to wait to take visions—until you're ready." He'd patted her dark curls after he said it, and she'd hated that idea then just as much as she hated it now.

What am I waiting for? She looked around at the trees that surrounded them, wondering if she could connect with them. Juniper stretched her arm, pressing a palm to the tree bark.

The bark fused with her hand, her eyes rolling as she was pulled into a vision:

The frosty air whipped at her face as her bare feet burned against the frozen ground. Juniper looked around and saw several adult Chattels standing in the snow— still in tattered robes, despite the winter weather. Her gaze caught on Grandmava. Juniper had arrived mere seconds ago, and she could sense that the mood here was heavy. The chill wasn't only from the climate. Her grandmother held the hands of two young boys—no older than eight years old. Silent tears ran down their cheeks; her grandmother's eyes glistened with despair of her own. In a flash, Grandmava's hands covered the boys' eyes as Juniper heard the sounds of a rope being tugged behind her, followed by a startling crack.

Screams ripped from the children's throats, like they knew what had happened even though their eyes were shielded from the sight. As if the sound was well-known to them. Her head whirled to see a man had been hung behind her; Juniper couldn't stop herself from looking at his face, though she wished she'd averted her eyes. He mirrored the boys in appearance and seemed to be in his late thirties, though it was hard to confirm with the slackened way his head drooped or the dead glaze in his eyes. That look numbed Juniper's limbs—sending her stumbling backwards. She landed in the dirt and crab-crawled back a few yards until she managed to put space between herself and his swinging, naked feet. She barely contained the scream fighting its way out of her own throat. Her head swam—she was not sure if it was from the impact of her fall or the stunning horror in front of her.

Out. I need to get out, *were her last thoughts as she recognized an otherworldly force shaking her body.* Leo.

With a gasp, her hand fell from the tree.

"JUNIPER!" Her sister shook her shoulders, yelling too loud.

Disoriented, mind reeling from what she'd seen, she answered, "I'm up!" To her dismay, her hands were shaking. "I'm awake."

Leola eyed her, taking her face into her hands as she checked for signs of injury. "What the hell was that? You touched that tree and the next thing I know, you're unconscious. I thought you passed out!"

"I had a memory of my training with Papa. Earthpowers can speak to the trees, especially ancient ones. I thought I'd try it out." She tried to hide her trembling hands. "Zero fucking stars. I don't recommend doing that, in case you were wondering." She tried to laugh, but the sound was weak.

"I wasn't." Leola grimaced, peering over her shoulder at the tree. "Bug, I couldn't do that if I tried." Her sister was silent for a moment as her eyes searched the trees beyond Juniper's head. "What did you see?"

She swallowed the lump in her throat, answering, "A man being hanged in front of his kids. The Overseers used this very tree, in fact."

Leola went quiet, a moment passed before she choked out the words. "*Fuck* these woods. Fuck this place. They see Mundaners as nothing here—and magic only *just* entered the world in this era—yet already, they are so hateful."

"Well, we aren't Mundaners anymore, Leo." She frowned at the realization. "Or we never truly were, I guess."

"We know how it feels to live as they do—as 'Lesserbeings.'"

"I hate that word," she whispered, eyes on the trees stretching above them.

"Don't look up." Leola grabbed her chin, tilting it down. "And yeah, well it's what they use to show where the power lies—and it's not with the Mundane beings."

"I don't see why Mundaners are their focus," Juniper breathed.

"Easy targets. Abundant in numbers, but powerless to magic-wielders. More fragile," Leola said, breaking her own rule as she glanced up and sighed. "*Assholes.* May the Gods curse the wrongdoers and welcome the souls forced to rest here. May those souls meet a peaceful end, while the Opes roast in Mors's garden."

Voices echoed in the distance. Both girls straightened. Juniper pursed her lips, stomach hollowing at the view of the carriage hobbling down the dirt path. "That must be the shipment," she whispered as she pulled the pocket watch out, holding it in her palm.

Leola reiterated the plan in a hushed tone, as if Juniper could have forgotten. "Wait until they get closer. You use the relic to freeze time. Then, we sprint to the carriage and shackle ourselves. Time unfreezes and we're on our way." She paused. "Am I missing anything?"

"Nope. You know, it almost seems too easy," she joked, flashing a smile at her sister.

"I wish I could use sarcasm to cope, Bug," Leola chided.

"You just did, Leo," she deadpanned.

She was terrified on the inside. She wished she could mind-wipe herself of the screams from the boys that had watched the hanging in her vision. But no, they'd seared themselves into her memory the second she'd heard them. The crack of the man's neck sounded in her mind again.

Juniper inhaled, shaking her head and forcing herself back to reality as she admitted, "I'm scared, Leo."

Leola nodded as she whispered, "They're getting closer. This is our chance."

They moved from their hiding place in silence until they were a few yards away from the carriage. The shackles dragging behind it sent a chill through Juniper's bones. She held her breath as she observed the newly purchased Chattels walk behind it. Juniper blinked away tears so her sister wouldn't notice her fractured resolve.

It moved on large round wheels—the ones in the back bigger than those rolling in the front. The square, cherry wood bodice was shaded, concealing the passengers inside, and looked to be made of leather. The carriage step, shaft, and lamps were adorned with gold. The Overseers sat in the driver's seat—one with russet brown hair that peeked out from under his hat, the other with a similar hat covering wisps of blonde hair that was pulled into a bun. Both of their faces were made obscure by dust coverings.

This is it—the moment of truth. Either our plan works or... we die. She clenched her jaw as she ran her finger across the face of the watch, hoping the relic would do as it had promised Benn—use that magic it possessed to freeze time. She still questioned the likelihood of this working but was left with little time to doubt. The relic warmed and the face transformed into a swirl of emerald green, like it had done in the deli.

The horses, carriage, men, and Chattels *froze*.

"Holy demons, Benn was right," Juniper breathed, dropping the relic in the hidden pocket of her layered skirt. She sprinted toward the carriage, hurtling over a fallen tree as she did. Leola followed in silent steps.

"There is no way to know how long the time freeze will last, so move fast." Benn's words echoed in her mind as she dodged the thick foliage.

She reached the dirt road and stepped into the shackles, closing them around her ankles in frantic motions.

"Gods. These are heavy," she huffed, straining as she lifted the shackles off the ground. She was able to clasp them around her wrists, where they threatened to dislocate under the pressure of the chains. At least she'd made it into the line of Chattels. She tossed a look over her shoulder and was relieved to see Leola had done the same. She grimaced, flexing her wrists against the cuffs that were already cutting off her circulation. Time unfroze and she stumbled forward, the carriage keeping its former pace as it pulled her along with it.

A breath later, the carriage halted.

Terror flared in her chest as her thoughts raged. *There is no way they saw us.*

Everything had gone as planned: the relic had released a time freeze and they'd intercepted the line of Chattels without disruption. The blonde man jumped down from his seated position in the carriage and stalked toward the line. Not a single one of the Chattels looked up as he approached, so Juniper dropped her eyes to do the same, keeping her head down. His steps were slow as he seemed to be examining each of the Chattels in the shipment. Sweat trickled down her neck. Urine leaked down the pants of the man in front of her and the one movement she allowed herself was retreating a step so the liquid wouldn't absorb into her slippers. She could feel her sister's shaking movements reverberating off her own shackles. Her anxiety reached its breaking point, and somehow, she was back in that vision, hearing the screams all over again.

Hearing the snap of the man's neck.

By the grace of the Gods, she kept her eyes on the red dirt as pointed boots came into view, drying her mouth up instantly.

"You. Eyes up," he said, his voice as demanding as it was demeaning.

She blinked, obeying, catching sight of the whip he held in his fisted grip. Her eyes slid up to meet a wide pair of emerald eyes. His eyes crinkled with a smile that she hated immediately.

His blonde hair was hardly pulled together by a leather band as it curled around his ears. He was taller than her, so Juniper craned her neck to look up at his face, fighting the urge to sneer at him. A piece of brown cloth covered his mouth and nose, so she could only see his eyes. Eyes that stayed glued to hers, like he was seeing beneath the glamour her grandmother had implemented last night. She prayed that he couldn't see her true face and forced that thought out of her mind; there was no sense in giving more life to her panic. He seemed to be no older than her, though that didn't make him any less intimidating.

His eyes raked over her, head to toe, making her skin crawl. He cracked the whip on the ground by her feet, sending dust into her eyes. She forced her eyes shut, unable to shield them with her shackled hands and coughed against the dust filling her throat. As her lungs desperately sought breathable air, the eye-crinkling expression that mimicked glee returned.

Opasteg garbage. Juniper resisted the urge to spit in his face—her mouth too dry to accomplish that anyway.

He spoke in a clear voice, still staring at her. "Seems we're moving slow back here and we're on a schedule. Pick up the pace, Lessers." He leaned so close to her that she refrained from backing up a step. He enunciated the words, lining each of them with disdain. "The next one to slow us down will be whipped to ribbons."

CHAPTER 12

— JUNIPER —

THE GRUELING WALK TO ROSWELL CAMP was made worse by the chains. Sweat dripped into Juniper's eyes, leaving a burning sensation in its wake. She yearned to lift her arms to wipe her sweat, but the chains were forcing her wrists toward the ground. She imagined that this must be similar to how it felt to be leashed, except there were thirteen people shackled together and the leash was made of weathered iron. The coppery scent seeping off of the chains was making her nauseous. Or maybe the nausea was a result of walking in this line of Mundaners for what had seemed to be miles.

She'd started this journey with her eyes forward, unwilling to look away from the carriage, fearful of another encounter with the Corruptor's friend. An hour later, she was unable to lift her chin as her eyes stared down at the red Laviegata dirt.

One foot in front of the other. She chanted that phrase one hundred times, repeating the words until they didn't have meaning anymore. She was never one to back down from a challenge, but today, her spirit was breaking. Her heartbeat pulsated throughout her swollen cheeks. She was so tempted to stop to rest—even if only for a moment. But then, she thought of the whip in the blonde kid's hand and the unsettling maniacal gleam in his eyes that would accompany it. Stopping was not an option.

One foot in front of the other.
One foot in front of the other.
One foot in front of the other.

— LEOLA —

The pudgy Overseer leaned down in front of her feet, using a large key to free her ankles; she almost smiled as she envisioned kicking him in the teeth. She couldn't see what lay under his hat—not that she wanted to—but she noted that he wore the same attire as the other Overseers. Unlocking the shackles was a painstaking process, or maybe he was moving slowly, or maybe she was eager to get out of these hellish bindings.

She stretched each of her legs, hearing the crack of her overworked ankles as the chains clattered to the ground.

The Overseer yanked her wrist shackles toward him, the metal digging into her already angry skin. She clenched her jaw, refusing to react to the pain. She tracked his hand movements, noticing the care he used to *not* touch her skin as he freed her. Which was laughable, considering she was the one wearing shackles.

Leola straightened her chin, her chest tightening at the thought. *They really see Chattels as animals here. Mundaners are nothing to them.*

He stepped away from her, not dismissing her... not acknowledging her at all. She shoved her free hands in her pockets and walked to where the other Chattels from the shipment stood, Juniper included, as they waited to be assigned roles for the day. Juniper didn't look at her, as her eyes were fixed on someone standing near the Master; her eyes followed her sister's stare.

Master Roswell was standing in the shade of a large tree nearby with three other men flanking him. She noticed the Corruptor first; he *was* the man they had met in the deli. She would recognize that jet-black hair and those piercing eyes anywhere. She felt a similar chill in her spine that she had gotten when he had first approached them while eating... Standing to his right was the same blonde man who had cracked his whip near Juniper's feet a mere hour ago. He had removed the cloth covering his face but kept the felt hat on his head. Leola found herself wondering if he was a man or if he was only a teenager. Her eyes shifted to the man to the right of the blonde. He wore a similar outfit but had shorter, mousey-brown hair. He looked to be in his 40s, and truthfully, he had a forgettable face. Leo would be trying her best to remember him, though, in case they were doomed to cross paths later.

The men walked toward the group of Chattels. Master Roswell reached them first, the Corruptor at his side. The other two men stayed behind them in the shade. Master Roswell walked a slow circle around the Chattels as he examined each of them. She and Juniper kept their heads down as Grandmava had instructed them to do. There were thirteen people total in the shipment—Leola, Juniper, ten men, and a girl. The Master's eyes caught on the young girl. She wanted to jump in front of the child—to protect her from whatever lurked in his predatory gaze—but she kept her feet planted, even as her fists clenched.

"Never make eye contact with the Master... or his associates. Never bring attention to yourselves, no matter what happens." Her grandmother's warning from this morning replayed in her ears.

He came to a stop, gesturing at the mansion looming behind them. "Welcome to Roswell Camp, your new home," he said as he let out a low laugh. "Well not *this*, of course; the Chattels' quarters are downaways." He looked toward the Corruptor, who stepped forward at Master Roswell's acknowledgment. "This is a mighty good lookin' group, my friend. I must thank you."

The Corruptor tipped his wide-brimmed hat in Master Roswell's direction. "No thanks needed. You've agreed to host us while I continue on my search for my prizes. Consider this repayment."

Prizes. Leola's teeth clenched.

Master Roswell chortled. "You've always been a generous one, Carole." He clapped his hands together, returning his gaze to the Chattels before him.

Carole. Carole is searching for us. She forced the name to etch itself into her memory. If she had to be in this creep's presence, she was determined to observe and report something; in her skirt pocket, she raised her middle finger. *Search for this, motherfucker.*

"Now, I hope y'all came ready to work; I've nearly given you half the day off already," he sneered as his cruel laugh at his own joke indicated that he really might believe that this day had been a *day off.* Contrarily, the walk up the dirt path had nearly sent her to the Gods. "I was expecting eleven of you, but we got thirteen here. No problem—there's always work needing to be done around the grounds." He glanced around, his tone bored as someone who had done this hundreds of times before. "Ten of you to the field and three of you to the house. Someone'll see you to the barracks when it is dusk. Don't be caught outside after curfew or I'll send the dogs after you." She swallowed her shock.

So that's what the dogs in the forest were for last night... She balled her fists to hide her shudder.

———

She and Juniper wordlessly made their way to the back entrance of the main house, refusing to spend another minute in the sight of the Master or his friends. On their way to the kitchen, Leola tugged the young girl's hand, indicating for her to follow. Her dusty face was tear streaked and Leola's eyes burned, imagining what kind of day this youngling girl had experienced.

What kind of life has she experienced? Is it even a life at all?

"I'll catch up to you," she murmured to Juniper, taking the girl's small hand in her own, branching off to the side of the house where a well pump stuck out of the ground. She stopped at the well, bunched up the edge of her skirt, used the pump to dampen the fabric, and took the girl's chin in her hand, using her skirt to wipe the dirt off of her face.

The girl was silent as she pulled her along the back of the mansion to where her sister waited for them. They had known that they couldn't enter the house through the front entrance, as Chattels were not permitted to use front entrances, but Leo was surprised to find herself relieved at that fact. The mere moments she'd spent near the Master and Overseers had been more than enough. Leola's fist rapped twice on the door, and her grandmother opened it with a smile.

"Welcome, my dear"—Grandmava's eyes darkened as she took in the sight of the child standing in front of Leola and Juniper—"*children.*"

She recovered fast. "Come in, come in. We could use the extra hands in here. Master is serving his friends a feast tonight."

They stepped inside the hot room, Leola taking a job cleaning dishes and Juniper taking a job in the gardens. The girl quickly became Leola's shadow. The prep kitchen was absolute madness. With every job they finished, another followed, and Grandmava seemed to be the ringleader of this circus.

Grandmava handed her a harvesting basket, uttering just one word: "Carrots." She pointed out the door toward the garden.

She wandered through the grounds as she attempted to look for the vegetable. She heard a familiar chuckle behind her and whirled to find Juniper, repeating what Grandmava had asked of her to find, "Carrots?"

"The carrots are out of season; they won't be ready for a few weeks. Grandmava must think the Master won't notice..." Juniper gestured to an area on the opposite side of the garden as she continued, "If they suddenly have carrots tonight." Juniper's basket was full of freshly harvested leafy vegetables, but no carrots, as she seemed to consider the idea. "She's probably right. I doubt he has ever considered where his food is coming from." Juniper snapped her fingers as she said, "That should work."

Leola flexed her forearm at the sudden weight of her basket and looked down to find it full of carrots boasting shades of rich purples, beiges, and oranges, with lush carrot greens growing from the tops of them.

Leola smiled, thankful she wouldn't be digging in the dirt to find these. "Thanks, Ju—" she said before she cut herself off.

Juniper smiled sadly. "No names."

"No names," she repeated, smiling but never letting it reach her eyes. She turned to carry the basket inside. She set it down on the wooden counter and wiped sweat from her forehead.

Wary of the other ears in this prep kitchen, Leola whispered, "The garden is doing *quite* well." She hated to be so out of breath from carrying vegetables.

"Mmm-hmm." Grandmava continued kneading the dough she'd been working on.

Their work continued for hours. It was a constant hustle; everyone had a place and everyone worked. Even the girl who arrived with them fell into the pattern of constant work. There were no breaks—in fact, it seemed these people had never been *given* a break before. It was like they couldn't stop—whether it was fear or instinct driving them, she could not be sure. There were only women and children in the prep kitchen and gardens.

Her grandmother didn't want them working too close in case it tipped anyone off that they were glamoured, so they separated. Leola had chosen to stay in the kitchen because if there was one thing she knew about her sister, it was that she adored her garden; she had no doubt that Juniper was now breathing life into the one at Roswell. Gardening was akin to therapy for Juniper, and after the last miserable 36 hours, Leola sent a silent thank you to the Gods for that small gift to her sister.

— LEOLA —

It was late afternoon when Leola took her first bathroom break of the day—which meant she was to go to the treeline and relieve herself outside.

Like an animal.

Exhausted, dehydrated, and angry, she stalked toward the trees, trying to hold onto whatever pride she had left. She was making her way through the gardens and back to the kitchen when she heard a loud whistle from inside the kitchen. Not knowing what it meant, she moved quicker. She opened the door and saw the Master's wife, Lady Louisa, standing in the kitchen. She was a short, round woman, and her face was splotchy with red patches. Leola guessed it was from the relentless heat of Laviegata and the lack of sun protection in this era.

"We will need extra servers for dinner tonight. Mr. Roswell has friends visiting," Lady Roswell said, speaking directly to Grandmava.

You forgot to say please, she wished she could say to the woman.

Her grandmother nodded, turning back to the vegetables she'd been chopping.

Lady Roswell spoke again. "My husband requested the two new girls help serve dinner... the ones who arrived with the shipment today. Not the child." She nodded toward Leola, adding, "I assume that means you. You're filthy; wash up and make yourself presentable before dinner."

Leola almost gaped at the harsh words, but she stopped herself and, instead, bowed her head. After that encounter, it was clear that Lady Roswell did not care for the Mundane Chattels, though she assumed that was the standard of this era. The shrewd woman left, and the Chattels resumed their tiresome work. Grandmava turned toward Leola and wrung her hands, her eyes darting around the mess kitchen. Her nervous energy spiked Leola's pulse.

"What is it?" she asked as her eyes narrowed.

The concern on her grandmother's face was clear. "I'm worried that since both of your presences were requested by the Master, he has other plans for you two than *serving dinner*."

She stiffened. "What do you mean by *other* plans?"

Grandmava chewed on the inside of her cheek, and Leola could see tears forming on the rims of her eyes. Plans could mean anything in this era—punishing them, killing them... whatever the Master meant when he'd referred to the *dogs*.

"*What other plans?*" she repeated in a horrified whisper.

Her grandmother's hands trembled. "The Master and his friends sometimes... call on girls to use for entertainment."

"*Entertainment.*" The word was a soft whisper, even as dread twisted in her stomach and her arms lost feeling. She gripped the counter to prevent herself from falling over. Her eyes traveled out the window to where Juniper sat in the garden, pulling at weeds.

No. That will not be happening. No fucking way. She refused to let her sister be violated that way.

Leola blinked and continued with her dish washing, trying to stay focused. There had to be a way for them to make it through this with their dignity—their autonomy—intact. She'd been following the plan that they had crafted last night, but she needed to keep her sister safe without exposing the mission or themselves. Now, she wondered if following the plan was still a possibility or if she needed to scrap that plan and burn Roswell Camp to embers.

She was still scrubbing when Grandmava put a hand on her shoulder and asked, "Why don't you two go to the barracks and get washed up to serve dinner? We'll finish up here."

Grandmava sent a pointed look toward the sudsy water around her hands. She looked down to find it boiling. She yanked her hands out on instinct, even with the knowledge that the heat couldn't hurt her. Wordlessly, she dried her hands and walked out to the garden, debating how to tell her sister what awaited them.

She grabbed Juniper, walking further from the house, so their conversation could be private. Once they were out of sight of the main house, she pulled Juniper close and choked out the words, regurgitating what Grandmava had told her.

"*What?*" Juniper responded, stopping in her tracks. Leola tugged her toward the barrack they had slept in the night prior. "First, I have to walk a mile in *chains,* and now the Master wants to *offer* me to his friends? You have to be kidding."

"I wish I were." She sighed, her palms heating. "We'll find a way out of this. It might be a game-time decision, but I won't let you be alone with that monster or any of his friends. I'll protect you, Bug."

"Just me, huh? And what about *you*? Who protects you, sis?" Juniper's voice was firmer than she'd ever heard it, Leo's throat burned when she noticed her sister fighting back tears. "The last forty hours have been vile and demeaning. I thought it couldn't get worse than the chains. Look at us now."

She snorted at her sister's sarcasm and pulled Juniper toward the Chattels' quarters. They had thirty minutes until they needed to report for serving duty.

"Who the hell decided to make all of the outfits in this era so frilly? People are wearing all of this with no air conditioning? It's like wearing a comforter," Juniper grumbled and fluffed her layered skirt. She opened a hidden pocket to reveal several apples, tossing one to Leola.

"You know, you could use your magic to grow those, right? Stealing is risky," she said as she bit into the apple.

"*Duh*. How else do you think I got these, by *picking* them? Ha-ha," Juniper chided.

They took turns using the wash bucket while the other kept watch. It was not comfortable, but it was nice to be rid of the dirt that had been caked to her skin since this morning. They changed into clean clothing in their barrack in silence.

Juniper broke the silence as she sniffed her armpits. "You know, maybe I should have left the body odor. Would that make me less attractive to the Master and his buddies? No man wants a *stanky* girl for nightly entertainment." She let out a laugh that was full of nerves and Leola hated it. She could count on one hand the times she'd seen her sister nervous.

Leola was a whirlwind of anxiety, trying to figure out how they would get out of this horrifying situation. However, she didn't want to show that to Juniper, so she joked back.

"Juniper, your pits could deter a pack of hungry lions. It is basically repellant." She tapped her chin for comedic effect and added, "You should ask Grandmava if that is another one of your *magic* powers."

Juniper rolled her eyes with a laugh. "Anything to save me from these nasty men." She sighed, blinking tears back as she pulled her braids into a band of leather at the base of her neck. "It's not funny, actually."

Both sisters were dressed, so that meant it was time to go. Leola wished she could stay in this temporary safe space she and her sister had created in the barrack, but that was not a possibility.

There were no words to soften the reality that lay ahead, so she only said, "It's horrifying."

Her sister looped her arm through Leola's and they walked together through the Chattels' quarters, passing the gardens, entering the house through the mess kitchen.

Juniper prepared to push through the swinging door that led to the proper dining room. Before she did, she turned over her shoulder, keeping her voice low, and said, "One wrong move toward either of us and I'm killing them all."

She stepped around her sister, beckoning her through the door, as she agreed, "Good. I'll torch the place while you do."

CHAPTER 13

— JUNIPER —

"STAND IN THE CORNERS OF THE ROOM so you aren't in the way. We'll serve dinner. Whoever is not filling the glasses will clear the plates," a steadfast Chattel woman named Margaret directed. "And be quick—don't wait for them to ask you to do it."

She held out a pitcher to them, which Juniper promptly grabbed so she would have something to do with her jittery hands.

"Guess I'll be on plate duty then," said Leola.

Margaret walked back out to the prep kitchen. The swinging door closed behind her with a soft swish. Juniper walked to a corner of the room, while her sister did the same.

Juniper's eyes wandered, the dust from the curtains tickling her nose. She sniffed, not daring to speak due to being wary of listening ears, though it was just her and her sister in the room. She took in the space around her. The dining room was grand with tall ceilings and a large oak dining table that could seat at least twenty people. The room was ornately decorated in shades of red complimented with gold accents. Beautiful, imported dinnerware sat on the three placemats set on the table.

138

This house is loaded with thrifted treasures. Juniper scoffed to herself, at her nomadic mind and its reaction to the absurdity that surrounded them tonight.

Despite being grateful to have her power and magic returned, the conflict raging within her was an untamable beast. The antiquity of the furniture left her mind reminiscent of the simplicity of wandering through the Mundaner-allowed stores of Poppycal with her sister. She wondered if they would ever get to be those versions of themselves again, or if those beings were now a facet of the past, left behind in perpetuity while this version of themselves navigated their new normal.

This can't possibly be our life now. We won't be here forever, right? Her eyes traveled down to the tattered frills of her ankle-length skirt. *I'm not spending my entire life here. Nope, no fucking way.*

Juniper took in a sharp inhale to calm her nerves, which backfired as it invited more dust into her nose. Her shoulder brushed the maroon drapes; Leola stood in the opposite corner, fists white-knuckled and clenched at her waist—her usual stoicism cracking.

The others served the feast, each one of them moving with swift purpose. None of the Chattels seemed willing to meet Juniper's eyes as she observed them. It was like they *knew* what her and sister's roles were in this dining room—not that they could do anything to change it; they were as blameless as she was. A man shouldered around her and she retreated further into the corner until her back hit the wall. As she took in the scene—of her and Leola standing in the corners, unable to leave until they'd been dismissed—it only confirmed that they were on display for the Master and his friends. Bile rose in her throat at the thought, but she kept her chin raised and waited.

Minutes ticked by as more dishes were brought to the table, the start time of the feast crawling closer. Violent, incensed thoughts raged through Juniper's mind as the table was prepared. She thought seriously about killing each of the men. Eyeing each plate, she debated if she had enough time to concoct an odorless, tasteless poison. Innately, her power could provide her with the ingredients needed to do so, but she didn't have the tools handy to bottle it. She blinked the thought of the risky plan away, knowing unknown variables presented abundant risk.

These bastards are Opasteg. The ticking of the grandfather clock to her left had the thoughts resurfacing. *They have powers of some kind. Poison* might *work, but the odds of us winning if a fight broke out—when we got our power back yesterday? Slim. Way too slim.* Juniper swallowed her sigh.

Voices boomed somewhere in the house, sending a chill up her spine.

Oh, seven hells. She held her breath. *No time for poison. The claws I summoned this morning will have to be enough. If it comes to lethal force, we will have to hold our own.* Her grip tightened on the pitcher she still held.

The voices moved closer. Three different tones of speaking, two that she recognized.

Aside from the mess kitchen, she had not been inside the house, so she hadn't cataloged the layout. Sweat beaded down the back of her neck, her palms annoyingly slick. She adjusted her grip on the ceramic pitcher so she wouldn't drop it.

A few yards to her right, the door swung open; Master Roswell entered with two men, their faces curdling her stomach with recognition. Once they took their seats, she filled their glasses, keeping her eyes on her hands the entire time; given that there was not a lapse in the conversation, and to her immense relief, it seemed the men were not paying attention to her.

Thank the Gods. Keep ignoring me. She managed to hide her trembles while she poured the wine. Keeping her footsteps light, she made her way back to her spot in the corner. At least here, her back was protected from any attack. *Nothing to see here.*

Back to the wall, she stole a quick glance at each man. She recognized Master Roswell, the Corruptor, whose name she now knew to be *Carole,* and the blonde bastard who had been driving the carriage, whose name she didn't know... yet. She lowered her eyes, considering the idea of poisoning them again. Violence was not a typical theme in Juniper's world, especially since she had lived a relatively Mundane teenage life, but that had all changed yesterday. She'd spent enough time under the thumbs of these men to know that society would do just fine without their involvement. The men removed their hats.

Huh, they have manners. Corruptor Carole's hair is totally dyed. Juniper wondered if the intention behind that choice was to appear younger or disguise his identity—or both. She swallowed the lump in her throat. *These guys must be important if he's throwing this feast for only them.* Her eyes went to the blonde's unkempt bun. *How old is the blonde guy anyway? He looks younger than Leo; hell, he could be my age.* If she poured her focus into observing, she would not succumb to her fear. At least that was a tactic Benn had recommended to her the night before. She listened to the quiet, yet firm, tone of the blonde's voice, as she poured more wine into his glass. *Are you even old enough for this?*

The Master's words interrupted her thoughts. "...the iron rusts so damn fast that they have been escaping. I've been using it as a training exercise for my dogs..."

Juniper blinked twice, burying her disgust. *There is still the option to trap them in shackles made of vines.* Her intrusive thoughts bubbled to the surface as she recalled her still sore wrists and ankles being shackled earlier that day... At least the rawness had subsided. She sidestepped, refilling Carole's glass before retreating back to her corner.

Master Roswell said, "So how are you liking Laviegata, Carole?" His fork and knife tore into the roasted chicken on his plate in a mannerless fervor.

Ah, the manners have already left, Juniper wanted to quip.

"I'm sure you mean Region 849, as we don't use the state names of the former republic," Carole said.

"Of course," Roswell said as he sipped his drink. "Still getting used to the change."

Carole's response was pragmatic. "It's nice here... could do without the humidity and heat, but 849 is fine." He shoveled food into his already full mouth. Juniper tried not to grimace as food particles flew out and onto the tablecloth as he continued, "Our work requires us to travel often, so we have seen a lot of this region. Never do get used to the climate though."

Master Roswell pulled at his trimmed facial hair. "Hmm, I was trying to learn a bit about your work from Levi here today, but he was… pretty tight-lipped about the whole thing." He flashed the blonde Corruptor from the carriage a smile that Juniper thought looked more like a side-eye.

The blonde returned it with a tight, unfriendly smile of his own.

The Master and I have one thing in common—we do not like Levi, his curly bun, nor the demons-blasted whip. Juniper's rage flared at the memory replaying from earlier today. Her eyes locked with her sister's for a fleeting moment, confirming that her sister noted the same.

Levi continued eating, notably unfazed by Master Roswell's passive-aggressive comment.

Carole's eyes flashed between Master Roswell and Levi, and he let out a resigned sigh. "Levi is right to be *tight-lipped.* The work we do is private. Only to be discussed in the right room with the *right* people."

Exclusive Ope business only, Master, Juniper commented silently; she was catching on to what Carole was saying, but the Master clearly was not.

"Sure," Master Roswell said as he sucked his teeth, his face flushing an angry pink. "How long have you been participating in this *private* work together?" Juniper had barely met this man, but it was obvious that his ego was hurt that they were not clueing him in. She pressed her lips into a tight line to keep from smirking.

"Levi has been my apprentice for nearly a year now. When I first started, I served an apprenticeship as he is doing now. I've been doing this work for 15 years, so I'll keep Levi around until he is seasoned enough." Carole paused, glancing at Levi. "Then he will venture on to a new territory where he will train an apprentice. It all depends on our orders; with the new regime in place, there has been a lot of magic movement. I'll move on, too, working closer to our leader if the Gods will it."

"Your leader, *Daemon*. I have received bulletins from him," Master Roswell answered. "To keep the Chattels as they are in this era—*Chattels*. Sounds like he has hopes of enslaving all Lesserbeings."

Juniper clenched her fists tight around the pitcher, casting her eyes down toward the fraying rug.

Master Roswell continued, "It is hard to trust a man I have never laid eyes on. But I must say, I like the way he thinks. I like the way he *dreams*. He wants a world where lowborn Mundaners serve their lives as Chattels. That would open up so many opportunities for magic-wielders. Hell, even the Overseers. Imagine the doors we could open if Chattels were more abundant and sold at a lower price. Middle class society could afford to own Chattels. Heri's economy would thrive with access to that kind of untapped labor. In all eras." He tipped his drink and downed it in one large gulp, slamming the glass on the wooden table. "To your leader. He is a smart man, and he has my full support. Please let us know how Roswell can be of service for you and your *private* work."

Leola cleared Master Roswell's plates as Juniper moved to refill his glass; he didn't acknowledge either of them.

Levi cleared his throat, but his voice remained softer than the other two men, "Yes, the opportunities are endless. We're thrilled to hear *how* Roswell is on *our* side." Juniper looked up, freezing as his gaze caught on her own and he smirked at her. "The *right* side."

Her jaw clenched so hard that she wondered if it might crack. Levi shot her another knowing glance and tilted his empty glass toward her direction. She lowered her gaze and moved to fill it.

Levi started talking again. "Enough of the niceties. We came to 849 to find those girls. Still *no* word on their whereabouts from you. We tracked them to Roswell. Daemon needs them found—alive." He traced the border of his placemat. "*They* are his number one priority. You understand full well that the first way to *help* our organization is to help us locate them, yet you've done nothing for the cause. You are wasting our time. If I was a betting man, I'd wager that you know where they are. I would wager you sent that neophyte search party, knowing they would fail."

Her knees quaked under her layered skirt. *Daemon knows we're here and sent these buffoons to sniff us out. Focus. Focus.* Her mental wheels were spinning out of control. *If Daemon knows we're here, do they know where Daemon is? Or—* She tried to cut off her hopeful thought before she failed and it flared to life. *Do they know where my mother is?*

Master Roswell sputtered, "N-Now, I don't know what you are implying. I'm not hiding and never have hid a Mundaner here—they are only here if they are a member of the Camp. I'm loyal to Daemon's mission. I follow all his laws."

Carole started to speak, but Levi interrupted. "We are not saying you are hiding anyone, but could they be hiding nearby? Maybe you haven't noticed their presence—I mean, who counts their Chattels every day?" Levi took a small sip from his glass.

Juniper wished she'd had time to poison it.

Master Roswell's hand hit the table, causing both sisters to look up. He spoke to Levi through clenched teeth. "Don't you *dare* imply something so *vile* would occur under my roof or on my *property*." His face was now flushed with rage. "I feed and house you, and this is how you repay me? You're just a disrespectful *boy*. Leave the talking to the *men*."

Levi smirked again—like he knew he was getting under the Master's skin. "Do not confuse my *age* for lack of wisdom. I'll find the girls one way or another." His finger swirled the rim of his glass as he continued, "Maybe you will help me or maybe I'll just tell Daemon *you* housed Lesserbeings, in secret."

Master Roswell threw his glass at the wall, missing Leola by centimeters as it shattered into endless, sparkling pieces. "Clean that up *now!*" he roared.

Leola ran to the mess kitchen and returned with a broom and dustpan. He wiped his sweaty forehead with his sleeve, straightened his clothes, and took his seat at the table again. His bloodshot eyes flashed to Juniper as he said, "You. I need a fresh glass."

Juniper pushed through the swinging door and into the bright light of the main kitchen. She reached into a sideboard where she assumed the glasses were kept, thanking the Gods when she found one.

A rush of air tingled against her arm. She turned the glass over in her hand, examined her wrist and saw that her glamour was starting to fade, her skin now showing through the magic. It looked like a missing piece of a puzzle. It was not exactly conspicuous, but the slight fade in her glamour made her stomach somersault.

No no no. Why is it fading? Her knowledge of glamours was limited, but she felt a distinct *tug* against her skin; pulling with it, another piece of her glamour... this time from her elbow. She let out a gasp and narrowed her eyes in the direction of the swinging door she'd come through. *It's one of them.*

Juniper schooled her face into a bored mask as she entered the proper dining room, fresh glass in hand. She set it down and refilled it, not daring to make eye contact with any of the men at the table.

The unmistakable tingle returned, this time moving across her neck. She retreated to her place on the wall, fear pooling in her stomach; someone in this room suspected her true identity, or worse, her sister's identity. The tingling crossed her entire face. Then, as if the person trying to remove her glamour had found what they were looking for, the tingling stopped.

Tears pricked Juniper's eyes, and she forced herself not to shake in fear. *Maybe they didn't see.*

Master Roswell had cooled down from his earlier tantrum, clearing his throat to speak. "Despite the rudeness of *your* guest, I have prepared some entertainment for you, as you are my guests."

He grinned, Carole smiling in return as he chuckled.

"I heard one of you is *inexperienced* and was hoping to give you an opportunity to sample my property," Master Roswell explained like this was normal conversation.

Juniper scanned the table for empty glasses, but none needed to be filled. In the process, she noticed that Levi's hands were folded in his lap. His knuckles were white with tension, contrary to his boss, who was relaxed.

He knows. Shit. Shit. He knows. Juniper kept her eyes trained on his hands. *Any sign of a weapon, and it's go time.*

Carole's voice filled the air. "Ignore the boy, he will be all smiles in the morning after he has had his way with one of yours. I don't suppose we may be offered options?"

Master Roswell laughed and said, "Obviously." He turned toward Leola, who didn't look up. "Get the girls from the prep kitchen. Hurry, girl."

Juniper kept her eyes glued to the hideous rug beneath her slippers. The thought of seeing the girls paraded in front of these men sent the apples she'd eaten right back up into her throat. *They get to choose a woman to spend the night with—violate—when none of them have ever had rights. Never born with them—or given the opportunity to choose* anything.

Leola spoke aloud, "Ladies." The room had grown a few degrees hotter—a surefire sign of her sister's rising temper—but it wasn't showing in her calm mannerisms as she held the door to let the women enter the room. Juniper looked up and noticed they weren't women at all—in fact, most of them were the same age as she was. Four Chattels stood in front of the dining table now. She expected relief to fill her at the mention of there being other options, but here she was, mourning the fact that she couldn't do anything for them or take their place. Juniper gritted her teeth, eyes back on the floor, determining the ground as the safest place to look.

The Corruptor stood first, circling the women and girls. He pointed at one of them before returning to his chair, and Juniper assumed that meant he had chosen that one. Her name was Mara—Juniper had met her in the gardens today. They chatted for a few minutes while pulling weeds. Juniper wondered if the gardens were where Mara went for reprieve after the horrors she endured with the Master's friends. Juniper's eyes pricked but returned to the floor once more.

"Take your pick, *boy*," Master Roswell sneered.

Levi's chair scooted across the wood floors, the only sign that he'd gotten up. Her pulse spiked as familiar snakeskin boots entered her peripheral vision. Despite his sudden closeness, her eyes remained glued to the ornate rug beneath her feet. Her anxiety made the room smaller, like each wall was closing in on her. She wished she could be outside where she could take a deep breath of fresh air and clear her mind. He moved closer still, until Juniper could feel his breath in her face. The tingling was back; her eyes rose to meet Levi's to see that his finger was pointed directly in her face.

He uttered one word: "You."

CHAPTER 14

— JUNIPER —

EVERYTHING FOLLOWING THE SINGLE word he spoke happened in a blur. She peered over Levi's shoulder to see Leola was frozen, her eyes ablaze— literal flames burning in place of her brown eyes. Juniper did a double take, watching her blink to regain her composure as she scrubbed one singular tear off her cheek. While the glamours they wore hid their physical similarities, any misplaced emotional outburst would jeopardize their spycover. Luckily, Leola's glamour seemed to be holding; another tingle cascaded along her arms.

Not good. Juniper nodded toward her sister, hoping to acknowledge the fear that had Leola standing as still as a statue in the dining room. She chanted the words in her mind, as if she could hear them. *Stay cool, Leo. We'll get out of this. Go somewhere else. Get somewhere safe.*

Levi's emerald eyes were still on her, as if they were pleading for her to look at him. She refused, eyes turning back down toward the rug. The tingling sensation intensified to the point of pain.

Shit. Shit.

The Master snorted. "Oh, that one. She is new. Came in on the shipment you brought in today. I'll admit, I was planning to break her in myself—" He trailed off, standing up, patting his round belly. "But I'll let you do the honors since it's a special occasion for you."

Sharp thorn-like talons erupted from her fingertips as she curled her hands tighter around the pitcher, hoping no one had seen the claws. Levi turned toward the other men for a single heartbeat—just enough time for Juniper to set the pitcher down and tuck her hands into her apron pockets, concealing her newly emerged claws. Yet, she remained poised, ready to strike. She bit her lip to mask her terror.

"Master, we will need her help cleaning up after dinner," Leola said, presumably grasping to salvage a private moment for them to talk before she was forced to go with Levi—when really, the prep kitchen had been cleaned by the others already.

"Nonsense, girl. We will not keep a virgin man waiting when he has a girl to bed!" Roswell clapped his hands with maniacal enthusiasm, shooing Juniper toward the door to the proper kitchen. "Now go and show him a good time, girl."

The other girls turned to leave as Master Roswell caught one of their arms, yanking her to a dead stop. "You'll join me tonight, Lottie."

The blood drained from her face. Master *knew* Lottie by name, so that meant she was selected often. Juniper might have vomited on the spot, but Levi grabbed her arm and tugged her through the swinging door that led to the main kitchen before she could form another thought. There was no escaping this unless she killed him— a choice she'd already accepted after overhearing that dinner conversation.

They were moving too fast for her to get a bearing on her surroundings. She noticed the fresh paint on the beams lining the vast two-path staircase that Levi dragged her up but was never able to make sense of the layout.

Gods, slow down. She contemplated pretending to pass out, simply to buy herself some time. *Running to commit a heinous crime against me? That's not happening.* She yanked against his grasp, but the hold on her arm was unbreakable.

She tried to plant her feet against the stairs, only to have him hook an arm around her waist, pulling her like a rag doll against his side.

At the top of the staircase, Levi pulled her to the left down a narrow hallway. She counted six doors before they reached the one they entered. The door creaked shut as Levi tugged her in, releasing her arm. Desperate to put space between her and this monster, she crossed the room, her eyes glued to him until her back pressed against the wall.

She surveyed the space around her. She was not looking for a weapon—no, she didn't need one to kill him—but she did need a place to hide his body. A place clever enough that no one would find him while they escaped.

How did I summon that bind magic? Her mind ran wild; she needed a plan. *I could restrain him. No, I should kill him. Then, we escape.* Her thoughts trailed off, catching on the doomed likelihood of her, Leo, Grandmava, and maybe even Benn, all escaping unseen. Not likely, but she dreamed anyway. *Benn can warp us out of here; he'll know what to do.*

Levi's ear was to the door, though he still watched her through his peripheral vision. He lifted a finger to his lips, indicating for her to be quiet.

Like I was going to talk to you, she wanted to snap. *You rush me up here, and now you want to take your time? Prick.*

Her eyes became slits as she asked, "Are you waiting for them to join us?" Her tone did nothing to hide the bite in the question.

His hand went up to silence her. "I'm trying to hear if they've left the main dining room. If you could keep your voice down, that would be helpful." He gave her a sideways glare, as if cooperating with him should be obvious to her. What was obvious to her was that his tone dripped with condescension that she did not appreciate, and more importantly, that his Laviegatian accent was *gone.*

Laviegatian drawl turned... Rosebay-ish? His accent was too unique to place— similar to Benn's, but much more curt. Either way, his response didn't answer her question. She took her hands out of her apron pockets, resting her hands at her sides as Benn had shown her. She decided she *would* be showing her claws. He stood with his back to her, in a similar stance as she, but was not looking at her anymore. Instead, he continued to watch the door.

Her reply was closer to a growl. "And why, exactly, would you be waiting for them to leave that dining room?" She picked at her thorn claws, trying to appear calm and to shift his focus toward the weapons at her fingertips. Intimidation might work here, especially since it would be wise to get information from him.

He waved a hand motioning her to be quiet again as he said, "*Demonspawn*, could you be any louder? There are eyes everywhere, and these wards are unfamiliar to me." He released an aggravated sigh. "We don't know who is listening, so no more talking. Let me focus."

She'd had enough of his attitude, becoming more confused by him by the minute. Grandmava and Benn had mentioned wards last night, but she knew them to be barriers; there was only so much she could have learned from the magic crash course she'd received yesterday—the memories that were returning from her toddlerhood needed some sorting through.

Play dumb. He doesn't know what I know. He still hadn't noticed her claws.

"*Eyes?* It's only us in here," she responded, in a softer voice.

"Yes. This house is crawling with enemies. You can never be too careful," Levi whispered. "This door has no lock, and I don't want someone I can't see coming in."

Surely he means "enemies" of Opasteg. So that would refer to people like Mundaners or Mundaner-sympathizers. Or me. Leo. Grandmava. Benn. She mulled over the dinner conversation in her head. Levi was definitely with Opasteg, so he must be worried for the safety of himself while he planned to violate *her*. *Nice, asshole. Real nice.*

She walked over to an oak desk in the corner, running a single finger over the wood. It was dusty like everything else in this wretched house.

Still playing the part, she whispered again, "I'm not sure who you mean by enemies, sir." She nearly gagged at the idea of calling him a formal name, but managed to keep her voice quiet, only obliging his request so that he'd keep speaking freely.

"You can quit with the act now," Levi said as he turned toward her, scowling as he crossed the room.

She moved to throw her hand up, to defend herself with her claws, but she was *stuck*. It felt as if her limbs were stuck in molasses, moving at a startlingly slow pace. Her magic was blocked, too, writhing to get free from under her skin, but unreachable. He got closer and touched her face, shocking her with the sensations of a thousand sharp needle-pricks.

She winced, knowing that the glamour was now gone from her face and body.

Levi's jaw slackened a bit like he was delighted—maybe shocked.

"*Juniper Runes*," Levi breathed, loosening his magical grasp on her limbs. "I've finally found you."

She took that moment to strike, slicing deep into his face with her poison-tipped talons. She'd dug into her power reserve to fill them with Nightshade poison; these wounds would be slow to heal or, if she was lucky, lethal. Benn had said that her magic would protect her, and damn, the smug magic-wielder was right.

"Owww." Levi grabbed his face and staggered backwards. He gaped at her. "*What in the Ancestral hell is wrong with you?*"

She whispered-yelled back, "Yeah, that's right, you prick. Think you can pick me out of line like cattle and bring me up to this *dusty* room to do Gods know what to me? Well, I have news for you, you Ope scum of Heri. Not happening!" She struck him again as cactus thorns shot out of her fingertips, splintering his face. She hadn't planned for those, but she was not complaining. He leaned against the bed, wounded. "Tell me where my mother is, *now*. Tell me where your *leader* is. I'll let you live so long as you're useful to me. You'd better start talking, *Levi*."

He held up a hand, and she considered shredding it. "I think you're c-confused," he stammered. "I'm not... Opasteg. I'm Conscripted. Underground. Undercover. Shit." He winced, reaching blindly into his pocket.

She struck him again, this time going for his arm, landing the hit on his shoulder.

He glared through his swelling eyes as he asked, "What the fuck are you doing?"

"What the fuck are you reaching for?" she shot back.

"My glasses," he said, his eyes reduced to slits. "They were in my pocket before you *hit* me."

"You think I'm an idiot?" she scoffed, leaning down to grab the glasses off the ground. "You haven't been wearing glasses this entire time." If he claimed to need them, they could be used as leverage.

"Obviously. These would've been..." His head drooped, his words becoming slurred as he questioned, "No one briefed you?"

Her eyes narrowed; she leaned down until she was eye level with him. "Like I'm stupid enough to believe a word you say. Give me one good reason not to execute your sorry ass right now. And who the hell would have *briefed* me? I just got here."

His face was a swollen mess of carnage; she'd struck his shoulder so hard that white bone and severed tendons were visible.

"Benn," Levi gasped out before he sank to the ground with a thud.

CHAPTER 15

— BENN —

"THEY WERE CALLED TO SERVE the Master's feast," Grandmava said in a quiet voice.

"Fuck." He scrubbed a hand across his face as he said, "Of course they were."

"I spoke to Leo earlier—she'll burn the house down before she lets anything happen to Juniper." Grandmava handed him a plate. "Eat this. I'll return in a few hours."

The food tasted like ash; it didn't help that his stomach was in knots. He cast his power to feel for any indication that they were safe. To his shock and horror, he was met with nothing.

Are they dead? Or are they lying in a room somewhere being subjected to nightmares and— He inhaled through his nose, cutting the thought off.

From the moment he had left them in the dreaded forest that morning, he felt uneasy. Around midday, he was grateful to catch a glimpse of the sisters when they arrived with the shipment. A few men from the same shipment had been sent to work in the fields alongside him. When the Overseers had gone to the Main House for lunch, he'd asked one of them where the ladies in the shipment had gone.

The Chattel had responded with one word: house.

That was all he needed to know. He had sighed in relief; the house was safe. The gardens were safe. Well, as safe as being Chattels in a Labor Camp could be. House Chattels at Roswell spent their days in the kitchen, gardens, or with the Roswell family. He had hoped their assigned role would spare them from the brutal work in the fields, but his relief had been misguided.

Nope. No mercy—no easy way out for the Runes sisters on Roswell; no, when you're spared from one brutality, you're rewarded with a different kind.

He sent out another burst of magic and was met with nothing again; it couldn't be the distance blocking his power, so it had to be a result of spellwork or wards. Benn *always* thought three steps ahead and he hadn't even considered the outcome—the worst possible outcome—that the sisters would become fancied by the scumbag Master or his sick Opasteg friends.

How long until their identities are discovered? Opasteg Corruptors will take them to Daemon in a heartbeat. The thought of failing his mission brought his pacing to a sudden halt. His limbs were cold, unfeeling, as his eyes darted across the room. He needed a reason to go to the house to check on them, but it was past curfew, and he was doing his best not to be hung by Patrol tonight.

He chewed on his fingernails, anxiety seeping through his body, drenching any sense of calm with immense dread.

If you could have been smarter, used your training to—

Leola materialized in front of him, and the relief at the sight of her nearly knocked him off his feet. Glamour and all, he knew it was her, despite the frenzied flames that consumed her eyes.

Flames. He'd seen the molten glow of her eyes last night, but the flames... those were new.

The relief was interrupted by her panic, which completely enveloped him. He couldn't breathe. Pure, unrestricted terror had taken over her mind and he realized that it was dangerously close to taking him as its next prize.

She grabbed his tattered shirt collar in one hand, choking out a ragged whisper, *"Juniper."*

She looked around at their surroundings, like she was processing the gravity of whatever situation she'd yet to clue him in on. A sob escaped her mouth, and she covered it with her free hand, tears escaping. The other hand maintained a scalding death-grip on his shirt, burning through the sun-worn material.

Her breathing quickened, and he had to resist the urge to step out of her grasp.

Shit, she's going to hyperventilate. He kept his breathing steady, even as he listened to her breaths become shallow.

He'd experienced strong emotions before, always relying on his shields to protect him but this emotion-pull was like nothing he'd ever encountered before.

As her panic rose, his mind mimicked that same panic. With each frenzied breath she took, he struggled to keep his hold on his sanity, sliding further into a bottomless emotional pit that he knew he could never claw his way out of.

He closed his eyes as he gently pulled her hand from his collar. His shield failed again, and he gritted his teeth, knowing that if the emotions were too strong, it would be impossible for him to will her mind to calm. They couldn't have that because her mood was interfering with his shield.

He willed his power over her mind, emulating a soft night sky, sending waves of calm into her headspace as he said, "I need you to calm down." His hand brushed over the back of hers, the one he had removed from his shirt. He hoped to sense tranquility, but instead, her palm heated more.

He narrowly dodged the flame that shot past his nose. He turned back to her, glaring.

"Don't you tell me to calm down!" she hissed. "My sister is *with* that Corruptor. "

His eyes widened as flames raced up her hands; this time, he retreated two steps.

"Stop time. Warp. Do whatever you do—go get her *now!*" The flames at her fingertips mimicked torches. Her voice shook and dropped to a whisper that dripped with malice as she continued, "If she's hurt, I'll burn them all."

He trusted that she would burn *anyone* who stood in the way of saving Juniper, including him. Hell, he needed to pause time and save Leola from herself.

"GUYS!" Juniper landed with a thud, Benn whirling in her direction as he zeroed in on the slumped kid that she was holding. His limp body hit the ground with a thud as she dropped him.

"Demons." His mouth gaped open. "Did you kill him?"

Leola went silent behind him.

"Nearly. He picked the wrong girl for evening entertainment." Juniper gestured to the kid as she explained, "He uncovered my glamour during dinner, so I knew something was up. He pulled me upstairs and started talking about 'enemies being everywhere.' Then he said something about... wards?" She scrunched her nose at the word, like it was new to her; Benn was once again reminded how new his world was to the Pair. "He held me somehow. I couldn't use my magic... I couldn't even move. Then I felt a burning sensation on my face; I knew my glamour was gone."

He took a step closer as he said, "He *removed* your glamour?"

"Obviously." She gestured to herself; the glamour was nowhere to be seen. "He seemed relieved to see me. I hit him with my claws before he could do anything else." She took a breath, swinging her braids over her shoulder, and continued, "I thought he was an Ope but then... then he asked for you, Benn."

Shock wracked through his body, top to bottom.

His eyes narrowed as he asked, "For me?" He crossed the room to the kid—his face unrecognizable from whatever Juniper had struck him with. He blinked and sent an inquisitive look toward her. "Gods, his face is shredded. What'd you hit him with?"

She answered, "Oh, I summoned claws this morning. On him, I used Nightshade thorns. Lethal, unfortunately." She inspected her black-tipped fingers, showing off the claws she spoke of. "Luckily for him, I have the ability to make an antidote... if he's worthy of being saved."

"Lethal indeed," he said as he leaned down to check the other boy's pulse.

157

It was weakening by the second. A cold sweat had covered his skin that was now a gray-white color. His face was shredded *and* swollen, bleeding red. The blood of a magic-wielder. A group of thorns stuck out of his nose. Benn was beginning to think he would never recognize him unless she gave him the antidote.

"His face is destroyed. Did you hear his name by chance?" Benn asked, lifting an eyelid on the boy to find dilated pupils.

"Levi," the sisters answered in unison.

Disbelief crashed over Benn as the name rang through him like a tolling bell. *It can't be.*

He reached down and yanked the high collar of the kid who lay motionless on the ground, recognizing the J-shaped scar that stretched the length of his ear to his collarbone.

His blood chilled. His head was spinning. Levi had been Conscripted nine months before Benn had—as Seers could enter Assignment earlier than other magic-wielders.

What is he doing here? Where was he even sent? He tried to rack his brain for any information to help him put the pieces together. He had no way of knowing where his best friend had been deployed after they said their goodbyes last year. The Underground kept Assignments classified. *No—I'd know if Levi was here. I would've sensed him, right? Is this some kind of trick?*

Juniper checked her nails as she spoke the devastating words with nonchalance. "His pulse is dropping."

Despair twisted his features as he looked up at her. "I know Levi. He is not Opasteg. He is Conscripted. He must have been working undercover—I'm not sure." He trailed off. "What are you waiting for? Make the antidote. We can't question him if he's dead."

Juniper sighed and flicked her wrist, manifesting a small glass bottle filled with green liquid.

Benn snatched it from her hand as he cupped the back of Levi's neck to pour the green mixture into his mouth. He emptied the bottle and tossed it back to her with a scalding glare. "Next time, question first, kill second."

He glanced toward a silent Leola, who stared at the brown wall in front of her, looking as if she'd seen a ghost. Benn knew that her stance had nothing to do with Levi and everything to do with Juniper. Her mind was subdued, and while Benn couldn't seem to shield from her, at least her emotions were not bleeding into his. The hysteria he felt now was of his own making. He brushed his hands on his worn trousers and returned his eyes to his friend.

"Give it a second to take hold, Benny. He was eye-to-eye with Mors, so he'll need a few minutes at least," Juniper mentioned the name of the Death God way too casually as Benn shook his head at her apathy. He kept his eyes on Levi, plucking the thorns out of his face with gentle care, waiting for the antidote to take hold.

Juniper broke the silence as she asked, "You know him?"

"He's my best friend. Like my brother, actually," he said. He was still trying to convince himself that Levi being at Roswell was a trick, but the J-shaped scar was unmistakable. It was him.

"He said he needed these to see." She handed him Levi's glasses and spoke in a quiet tone, but Benn didn't lower his shield to determine what that meant. "I hope he lives."

Benn let out a sigh of relief when the color began to return to his friend's face. The wounds from Juniper's claws were healing, the swelling improving as his bone structure became visible again.

Levi coughed, leaning over onto his side. He inhaled a ragged breath, grasping his chest like he thought he could rip it open to intake more air. Benn sat back with his tailbone against his heels as Levi struggled to breathe.

Benn shot a look in Juniper's direction, at which she merely shrugged before sending her own unforgiving scowl toward his friend. That was a clear indication that he had not earned her trust, even though he was fighting for his life on the ground.

Levi gasped again, but was able to sit up, pointing a finger at Juniper. "You—" He choked on the word. "*Witch.* You nearly killed me." He shot a furious look toward her that looked more akin to pain than anger as he choked again.

"*Witch?* Must I remind you of our first encounter this afternoon?" She threw her hands up. "I'm sure you haven't forgotten the *whip* you used to send dirt directly into my face."

"I was instructed to whip you *all*—which I was never going to do—so I hit the dirt once to demonstrate that I—" His wet cough interrupted his speech, which had Benn wincing. "To show *Carole*, not you, that I could do it. I'd die before abusing someone like that."

Juniper glared at him in disgust, scoffing, "Well, calling us *Lessers* really helped your case, dickhead."

Levi rested on his elbows as he explained, "My hands were tied."

"And mine were shackled," Juniper snapped.

Levi raised a shaky hand. "I sensed Carole was listening and couldn't risk *him* sensing that I had empathy for you. I haven't used my whip before, and Carole knows it. I had to do something with it, simply so he wouldn't get suspicious. If he had, he would have done so much worse. Trust me."

"I would rather do anything else, actually," Juniper sneered. Leola watched the entire exchange from the other bed, but her mind was riddled with distrust that triggered Benn's power.

Benn rose, watching the heated exchange. "Leola, Juniper—meet Levi, my best friend." Benn gestured toward his friend. He extended a hand to help him up, hoping to ease the tension with a proper greeting or introduction.

"We've met," Juniper snapped.

"I already know who you are anyway," Levi countered, wiping his leathers off as he rose to his full height. "No introduction needed."

Juniper's tone dripped with disdain. "Oh, good, that's *so* comforting."

Benn sighed and leaned against the wall, motioning for his friend to sit on his cot as he handed him his glasses. Levi took the glasses, cleaning them, before putting them on. He flexed his arm, rotating the joints in his injured shoulder that was already beginning to heal.

"I was trying to protect you. Carole sensed the freeze in time around us. Luckily for you, he didn't read the documentation for the shipment and remained inside the carriage while I rode with the Overseer, the one that was driving. He didn't notice that two people joined the shipment after the time freeze, but I did," he said as he huffed out a frustrated breath. He let his hair loose, releasing a mass of golden curls. "Carole possesses powerful time magic, almost as powerful as Benn's. The instant he sensed the shift, I knew we were in deep shit. Like the *hang-us-all* kind of shit. Before he could react, I hopped down from the carriage and was able to sense three magic trails in the trees—time, fire, and earth. I saw nothing in the trees, so I looked toward the Chattels we'd picked up with the shipment, seeing you two had shown up." He pointed to the sisters as flames returned to Leola's eyes. "You were expertly glamoured, but it only took me one glimpse to see your true features beneath. I knew who you were right away. Worse, I knew Carole would know who you were, too. He saw your faces. Opasteg knows your faces, and you're the Prophesied Pair, for demons' sake. He can't see through glamours, but he's been watching me. Wary of me. I couldn't risk him seeing me take any mercy on you, especially when he's been hunting you two for days." He crossed the room. Juniper bared her teeth as he approached her.

He ignored her as he waved a hand in her direction, sending a bind of magic to retrieve the pocket watch from her apron. It flew to his hand. "And *this*. You can't carry relics on your person. That thing has been calling to my magic all day. Like an incessant mosquito buzzing in my ear. I nearly lost focus while I was analyzing

Carole's plans today. Thank the Gods that Carole does not have an Opasteg Seer with him—which is what he thinks I am. This relic could have jeopardized the entire mission. If an Ope Seer had been here, you would've been in Daemon's prison by now," he scolded her through gritted teeth. Levi's tone was clipped. "The relic has been asking for his 'friend of time' all day—I'm going to assume that's you, Benn, since you can speak to time relics. Please shut it up so I can have some damned peace." He handed the pocket watch to Benn.

Admittedly, it was foolish that he had not considered the possibility of the pocket watch speaking to any Seers in the area. Then again, he hadn't expected any Seers to be here, and they hadn't had many options to get the sisters into the shipment. He nodded at Levi, acknowledging that it was a misjudgment. Levi inhaled a deep breath, trying to calm himself.

My friend. The pocket watch greeted Benn in that strange, wiry voice. *I did as you asked. I kept the Prophesied Pair safe.*

Benn shuddered as the voice whispered to his mind, but he cut it off before it could continue. *Thank you. Are you speaking to all of the Seers in the area, or only to the ones you can trust?*

I recognized the connection between you and the blonde Seer, so I decided he was someone to trust. That connection is something I yearn to have, the relic answered, the words swirling.

So even relics get lonely, Benn noted. *You were right. The blonde Seer is my best friend. Thanks for helping us.*

The pocket watch warmed in his hand. *Talk soon, friend.*

Levi's continuing rant interrupted his conversation with the relic as he said, "I knew from the moment I sensed your presence that the prophecy was alive and prospering here. I've worked my ass off since I was deployed to spy on that wretched prick, Carole, all to protect you two." He pointed accusatory fingers in the directions of the sisters. "It's been damn near impossible to keep that protection going. Every day has been more challenging than the last. I was *so* excited to sense you both here.

I was so grateful I got to choose you at dinner. Grateful that Roswell or Carole didn't. I was thrilled to keep you safe—to keep the prophecy safe—for a moment longer, and when I finally get into a room with you, Juniper, what happens? Well, you strike me with poisonous claws!" He let out a hollow laugh, shaking his head as he finished, "You have no self-control."

"Relax," Leola warned, her fingers turning to torches again.

"I'm not used to being treated like livestock. I was subjected to chains, shackles, and whips today—you had a hand in all of that, by the way." Juniper crossed her arms and scoffed. "I'd have been a fool to trust you once we were alone."

"You could have given me ten seconds to explain." Levi leveled a vicious stare at her.

She sent one back, claws out again. "After you stripped me of my glamour? Fat chance. Strike first, ask questions later. Survival hack 101, or did you not learn that lesson at your fancy magic school?" She spat the words.

Levi rolled his eyes, picking his discarded hat up off the floor. He paced the room while Juniper looked in the opposite direction. Benn found himself watching them reach a stalemate, *again*. In the coveted silence, he fought the urge to glance at Leola. Distress was coming off her in deep, dark waves—filling his mouth with a tar-like taste.

Levi broke first, sighing, "This isn't productive. As I was explaining, I'm a Seer. Carole is not, thank the Gods. That's what saved our asses today. Now that I'm here, we need to establish a few *ground rules* to avoid being caught by someone like me. And then, we need to get the fuck away from here as fast as possible." He clapped his hands together before speaking to the sisters again. "First, no relics on your person unless you command them to speak to you and *only* you. I don't need to tell you that you need to be glamouring yourselves, as you were glamoured all day, but second, you need to be glamouring your magic, too. I have studied methods of tracing Opasteg magic. I'll show you how to mimic their glamours and magic trails. Third, trust no one unless you have confirmed with an Underground Fa that they are vetted;

that means it is indicated in a vellum. Finally, restrain first, interrogate second, and kill last. You never know when someone might have information for the Underground. That's what I learned at my *fancy* magic school."

Neither of the sisters answered; Benn doubted they trusted his friend because why would they—the circumstances under which they had met had been threatening. Traumatic, even.

Levi closed his eyes, clasping his hands together again, as he turned toward Benn and said, "That's enough for now. My man—it's been way too long!"

Tears pricked his eyes as they hugged. The dual-power hadn't allowed himself to think of his closest friend in some time, as it had been nearly a year since Levi left on Assignment. Benn hadn't been able to contact him—nor could he know of his location in time or space. It was a safety risk to contact the Conscripts outside of Fas. He couldn't contain the joy that he was feeling, a stark contrast to the utter despair he'd endured over the last few months.

"I hoped your Assignment would be better than mine, but seeing this room and this place... I can only assume it's been a *nightmare*." His voice broke on the last word.

"Yeah, man, you wouldn't believe what it has been like," Benn said as he pulled back, not caring to reflect on his time here. "It got better two days ago, when they arrived. Before that, it was... lonely," he explained as he swallowed the lump forming in his throat—he would not break in front of the sisters.

Levi and Benn had been best friends at the Academy; having shared a room for twelve years, the Seer could read any emotion playing on his face. Levi nodded, a hint of sadness gracing his features. Benn was thankful when Levi said nothing, and instead pulled him into another embrace.

Benn cleared his throat as a way of indicating he was done with this conversation. "So, how'd you get stuck working with that prick?"

"My spycover was to work with Carole as his 'apprentice.' To learn the ins and outs of Opasteg's training techniques, information exchanges, HQ locations, that kind of stuff. I learned a lot—some Seers would probably call it a good Assignment." His mouth twisted. "The hardest part is that Carole is a creep—loves to abuse women and girls. I've been listening to that horror every night, helpless as I scheme up ways to kill him. Assignment be damned, he deserves to rot with the Gods. I was ready to kill him just so I got recalled to Headquarters, but then, I got a vellum. It told me to get to Roswell Camp—no explanation as to the why part—and the schemes morphed into how I'd convince the pervert to come here." He turned toward Juniper, addressing her as he spoke. "See, that is why you always wait to kill."

"Do you love to hear yourself talk?" Juniper shot back.

Benn asked the next question before their bickering could ignite. "What was the message on the vellum?"

"That the prophecy was coming to fruition—always so fucking vague. With my spycover, I was intercepting vellums and missives from the enemy daily—the Underground only sent vellums once a week, maybe. Five days ago, Carole threw an Opasteg vellum at me. It demanded he return to the Modern-Era for a meeting concerning the prophecy. They gathered all the Opasteg Executives and Corruptors, saying they'd received news that the powers of the prophecy would be revealing themselves somewhere in the northeastern region of Heri. He asked what I thought about it. I told him I was skeptical, but I really wasn't. He traveled to the Modern-Era and returned the next day totally irate. He'd sensed a powerful time relic being used in Poppycal and attempted to intercept two sisters, the ones he believed to be the Prophesied Pair. He said he approached them to purchase the relic, hoping he would actually have a chance to touch one of you. To *mark* one of you. In addition to being a timepower, he is a sleuth. Once he leaves his mark on someone, he can track them through all eras and travel to reach them anywhere, anytime." Levi shuddered as he explained.

"A dual-power. Shit." Benn grimaced.

"Yeah, shit. I feigned excitement, though I was quaking with fear. I asked if he had done it—if he had left his mark on either of you. He said he had only grasped one of your jackets before the relic transported you both. With the touch on your jacket, he left a partial mark and was able to see which era you had traveled to and the general area you were in, but he couldn't seem to track the exact location. He said it was somewhere in 849. I still hadn't figured out why I was being told to get to Roswell Camp, but I had figured out that the camp was here in Laviegata." He shrugged. "I needed to get Carole here, so I made it seem like his idea. I glamoured the vellum from the Underground Fa that I had received days earlier to look as though it had come from Opasteg, leaving it in a place for him to find it. Thank the Gods, he believed it had been sent to him by Opasteg, so we headed to Laviegata," he continued as he pulled his thick frames off to clean them. "Last night, I received a vision that I was hugging Benn. In the vision, I could sense fire and earth magic, and I guessed that you both would be here, too. I assumed we were either reuniting at Roswell or that we were all dead." Levi chuckled at that. "Thank the Gods it was the former. Once I realized Juniper was indeed stronger than me and intended to kill me, I mentioned your name, Benn, hoping she might know you—might even trust you."

"A vision?" Juniper questioned with a raised eyebrow.

He gave her a perplexed look. "Well, yes. I'm a Seer."

She cocked her head as she replied, "You've said that."

Levi's eyes brightened, the otherworldly signal that indicated he'd learned something. "Right, uh, I do some of my work off vellums sent by the Underground Fas, and as a Seer, I receive visions that guide me. They help me make decisions." He paused. "Over the last year, I've tried to coax Carole into telling me where Daemon is to no avail. I tried to get the information from each and every person he introduced me to, but all were tremendous failures. I've been having this recurring dream lately, though."

Benn leaned in closer as Levi kept talking.

"There's this darkness that swallows me whole—darker than midnight and colder than Mors' winter. When I'm there, the weight of the place is heavy, like I'm under the pressure of the sea. The air is ancient and stale. It reeks of evil magic, like rotting flesh and sulfur. For a bit, I assumed that I was dreaming of Daemon's lair. But as I was walking through the vision, something had changed there. I noticed light coming from a pit I hadn't noticed before. I walked toward the pit, and within it, I noticed levels of shackles and the brightest light. It blinded me, which caused me to fall back, unable to see. However, I could sense... magic. It made my bones light and it carried a floral fragrance—*benevolent* magic—magic that was trapped in this darkness. I studied the vision until the pieces started to come together—it was magic of all kinds being harnessed. I had read something about it in a vellum a couple months ago, but I didn't know what it meant. It told me nothing at the time, but now I have a theory." Levi looked around the room. "The vision is showing me where Daemon is keeping his prisoners from the ambush."

The room went still. The energy in the room was charged although no one spoke. No one dared to breathe even.

Leola broke the silence when she asked, "Could you see anyone at all?" Her silence had been bothering Benn, so he was relieved to read the curiosity floating at the edges of her mind.

"No, the light was blinding. I could only see shackles, but there were hundreds of them," Levi answered, his voice dropping to a chilled whisper. "The power had been harnessed somehow—it was so powerful, like nothing I have ever felt before. Nothing has ever drawn my visions to the same thing repeatedly. For whatever reason, the Gods want me to see what is there."

Juniper shifted her hands to place them on her knees as she said, "Grandmava mentioned that magic can be tracked. If there is this mass of power being harnessed, then it can be tracked, right? There has to be a way for us to find it."

Benn twisted his hair in his fingers. "We could send a message to my grandmother. She should be able to detect a massive gathering of power. When she was elected our leader, she was gifted increased sensitivities to magic—"

Leola cut him off, eyes far away, as she said, "In use."

Benn raised an inquisitive eyebrow toward her.

She elaborated, "Leader Wyndmere was gifted increased sensitivities to magic... in use. She can't detect magic that has been gathered until it *is* used. Daemon knows that. He's storing the magic for some purpose, but he knows she won't be able to sense the location until it is used."

Benn's hand scrubbed his face as he whispered, "He's orchestrating a blind attack."

Heat radiated off Leola as he sensed her incensed emotions, but her voice was soft. "With that much power, he could do whatever he wanted to do. He could imprison us all. He could imprison the entire Underground."

Fear squeezed his chest. "And if he imprisons us, he imprisons Heri. Beyond, even."

They were silent for a few beats until Levi said, "Of course he is. How did I not see that? We have days—maybe a week— until he harnesses that power. We've got to find that prison."

CHAPTER 16

— BENN —

B ENN LISTENED IDLY AS LEVI reiterated his vision countless times to Grandmava. In some cases, illusionists and Seers could combine their powers to build illusion portals; they were aiming to do that. If she could create a replica of his vision, they would be able to enter the illusion portal—they'd be able to project into Daemon's prison. Aromas of lavender filled the room as she projected scenes from his visions onto the mud-caked walls. Levi then combed through the details of the illusions to determine what elements were missing.

Grandmava tweaked the details of her illusions each time, saying, "Tell me again, child."

Benn attempted to pay attention to the visions, but his power was needless in this situation and his focus was being siphoned by the auburn-haired woman sitting in the room—how her fear earlier that evening had invigorated his senses. It was not a burn of fire, but rather of something mimicking electricity, like a lightning bolt that had struck through his entire body, shocking each of his senses tenfold.

In the time since he was initiated, surges of emotion in his presence had strengthened his power. He was able to draw power from the emotions playing out around him and work them to his advantage. His grandmother possessed the same

169

emotion-bending powers and had trained him as soon as he'd shown signs of this power manifesting in him—how to wield it and how to protect himself or protect others.

However, what had happened tonight with Leola was... different. He had an impeccable shield—so strong that it had become instinctual to him to have it in place at all times. He'd spent years learning to shield at the Academy, and being a Conscripted whose spycover was in a Chattel role only taught him to strengthen his shield even more. After all, negative emotions like sorrow or grief tended to have a negative effect on emotion-benders... and that was all there was at Roswell.

None of the Chattels around him utilized shields—Mundane beings did not have the ability to shield their minds. Benn could shield from them just fine, so why couldn't he shield from Leola? Even with the power block in place, his shield always failed. Now with her power present, his shield failed even quicker. She didn't have shielding skills; he'd checked. Multiple times.

But I should be able to shield from her as easily as any other magic-wielder. Benn mulled the thought over, pulling at his hair.

His grandmother had never mentioned a situation like this to him. In Leola's panicked furor, he'd been paralyzed—not able to breathe or think. The emotions hit him like a tsunami, obliterating everything in its path, leaving his mind a chaotic wasteland. He'd chosen to ignore the problem when he first met her, but after tonight, that was no longer an option.

He had wished daily to see his sister, but now he found himself wanting to speak to her so she could offer some knowledge from that impressive brain of hers. Asha was a Fa, so in addition to being intellectually inclined, she could reach out to the Ancestors or Gods to ask for advice or answers. At this point, Benn was prepared to trade his soul for an explanation.

Could someone else hinder me like that? Benn wondered, chewing his cheek. *No. There must be some sort of tether.*

He didn't love the idea of being tethered to a woman he just met, but he found more peace in that idea rather than the thought of enemies having the ability to unseat him. Or worse. What if the hindrance was a result of his own power malfunctioning?

Benn grimaced, as the uncertainties sweeping through his mind were met with several aftershocks of unease. *Either Leo unknowingly turned my power on me, or we're connected.*

His gaze drifted to Leola, who sat away from the group on the floor on one of the cots. Her mind was withdrawn, her cheeks rested on her knees, which were pulled to her chest. She'd turned in the direction of one of the walls, but he had a clear view of her face from where he leaned against the opposite wall.

Without meaning to, Benn took in her features now that her glamour had been removed. Her auburn curls rested on the middle of her back. The coils fell in different lengths and framed her face, showcasing her high cheekbones and full lips. Her unique freckles danced around her cheeks and nose in patterns that rivaled the starry night sky.

Leola caught him staring at her and frowned in response. She turned her eyes back to the wall beside her. Her emotions weren't screaming at him anymore; they had taken on a subdued tone. He was not sure if that was his doing or hers, but he found himself wondering what she was thinking nonetheless.

He crossed the room, stopping at the edge of the cot she sat in as he said, "You removed your glamour." He kicked himself at how idiotic and irrelevant that comment was.

"Yeah, I figured I could live in my own skin tonight. At least, in here, it is... safe," she replied dryly.

It was not lost on Benn that she didn't turn her head to look in his direction as she spoke. The air around them heated as Benn sensed her frustration, but there was something else there. Her emotions quieted again.

Imbecile, he thought about himself, abhorring the idea that he'd upset her.

Benn changed the subject, not wanting to give her more time to consider that he'd been paying attention to her appearance. "I can feel your—" He cut the words off.

Nope. Not about to tell her I can feel how hot she is, literally, Benn scolded himself.

She still wouldn't look at him.

He tried again. "How are you doing?" A neutral question seemed like the best way to approach the firepoweress.

She leveled a flat stare at him as she replied, "I was shackled and overworked all day. I thought for the better part of 20 minutes that my sister was being assaulted by an unknown man—who is apparently your *friend*. I learned my mom is in a dark pit in some unreachable location. I must say, I've been better." Her tone was sarcastic as she looked back toward the wall.

Benn nodded, lowering his eyes to the floor as he responded, "Roswell is terrible. 1855... is and was not a good time for Heri." He sighed, ignoring the tightening in his throat. "But, I never really thought I'd see my mother again. I never considered that as a possibility." His chest squeezed at the thought of seeing her one day, if somehow she'd survived through this time in Daemon's prison. It had been so long since he'd last seen her; he hardly remembered her at all.

Leola was silent, so Benn was surprised when he looked up to find her watching him, her honeyed eyes glistening with tears.

"I never thought that either. I'd accepted that my mother was gone forever, never to be found. Happy to say I was wrong." She paused, then added, "And I hate to be wrong." A smile played at her lips as Benn found his chest squeezing for a different reason.

Gods, you sap, when was the last time you saw a beautiful woman? Benn chided himself, but returned the smile nonetheless. *Keep it together.*

"Well, it doesn't count if you don't admit it, right?" He raised an eyebrow at her and she smiled—a full smile that didn't eradicate the despair in her mind, but didn't indicate it either.

"The key to never being wrong is to *never* concede, Benn." She looked down at her hands, wringing them. "Thank you—for earlier. I was so scared for my sister that I warped straight to you. I needed *help*. I knew, somehow, you would know what to do even though I felt powerless." Her voice dropped to a whisper by the end of her sentence. "I'm not used to feeling that way. It seems more common these days—with the new regime and the sanctions on Mundaners. And now, I have the power Mundaners crave... yet still, tonight, I couldn't save the person I love the most." Her voice broke as she looked down to hide her gaze.

He lifted her chin until their eyes met. "You wield enough power to be envied by not only Mundaners, but the most powerful beings of the magic-wielding world. You and Juniper are the most powerful poweresses *alive*. Despite needing my help tonight—and I didn't do anything to help, by the way—you know that changes nothing, right?" Benn asked.

Leola shrugged. "It doesn't feel that way. I don't like to ask for help from others. Can you just accept my 'thank you' so we can put my emotional outburst behind us?"

"Sure." He chuckled. "In exchange, could you not shoot fire streams at me in times of duress?" He was only half joking.

She laughed, raising a hand as if to check her nails, but the torch hands had returned. She flashed a smile as she joked, "No promises."

He smirked, refusing to give in to the instincts screaming at him to back away. Like any sane being, he wanted to run from those torches, but she didn't need to know that.

Her smile dropped as she admitted, "Usually, I'm in control of everything. I can face any challenge and solve every problem. Today, everything stopped when I lost sight of my sister." Her hands shook in her lap, although they were now flameless. "Today, I was weak."

"Asking for help is not weak," Benn said, his hand yearning to touch one of her curls, but he let it drop to brush her arm instead. "You can't control everything and solve every problem. You'll drive yourself mad with those expectations. We're all working together now, battling every battle, facing every obstacle, solving every problem together." He gestured to the others who sat on the floor. "You, Juniper, me, and now Levi. Even in the prophecy, there are *two* of you. The Prophesied *Pair*, remember? You're not alone in this. Lean on us. Lean on me, Leo. I trained for this; I can take it."

She didn't look up, but the corners of her mouth tilted up as if she were accepting a challenge. "Maybe I will."

She pushed her palms into the cot and stood up, crossing the small room to Levi as she said, "Show me these—um—what did you call them?"

"Illusion portals." Juniper smirked at the Seer, fluttering her hands. "The floor is yours, blondie. Take us on a tour of your spooky vision."

CHAPTER 17

— BENN —

E XHAUSTION HUNG LIKE A WEIGHT as they struggled to recreate Levi's vision. Each attempt revealed the same darkness, the same twisting path, and the same rotting stench, all culminating in the shackles bathed in blinding light. Levi called it "benevolent magic," but the moment the light appeared, the portal collapsed, severing the connection.

Grandmava sighed as yet another illusion shattered, disrupting the astral projection and as they abruptly dropped back onto the dirty floor of the barracks. Benn fought the urge to rub his eyes as he glanced at the tired expressions he saw around the circle.

Leola's face was blank, but there was a faint blaze of fire surrounding her retinas. She nudged her sister; in response, Juniper stretched and sat up straighter against the post of the cot. Levi rubbed his temples, his hair hanging toward his eyebrows.

"Yes!" Grandmava clapped in celebration. After what seemed like hours, the illusion solidified into a shimmering, oblong doorway that opened up to a midnight-dark path. She'd done it. The edges of the illusion portal glowed with glittering onyx and the temperature of the room became frosty.

"This illusion portal will take you to Daemon's prison. They're different from time portals—we can use illusion portals to determine exact locations, but we can't travel through them. Spend enough time inside to figure out its location, then we can go back there when the time is right. I warded the portal so it will cloak you all in shadow; so long as you're completely silent, you won't be discoverable. There were no guards in Levi's vision, so we don't know who is guarding this place, or if it's being guarded. Depending on *who* is in the prison, they may be able to detect you. If you make any sound, the cloak will wear off. Your scent will be tracked first, then you will become visible. If that happens, you need to leave right away." Grandmava voice was firm. "Do not linger. Don't let them see you. Daemon wouldn't leave this place vulnerable. Be prepared, not scared, and you'll do just fine."

Benn asked, "Will the illusion portal weaken once we reach whatever that source of magic is? The vision and illusions seemed to crumble whenever we reached the light."

Grandmava considered his question and responded, "Potentially. My power reserve used to be stronger... I could repair faltering portals, but I've been at Roswell a long time and it has been impacted." She flexed her wrists as her joints popped in the silence.

Levi looked between them, offering, "We've walked this vision dozens of times. We know the scents and scenery. We know the path. We know the illusion falters once the light is too bright for our eyes to behold. What if we get as close to the light as possible, then continue the rest of the way with our eyes closed? Would that help the connection hold?"

Benn looked toward the illusionist as he questioned, "Is it possible to go through the portal with our eyes closed? Will it interfere with what you're casting?"

"No, I'll be here. The illusion portal was breaking due to its impact on you—not me," Grandmava said as she stared off into the distance like she was looking years into the future and eons into the past, as if she was searching for any information that might give her a clue as to whether or not walking through blind would endanger them. Finally, she said, "It should work. Hold hands the entire time, squeeze each other's hands once to move forward, squeeze twice to move back. Once it is time to retreat, snap your fingers. I'll take that as a signal to pull you out of the cavern and bring you back here."

"I'll lead. I have walked this place hundreds of times. I'll snap my fingers when we get what we need, but if there's ever a time where one of you feels we must retreat, whistle once so I can snap," the Seer said as he looked toward the sisters, catching on that they were unfamiliar with this practice. "Each of your hands will be holding the other and you *can't* let go, no matter what. We can't risk leaving someone in the cavern or ripping open the portal."

Benn kept his voice soft as he said, "I'll walk at the back so you two can stand in the middle of us. Let your lack of vision heighten your other senses. Nothing is irrelevant; any detail could help us determine where the prisoners are being kept."

They all exchanged glances, nodding at each other as an understanding passed through them. An understanding that they would step into their enemy's territory — a place that had likely served as their parents' dungeon or demise, in Levi's case—and were choosing to walk through it blind.

"I'm holding your hand out of obligation, Levi. I still think you're repulsive," Juniper said, breaking the silence, her hands outstretched toward Levi and Leola. "Let's go."

Levi almost grinned as he said, "Noted, Earthpoweress."

Leola nodded, lacing her fingers into her sister's and then reaching toward Benn, as she quipped, "Lead the way, Levi."

Her palm was hot in his, her power readying itself for defense. He had expected that, but what he was not expecting was the apologetic grin she flashed toward him. She mouthed 'sorry' as her palm cooled against his.

He winked at Leola, before turning to the other sister. "Juniper, claws away?"

She let out a short laugh that mimicked a cartoon villain. "Tamed but ready, Benny."

Hands held, Levi stepped through the illusion portal and led the group down the obscure path, further and further into the darkness.

— JUNIPER —

They crept through the cavern in silence, hand in hand. The only sound that could be heard was the constant dripping down the cavern walls. She blinked, hoping it would help her eyes adjust. Eyes open or closed, it was impossible to see even her palm in front of her face.

Cold wind whistled around them—a vicious cold that had her nose running and her snot freezing. It seeped into her bones, making them ache. She kept her jaw clenched, forcing the chattering to cease. A sudden shiver passed through her; she tightened her grip on Leola's and Levi's hands.

How could anyone ever survive here? she thought as they walked; she found herself hoping her mom was here, yet also wishing she was *not*—that she might have ended up somewhere safer. Though, the probability of her surviving or recovering from being imprisoned in a place that lacked any suggestion of warmth or light was... slim.

She yearned to have a free hand so she could touch the dripping walls, wondering if she could gain knowledge from them in the same way she'd done with the hanging tree. She had yet to try it with the walls of a cavern, but that was only because her hand was stuck in Levi's, which she loathed. She wanted to tug her hand out of the Seer's—who she was still apprehensive to trust. Despite her grievances with the guy, she preferred holding his hand to breaking their connection with the illusion portal and getting lost in the middle of time and space, so she kept her hold on his hand. At least they were on the same side, or rather, that's what Benn had confirmed when she'd interrogated him about it.

More than once.

For comfort, she tightened her other hand on her sister's.

The aromas of the cavern started as a scent similar to the rotting flesh of a dead rodent, then slowly, it morphed into the scents of sulfur pools met with stomach bile. It was impossible to decide if it was better to breathe through her nose or mouth—neither option was serving her well. She opted to breathe through her mouth again, quieting her gag.

But then I'll taste it. She grimaced in the dark, keeping her jaw clenched. At this point, it may as well have been wired shut. *Absolutely not.*

A small kernel of light sparkled ahead. Levi picked up the pace, tugging her arm in the process.

— BENN —

The light illuminating the cavern was creamy and buttery and sparkling. It had the likes of a crisp glass of Chardonnay on a summer afternoon. It was as beautiful and all-consuming as it was impossible to look away from.

Benn forced his eyes closed, encouraging his other senses to take the lead. Relief washed over him when the scent of sulfur that lingered in his nostrils was replaced with the scent that he was familiar with—the invigorating scent of good, clean magic. It smelled like endless bundles of lavender, like fresh squeezed citrus, like sprawling fields of roses. It smelled like Rosebay. Home.

A fizzing sound danced along his eardrums, mimicking the sound of popping candy. As they got closer, remnants of magic ricocheted off the walls, alive and bubbling. He expected the magic around them to feel desperate in their presence, but instead, it was excited, as if the minds trapped here knew someone had finally found them.

CLANK. CLANK. CLANK. Metal met the stone walls, echoing so loudly that Benn flinched. Next to him, Leola went as stiff as a rod.

The sound was unrelenting—so loud that Benn used his free hand to cover his ear. Someone was hitting their shackles against the cavern wall but that meant... *someone knows we're here.* His blood ran ice cold. They weren't supposed to be detectable.

A bloodcurdling scream reverberated through the cavern, replacing the clanking. A wet thud echoed through the cavern next, silencing the scream at once. Whoever had sensed them, whoever had made the clanking sound, had risked everything to do so. Now they were dead. A deathly quiet settled in the cavern; there were no other sounds save for the fizzing of the benevolent magic and the occasional drip along the walls.

A chill sent icy fingers down his spine—the kind that comes from the primal response invoked by some unseen entity watching another. Benn angled his body toward the direction they'd walked from, straining his ears to listen for a faint sound to confirm his suspicion. The drumbeat in his chest was a rhythmic reminder to stay alert. Leola's palm heated in his. She sensed it, too. In a move he hoped would be imperceptible to whatever lurked behind them, he turned his body as he shifted Leo behind him before taking two steps backwards, pushing her closer to Juniper. All the while, hoping that the move would leave the Pair less vulnerable.

Whispers of many voices—toneless and haunting—slithered into his ears.

"*Who are you? Where do you come from? How did you find this place?*" He flinched at the incessant questioning. "*Bennjamin Wyndmere. A descendant of a Founder. How did you find us?*"

The questions swarmed through his mind—like a crowd of one hundred was speaking to him. He reinforced his shields, blocking out everyone but Leola.

"*Bennjamin.*" The voice was a piercing whisper, close enough that there should be a faint exhale of air accompanying it, but there wasn't. "*How did you find us, legendary lineage of Josephine?*"

He opened his shield a slither to search for the essence of these *things*. Nothing. No emotions.

These are... soulless. His breathing ceased. *Darkbeings.*

The volume crescendoed to a boom, swarming them. *"WHO ARE YOU? WHY ARE YOU HERE? WHO SENT YOU?"* The shouting clung to his skin, making the space around him constrict as the Darkbeings roared. *"WE CAN'T SEE YOU. WHO ARE YOU? COME PLAY. WHO ARE YOU? WHERE ARE YOU?"*

Keep your eyes closed. He needed to tell the others but forced himself to stay silent. He repeated the only thing he knew would keep him safe, *Eyes closed. Eyes closed.*

He tried to dodge the shouting, but it was hitting from all directions.

"OPEN YOUR EYES. OPEN YOUR EYES. OPEN YOUR EYES. OPEN YOUR EYES, BENNJAMIN." The voices morphed from screeching gasps and sinister whispers to enraged, violent, thundering snarls—each one a different tone, each one closer than the former. *"OPEN YOUR EYES. OPEN YOUR EYES, BENN. OPEN YOUR EYES. OPEN YOUR EYES. OPEN YOUR EYES. OPEN YOUR EYES, BENN. BENN, BENN, BENN."*

He swatted his open hand around, trying to defend himself from the monsters, but was met with nothing but frigid air. He held the back of his hand over his face to block it from the voices—the demons—apoplectic around him. Seconds turned into minutes as they stayed in the narrow cavern, tormented by the screaming creatures.

Don't open your eyes, he repeated, raking his mind for information about Darkbeings... anything that could disarm them. *They can't get in if we don't open our eyes. Eyes clo—*

Leola jolted forward and his eyes flew open on instinct with no time to consider the consequences. A breath's distance from his face was a demon. Hundreds of unblinking, beady eyes met his, way too abundant, and looked closer to a fly's than a human's. Each eye was a deep, dark void. With a face made of white bone, the old blood dripping from its jagged teeth was the only contrast in its drooling mouth. Benn didn't need to look away to figure out they were surrounded by these beasts.

Hunger flashed in each independent eye; its wet mouth stretched into a Cheshire smile. *"THERE YOU ARE, BENN. COME PLAY. LET US SEE YOUR POWER. STAY FOREVER."*

No. No No. His limbs started to rise, feet lifting off the ground. The monster's gaze was a magnetic force pulling him toward the demon. His vision blurred, his chest closing in as the sound of the voices faded into a resounding, unintelligible ring. His thoughts turned to mush as the demon's power paralyzed his movements. He needed to use his magic to defend, but his power reserve was drained so fast that he chose to focus all his will on keeping hold of Leola's hand. The demon was feasting on his soul, and while it wasn't painful, nothing compared to the pain of the knowledge that his companions would soon meet the same fate.

Snap.

CHAPTER 18

— LEOLA —

WITH A JOLT, SHE GRIPPED her chest, eyes darting around the room, looking for something while seeing nothing through the disorientation. She pushed up off the floor and leaned back against the closest cot, pulling her knees to her chest. Her hands dropped to grip the hard floor as though it could act as an anchor to reality.

Benn and Levi lay in two of the cots; Grandmava prayed in soft whispers over Juniper, who was tucked into the other one. Her mind was in a haze as she tried to make sense of her foggy memories.

Cavern. Voices. Demons. The words played on a constant loop, but all her memories ended at the same point.

Cavern.

Screeching.

Demons.

She forced her lungs to take one deep inhale, followed by a second and third.

Juniper fell forward and I... slipped. Her mind cleared as the sound of Benn's slippers failing to gain purchase on the ground in the cavern resurfaced. *Demons... some kind of* monsters.

"Grandmava," she called through a constricted throat, eyes moving toward where Benn lay. "Are they hurt? Are they—?"

"Alive. Levi and Bennjamin should wake at any moment. They were in worse shape than you were when you all returned." Grandmava sighed, stroking the braids out of Juniper's face. "I believe Junebug is in a vision or another portal. She's connected with the cavern somehow, so I'm not sure when she'll return to us."

Leola flinched. She reached down and peeled the worn slippers off her feet. They were wet and cold, and she tried not to frown at the blistered skin marring her heels and toes.

Grandmava cleared her throat, her grandmother's gaze harnessing her focus as she asked, "Leo, has she been using magic to take visions from the Earth?"

Yes. She swallowed her response and Grandmava's eyes narrowed to slits. Her grandmother already knew the answer, so she relented.

"Yes, she has." She tested the vague words. Juniper would hate her for sharing that secret—no matter the vagueness. Her heart pained as she took in her sister's peaceful face. She wondered where her sister was—or rather, where her *mind* was.

Sorry Bug, you can hate me later when you're back.

Despite the strength that both she and her sister possessed, it was common knowledge that eliciting visions from the Earth required strong magic, even stronger restraint, and hours of training. While it was a power that came innately to Juniper, she still lacked proper training on how to use it. They had only received their powers back days ago and she'd seen Juniper slip into a vision from the trees in the forest. It had taken everything for Leola to pull her out of that vision. The memory of shaking Juniper awake made her stomach churn.

As if Grandmava heard her thoughts, she hissed, "The Poplar trees are for hanging. Why would she do that? The terrors she must have witnessed—"

Her eyes snapped to her grandmother. *Did she just read—?*

"Yes, child, I read your mind. Illusionists can do so. Normally I'd ask your permission, but seeing as though I'm not being given the whole picture..."

Grandmava crossed her arms over her chest, shaking her head. Her tone was dismissive. "I'll be taking matters into my own hands. You should have told me that your sister was doing that. She should've asked me first. I thought she would understand the dangers."

"Should have told you." Leola scoffed at the irony of that statement. "I didn't feel it was right to tell you; I've barely had time to think. I don't want to hold Juniper back. I don't want to govern her and the last few days have been..." She trailed off, her hands picking at her worn clothing. She cleared her throat and continued, "You know how the last few days have been for us. You know she wouldn't have listened to me anyway."

A few heartbeats of silence passed before her grandmother spoke again. "You're right, I should not have been so harsh; you're under enough pressure. I'm sorry." Grandmava attempted to hold her gaze, but Leola kept her face down. She sighed. "As I'm sure you know, granddaughter, I can sense emotions when I peer into the minds of others."

Leola said nothing.

Looking away, Grandmava mused, "You toe the line of protecting your sister and staying in her good graces. You're both *so* stubborn. You've always had a fierce, protective nature, ever since you were a girl."

Leola's face was neutral, her eyes unblinking as she listened to her grandmother. She refused to see that protective instinct as a bad trait. She would die for anyone she cared for, and Juniper happened to hold the number one spot on that list.

"Ah, yes, my dear child of fire. You protect the people around you, constantly feeding your hearth for others." Her grandmother smoothed her wrapped hair. "But, who, my little flame, protects you?"

Her eyes flicked to Benn, fast as lightning, and then back to Grandmava's. Leola regretted the glance, though she couldn't help reflecting on her conversation with Benn, where he'd encouraged her to lean on him.

185

A knowing grin crossed her grandmother's features as she asked, "A twin to your flame, perhaps?"

Where the hell is she going with this? Leola remained silent, worrying Benn might somehow hear this conversation, causing her an embarrassment-invoked death before she'd even had a chance to fulfill the prophecy. She knew that her grandmother was sensing some sort of shift, though Leola, herself, didn't know what to think. He was a stranger, and she was ignoring any and all feelings that weren't vital at the moment. For Gods' sake, she was sitting in a Camp in 1855, and her grandmother thought this was a time for... *romance?*

Pointless. Pathetic. The words clanged through her mind as she reminded herself that this was the worst possible time for a fling to start—despite Grandmava's wild ideas.

Her grandmother interrupted, "Shh. I think the word you're looking for is fearful, my girl. A bit fearful. A bit unwilling to trust. I might call that wise. You lost your parents, your grandmother, your memories, and it has all returned to you in the last few days—right as you find yourself—"

"Don't you finish that sentence, Grandmava," Leo snapped, sending a pointed glance to the other cots. Her grandmother chuckled. Leola straightened, molding the words and firing them back at her. "I *find* myself on a mission. I *find* myself on a journey that is bigger than *me*. I *find* myself with an impossible task." Her voice dropped to a whisper. "I find myself tasked with saving people I hardly remember— and fulfilling a prophecy I didn't know existed until two days ago."

"Mhmm, you do. *The Prophesied Pair,*" Grandmava said in a sing-songy whisper. "I pray for anyone who dares stand in my grandbabies' way." She grinned as she touched Juniper's forehead again. "May they all meet Mors."

She was quiet for a moment, and then she asked, "If you can peer into my mind, can you do the same for Juniper?"

"Yes, but it's a great violation. It takes more power to do when someone is in a vision—it is not something that is encouraged. I'd only do it with Juniper's consent.

ECHOES OF HOLLOW AND EMBER

I can't get that from her, so I've been waiting for you to wake. You're the closest person to her. I was hoping you'd consent on her behalf," Grandmava said as she wrung her wrists.

"Well, why didn't you say so? No need to waste time on *topics* that don't matter," she quipped as her traitorous eyes wandered toward Benn again.

"Nonsense," Grandmava said. "I took the opportunity to ask my granddaughter about a *topic* I'd ask about in another life. Especially if we'd been given the chance to have... a normal conversation. A conversation about *boys*. One that didn't revolve around her saving her sister and her mother and, well, the world." She winked.

Leola sighed, sending her a loving, yet censorious look before she said, "I prefer not to consent *for* Juniper but... if I must." Stones dropped in her stomach as she prayed to the Gods that her sister would forgive her for granting their grandmother passage into her vision.

Grandmava nodded, taking a seat on the floor next to Juniper's cot. "I'll peer in for a moment, make sure she is safe, and return as soon as possible. If she touched the walls of the cavern, she is likely learning something there. Rest now, and I'll wake you when I return," she said.

Leola scowled, putting a hand up to stop her words, as she said, "I don't love that plan. What if something goes wrong? What if you need me?"

Grandmava shook her head. "Need you? You aren't the only powerful poweress in this room, child. Now get in that cot and rest."

***

She awoke to the sound of hushed male voices. She had no sense of what time it was or how long she'd been sleeping. Juniper still lay in her cot, and Grandmava was nowhere to be seen. Benn pulled at his twists while Levi lay under a thin blanket, his body trembling. Neither of them noticed her watching them.

"Hey," she said as both of their heads snapped to her, startled by her words. She cleared her throat, feeling the need to fill the silence. "I was awake earlier. You guys weren't up yet. My grandmother said you were in pretty rough shape when we got here. How—how are you feeling?"

Benn sent a sideways glance toward Levi, dropping his voice to a whisper. "One of the Soulsiphons damn-near separated my soul from my body. I still feel a bit off, but I'll be fine. Levi might need a moment."

"I felt you rise into the air. I could hear your feet slipping, like you were trying and failing to stay on the ground," she said, recalling the memory. A tremor ran through her limbs as she thought of it. "That was a Darkbeing, wasn't it?"

"A form of one," Benn murmured as his jaw ticked, his hand scrubbing across his cheek. His words came out intentional and informative. "Soulsiphons are *vile* creatures. They feed off the souls of the living. They can take a soul just by looking into the eyes of their victim. For more skilled individuals—ones who have had training against their type of power—they show them their worst fears." He swallowed. "Fear is... powerful. It can have lasting effects on the mind and the soul. I opened my eyes when you fell forward. The demon was right there—breathing into my face. It drained my power almost immediately. I lost my footing... then I lost my hearing. From there, everything gets a bit blurry. It was a close call." He shot another glance at Levi, checking on him. "Levi saved us. He—uh—we think the demons knew that Levi was the source of the vision, so they did everything in their power to dismantle him. Levi fought back, they failed, and he snapped his fingers so we could return before things got worse."

She glanced between the two men, wondering why Benn wasn't using his emotion-bending power to calm Levi. Maybe Levi had refused the help while she'd been asleep... or maybe he'd already tried and the trauma was too much to alleviate. She hardly knew the Seer, but he looked like he'd seen a ghost. She frowned because maybe he had. Or, maybe, he'd seen something worse.

She pressed her back into the wall so she could see the shaking blonde fully. "And you, Levi, how are you doing now?"

His eyes were as wide as saucers, staring at the shadows that the lanterns were casting on the ceiling as he answered, "I arrived here with my soul detached. I watched as you all landed back here. I landed with you... but I was outside of my body. It was—" He swallowed. "Horrifying. I watched as your grandmother realized my soul had been separated from my body. She couldn't see me, but I could see her. She must have asked the Ancestors to return me. My body didn't know where to go, but I didn't want to leave, so I stayed here. After a while, I felt a force pulling me back toward my body, and once I got close enough to myself, I was pulled back in." He shuddered. "To dismantle my vision, the monsters showed me my nightmares. I've been trained to withstand that torture, so I thought I was prepared. The nightmares were... different this time. I—I don't have any living family. My grandparents were assassinated by Opasteg. I was orphaned after Daemon's attack; he killed both of my parents that night. My brother and sister were killed in an accident shortly after."

Her mouth fell open. "I am so sor—"

"Don't be." His mouth twisted. "Families of high power are targeted so they can stop the family line, but Daemon couldn't find me—or rather, didn't care to. After that accident, I went to an orphanage with the other children who lost their parents and lived there until it was time to go to the Academy. Over time, Benn, Asha, and Sena became my family. I was expecting the torturous imagery to be of the Wyndmeres being hurt once the Soulsiphons entered my mind." His voice cracked. "But Juniper's screaming is what caught me off guard. I couldn't tell if the screams were real, or if they were being created by demons. I felt her lean forward, right as the screaming started. It paralyzed me, and I couldn't feel her hand in mine anymore. I thought her soul had detached. I still can't see her... I can't make sense of where she went, but I can still hear the screaming..." Levi trailed off, choking on the last sentence.

189

She smiled, hoping to comfort him. "She wasn't screaming, Levi. I would've heard her screaming." Levi said nothing, his eyes were boring into Juniper's face in a way that made Leola shift her weight forward to get a better vantage point.

What is he looking at? She searched her sister's face for any signs of pain.

Benn spoke quietly. "Why is she not awake yet?"

"When you felt her lean forward, she did that to put her hands on the cavern wall." Leola sighed. "She can take visions from the Earth. I'm guessing she tried to do the same with the cavern. She was probably hoping she'd learn something so we could leave."

"*No,*" Levi hissed. "You've both been *hidden.* Has she had any vision training? Any power reserve training at all?"

She tensed, not familiar with the training that Levi was referring to. "No, we weren't given the opportunity to train, aside from training we did before we went into hiding—but Juniper was in toddlerhood at that time. Our powers were returned to us after we got here, and we haven't had them long enough to train."

"Shit. She won't be able to make it back. This could be a trap, one that is set by Daemon. It must be. If he does trap her, we may not even know. He could torture her. He could *kill* her from a remote location." Levi's voice was thick with emotion, his fingers twisting the thin blanket that was wrapped around his midsection. His eyes never left Juniper's body.

She flinched, anxiety creeping into her marrow as she continued, "No... Grandmava was here earlier. She said she would peer into her mind and wake me if she needed help—she would have woken me up if something was wrong."

Benn scanned the door. "She'll tell us more once she comes back."

Her feigned calm hung by a fraying thread.

Levi's whisper was strained. "We have no idea where she went when she connected with that cavern. What if the screams *were* real? And they were just not in the cavern with us. The illusion portal was built from my vision, so I may have been able to hear her screaming when she... left."

She shifted her wide eyes toward Benn to see that his watchful eyes were on her sister. She had no doubt he was using his power to read her emotions.

"Benn." She hoped that he would perceive her saying his name for what it was—a request.

He flinched and his brown eyes sent a horrified look toward Leola. "She—I can only feel remnants, like she is far away. Juniper's body is here, with us, but her mind couldn't be further from here. She's feeling distress, panic, and heartbreak." His brows drew together as he continued, "I'm also reading... peace."

Her hand shook. "Peace? How can she feel all of that and peace? What place would she go where she could experience all of those emotions?" She shook her head, pointing at the Seer. "You said Daemon could *kill* her from a remote location? I'm going to need you to elaborate on that. *Now.*"

Her tone was fierce, but internally, her thoughts raged. *No. Not death. She can't be dead. Juniper is not dead. I would know. No, please, no.*

"There are other possibilities than death," Benn muttered, presumably reading her own emotions as well, though Leola was too far gone to scold him for that intrusion again.

"Not many," Levi said. "We need to wake her. Now. Every second we spend debating is wasted. The longer we leave her there, the longer Daemon might have a hold on her. We *need* to wake her." He leaned toward Juniper's cot.

"How?" she asked. "I pulled her from a short vision in the forest this morning, and that alone was nearly impossible. That can't be good for her, to wake her like that."

Levi groaned. "She used her vision power *twice*? She is not trained and she has barely had any time to recover. Her power reserve must be entirely depleted. It's low—shit. 18%. How could she be so reckless—so careless?"

"She was never warned," Leola hissed with venom. Her horror was growing by the second, her palms burning in response. "I'm not going to wake her up until I know it won't hurt her. Let's stop talking about what she should have done and start figuring out how to pull her out of her vision. *Alive.*"

Levi shook his head. "Waiting doesn't keep her alive."

"Last I checked, we just met." She sent him a glare that promised murder. "And you don't know us, so I'll be sending any feedback of yours on how to help *my* sister straight to the trash."

"Last I checked, you've both been hidden for not only your safety, but the safety of the realm. We both have a vested interest in Juniper's life, and I won't let your ignorance result in her death."

"Ignorance?" Her hands turned to flame.

"Yes," he replied as his emerald eyes hardened. "Through no fault of your own, your knowledge of our world is limited. And before you ask how I know that"—he gestured to his eyes— "just trust that I can fucking see it. Now let me make the call because I'm the expert here."

Benn cursed, catching both of their attention. A vellum had appeared on his cot.

Her mouth parted. She'd only heard of vellums, but this was her first time seeing one with her own eyes. The small paper was yellowing on the edges and was sealed with red wax that boasted the symbol of the Underground—the letter U in antiquated cursive.

Benn opened it, breathing the words out of disbelief, "My sister sent it." His eyebrows furrowed, as he twirled the parchment in his hand. He read it aloud, *"Please send an update on your Assignment and a precise location. Talk soon. Remember the Underground. Asha."* He looked toward Levi as he spoke. "I thought they couldn't sign their name at the bottom of the vellums. I also thought that... Asha couldn't send me vellums."

Levi's frown deepened. "They can't sign them. Or at least, they haven't been able to before. Family members can't send vellums to Conscripts."

Benn examined the weathered paper. "Since when do they ask for location updates? They sent me to this wretched Camp. They send me kill cards. They know where I am."

The Seer's question was tentative. "Could it be... compromised?"

"Impossible." The dual-power reared back, like the vellum had caught fire in his hand.

"Think about it. I've been intercepting vellums for months. With the right power, anyone could send a counterfeit vellum." Levi stood on shaky legs to take a few steps toward Benn's cot, where he sat down and took the vellum as he continued, "The Underground *never* signs the names of the Fas. Asha would never risk contacting you for—what—an update? She knows how vital the vellums are. They are only used when absolutely necessary."

"If someone glamoured this, you could see it, right?" Benn asked.

"I can try. Typically, yes, but if this is glamoured, it is likely done with Seer eyes in mind," Levi said. He closed his eyes for a moment as Leola noted a faint pine-scented breeze floating through the room. Levi rolled the vellum over in his fingers, holding it up to the light while rubbing his fingers over the edges. "Everyone has a scent and anyone can trace a scent, but Seers can see scents or *tracks*, as we call them. *Tracks* are like fingerprints of a magical being, and Seers can track those innately. On this, I can't—I can't scent who wrote it, but it was not Asha. I know her. I know her scent, and I'd know any tracks she left behind. This scent has been glamoured beyond recognition and Asha would have no reason to hide her scent from you. This vellum is not from her. She never touched this. Whoever's scent lingers on this vellum—the tracks on this vellum—they reek of death."

"I should have known it was too out of the ordinary to receive a vellum from her. I miss her so much. My excitement took over the moment I read it. I should have known," Benn murmured, his voice breaking on the last word.

Levi shook his head, putting a hand on Benn's shoulder to comfort him. "Asha is your most trusted person, besides me, obviously," he added with a smirk that quickly dropped. "Whoever sent this knew you would accept a vellum from her. They planned it that way. Manipulative Ope *bastards*."

Leola watched them from her cot, wondering how long these two had been best friends. Their bond reminded her of two brothers. They moved, thought, and acted in similar ways.

It was endearing to watch. She didn't realize she was smiling until Benn sent a quizzical look toward her and asked, "What?"

She jumped as a soft scowl returned to her face.

She was interrupted by a whimper from Juniper. "No, no, no, please. *Please don't die.*" Leola moved to her bed so quickly, she thought she may have warped without meaning to. She ran her fingers through Juniper's braids as she continued to whine, "It was an accident."

"Bug, can you hear me?" she whispered, gripping her shoulders.

Silence. Juniper's entire face then twisted into a scream, but there was no sound. Warmth cascaded down Leola's cheeks, the dam finally breaking on her tears.

She didn't know how long she'd been leaning beside the cot as she watched her sister's face remain frozen; she jolted as Benn's arms surrounded her in a featherlight touch, which he quickly pulled back from.

"I didn't mean to startle you. Your stress is exhausting your power reserve," he said, his voice soft. "Come sit for a moment; let us figure out what to do."

She took one step back, the exhaustion sinking into her like a brick through water.

Levi took her place, leaning over the bed while taking Juniper's hand in his. She watched as he rubbed small circles over her hand, his sad eyes never leaving her face.

"How did I let this happen?" Her uncontrollable panic—the bane of her existence—reared its gnarled head. Her nightmares were coming to fruition; Juniper was hurt, and she was powerless to help.

"You have no responsibility here," Benn murmured, close to her ear.

Wake up, Bug. Wake up. Wake up. Wake up. She chanted until her mind screamed the words.

She kept her eyes on Juniper as Benn pulled her back toward the cot she had slept in earlier. A thin blanket was wrapped around her shoulders as she leaned against the mud wall. Always watching Juniper. She could not—would not—take her eyes off her sister. Benn held her hand as they sat and waited. Waited and sat. His embrace would have made her feel safe, if she had the mental capacity to think about anything other than her sister's limp body.

"She's damn near convulsing with anxiety," Levi said to Benn. "She's seconds from burning herself alive."

Leola's eyes flicked toward his when she realized he was talking about *her*, not Juniper. She glanced at her trembling hands, recognizing the signs of an impending panic attack. Her fingers turned to torches again.

"Not helping, Levi," Benn snapped, though his voice stayed quiet.

"I could do that?" she asked in a whisper that embarrassingly shook.

"Theoretically, no—" Benn answered before Levi cut him off.

"Theoretically, *yes*," Levi murmured. "Firepoweresses who lack control can burn themselves alive. Similar to how when an Earthpoweress lacks control, she can get herself trapped in a vision. Who would've thought the most dangerous threat to the Pair would be themselves?"

The Seer had a point, and she hated it.

"Enough," Benn said, slightly louder this time. "You're being rude because you're stressed. You're not the only one. Now channel your energy into something useful like finding Juniper." He lowered his voice to a volume only she could hear. "Rest, Leo, and I'll wake you when something changes."

Sleep took her before she could protest.

CHAPTER 19

— JUNIPER —

Year: N/A
Location: Unknown

*H*ELLO EARTHPOWERESS. A sweet, calming voice echoed in Juniper's mind. *Wake now, dear. Wake, please.* Her eyes opened. Light, warm hands cradled her face as she peered up into a honey-colored gaze.

"There you are, my darling Earth child," the angelic voice spoke to her again.

Juniper flinched out of the hands and away from the voice, readying herself to defend. She spun her body so that she landed facing the threat, her palms pressing on the grassy Earth below her. It was a *woman*—a beautiful brown-skinned woman with braids of varying shades of chestnut. The woman sat on the ground, palms in her lap facing up toward the sky. Juniper assumed that was where she'd been lying moments before. The woman seemed calm and inviting, but Juniper wasn't in the most trusting mood. Not that she ever was, but the last few days were only fueling her apprehension. And this reeked of a trap.

"Who the hell are you?" she questioned. "What am I doing here?" She'd already decided that she did *not* like this strange situation, this strange place, or this strange woman.

The woman's sing-songy laughter sounded around them. "Our power calls to each other, Earthpoweress. You are a child of Earthmagic. We can speak wordlessly—telepathically if you will, mind-to-mind, if that's what you prefer."

"No thanks." She huffed a breath, still in her defensive position. Those Nightshade claws were now showing like a fresh onyx, almond-shaped manicure. "I *prefer* you answer my question."

The woman's laughter sounded once more, and she flipped the waist-length braids over her shoulder as she said, "I can speak in any form I please. I could speak to you in your mind because I like your mind. It's comfortable there, but I'll honor your wishes." She rose to her feet, standing eye-level with Juniper. "You being an Earthpoweress, and me being Gaia, the Earthgoddess—we are similar in some ways. I would not talk to all of your kind like this, and you would only be able to use telepathy with someone who you had an extremely strong bond with. And, me, of course." Her voice was soft, but her eyes were clear—alert—as she held Juniper's gaze and continued, "You need not fear me, young poweress. I mean no harm. In fact, I'm elated to be meeting you here now." She bounced on her feet.

Juniper relaxed, shifting out of her defensive position. She smoothed her hair, reeled her claws in, and used the lapse in conversation to give herself a moment to consider her words—not totally convinced that the Mother of the Earth was standing in front of her.

She pressed, "And why is that? Why would you be happy to meet me, Mother Gaia?"

"Well, because you summoned me! I'd planned to summon you soon, but you came to me. For that, I am thrilled. I love visitors! I anxiously await to learn your motivations for doing so." Gaia flashed a radiant smile, showing off teeth that were white and straight. Gaia may have been as old as time, but she looked vibrant, youthful, and full of life.

"I appreciate that." She winked at Juniper. "I live my life by the Earth and its inhabitants. I provide for them, keep them safe, give them what they need to prosper, and in return, I have aged well. Legend says that kind Gods age gracefully." She motioned to herself. "I'll let you be the judge of the truth that legend holds."

"Did you say that I summoned you?"

Shit. I hope I'm not dead. Please don't be dead. Leo will be pissed if I'm dead. Juniper ran her hands over her midsection as she felt for any fatal injuries.

The Earthgoddess's nose wrinkled as she answered, "You're not dead. You are very much alive, Earthpoweress."

Juniper wasn't convinced. *If this woman is actually Mother Gaia and not a trap set by Daemon to kill me and threaten everything I hold dear, then I'm in a room with my actual hero. Maybe it would be worth the risk to talk to her—whether she is a hallucination or not.* Her thoughts trailed off, but her skepticism remained. Juniper thought as she took a step toward the goddess, who still smiled at her expectantly.

She held a hand out toward the Earthgoddess. To her thrill, Gaia took it.

"If this isn't a trap... I think it would be best if we start over," said Juniper. "I'm such a fan. You are absolutely dreamy... the true Earthgoddess. And can I just say that your hair looks phenomenal? That braid style is super popular in Poppycal these days." Juniper grinned, battling with timidity and tentativeness to trust the goddess. She cleared her throat, her voice taking on a serious tone that was rare for her. "I may have summoned you, but I didn't mean to. I'm not totally sure how I got here."

Consideration crossed Gaia's features as she finger-combed her hair, asking Juniper, "Tell me of the moments before you arrived here. What do you remember?"

Juniper pressed her lips into a thin line as she attempted to explain, "I was—in a cavern with my sister and two new-ish friends of mine. These awful monsters were swarming us. I assume they were monsters, anyway; their magic was slick and oily and evil. They were chanting at us to open our eyes, but I was too afraid to do that.

My grandmother had projected a portal for us to enter. We were trying to find something in the portal to use to track Daemon's prison." Juniper's eyes went wide, regretting the admittance of information. Her magic thrummed in defense in case this went south.

"Speak freely, child." Mother Gaia waved a hand in the air. "I know of the threat that is Opasteg."

As if being commanded, the words were out before Juniper could reconsider. "I've been able to take visions from trees, so I took a chance and touched the wall of the cavern. I thought I might be able to get a vision from it." She released a breath, willing her racing pulse to slow. "Then I awoke to your voice, here... in this place. Wherever we are."

"You're sure you did not break contact with them?" Mother Gaia's question was soft, her voice laced with concern.

"Yes, I kept my arms looped in theirs the entire time. I couldn't risk separating from them—from being trapped in that place. No way," Juniper explained.

"Then your body is with your companions. Assuming they left the portal intact, your body would have gone with them. As for your mind, well, your mind is here—with me." Mother Gaia offered a conciliatory smile.

Juniper's eyes stayed locked on the Earthgoddess as she asked, "Right. And where is *here*?"

"My home—the Center of the Earth." Gaia's tone matched the wistful look in her light brown eyes.

Juniper's eyes wandered; she had never given much thought to what the center of the Earth would look like. If she had, her imagination wouldn't have conjured up something as magnificent as what she could see. A place so... heavenly. It was celestial; it was ethereal. A vast forest surrounded them. The balmy air held aromas of damp wood and pine needles. A winding stream bubbled near Juniper's slippers. The trees towered so tall that she found herself straining her neck to look up to see their tops. Soft rays of sunlight peeked through the trees, lighting up the dew and mist floating in the air.

Her fingertips moved mindlessly toward the sparkling mist. Her skepticism stopped her hand as she questioned, "If we're in the center of the Earth, why can I see the sun?"

"Magic, dear; an ancient Sun God favored me. He was a bit grouchy, but it pays to be nice." Melodic laughter flitted through the trees. "He noticed me traveling up to the Surface—the world in which Mundaners and magic-wielders reside—to see the sunrise and moonrise each day. He offered me an enchanted pocket here. The enchantment shows me a glimpse into the sky, no matter where you are in my territory. Now I can watch the sunrise and moonrise every day, without leaving. Unless I want to."

"What a gift. This place is stunning." Juniper's voice carried notes of emotion, yet still held a tone of skepticism.

"Indeed. It is enchanting." Gaia beamed. "Walk with me, Earthchild. Let me answer the questions that **impatiently** bounce on your tongue."

The forest floor poked Juniper's feet through her tattered slippers; she wished she'd been able to wear shoes with soles. Her feet were torn up from the walk to Roswell and the work that followed. While she did not want them to get any worse, she couldn't bring herself to deny the Earthgoddess's request.

She simply answered, "Okay," and fell into stride with Gaia.

———

Gaia spoke of her construction of the Earth, her mate's building of the sky, and her brother's crafting of the sea.

As they explored Mother Gaia's serene home, Juniper nearly wept at the beauty she beheld with every step. Gaia explained that she built what was necessary in the Center to preserve the landscape of the Surface, and that her magic kept the foliage trimmed and shaped to divinity. Every inch of this palace was transcendent, like wandering through a sprawling tropical greenhouse that rivaled an amusement park in size.

Gesturing to the flourishing gardens they'd entered, Mother Gaia explained, "As the Mother of humanity, I gave humans everything they needed to survive and thrive. I'm sure you have that figured out already, as I am aware that you're quick with your antidotes." She gave a pointed nod toward Juniper's hands.

"Oh, you mean the Nightshade claws?" Juniper beamed, admiring the claws that had retracted to form an oval-shaped manicure. "Yes, I have learned to make antidotes for any poison I use; I have dozens of poisons in my arsenal."

Gaia raised an eyebrow at Juniper as she said, "I'm sure you already know that the use of poison is strongly advised against. You know, it is kind of like a 'they go low, we go high' principle."

"Yes, I do know. I may use deadly poisons, but I don't prefer to kill. That is why I keep the antidotes on me. I'm new to this... but, I prefer to show someone I can kill them, and then determine if they are trustworthy enough to spare." Juniper sighed, rolling her eyes. "Truthfully, I have only used the Nightshade claws on one person— someone I now consider an acquaintance. So, it's a damn good thing I had the antidote ready."

"You mean Levi," the goddess chirped.

Juniper's eyes narrowed. "Uh, yes, I do mean Levi. Do you know him?"

"I know all of my children," she answered with a smug grin. "However, I must admit that I've paid closer attention to some than to others. Not all of you are interesting."

Despite herself, she wondered if she found *her* interesting.

"Yes, child, or else I'd never have invited you to my home," she answered after reading Juniper's mind. "We could have had this meeting elsewhere, you know. I pay attention to many humans, especially the magic-wielding ones. I love to watch Seers, for example. I've studied their power for millennia; how frustrating it must be to be able to see current or future happenings, but never receive any context about those happenings. Seers have so much power and exist in a constant battle with ethics; they are a wonder to me." Her lips were pursed as she mused, "Levi Miravale's visions are particularly interesting to me. I have had my eye on him for a while. I've been watching you, too, dear. I knew you two would eventually cross paths."

Juniper's jaw dropped as she asked, "You've been watching me?"

"Of course. You are one of the legs of the Prophesied Pair. I'd be a fool to not have been paying attention to you." The Earthgoddess smirked, like her admission should have been obvious to Juniper.

"I—I guess that makes sense."

She turned, taking Juniper's hands in her own. "Juniper, you're essential in winning this war. Your power is unmatched, and while they were forced into dormancy for years, they now claw to get free, literally. Your grandparents' decision to hide you blessed you with an insurmountable power reserve—the same goes for your sister. Two poweresses hidden until they were needed the most. It was an ingenious plan on their part. Thanks to them, you have both remained unseen and untested. You and Leola give us an opportunity to catch Daemon by surprise. That might just be what we need to defeat him." Gaia inhaled a breath and straightened her chin, continuing, "You are confused—I assume you did not know of your relevance?"

Juniper had been told that she and her sister were the Prophesied Pair, but she had only just discovered this information. A few days ago, she'd been living as a Mundaner.

"I have not had much time to process the news. If you were watching, I'm sure you know that the last couple of days have been... strange," said Juniper as she stared beyond Mother Gaia's shoulder, seeing nothing.

She frowned, looping her arm in Juniper's as they continued their walk. "You're right. I apologize for my directness. Perhaps that is why you summoned me, for more knowledge of your role in the prophecy?"

Juniper lifted her eyebrow in question, not able to confirm if she had really meant to summon her at all. They slowed. They'd reached a lush garden with a seating area and Gaia motioned to the table in front of them. "Sit. Let's have tea."

She glanced around and said, "I should be getting back."

"Not to worry, poweress, time doesn't exist here as it does on the Surface. We'll have tea," she said as she waved her hand. An afternoon tea spread appeared on the teakwood table. They sat in comfortable silence for a moment, the only sound from the teaspoons stirring in the milk glass mugs. The tea left a scent of rose in the air. It reminded her of her favorite tea shop in Poppycal. Her throat tightened as she wondered if she'd ever get a chance to sip tea in the tea rooms again. She forced the thought out of her mind with a decisive shake of her head. Now was definitely not the time to deal with those emotions. She would process them later—when she had a private shower to cry in.

Juniper sipped the tea and was pleasantly surprised to find it was similar to what she preferred back home. "Rose Earl Grey?"

"Yes. Homemade. I grow the roses, of course." Gaia nodded, gesturing to the rose blooms surrounding them. She refilled Juniper's mug, eyeing her with a look that shone with determination. "Now—back to the prophecy. You, Leola, Bennjamin, and Levi all play a vital role in defeating Daemon's army. Each of your skills is fundamental to our success. Bennjamin and Levi have the power to get you and your sister where you need to be to stop Daemon. Bennjamin is a highly-trained, well-practiced dual-power. He has multiple capabilities, which is rare to see. Levi's visions are clearer than what I had previously observed in Seers, and his power with wards and spellwork is incredible." She paused, sipping her tea. "What I have not been able to figure out is how he is seeing into Daemon's dungeon. The magic of that cavern is ancient—impeccably and dangerously guarded. It is defended by wards that have withstood the test of threats and time. It is difficult for anyone to enter the cavern unless Daemon has approved their visit. But the four of you used an illusion portal and walked right in without his permission; you almost went unnoticed, too."

"You are with the Underground?" Juniper's tone was full of wonder.

"No, child, I don't join organizations created by humankind. I believe in justice, though. I have seen Daemon's plans, I have seen his heart, and I have seen his ambitions. I can't tell you everything, but I can tell you, if he wins, we all lose. I'll do everything in my power to ensure justice and good prevail in this war—I am on the side that benefits the greater good. The Underground *happens* to be on the same side as me." Gaia sighed. "Years ago, I was plagued with horrible regret about my creation of humankind. I'd always feared that their proclivity to selfishness would taint the species. Once humankind began the practice of Labor Camps, I was *sick*. For years, I could hardly bring myself to peer into the happenings on the Surface. My visits to the human world became infrequent, changing to yearly visits. When or if I did visit the Surface, I chose to pop into areas where people of all backgrounds would be interacting—it helped heal the brokenness of my heart. Everything was dark. I was devastated that my own creation would end up ruining the world that I built. There were years of death and mistreatment—and I had to watch it all. I was lost and hopeless until I started to witness the work of the Founders. That is what brought me to the Underground." Gaia's smile was tearful.

"This was the first time any Chattels had a chance on the Surface. I felt the ask from the Founders to be blessed to join together—to stand for a cause that was bigger than themselves. I chose to support this group in their endeavors. I was so enthralled by the possibility that humankind had a chance at being good again, so much so that I chose to gift my Goddessblood to their cause. When the Founders of the Underground performed their sacred initiation to form 'the Underground,' my blood blessed them with unique gifts, gifts that they could use to continue this fight against evil. Despite warnings from other Gods, I gave the humans magic." Her face darkened and the mug shattered in her hands. "But then Daemon, a Founder himself, became overcome with greed. I could have never foreseen the twist his soul would take. Magic likes balance and... I learned the hard way that the principle applies to both goodness *and* evil. Even there, magic will side with whichever is less to restore balance. For without evil, goodness cannot shine." The mug turned to sparkling mist in her hand and then quickly repaired itself as she sighed. "Daemon was able to create his organization and mimic the magic sharing that my Goddessblood gifted. His ideal world protects the oppressors and thrives in an environment where bigotry is rewarded. He has no limits to how far he will go to control people who do not agree with his ideologies. The cavern you visited is a prime example of that—and I fear that it is just the beginning."

"The cavern?" Juniper's whisper filled the air. "I don't understand. We've been told of the prophecy, but any communication from the Underground is so vague. How do we help—?"

Mother Gaia interrupted, "You were correct in your guess. Your mother is in that cavern, Juniper. That entire generation of magic-wielders from the Underground were captured by Daemon in battle, and he is using that cavern to store their magic. He has the magic of 288 powers and poweresses stored and ready to be used for his dark endeavors."

"You have all of this power. Why didn't you stop him?" Juniper gritted her teeth. She hardly remembered her mother and she'd been kept in a prison most of her life. Mother Gaia had *known*. Not just about them, but she had known about all of Daemon's heinous acts. Tears burned her eyes as she asked, "You saw his heart. You saw what he's done to Mundaners on the Surface. Why did you do nothing while his power raged?"

"As a Goddess, I'm blessed to be able to create life and give gifts, but once I create it, I can't destroy it. That is the cost of my power. I am able to give a life, but then I must stand back and watch that life take others while I remain powerless to intervene," she said as her eyes saddened. "Long ago, I used to love that cavern. It is close to the Center, so I often used it as a channel when visiting the Surface. Some of my followers would even visit the cavern to feel closer to the Earth—to me. The worship and happiness from my followers and my frequent trips there left a lot of remnants of my magic—my powers—there. Worship is an incredibly powerful and beautiful thing. I'd never considered the fact that the cavern could *imbue* magic. Until one day, that all changed. Daemon had summoned me—many times. I knew what he wished to ask and why he was calling upon me. He wanted me to show him how I'd granted gifts to the Founders. He wanted to bargain with me, simply so I would support Opasteg instead of the Underground. Instead of outright declining him, I ignored his summons. I thought he would give up," she said as tears fell from her honey-colored eyes. "Daemon must have visited the cavern, hoping to reach me. When he did, he noticed the remnants of magic left behind. Daemon is clever. He knew that the remnants of my magic were malleable—like clay that he could shape. Initially, they were weak, so he called unto his worshippers to revere him in this cavern. The magic liked the practice of worship and it became stronger with each worshiper. Daemon continued this practice until he had gathered enough of the remnants of magic to transform the cavern into what it is today—a prison. He enlisted demons to guard it. The only people who are granted entrance are members of Daemon's trusted circle. The cavern only has one true entrance, and he has used his power to create wards that prevent anyone who enters from exiting. His permission must be granted to open the wards or leave the cavern. Entering via warping or portals is prohibited by the wards—anyone who enters must walk in and out. You and your companions found a way in and out of that cavern—you four may just be able to free the people Daemon has trapped there and prevent him from using the stolen power."

Juniper traced the rim of her mug, digesting the information. "When he trapped all of those people, how did he do it? What happens if he's able to trap us there? Who will fulfill the prophecy and defeat him if we become trapped?"

"I can tell you that Daemon was gifted the power of illusion when he assisted in forming the Underground, similar to your Grandmava, but he is much more powerful. He was able to show every Conscript their worst nightmare as it played out in front of them—the people who were trapped saw their children or loved ones being imprisoned and tried to stop it. He then created a portal that led directly into the entrance of the prison, then warded the prison to trap anyone who entered. Soldiers ran into the portal, unknowingly trapping themselves inside. Once he had trapped them, the Soulsiphons drained their magic and locked them up in chains. Daemon is old; his power reserve is extensive, and he has since found various ways to make himself more powerful. I do not know all of his powers, but I must warn you not to underestimate him. I hope to show you some inside knowledge of the cavern—of Daemon. To do that, I must ask you to re-enter the cavern through the eyes of one of the prisoners."

Juniper flinched. "How would I even do that?"

Gaia held out her hand and said, "I can show you, Earthchild. Take my hand. I'll stay with you and pull you out when it is time. It is the only way that you can adequately warn your companions of Daemon's power and learn the ways of the cavern before you attempt to rescue anyone. You entered to find something to help Levi identify the location of the prison—I know that you didn't find it."

Juniper chewed on her lip, nodding. She gripped Gaia's hand in her own, pulling her forward so she was staring directly into her eyes as she said, "You betray me and I'll destroy everything you love, starting with this place."

Gaia threw back her head in laughter, squeezing her hand gently. "Oh, I know you will. That is why you're my favorite Earthpoweress. Ready?"

Juniper smirked. "Obviously."

Fulfilling the prophecy was a motivator, but she was embarking on this doomed adventure because there was nothing that would deter her from saving the people she loved. The world she'd known had shifted under Daemon's regime—into ugliness so profound that she couldn't look directly at it. If she were not meant to use her powers to destroy the looming threat, why would the Gods have granted her such immense strength?

Part II:
The Pair

CHAPTER 20

— JUNIPER —

Year: Unknown
Date: Unknown

CHAOS.

Chaos that spiked her pulse and forced her eyes to dart around, looking for something—anything—that made sense.

Whiz. She shifted too slow; the arrow caught the tip of her ear. With no time to react as another one shot toward her throat, she blocked it with a rush of vines, detouring it just enough so it didn't meet its target. Rolling onto her knees in a defensive position, she touched her ear, shocked to be met with hardly any blood.

What the fuck? She dropped to her stomach as arrows whistled toward her from all directions. Her eyes darted, not sure what to focus on; there was too much happening. People screamed, others sprinted, some heaved, dozens bled. A man stumbled in her peripheral, hands grasping his midsection as his intestines bounced over his shaking arms. The screams were endless—pain, terror, and desperation raged in her ears.

Move. I need to move. She shuffled backward, slamming into a boulder as she crawled frantically across the ground. The air was thick with the metallic tang of blood and the scents of all kinds of magic—good and bad.

She threw up another wall of vines, catching an arrow that came inches from her chest. *What is this place? This isn't the prison.* She shrunk further against the boulder, biting her cheek as she took in clues from her surroundings. *Gods, Gaia really sent me here.*

Beyond the arrows whistling and the swords clashing, magical-beings were *fighting* with magic. Illusionists dismantled their opponents by thwarting the scenes in the meadow; elemental powers wielded their power against the enemy in various forms—earth exploded, wind roared, steam plumed, ice cracked, fires raged. Wind whistled in all directions as the battle continued, people in both hunter green leathers and blood red leathers—all matched in power and numbers. Her eyes widened at an Underground power using telekinesis to lob boulders at Ope forces.

Juniper cringed at the cries of one unlucky male in red being crushed. *Gnarly. But effective.*

A fire stream shot centimeters above her head—a signal that it was time to move again. She turned back toward the Underground forces and ran in that direction—to safety, she hoped.

The goal of this visit is to learn something—not die. Her surroundings blurred as she sprinted faster than she'd ever moved before. The arrows were faster, dropping with eerie thuds as the air of their descent brushed her arms and ankles as she zigzagged. *Thud. Thud. Thud.* Her eyes caught on one that landed right in front of her foot as the world tilted.

She landed face-first in thick mud. The mud squelched under her palms as she tried to push herself onto her feet, but she couldn't get enough power to rise from the yard deep, swampy earth. Rolling onto her side, she lay face-to-face with an Underground soldier. She swallowed the scream that yearned to rip through her teeth. The man was fair-skinned with chestnut curls and hazel unseeing eyes. He was dead. His jaw was slack, his white teeth and colorless lips covered in fresh blood. He might have been handsome if she were not meeting him like this—lifeless—for the first time. Juniper put out a shaky hand, touching his eyelids to press them closed.

Her hand was different—similar to her own, but much more weathered. She turned her hand over to reveal badly scarred skin that was definitely not her own.

I must be glamoured. She looked down to see herself in an Underground uniform. Gaia seemed to think of everything before sending her here—except maybe a warning of where exactly she'd wake up. Swords clashed nearby, dropping her right back into reality. A reality in which she really needed a weapon.

Thank you, sir, for your service and your sacrifice. She reached over to the fallen soldier's tactical belt. *I need to borrow this.* She inhaled two deep breaths, stood up from the wet mud, and started running again.

"RETREAT!" someone shouted. "Retreat to the tree line!"

She ran for the tree line—hands shaking in anticipation for what she'd see once she got there. She'd agreed to come here, but holy demons, did she regret it.

Perhaps this should have been something for the Pair *to do together.* She picked up her pace. *Leo will be so pissed.*

"GO!" A man in front of her waved his arm, motioning for her to move. "GO, GO, GO!"

"Yep," she said, sheathing the dagger she'd borrowed from the soldier into her leathers, using a vine to snag another one from a different fallen body. She winced. "Sorry."

Despite the cover of the trees, the drizzle had escalated into a torrential downpour. Juniper blinked the falling water out of her eyes, coming to a halt as she reached the tree line. Forces waited in organized lines for orders from leadership who sat on horseback ahead of them. She followed suit. She knew nothing of war or battle, but what she did know was that the important people got to ride the horses. The frigid rain dripped down her chin, making her teeth chatter, as she kept her eyes trained on the magic-wielder in front of her.

"JUNIPER!" Her head whirled only to see Leola calling for her. "JUNIPER, RUN! You have to go now!" Her sister hissed the words, dressed in leathers the same as she, yards away from her.

Shock numbed her limbs and depleted her judgment as she took two steps toward her sister.

"Look out!" Leo screamed, but Juniper was already on the ground. Leola lay on top of her.

"What are you doing here?" Juniper said, shoving her arms into her sister.

But she didn't speak; she didn't move. A sensation of warmth covered Juniper's arms.

"Shit." Leola's whisper was near silent against the roaring wind and rain.

Juniper shoved again, pushing out of her sister's grasp, but Leola didn't rise to her full height; they knelt eye-level until Juniper's eyes caught on the red that soaked through her leathers.

"What the—" She ran her hands down her body. "This isn't my blood."

"I know," her sister croaked, her body slumping. "Thank the Gods."

Juniper crossed the small space separating them, catching her before she could hit the ground. Deep, red blood covered Leola's uniform—a twin to her own—except, on her sister's, the blood spurted out in rhythmic bursts. A splash of blood hit Juniper between the eyes as she looked toward the source—there were three thumb-sized holes in Leola's chest with a fourth plugged by an arrow.

No. Blood from her sister's mouth splattered her cheeks; to her horror, the liquid met her tongue, filling her mouth with an earthy, rotting taste.

"NO! You're okay. Y-you're okay," she repeated, clawing at the arrow. When she looked back into her sister's eyes, she recognized the same lifeless gleam she'd seen in the soldier's on the battlefield. Her hands shook and she screamed, "NO! NO, LEO!"

Nothing changed—the lifeless gleam now overshadowed by her blown pupils. A combination of rain, tears, and blood ran down her face and hands, as she rocked her sister's body in the glacial mud.

A strong hand gripped her shoulder as someone said, "There you are!" She looked up into a pair of familiar emerald eyes, eyes that were surrounded by black frames. "Oh gods. Wh—what happened?"

How—? She kept her hold tight on Leola, unsure how the Seer could be meeting her in this vision as well. He was not high on her list of people she wanted to see… but he was familiar. *They are here because of… me.*

"Levi! You have to leave, *now.*" She scrambled to her feet, pulling Leola up with her, ignoring the scream in her muscles protesting the deadweight as she continued, "Get out! Tell Grandmava to take you out. Go through the portal—whatever you have to do. Take Leo. Go. Go *now.*" Her teeth gritted as she sobbed the command. She tried to thrust Leola into his arms, but her feet began to slip as he caught them both in his arms.

"*No.*" The sorrow in his voice was unbearable, taking her out at the knees. "I can't do that."

Juniper's arms shook as she fell into his embrace. *This isn't real. She's not dead.* She wanted to believe the words, but the blood that soaked through her uniform told her otherwise.

"Juniper," he said as he tilted her chin until she could see his face through her tears. "Listen to me. She's gone. I'm here to get you out. We can't lose you both." He tugged on her arm. "You have to come with me. Mother Gaia made a mistake sending you here. It's not safe. This position is too vulnerable."

She dug her heels into the ground, shaking her head at him as she said, "I'm not leaving. I need to stay here and complete my task from Mother Gaia. For the prophecy. I'll return when I'm finished." Her sobs were choking her. "Get to safety. Go! Take her with you, *please.*"

She stepped back, making the devastating mistake of looking at Leola's limp body in his arms. Denial overtook her senses as she took in the image.

Her sister was dead. Leola was dead.

Dead.

"Juniper!" he shouted through the rain. "Listen to me! You are in *danger!* Gaia fooled you. She fooled all of us. I'll explain later—please, we have to leave." Levi pulled her forward.

She exploded, "NO!" She pushed back from him and he grunted, stumbling backward. She looked up to see his face shredded to ribbons, then down to her Nightshade claws that she didn't remember summoning. She flipped her weathered hand over to see that her claws were exposed, dripping in fresh blood.

When she looked up to see his face, it was already swelling. In fact, he was swelling much, much faster than he had the first time she'd used the claws.

He choked, dropping Leola to the ground as his hands reached up to his destroyed face. "You didn't mean to," he said in a hushed tone.

She whimpered, "No, no, no, please. *Please don't die.* I—it was an accident."

"I know," he coughed, his words slurring, "I know it was."

She dug into her enchanted pocket, feeling for an antidote that wasn't there. He needed help, now. She looked around, desperate for an escape route or for something to give to him to slow the effects of the poison.

"*Juniper,*" he wheezed. "Let's get out of the rain—you can wait for Benn there—he'll take you back." He pointed beyond her shoulder, his eyelids beginning to flutter.

"*What?*" Her voice raised to incredulity. "No, we need—" Her eyes followed his finger.

Then she saw it—an entrance to a tunnel—the prison. She squinted through the rain, taking in her surroundings with fresh eyes. She was living her worst nightmare; this was all an illusion.

"Juniper." His breaths were labored. She eyed the Levi that stood next to her; he certainly looked authentic and not like some kind of illusion. He even had the same scar Benn had used to identify him. This was definitely the Seer she met at the Camp, the Seer who was Benn's best friend, the one she semi-trusted and only slightly despised after working together tonight. However, if her theory was true and what she'd just experienced was, in fact, a nightmare and not her reality then that meant...

Leo is alive and Levi is not dying. She straightened, glancing toward him again. *None of this is real.*

She touched his swelling cheek, her finger met with the tattered flesh she'd caused as she said, "You stay. Stay out of sight." Her chest squeezed as she lied to her companion. "I'll come back with the antidote."

She sent a silent prayer to the Gods that she was correct in assuming everything she'd just lived through was a product of an illusion. She prayed that her sister was alive somewhere and that she hadn't just turned her back on a dying Levi. She prayed that she would escape the cavern with what she needed, leave this vision, and hug her sister once again.

"Juniper!" he called out.

Too late. She was running again.

———

She blinked, her eyes adjusting to the pitch-black of the cavern. She'd just been in this wretched place so the stench should not have surprised her, but she grimaced anyway.

The thick, wet air was the same as she remembered it but, this time, there was movement everywhere. Soldiers in Underground leathers were sprinting around her into the prison. She flattened her body against the tunnel's wall to keep from being trampled. She bit her lip, fighting the urge to tell everyone to turn around and *leave* the tunnel—while they still could.

They really walked right into his trap. Tears blurred her vision as she took off into a jog down the path, following the others. *And I need to do the same.*

She observed powers and poweresses using their magic to light the path and to shield themselves. She shuddered, wondering what kind of nightmares each person was seeing—what they were running toward... or away from.

Faster. Faster. The sooner she left this place, the sooner she could see Leola. The image of her sister's dead eyes would be burned and looping in her memory in perpetuity.

Reaching the end of the path, the orb of benevolent magic she expected to see was not yet present. She was prepared to shield her eyes from its bright light, but only saw infrequent, faint sparks in its place. A spark of light whizzed past her face as she staggered backward. It landed in the area where the orb should be.

Gods, the prisoners are starting to lose their magic.

A voice yelled, "My power—is gone! Stop! Stop! All of you! This is a trap!"

Juniper ran to the side of the path so she could see where the voice was coming from. She peered down, down, down until she caught sight of the man responsible for the warning, right before he was yanked out of sight. The unmistakable sound of shackles snapping into place echoed throughout the spiraling levels of the prison.

"It's a trap!" he yelled again. "Run! Run now!"

A thud reverberated in the cavern; the screaming prisoner fell silent.

She stayed in the shadows, using the dark pockets to move through the prison unseen. She flinched every time she heard the metal shackles close. She held her breath, watching the *things* doing the shackling. Some kind of demon, she presumed, not wanting to spend too much time looking at it. Gods forbid one of them *see* her. Whatever these things were... they were strong. The magic-wielders were fighting back, and they were *losing*.

I'm here for research; I can't save them from this. She needed to get her hands on an item that Levi could track—that's how she could help them. *Get in and get out. I'm not dying here.*

She ran her fingers over the cool metal of the shackles nearby. The metal was hot to the touch. Not hot like fire, but hot like an ice burn.

Ouch. Grandmava spoke of enchanted, power-blocking metals. She sneered into the darkness. *No wonder they can't fight back. Being shackled to these would subdue the magic and burn the skin at the same time. Cruel bastard.*

She looked over her shoulder, hearing the screams of another magic-wielder. *"Get your hands off of me!"*

Her blonde curls were caked in blood; she thrashed against two demons as they dragged her deeper into the cavern. Juniper admired her fight, wishing she could help her as she kicked and fought against them. This woman was everything she hoped to be in this life—untamable and fearless. One of her kicks landed, knocking the thing to the ground. She threw her shoulder into the other one, standing as it released her and crawled up onto the wall like a spider.

The blonde warrior spat, "Leech. You'll die here, demon."

Whatever it said back, Juniper didn't hear, but the woman simply responded, "You think I don't know that?" She kicked another approaching demon, square in its chest—if it could be called that. "I know it's my time. It's *my* job to know that. I'd be a lousy Seer if I didn't."

She tensed.

"But first," the woman said as her wrist twisted, suspending the demon in the air, its tentacle-like limbs flailing. "Useless. You don't have what I need."

The thing *whimpered*. A crack sounded, splitting it in half. She dropped it to the ground. In pieces.

Badass. Juniper's eyes flashed. *She killed one.*

"But you do." She sighed, beckoning with her finger into the shadows beyond Juniper. "Come on, then. Best get it over with." Her accent was proper and thick.

Articulate and smooth-tongued, even as her words dripped with venom when she said, "If you must be the one to kill me, best get on with it. Funny to think *you* could catch me by surprise."

The darkness slithered toward the woman, her emerald eyes unblinking as the demon rose from the darkness to its full height. "My, what a lovely parasite you are," she said before she struck, sending it careening into the wall. It rose quicker than an arrow, its clawed hands latching onto the woman's face. She choked out, "You can take me, but you won't take *him*. Which will be a... colossal... mistake for you."

The snap of her neck rang like a gong in Juniper's ears. The woman slumped forward, a mass of curls following her drooping head. Juniper swallowed her scream, watching the demon drag her body toward a pile of dead soldiers, where it dropped her there as though she was a bag of garbage. Her eyes went back to the area where the demon had landed, her eye snagging on a small glint of silver.

A key. She tossed a look over her shoulder, checking to see if any*thing* was paying attention to her, and sprinted toward it. The metal burned her hand as she picked it up. Wincing, she shoved the key into her pocket before any demon could notice.

Was this *what she meant by what she 'needed'? She couldn't have known I needed the same thing.* She returned to her spot along the wall near the shackles. Her throat burned at the idea that the woman had been trying to help her... and she was dead now. She shook the thought away, throwing her braids over her shoulder. *I came in here for an object—now I need a way out.*

She thought back to the key and its unique shape but didn't risk pulling it out of her pocket. There was no keyhole on the shackles that she could see.

If a demon-guard holds a key, there must be a reason that key exists. She moved through the darkness. *Gaia mentioned* one *entrance, but there must be another door somewhere.* She pondered this as she scanned the walls looking for a hidden door, but she saw only shackles on this level.

She looked over her shoulder to see the demons preoccupied with fighting the magic-wielders around them. She peered over the precipice to the lowest level, channeling her power into a thick vine. It slithered from her palm, wrapping around one of the shackle anchors on the wall. She held her breath, stepped off the ledge, and lowered herself to the pit level. Her feet met the ground, and she reeled the vine back into her palm, moving in the shadows again.

Each prisoner was drained of energy, their powers stolen in the brutal ambush. Some yanked at the shackles tethering them to the walls, refusing to accept defeat. Some were injured—missing limbs or actively bleeding out—but the guards showed no mercy.

All this death and gore in the name of the new regime—before they even led. Her anger transformed into rage. *I'll return and kill every demon in here.*

Juniper reached the end of the walkway, counting 127 imprisoned Underground soldiers on her way, knowing there were more in the other levels. It was too dark to make out the design on the door in front of her, so she ran her hands across it. Finally, her finger met a keyhole.

A menacing voice froze her movements. She let her palm drop to her side, leaving the key in her pocket.

"*Young poweress.* You are back in my prison once again," the tenor voice called into the darkness. "I didn't think you would return after your last visit, but here we are. I sense your presence. I sense your *fear.* I sense your foolishness."

She kept her hands relaxed, but fear shook her to her bones. She was outnumbered; she was vulnerable. She had literally walked into a place designed to trap magic-wielders. She'd found what she needed. She may have the key that could lead them to this place... that could help them locate and free these people. Yet, here she was, cornered by her enemy, alone. All a mere frustrating yard away from the fucking door, the one that would have been her way out.

She breathed one word in response: "Daemon."

"So harsh. Where are the pleasantries?" His twisted, grating laugh echoed too loudly in the tight space. "Not happy to see me? I, for one, am thrilled to meet you and only you. I didn't think I'd get the chance to meet you under such wonderful circumstances, though."

"Is that what you'd call this?" she seethed.

"But of course. This 'ambush,' as you may call it, was only the beginning of an impeccably executed plan," he said. "Which you should take note of—considering you are now trapped here and I'm the ruler of Heri. Both happenings undermine the credibility of the prophecy—as I'd planned."

She pressed her mouth into a tight line.

His voice darkened as he continued, "I've been waiting a long time for you, Juniper Runes."

"Have you?" She chose to keep her answers short so he wouldn't hear her voice shake. She shuddered, eyes darting all around, still unable to see him. Darkness filled her vision, and she wondered if this was part of his illusion power.

"Yes. I read the prophecy. I know the Underground is relying on you and your sister to defeat me," he said, his tone smug. "Fools. They were always so *disagreeable*, but now that I have you here, I'm hoping for something different with you. Maybe you're more evolved than the company you keep. I was hoping we could come to an agreement together. That was the problem with the Founders; they would not work with me. They were turned off by my ambitions." A hand she could not see touched her face, a long nail caressed her eyebrow as the voice continued, "Perhaps we could work together, Juniper Runes."

She schooled her face to an unreadable mask, using all her willpower to resist pulling away from the phantom touch. "I'm listening."

"You are young."

She lifted her chin as she said, "I'll reach Maturity next summer."

"Two summers from now, if my spies are trustworthy," he corrected her, sensing her lie to her dismay. "You are untested and unseen by the world—previously hidden in the Mundaner world. You are unpredictable. I hear you are powerful, but that remains to be seen. You have limited exposure to my world. Your powers were taken from you and your sister at a young age. You were forced into hiding and never got to know your true self. You were robbed." The voice surrounded her, reeking of deceit. "You work with me, darling girl, and I can assure you that that will never happen again. You work with me and I can show you *real* power. Rule Heri with me, Juniper Runes."

He appeared before her, silver-haired and centimeters from her face. His trimmed facial hair matched the silver on his head, his locs resting on his back. He was dressed in a silk, white button down with matching slacks—starkly different to the blood-red uniforms she'd seen his soldiers wearing on the battlefield. In fact, he looked pristine, like he had never even been there at all.

She almost choked at his ridiculous words that did not match his shocking appearance. She hadn't expected him to offer to work with her, and she had not expected him to be so handsome. Old enough to be her grandfather, but still handsome with a smile that could easily be misinterpreted as warm. Every speech she'd listened to him give, every anti-Mundane bulletin he'd signed, every discriminatory sanction he'd placed on Heri... Well, she had envisioned the man who led the new regime to look as slimy as the demons he employed. Especially since he chose to keep his face hidden. Yet, here he stood, not at all how she'd pictured him.

She smiled, biding her time so she could think and respond appropriately. "So, I work with you, we slay our enemies and then, we rule Heri? Would we be doing that side-by-side?" she asked with a hint of playful defiance.

"Simple as that. You'd be my right-hand. I could use an Earthpoweress like you in my arsenal." His answer was quick and condescending.

"You said 'rule with you,'" she replied, "if I remember correctly."

"Yes, yes. Don't get carried away. There can only be one ruler, Juniper Runes." He smirked.

"Mmm-okay." She nodded, half-listening to him and half-plotting how she would get out of this prison alive. She couldn't warp herself, as Daemon had warded the cavern against that magic. She needed... Her hurried magic knowledge hollowed as she realized that she had no idea what she needed. So, she stalled a bit longer. "I see. Is this an *invitation* to work together, or a threat?"

"That depends on your answer, my sweet."

Gag. She covered her grimace with another smile, growing desperate for a way out. *Mother Gaia! Pull me out of here, please. Hello! Gaia!*

"Interesting," she said, fingers grazing the dagger she had sheathed in her uniform. "What if I need time to think about it? I'm intrigued, but my sister would be suspicious if I didn't return to her."

What are the odds I can goad him into letting me out? She kept her eyes on him.

He stepped toward her, keeping his hands behind his back. "I'd hate to let you leave. Once you return to your lair, you will be surrounded by hateful words about me. It's all unfair propaganda, Juniper Runes. They all hate me." He scoffed as if he couldn't believe they felt that way toward him.

Narcissist. The word hissed through her mind. She had watched this magic-wielder kill and imprison people for his own interests, lead a Coup that resulted in countless loss of life, and followed it all with an assault on Mundaner rights. Her own mother was trapped here somewhere and this man was seriously attempting to glean sympathy from her?

He's not letting me out. She almost scoffed back at him, pleading silently, *I have what I need. Gaia, please help me. Please, please.*

He stared at her; she stared back. A woman groaned a few yards away from her, causing them both to break eye contact.

"Ignore her," he muttered. "Come, Juniper Runes. It would be such a shame for you to die in this war. Think of what we could be together—what we could *do*. Rule Heri and all the worlds beyond. Join my team—the winning side."

The groan sounded again, and Juniper's temper flared in response to her pain, claws forming on her fingers.

If he's going to kill me, I'm going to go down speaking my mind.

Her voice dripped with rage as she seethed, "I would *never* work with you. I'd never represent this kind of carnage and violence. Your side may have had a win today, but remember: my sister and I are coming for you. You, you cruel, evil *fool*. You are dead. Hear my words: you will *die* in this prison, even if I have to drag your almost-dead body back here and deliver the killing blow myself. You will die here, Daemon." She crept close enough so her nose touched his. "And I will fucking laugh once I am through with you. And so will my sister. And so will everyone you have imprisoned here. You will die here, and *no* one will mourn you."

A smile crept over his tight skin as he chuckled. "So, shackles it is then?" His laugh was short as he gestured toward the higher levels. "Or, even better, I can string you up at the entrance of the prison so your sister can look at your limp body when she undoubtedly, foolishly comes to rescue you. I think I'll do that instead."

She pushed that thought out of her mind, returning her attention to the woman whose palms now faced the wall. A dim light cast from them. It flickered a few times, but Daemon was too absorbed in his own rambling to notice her movements.

What're you doing, lady? She kept her eyes on Daemon and only looked away when he looked back up toward the tops of the towering walls.

The wall behind Daemon rippled unceremoniously. A portal cloaked in some kind of obscure magic—but not an illusion portal; this portal was clear and bright. Illusion portals had a bit of a haze to them, but this one did not. Plus, if it were an illusion portal, it would have the trademark ovoidal shape.

Her eyes rose to meet the woman's along the wall; she perked up, jutting her chin toward the portal. She tilted her head to the side and Juniper realized she knew that smile—that *face*. The woman's resemblance to Benn was uncanny. Grandmava had mentioned that Benn's mother was trapped here, too; she was a legendary time-wielder, stolen by Daemon. Juniper's eyes widened. The woman gestured imperceptibly toward the wall again.

No, that's... a time portal.

She caught the end of Daemon's words. "—or I'll kill you right now. Strike you down and end any chance of the Underground defeating me." His cold hands gripped her neck and she struck, slicing into his face with claws that had grown to the size of blades.

Daemon stumbled to the side, hands reaching for his face as he sneered at her.

Juniper flicked her wrist, shackling Daemon in thorny vines that anchored his body to the wall.

He let out a deafening roar that caused the entire cavern to tremble. "You won't escape me."

"I just did," she said as she took two steps around him and dove into the portal.

CHAPTER 21

— BENN —

Year: 1855
3 July
Laviegata, Heri

THE DAWN HOURS WERE APPROACHING, and Juniper still lay motionless. Grandmava peered into her mind a few times and was met with a steel-like barrier over and over again. He'd gotten nothing but the feeling of peace on every attempt to read her emotions.

Benn watched Leola, who remained silent and still—the only hint of emotion being the indiscernible shaking of her hands. Her despair was like a melancholic screeching in his mind. Not able to withstand the pain she was in, he'd sent gentle waves of sleep to her mind. She was so exhausted that in minutes, she was asleep in his arms; despite what he wished to do, he shimmied away from her and tucked her in so he could be closer to Juniper and Levi. If there was a flicker of emotion, he wanted to be there—focused—to sense it. If there was a threat incoming, he needed to be there to detect it. His eyes flicked to his friend, who sat with the dark-haired sister's clawed hand in his.

Claws?

The claws stretched, morphing into blades.

At the same time, Levi broke the silence. "Her claws are back. Sharper this time."

Leola was at his side in seconds. "What does that mean?"

Benn sent a surge of his power into Juniper's mind, listening for a scream, a plea, a reassurance—anything that would give him a sign of what was going on. He was met with a dreamless, quiet once again.

The back of his neck tingled. *Different* magic was present. His brow furrowed as he cast a stream of power that had nothing to do with her emotions and everything to do with time.

This has to be the work of a timepower. He patted his pocket that still housed the time relic. *It can't be the relic. She'd need to have it to travel through time—*

The tingling on his neck snaked down his spine as the room around him blurred. His vision cleared and he was surrounded by complete darkness save for a cerulean stream of light. He squinted into the light and, at last, there she was, encased in a time portal. Juniper looked to be sleeping, suspended in the sparkling orb of benevolent power. Her braids floated like she was beneath the surface of a pool. The magic here was strong and familiar, but he'd never seen anything like it; he'd made time portals before, but he'd never been able to see someone else using one to travel.

Someone made this portal—but who? And why can I see it? Now that he'd found her, he understood why he'd sensed peace in her emotions. She looked peaceful indeed, but she also looked... stuck.

He cast his power toward the sapphire magic that held Juniper and it landed. He tugged, hoping to jostle her. The orb shifted; her eyes opened at the movement.

She whispered, "Hello?"

He didn't need to wield emotions to recognize the fear trembling in her voice.

"Juniper! It's Benn. I'm going to open a time portal. Tell me if you can see it," he shouted to her. He kept his tether on the orb, inhaling, as he opened a time portal of his own and cast it toward the orb. She was far away; all of his effort to bring the orb closer was like pushing a ball through a tub of molasses. His teeth gritted as he willed the portal in her direction.

"I see it!" she yelled as she turned, swimming through the orb, toward his time portal. She disappeared into the darkness as his hearing became muffled, like he'd been submerged in a tub.

"Benn! Benn, wake up!" His eyes blinked open to see Levi standing over him, shaking his shoulders. "Welcome back, man, and good work." Levi side-stepped and gestured to the cot next to him.

There, in her cot, Juniper was sitting upright, alert, staring wide-eyed at Benn.

———————

She wasted no time spilling the details. Benn and Leola sat on his cot while Juniper sat on her own. Levi knelt nearby on the floor.

"I saw you guys." Her voice dropped to a whisper as her tearful eyes landed on Leola. "You were dead, Leo. Killed by an arrow right in front of me. I had your blood on my face. I tasted it in my *mouth*."

Levi reached up to touch her shoulder, but Juniper grabbed his hand. "*And you.* I..." She trailed off. "I thought I killed you."

Levi chuckled, teasing her. "Would you have even been upset if you had?"

She touched his face with a light caress, wincing like she was remembering whatever injury she'd seen him with in her vision. Benn raised his shields to give privacy to Juniper while she processed her vision, but the tenderness in her eyes was clear. She didn't answer Levi's teasing question.

Leola cleared her throat. "I'm definitely alive, sis. So is Levi. You were right—it was all an illusion. Daemon's even more heartless than we thought."

"Gaia told me that Daemon showed all of the prisoners their worst nightmares. Somehow, whatever illusion he spun for each person led them into the cavern. Once they were inside" —Juniper snapped a finger— "just like that, they were *trapped*." A single tear ran down her face.

Levi squeezed her hand again as he said, "No one is dying. I'm not going anywhere, Juniper. No one in this room is. Does it make you feel better that I—we— were just as worried for you as you were for us?"

She straightened but avoided his gaze. "Of course not."

This was the most serious he'd ever seen Juniper, and he didn't need to lower his shield to sense a shift in her. Her bubbly personality was nowhere to be found, likely subdued as she processed what she'd witnessed. Soft hues of the morning sky glowed through the small window in the barrack.

Benn sighed as his stomach pitched. "It's almost dawn. I hate to bring it up, but we're still playing the role of Chattels here. I have assassin runs, and we need to get to the orchard for jobs. And Levi—"

"Shit. Carole will be expecting me. I'll warp back to the house. I can come back here after dinner; we can decide our next move then." Levi scrubbed his face, giving Juniper a once-over, as if to confirm she truly was unharmed, but he stilled. "What the hell happened to your neck?"

Benn followed his gaze, immediately catching on a silver mark the size of a fingerprint above her pulse point. Her hand moved to the spot, flinching when her finger ran across it.

Leola shifted off the cot to examine it further, but Levi was there first.

Pausing with his hand outstretched in the air, he asked, "May I?"

She nodded, shifting her braids to the side, fully exposing the mark. Heat radiated off of Leo, her fists clenching and unclenching.

His hand trailed on the mark, tracing it. "It is the mark of a Tracker—a strong Tracker. *Fuck.* There is another one on the other side." Benn noted the rage that leaked through his friend's quiet voice. "It is *burned* into your skin, Juniper. Who left this mark on you?"

229

"Yeah—well, I was getting to that." She glanced at each of them. "I ran into Daemon."

Benn stopped breathing. Levi went stiff as a rail. Fear clouded Leola's mind, and to his dismay, Benn's mimicked the emotion.

"He offered me a position in his circle. He said he needed a *strong poweress* like me in his arsenal. I declined, obviously." She grimaced. "He wasn't thrilled. He grabbed my neck and let go after I struck him." She held up a clawed hand that still shook.

Leola erupted at his side, "*That monster.*"

"Did you injure him?" Benn asked, his strategic mind whirling. "Maybe we could use the blood or skin from your claws to trace him."

"No, that won't work; my skin is also under her claws, and it will interfere with any tracking I try to do." Levi gestured to his now healed face. "But... I sense something ancient in this room."

"Oh! I was worried at first—Gaia glamoured me so I was in leathers, but it must have made it back with me," Juniper said, opening a pocket hidden within her skirt.

Levi's eyes flashed. "What else did you bring back, Juniper?"

"Oh, you mean this old thing?" She dropped the key in Levi's waiting hand. "Just a key to the *only* entrance and exit of the prison. A demon dropped it. Careful, it burns when you hold it."

Benn chuckled. "Not bad for an Earthpoweress."

"Ah. There is strong, ancient magic here. Nothing one of my concealing spells can't fix." Levi held the key up to the morning light. "I can track the location with this. I'll need some time—"

Grandmava burst through the door of the barracks. "Younglings. You need to go now. All of you. You must leave!"

Benn lowered his shield, making space for the terror that whipped through Grandmava's mind.

Leola moved to her. "What is it?"

"I was eavesdropping on Carole and Master Roswell. They know Levi's not in his room; they also, somehow, know that Juniper is *here*. I warped as soon as I overheard. You must go. You have minutes, at best, before they round up the Chattels. They plan to question us all." Grandmava gathered the sisters' belongings into a small pack. "I can cast an illusion that will cover your magic, but Juniper— your magic is being tracked. Use it wisely."

Juniper grabbed her hand. "I know. Daemon left a mark on me. I—I went back to the prison. I know how to free the prisoners."

Grandmava looked at Juniper with a proud smile. "Of course you did. Stopping Daemon is in your hands. And that is why you are leaving. I'll stay and cover your tracks."

Levi spoke first. "I'll warp back to the main house and grab my pack. Carole can use anything I leave behind to track me." The light breeze announced his departure.

Benn blinked, his internal conflict slowing his strategic thinking.

"Bennjamin!" Her voice was urgent. "Pack your things. I'll pack theirs."

In robotic movements, he collected his belongings. He'd ditched his Modern-Era clothes in the forest, but had held onto his sneakers, wallet, and a few other keepsakes. He reached under his cot to lift the plank of wood he'd used as a hiding spot all these months and grabbed the items, along with the enchanted pack that Grandmava gifted to him a few days ago. As he dropped the items in the pack, he tried to shield before the emotions blazing around the room overtook him—terror, apprehension, hesitancy, despair. In the same breath, he knotted his sneakers and discarded the vellum-thin work slippers. He ran a hand over his hidden sheaths, counting the daggers there; some he'd brought from the Modern-Era and others... he'd stolen from the people on his kill cards. Tears burned his eyes as the sisters began to plead with their grandmother.

"We can't leave you here—*no*—they'll kill you!" Leola screamed, pulling out of her grandmother's embrace. "You know they will!"

"That's our only option, my fiery girl," she explained as she hugged the sisters hard. Grandmava pulled back to wipe her granddaughter's tears. "Our reunion was short, but so monumental. It was a gift from the Ancestors."

"Come with us," Juniper sobbed.

Leola's whisper cracked his soul in two. *"You just came back to us."* Her reluctance faded, as she dropped her arms, crossing them around her midsection.

His throat was tight as Levi warped into the room, appearing next to his side with a compact leather duffel in hand.

"Carole and Master Roswell are rounding up the Overseers. There is a mob gathered in front of the main house. We need to leave, *now*," Levi said quietly, jerking his head in the direction of the door.

Grandmava pushed both the sisters out of her grasp. "Enough tears. I packed all of your things in this pack—it can hold anything you put in it." She kissed both their cheeks, and powerlessness drowned Benn as their sobs filled the room. Leola pulled her sister into her arms as she took one small, but decisive, step away from her grandmother.

Grandmava looked to him. "Bennjamin, it has been an honor serving with you. I know Sena is *so* proud. You'll do so well, my boy. You already have done so well." She touched his cheek, and he pulled her to his chest. She whispered in his ear, "Take care of my fire child."

Before he could respond, she side-stepped him and took Levi's face into her hands. "While we only had a few hours together, I have never met a more powerful Seer. Your power is admirable. I'm so grateful our paths crossed. Your mother was a marvel, and so are you." She squeezed his chin. "It was a pleasure to meet you, Levi Miravale."

"The pleasure was mine, Grandmava," he replied, his voice tight with emotion.

A chaotic roar sounded in the distance—a cacophony of guttural shrieks and sharp cries shouting indistinguishable words. Benn lowered his shield, the determination and rage wafting from the mob chilling his blood—the mass of noise was nonsensical, carrying an unsettling rhythm of curses, jeers, and the occasional syncopated rant. There was nothing more dangerous than giving hateful people a platform to unify on and then arming them with weapons—or in this case—flaming torches.

Leola peered out the window. "*Flames.* They have torches. I can slow them down. *Please,* let me give you a *chance—*"

"No." Grandmava shook her head, cutting her off with a hand.

Juniper's face hardened as Nightshade thorns, sharp as daggers, grew across the exterior window, blocking the entrance to the barrack. "If they have to come in here, we'll make them fucking work for it."

The crowd drew closer, becoming so loud that the chanting vibrated Benn's chest.

"Sweet girl, I know you could take out that entire mob on your own, but now is not the time to show your strength. Or yours, Leo. We've done everything to keep you hidden, though I don't mind this at all—" Grandmava broke off a limb of the thorny plant, avoiding the thorns with care, swinging it around like a sword. "This, I'll take. Do not fear for me, or did you forget who you got all that power from?" Grandmava smirked, gesturing to herself. "Go. Save your mothers. End the man who has destroyed Heri. Know that I love you." With a flash of lavender magic, she warped out of the room.

The sisters choked on tearful sobs; bile rose in his stomach as he watched the empty space where his only friend at Roswell, Grandmava, had been standing.

"Benn, can you take all of us?" Levi asked softly. "We need to travel through time; we can't stay in this era."

He understood what his friend implied. Benn nodded, still exhausted from nearly losing his soul earlier tonight. They would need to warp through time on a few trips, and with the added weight of the others, he could not risk going too far. He couldn't jeopardize breaking the time continuum, misplacing his friends, or exhausting his power reserve.

The orange glow from the torches shone through the thorns covering the window.

"They're here," Levi said. "We need to move *now*."

He'd envisioned himself leaving this wretched hellscape countless times. He'd looked forward to it... but in this moment, the sadness was immeasurable—he was leaving Grandmava behind in this desolate place. Their lit torches touched the vines, setting them ablaze. The toes of boots hit the door at an unyielding pace. *Thud. Thud. Thud.*

"JUNIPER!" Through all of the harsh indistinguishable yelling, one word was as clear as it was horrifying: "JUNIPER!"

Hearing them yell for her turned his vision red—he considered delaying so he could watch Leo burn them all.

"BENN!" Levi's warning yanked him from his thoughts. "We delay any longer, we'll have to fight our way out of here. I don't see that going well."

He inhaled and cast a long line of time magic as far as he could reach, struggling to find the safest spot. Benn and the sisters needed to rely on their spycover as Mundaners; that would be the easiest way to remain inconspicuous to anyone hunting them. Levi's jewel-toned eyes would tip off any magic-wielder. Since he would be coming with them, Benn needed to choose an era where Mundaners and magic-wielders could interact. He could not risk landing in another decade where the rights of the Mundane people were limited, which left him with several options—all within the four decades of the Modern-Era. Anything earlier than that, and Levi wouldn't even be allowed to hang out in Mundane areas—thanks to the Libata and Separation clauses.

He gritted his teeth and pushed his time cast a bit further. He managed to reach the 1990s. He used another distance cast as he aimed for Rosebay, but it stopped short in Papaver City. The block on his power was a clear indicator that he'd reached the end of his power reserve.

He looped an arm into Levi's and reached for the sisters, tucking them into his side as he said, "Hold onto me; do *not* let go." The scent of his magic filled the room, whipping around them like a wind tunnel. "No matter what happens, don't let go."

The mob breached the door. In his last glimpse of the barrack he'd shared with his friend all these months, Benn watched as Nightshade thorns erupted from the ground, impaling the first five men who rushed the door. The other men found their torches incinerating their limbs; the sounds of their hateful chanting changed to wails, chasing after them as they warped from the Roswell barrack.

CHAPTER 22

— LEOLA —

Year: Unknown
3 July
Papaver, Heri

THEY HIT THE GROUND WITH A force that rattled her teeth. Benn gasped for breath, as if the wind had been forced from his lungs. He'd gripped the brick wall to steady himself, swaying toward the ground.

Levi was walking as soon as they landed. "Stay with Benn, Leo. Juniper, check for threats to the west. Hug the wall. I'll go east."

She still gripped Benn's hand as she'd done the entire journey here. She leaned down to catch his gaze in hers, but his grip weakened on her own as she felt him falter. "Benn?" She shook his shoulder with her free hand. He collapsed against the wall. "*Benn!*"

Levi was next to her immediately, concern written across his face. He ran his hand across Benn's forehead, cheeks, and chest. He was *searching* for something.

"His power reserve is dangerously low. He took us too far. *Shit*. He needs food, water, and rest." Levi ran a hand through his thick curls, letting out an aggravated sigh as he continued, "We need to keep a low profile here. Daemon's men will be

236

hunting us through time, and we can't move again until Benn is well enough to warp us all. We'll need a place to stay and new clothes to wear. The 1855 get up won't fare well here. We don't need more eyes on us." Levi lowered Benn to the ground, setting him against their packs so his limp body wasn't fully on the ground.

She frowned at Benn, not hiding the worry etched on her face, though she knew it looked more like a scowl. "Any idea where we are?"

Juniper chirped up over her shoulder, "I think we're in Papaver. I can't tell what year it is. I see sneakers and thick-soled boots, so it could be the late 80s. Or, early 90s, perhaps?"

Levi smirked. "Basing your timeline off shoes? I like it."

Juniper shrugged, looking up to the tops of the buildings as she explained, "Shoes are a universal interest."

"Right. Do either of you have banknotes on you?" Levi asked. "I have my wallet, but any notes I had on me are long gone. I've been living in the 1800 era for the past year and they only used coins."

Leola reached into the enchanted pack and pulled out her wallet. "I don't carry cash. I have Papa's bank card—"

Juniper cut her off, "Leo, we're decades away from the Modern-Era, bank cards aren't going to work."

True.

Levi nodded. "Juniper is right. Even if we could use bank cards, his account is undoubtedly being tracked. Too risky."

She sucked the inside of her cheek, debating, "Without Papa's bank card, I don't have access to any banknotes. We lived as Mundaners, remember? Controlled funds."

"Looks like we're getting those clothes with the five-finger discount." Juniper wiggled her fingers, nails now tipped in blood-red. The laugh she let out was hollow.

Leola did not smile at her attempted joke.

Levi, however, chuckled. "Warp into a nearby store. Only get what we need, then get out. Juniper, no magic until Benn is awake. He is our only shot at outrunning Carole or Daemon, if you set off that Tracker on your neck. Rely on Leola's magic only."

She had not decided if she respected his matter-of-fact tone or despised it. Currently, she landed somewhere in the middle, unsure if she was willing to trust the Seer.

Juniper rolled her eyes at him. "I know."

"I'll stay with Benn and work on lodgings for the next night." He winced, looking at Benn. "Or two."

He nodded at them—a nod of dismissal—that had her brows raising. Nonetheless, she grabbed Juniper's hand and warped them into a store.

———

Leola grimaced at the dust filtering through her nostrils. They'd landed in a storage room, but the scent of mothballs was unmistakable. This was one of the last Mundaner-allowed places she and Juniper had been before they were sucked into the Laborist era.

"Oh yay, we're back in a secondhand store." She kept her voice at a whisper as she rolled her eyes.

Juniper snorted. "You told me we could visit all of them in Poppycal. Even better, we can do it in Papaver."

Leola shot her sister a look and ran her fingers over a box labeled *"Donations."* On top of it lay two oversized shirts; she grabbed one and tossed it to Juniper. She shoved her hand deeper into the box, feeling for pants or something alike. She pulled out two pairs of athletic shorts that she was not remotely interested in wearing, but they sure as the Gods beat the ankle-length skirts they currently wore. She set them on the side table next to her, yanking off the layered skirt and tattered shirt she'd worn at Roswell. She pulled the shorts and oversized shirt on; her sister did the same. Leola shoved their discarded clothes to the bottom of the donation box.

"Gods, it feels good to be out of all of that fabric," Juniper whispered. "Now, let's go already; I want to explore."

Her eyes flared. "Bug, we need to be fast and, if possible, unnoticed."

Juniper winked at her and reached for the handle of the door that led out of the storage room.

"I'm serious, Bug. No dilly-dallying."

"Sure, Leo." She pulled the handle, swinging the door open. "Maybe just a little dilly, a dash of dally."

The sisters were tall, but the racks were taller—which was wonderful luck as they concealed them as they walked through the store. She rushed through the racks so that she could keep her sister on task.

Leola's hand landed on a pair of canvas-like pants. They were baggy— parachute pants. She pulled them off the rack and did a length test. A smile spread over her face, seeing that the pants were long enough to reach past her ankles. *Mine now.*

She dropped them into her enchanted pack and noticed the same pair in a black-washed denim. She grabbed those, too. On her way to the shirt rack, she plucked two sherpa bucket hats off the hooks and dropped those into the pack. She was not one to steal, but there was no guarantee they would have another chance to get clothes to wear and she had been wearing Chattel attire for the last 3 days; today, she was treating herself.

She met Juniper at a coat rack near the back of the store, brows raising at the heap of clothes in her hands. They had been in this store for all of eight minutes, and thank the Gods, her sister was moving fast—for once.

Juniper started shimmying the clothes into the enchanted pack, explaining, "They're not all for me! I got things for you, for Benn, and for Levi. Some extra things for me." She smiled. "Grandmava said the pack was enchanted—she said it can fit *anything* we put into it." Juniper's hand froze, a tremor moving through it as grief flickered across her face. Juniper rolled the last item in her hand, a lavender pashmina, and whispered, "Later." The sad smile that overtook her face confirmed her sister was pushing out the pain of the loss they hadn't had a chance to process yet.

"The shoes we got transported in are wrecked and I'm not wearing these slippers any longer." Juniper pointed toward the wall where a neon "Shoes" sign hung. "Let's get shoes and then we can get out of here."

Leola lifted her chin so she could see the employee at the counter. His red hair was worn in locs and he was preoccupied, if not flirting, with the olive-skinned man who was checking out.

She nodded toward the shoes. "It's now or never."

"Levi said he and Benn were good on shoes, so we just need some for us." Juniper pressed onto her tiptoes, reaching for the first pair. "Boots for me," she said as she dropped them in the pack, followed by a white high-top pair of sneakers with burnt orange laces. "Perfect for you, flamethrower." With a quick movement of her hands, she grabbed two identical pairs of chunky, white sneakers. "I'd never be allowed to buy these in the Modern-Era, so now, we both shall have a pair. They are supposed to be super comfortable. Good for battle, I'm sure." She winked.

"Let's go," she said as she took Juniper's hand, wind whipping as they landed in another store.

"A *pharmacy?*" Juniper sighed. "How boring."

"Yes—for the essentials. Toothbrushes, hair wraps... underwear." She was walking as soon as they landed, pulling Juniper along with her.

They paused once to swap their nasty Chattel slippers for the new sneakers, grabbed what they needed from the pharmacy, and quickly left the store.

The sisters landed in the alley, where they'd left Levi and Benn. Benn was still sleeping against the wall.

Levi rose to greet them, motioning toward Benn. "I checked a few minutes ago. His power reserve is still low—under 2%. It's going to be a while before he wakes up." Leola ignored the worry gathering in her stomach.

"We need somewhere to stay for a few nights. I know there are Underground safehouses in Papaver, but I would need to look around to see where. If not, we'll have to hide out here until Benn wakes up." Levi's emerald eyes looked past the alley, but more so like they were looking far to the east, west, north and south—as if he were scanning the city of Papaver for a place for them to go for the night. She truly needed to brush up on her knowledge of Seers and their power. "Benn has the funds we'd need; Sena is bound to have cash stashed somewhere in the city for us to use to rent a place. But I can't ask him right now." He frowned.

Juniper piped up, shifting her voice to a deeper tone to copy Levi's, "What do you mean, '*Benn has the funds*'?"

He gave her a sideways glance. "You know. His grandmother leads the Underground. He's a direct descendant of a Founder. The funds come with the gig." Levi chuckled. "That as well as a constant stream of crushing pressure and waves of impossible expectations."

Her chest pained at the comment as she looked toward him again. He looked so... vulnerable, so peaceful as he slept. The calculating mask of the dual-power was gone. She had a thousand things to worry about today, but what she really longed to do was sit down in a cafe and learn about Benn.

"He'll wake up. Don't worry," Levi said gently.

Her trademark scowl returned. "Who said I was worried?" Her voice was not remotely convincing.

"You didn't need to say it; it's written all over that scowl of yours." Juniper shrugged.

Thunder cracked in the distance, and they all jumped. Hard rain followed. Leola reached into the pack for jackets for each of them.

She shoved two jackets toward Levi. "Here. One for you and one for Benn," she yelled over the volume of the storm; shivers overtook her body as a wet wind blew through the alley. "So, how does that Seer power of yours work? We need to get to a place to stay tonight—" Thunder interrupted her words. "And fast."

Levi pulled his jacket on, leaning down to his friend to put the jacket over his shoulders before leaning him back against the packs. "All I need is a quick walk to scan the streets to find a place for us." His tone darkened. "Carole is tracking me, and Daemon is tracking Juniper. We need to stay somewhere with someone who will be discreet. Someone who won't be weirded out that we traveled here from 1855 and are from the Modern-Era ourselves."

Juniper leveled a deadpan stare at him as she asked, "Well who would be *weirded out* by that? The options are limitless."

"Your sarcasm is as relentless as it is unhelpful," Levi bit back.

Juniper used a dagger to pick her nails. "Get used to it, blondie."

"Where in the Ancestral hell did you get that?" Leola snapped.

"It's a dagger. I got it from a soldier in the Underground—when Gaia sent me to the battle." Juniper flashed the dagger as she said, "I wish I hadn't had to take it from him, but it's kind of cool, right?"

"Absolutely the fuck not." Leola was abrupt. "Put that away before you hurt yourself."

"There's the In-Charge Marge we all know and love," Juniper quipped as she sheathed the dagger and put it into the pocket of her shorts.

Leola narrowed her eyes at the nickname and the dagger placement. They were grumpy, exhausted, and freezing, but she was too tired to argue with her sister, so she dropped it. "Let's move. We're too exposed in this alley... and I'm pretty sure I saw a rat over there."

"You did. They basically run Papaver." Levi tossed Benn over his shoulder and started walking, his bag held in his free hand. "We're going ten blocks east. Leo's right. Lose the dagger; you can do more damage with the claws anyway." He directed his words toward Juniper.

Juniper threw Benn's pack over her shoulder while Leola carried their pack. The sisters followed close behind the Seer.

"You know, my magic is being tracked." Juniper cracked her knuckles. "It's time I learn other ways to defend myself."

"Bug, you have so many talents, but you wouldn't know the first thing about how to use that knife." Leola smiled and bumped her sister's shoulder.

Levi stopped walking, turning back to them, his emerald eyes wide. "You can't wield a dagger?"

Juniper raised an eyebrow, laughing like he was joking. "I'm from Poppycal; I went to an art school for Mundaners."

Levi's gaping mouth shifted to a frown at her answer. "That tells me nothing."

Juniper put her hands on her hips, responding, "No. I don't use weapons. Never needed them—except the claws. But those are new."

Levi raised his eyes in question to Leola, who shrugged. "I took a kickboxing class once."

"Even after the Coup—never mind, I expected you would have picked up some skills," Levi said as he pinched the bridge of his nose. "At the Academy, most students don't have magic yet—they learn combat training, potion making, botany, spellwork, you know, the usual. Except Seers, of course; we get our magic early as do the descendants of the Founders."

"Well, I didn't learn that on the way to chemistry or physics. We were in *hiding*, remember? No magical Academy for us. Though, we did play sports," Juniper added as she pulled her hood tighter as the rain pounded overhead.

"Makes sense," Levi said, picking up the pace. He took an abrupt turn up a side street to the right. "First, find a safe house. Second, teach you ladies how to fight."

Juniper chirped, "Third—get sandwiches!"

"Let's bump that to first." Leola's stomach grumbled.

"Boyd will feed us." Levi walked faster. "And we can't risk being seen in a deli."

"Are we supposed to recognize that name? *Boyd?*" Leola repeated the name, testing it on her tongue.

He scanned the crowded street again. "Boyd. Yeah. And no, *you* shouldn't. Technically, I don't even know him. Yet. But he knows us." He paused for a heartbeat, then took a hard left. "Well, he knows we're coming."

"Can you read minds?" Leola blurted, not sure if she wanted to know the answer.

"No. I can see situations, occurrences, encounters, intentions, and circumstances. That's kind of a flex, by the way. Not many Seers can see intentions or circumstances. Not any that are alive actually. Daemon made it his personal mission to hunt the Seers to near extinction—only some remain," he explained, then he cleared his throat. "Some emotion-benders can read intentions, though, but only at close range."

She looked toward Juniper who sent a shrug in her direction. She blinked rain out of her eyes and picked up her feet to keep up with Levi's quick steps. "Could you elaborate on that? The intentions?" From the quick subject change, she didn't want to ask about the *hunting*.

"It's like a path with many strings. They can change, but I've learned to compare the probabilities. I know how to sense a threat hiding along the path."

She blinked at him.

"I *see* us meeting Boyd. I *see* him being happy to see us. I *see* him mentioning he was waiting for us. I *see* him welcoming us into his home," Levi quipped, annoyance obvious in his tone.

"I get it," Leola huffed. "That's impressive. You know—lowkey."

"Poppycallians have the most bizarre slang." Levi laughed. "*Lowkey*, your flames are impressive."

"No love for the vines?" Juniper cut in with a sideways smile.

He threw back his head, laughing. "When I go a week without feeling the thorns in my *face*, I'll give you my opinion." The storm thundered around them and Levi sped up. "Walk faster—my vision shows us eating in Boyd's kitchen, and I need to get Benn to a bed fast."

CHAPTER 23

— LEOLA —

Year: 1996
3 July
Papaver, Heri

"B UT, HE KNOWS *YOU'RE* COMING. Shouldn't it be you?" Leola asked.

"No, it shouldn't." Levi sighed. "Better if they see you first."

She loathed the idea.

Juniper chirped in, "I should do it; I'm the friendliest. Also, the youngest, and people always feel bad for children."

"You're no more of a child than I am," Levi snapped. "And still no, actually, all my sight is pushing us toward you, Leola."

"Seriously? I love Leo, but that scowl could repel a witch."

"Good, then it's working," Leola deadpanned, shooting a snarky smile toward her sister.

"You're too spicy for first impressions, Juniper," Levi said, adjusting Benn on his shoulder.

"Spicy?" Juniper scoffed. "Have you ever considered that I just don't like you?"

"That's half the issue." Levi peered around the corner. "The other half can be attributed to a personality flaw."

"You know what? I regret giving you the antidote."

Levi grinned. "There she is."

———————

So here Leola stood—her fist rapping against the wood—as the lucky chosen one to knock on this stranger's door. Pulling back, she rubbed her palms together, both in anticipation and in an effort to warm her cold hands.

"No answer," she mouthed toward Juniper and Levi, both of whom stood down the steps from her. She sighed and lifted her fist again, but the door swung open, revealing a man with strawberry-blonde hair, a porcelain complexion, and ice-blue eyes, all packed into a petite figure. His eyes tightened, moving past her to the others behind her.

Exhaustion had stripped away her manners, so she let the question slip. "Boyd?"

The man's answer was gruff. "Who is asking?"

"My name is Leola." She gestured down the steps. "That is my sister, Juniper, and our friends, Levi and Benn."

His face pinched like he had smelled something odorous as he questioned, "Is he dead?"

She sucked on her cheek. *"Benn* is fine—just a bit tired from our journey here. We traveled a long way." The man gave her a deadpan stare, which prompted her to overshare. "We are with the Underground."

His eyes rolled. *"Fool.* Never speak of the Underground. If I were an enemy, you'd be as good as dead."

She braced herself for the door to slam in her face, but he beckoned them inside. "Hurry up out of that rain," he said, his accent completely changed. It sounded a bit Laviegatian, with an abundance of vigor. "Well, come in already. We've been waiting

247

on you lot for *hours*. Shoes off at the door; these floors are *new*." They entered into a wall-papered mudroom, discarding their shoes. "Boyd worked way too hard on dinner for us to let it get cold. Follow me, younglings, Wait—" he said abruptly. With a wave of his hand, the rainwater evaporated from her coat. "That'll do for now."

"Waterpower?" Juniper whispered over her shoulder, braids no longer dripping.

"Naturally," the man replied as he sauntered past them to a narrow entry hall. "Keep up, please."

Leola dropped the pack in the mudroom and took in the luxurious home. She looped Juniper's arm in hers as they followed him. The towering ceilings made *her* feel as petite as the man they followed. Every inch of the space brimmed with exquisite decor centered around rich colors—fuchsias, emeralds, sapphires, all embellished with gold—of all different textures and depths. The man sped through the hallways with expertise. They walked so fast that the rooms blurred into varying bursts of color.

In a puff of ethereal magic, the man's nondescript outfit transformed into beige slacks and an emerald silk polo. His belt, adorned with golden seashells, matched the gold of his boots. He pushed open a bubblegum pink door, revealing a kitchen as beautiful and immaculate as the rest of the house. The black and white checkered floors complimented the coral backsplash and pearl-white cabinets—it looked straight out of a display in the furniture store that Mundaners weren't allowed to shop in.

"Boyd, our guests have arrived," the man called out, walking straight to the multi-compartment oven, where another man—who Leola presumed to be Boyd—of similar stature stood. Aside from height, these men were perfect opposites. Boyd had deep bronzed skin and a wide smile with eyes that shined like amethyst—his short, styled waves the color of silver.

Boyd's voice rang out, inviting and clear. "Welcome, welcome!" He clapped once, dropping his hand to caress the other man's back. "Gordon and I are so happy to welcome you into our home. Make yourselves comfortable; dinner is almost ready."

Rich aromas of spice filled their nostrils as Gordon motioned for them to sit at a breakfast nook. Boyd poured ingredients into a drink shaker, then proceeded to shake it in one hand.

Levi spun a slow circle around the room. "Is there a place I can put my friend?"

Boyd eyed Benn, whose limp body was still draped over Levi's shoulder. "Ah — a low power reserve. That is *the worst*. We've all been there. You must use your powers responsibly, kids." He poured the mixture into a glass and pushed it toward his partner as he asked, "What did he do to tucker himself out?"

"Took on a Soulsiphon, then warped all of us here from Laviegata, year 1855," Levi deadpanned.

Gordon sputtered, choking, while Boyd fumbled a plate that clattered to the floor.

"*Gods.* Let's find this boy a bed." Gordon tugged on Levi's sleeve, leading him back through the door, which swung shut with a swoosh.

Boyd snapped his fingers and the shattered dish was gone. He declined their offer to help and ushered the sisters to the breakfast nook, where she finally unlooped her arm from Juniper's.

He pulled an iridescent pitcher that boasted fresh-squeezed lemonade out of the fridge. Five colorful glasses and matching place settings appeared on the oak table.

"Hope you all like chili," Boyd said. "In case you don't, there's some sides as well."

Levi and Gordon returned, taking their seats at the table, while she found herself wondering where Benn had been sent to sleep off his power reserve coma.

"He's okay," Levi said between sips of lemonade. "He's upstairs sleeping in the room we will stay in. You'll stay across the hall."

She blinked to mask her confusion, but Levi gestured to his head and flashed her a smile that looked suspiciously empathetic.

No one spoke—too preoccupied with their meals—until second helpings were being passed around.

Gordon wiped his face with a napkin, then broke the pleasant silence. "So, how did Benn manage to pull off that stunt? That's near impossible—especially for a young timepower."

Levi scooped more chili into his bowl and answered, "Ancestral lineage."

Boyd nodded. "Ah, that makes sense. Every now and then, Ancestral power really shows out in the genes. I have not seen that kind of power in a youngling in decades."

Levi looked strangely unfurled, as though something within him was coming to light. Leola didn't think the expression was jealousy, but thought the blonde Seer might be reluctant to share details about his best friend without him present. Her eyebrow raised in question, meeting Levi's gaze. His lips were in a tight line as he turned back to Gordon.

He straightened. "I should've been more specific. Josephine Wyndmere is his mother."

Their hosts stilled, exchanging looks of melancholic understanding.

Boyd's voice was soft. "Now that is a name I have missed hearing."

"*Josephine Wyndmere.* I haven't seen her since before—" Gordon blinked tears away, abandoning the words he was about to say. "She and I were best friends at the Academy. We stayed in touch through years of Assignments and training. I knew she had children, but I tried not to be aware of the specifics—in case Daemon ever came for me. She was a marvel. In all my time, I never met a more humble poweress."

Leola picked at the rosemary bread in front of her, wondering if Benn had inherited his humble nature—the one that she admired so much—from his mother.

Boyd chuckled. "You know, she is the strongest time-wielder to exist in our history. Records say that she is stronger than any elder time-wielder she went up against." Boyd swirled his glass of wine, a thoughtful expression crossing his features as he continued, "But I'd wager that Benn is even more powerful. He risked everything—his life—for you all. He was willing to pay the shining price to get you here."

Levi's reply had an edge, making it clear that he was still pissed at Benn for nearly killing himself. "His power reserve was at 1.5%. He collapsed as soon as we landed in Papaver. I'll have to scold him when he wakes up."

Boyd frowned. "When it hits 1%, you're dead. He either didn't understand the consequences—"

"Believe me, he did," Levi interrupted.

"Hmm." Boyd's amethyst eyes twinkled. "So, he cared more about your well-being than his own life. You can't deny that self-sacrifice is honorable, but it would have been a shame to go out like that."

His words hit her like a freight train.

Juniper said gravely, "There was a mob of Opes and Overseers coming after us. They were definitely out for our blood."

Levi's tone mirrored Juniper's as he explained, "That and tracking magic at play. We would all be dead if we had stayed a second longer. Benn saved our asses."

The glass of lemonade reached a boiling point in her grip as the conversation continued around her. She set the glass down, willing her palms to cool.

"Well, we're grateful you landed here. You're safe here. Use the next few days to rest, recover, and reset before you travel again." Gordon looked at each of them with a grin, fluttering his fingers. "Now, tell us about your power. Your magic, its *depths*. Tell us *everything*; we don't spare details here. I love meeting younglings."

"Well, you know I'm a Seer already; the eyes give me away." Levi's expression turned sheepish. "Additionally, I have a knack for wards and spellwork. I picked it up at my foster home, then nurtured it at the Academy." Levi's tone was matter-of-fact, like he'd said nothing of consequence.

Gordon tensed, "You were fostered?"

"At one of the main Underground houses." Levi's tone stayed even. "I was orphaned after the ambush."

"Miravale lineage?" Boyd's eyes darkened.

"That's the one," Levi said as he flashed a wry smile that looked anything but happy.

"May your parents and siblings rest peacefully." Boyd tilted his glass. "Seems you're living up to the name."

Levi's jaw ticked as he shrugged. "Attempting to."

Juniper eyed him, leaning forward. "He's being modest. Mother Gaia told me that he is the most powerful Seer she has ever observed." Juniper flipped her braids over her shoulder in nonchalance.

Boyd considered, before turning his attention to her. "You aren't a Seer. Are you an illusionist? Did Mother Gaia speak to you in a vision?"

"No," Juniper answered. "I visited her palace."

Gordon's hand dropped to the table. "How in the Ancestral hell did you do that?"

Juniper finger combed her braids. "I took a vision from a cavern. She summoned me—or she said I summoned her. I guess the jury is still out on that one."

Gordon's jaw neared the floor. "You're an Earthpoweress, I imagine?"

Juniper nodded, beaming. "Oh yes. My *knack* is with the plants."

Gordon pushed a vase of wilted flowers toward Juniper. "Oh lovely. Could you fix these for me? I wanted to give them one more day, but a waterpower and a Seer can't do much in that department."

Her bright smile dimmed. "I'd love to help, but I can't." Juniper's eyes flitted around the table as she whispered, "There is a tracker on me."

"*Rude.* Who would do that to such a vibrant, kind poweress like yourself?" Gordon gasped.

"Daemon," Juniper muttered, shrinking a bit. She tilted her neck so the silver marks Daemon had left there were visible.

"Fucking hell," Gordon hissed.

Boyd's eyes were as wide as the serving plates. His fingers pointed between Leola and her sister. "Gods—you two are the Prophesied Pair, aren't you?" His voice caught and he swallowed. "I saw that we would get visitors today, but I was not shown how special they would be. All of you—you hold such strong powers in this room. I can see it thrumming through your veins." He turned to Leola, pointedly saying, "You never told us of your power."

"Fire—well, my grandmother believed it stretched to all of the elements. But fire seems to be the strongest."

Boyd sipped his wine, shifting toward her. "Yes, I sense it, too. The flame calls to you. The other elements are also there, just beneath the surface. With proper training, you could master all of them. Who were you training with?"

Her cheeks prickled, not enjoying the number of eyes that watched her. "I wasn't training, actually. Neither of us were. Our grandparents knew Daemon would hunt us down to interfere with the prophecy, so we were hidden and raised among Mundaners." Her throat burned as she spoke of Grandmava. "Our grandmother put a block on our powers so we couldn't be tracked," she explained.

"Amazing. That is why Daemon couldn't find you all of those years. Thank the Gods. And as far as you know, Daemon still can't track *you*?" Boyd kept his amethyst eyes on hers.

Leola was grateful for the subject change. "Yes. He hasn't caught up to us yet, and I've used magic all day."

Boyd nodded once, continuing, "Good. Well, if you didn't attend the Academy and you didn't receive any training, what can you do? Aside from wielding the flames, of course."

She blinked at him, not understanding the question. "Sorry? What are the other options?"

Boyd tapped his chin, explaining, "Hand-to-hand combat training. Horsemanship. Cavalry tactics. Archery. Martial arts. Spellwork. Those sorts of things."

Leola perked up, eyes trailing toward her sister's as she said, "We were athletes growing up."

"More modesty there. We did archery and fencing until... well, until our grandmother left on Assignment." Juniper's smile faded. "But Leo was the best Archer at our school. She set records."

She added, "And you're still the best fencer, Bug."

"Well, those are skills that can be utilized," Boyd said as he tilted his glass toward Leola, and she grinned.

Gordon drummed his fingers on the table. "Y'all will need a few days to recuperate until you get your next vellum. Let's use that time to train your other skills. I can help you learn the water... and then the ice. I'm not able to access each of the elements—as you may one day be able to. However, I have many skills in my arsenal that will be useful to you." He turned toward the others. "In addition, we can refresh *all* of your combat training. You will need it, even more so now that your magic is being tracked. In a few days, we will send y'all on your merry way, ready to kick some Opasteg ass. That is, if you're interested in learning."

Levi grinned. "Absolutely yes," he responded as his knuckles cracked between his hands. "It feels like years since I've sparred."

"Great, we'll start tomorrow then." Boyd returned to the table with what looked to be some kind of decadent dessert. He flashed a fond smile toward each of them as he said, "Tonight, we dine on Chocolate Mousse. Tomorrow, we will train the younglings who will save us all."

Each of them delved into the rich chocolatey dessert while the men shared hilarious stories. At one point, Juniper even laughed so hard that water came out of her nose. They lasted for about an hour before the adrenaline of the day wore off and they were forced to give into their exhaustion and retire to their sleeping quarters. Boyd denied their offers to help with cleaning the kitchen as Gordon led them to their rooms. Levi excused himself to prepare for bed—and to check on Benn, presumably. Leola wanted to do the same, but stopped herself and followed Juniper to their shared room instead.

Leola wrapped her freshly-washed curls into a silk wrap. She'd considered glamouring the curls to a blown-out style, but had decided against it, the wet hair granting her a sense of normalcy that she clung to with an iron grip. She leaned back on the plush gold bedding, waiting for her sister to finish her shower in the en suite bathroom.

Her mind drifted to her grandmother—to her unknown fate. *Did she escape? Will we ever know? What will I tell Papa... if I see him again?* The sounds of the mob shouting Juniper's name filled her mind, and she had to clench her fists to prevent flames from erupting.

A light knock sounded at the door, distracting her from her anxious mind.

"Come in," she called.

Levi padded into the room and sat on the edge of Juniper's bed. "Hey, how are you doing?"

She figured he knew the answer to that. "Meh," she replied.

"Yeah." His eyes trailed over the room, and he sighed. "Benn's power reserve is replenishing—slowly, but he will recover. I had Boyd take a deeper look at him. I'm trying to keep my magic trail minimal. Luckily, Carole didn't have a track on Benn's power, so it would be impossible for him to track us this far into the future. Especially because no one knew where we headed—not even your grandmother. Gods, I don't even think Benn knew where we'd land. I can't ask him, though, because he nearly killed himself with that power use."

"So, it's true. He almost died then." Her voice was so hollow that she didn't recognize it.

Levi laughed, but it was weak. "I'm actually surprised he survived. I tried to play it cool in the alley, but it was... it was a really close call."

She looked away, her thoughts roaring at the possibility of losing Benn. She scolded herself for all of the emotions that swirled within her and tried to pretend they weren't there. She kept her eyes straight ahead, seeing nothing.

"He'll live." Levi seemed to sense what was going on within her mind and he whispered, "He's done this once before, but it wasn't this bad. He should be awake by tomorrow." Her eyes snapped to meet Levi's as he shifted off the bed.

She hissed, "Nearly *killed* himself for people he barely knows? Is this common in your world?"

"Well, I *am* his best friend," he clarified, before his shoulders deflated. "And yes. But that is a story for Benn to share. Not me. And it's *your* world now, too." He trailed his fingers along the angles of the room, moving to each corner.

"Should I even ask what you're doing?"

"Looking," he answered, not sparing her a glance, tracing the window. He flashed a knowing grin. "*Seeing.*"

"That pun was painful."

"I'm looking at the wards and the architecture. Making sure we're protected and have a way out of here, if needed. Always, always, *always* have an escape plan. In fact, you should have three." He then turned toward her with a serious look on his face. "These males are trustworthy, but we should be wary of anyone else we meet. Keep any information about our plans vague. Stay alert. Watch your back. Tell Juniper the same."

He walked out of the room, his parting words leaving her chilled to the marrow.

CHAPTER 24

— LEOLA —

Year: 1996
4 July
Papaver, Heri

L EOLA PEERED OVER HER SHOULDER to the vintage analog clock on
the nightstand. Blinking, she attempted to clear her blurred vision. She'd slept
for over twelve hours. She stretched and sat up, pulling her knees close to her chest.

She assumed her sister would still be exhausted—much like the others. Leo had
been the only one to return in decent shape after their visit to Daemon's cavern. Benn
and Levi had nearly lost their souls. Then, Benn had nearly died warping them to
Papaver, a feat that she wanted to throttle him for.

Her mind snagged on Benn. Not hearing his voice for all of these hours had left
a strange void in her chest. It was a new feeling, one that she didn't care for. She
cracked her neck, trying to pull herself out of whatever haze that worrying about his
well-being had put her in.

Not the time to worry about a stranger. Not the time. Not the time, she repeated.
He's a stranger.

She shoved that thought aside, as she'd done dozens of times since they escaped. She tried to lock the thoughts into the little box she kept in her mind, but it popped back open, pulling her deeper into the chasmic space of her anxiety. Her hands numbed as she thought of the moment she'd thought Juniper died—she'd hardly recovered from that. And because her mind was cruel to her, her grandmother's face popped into her mind.

I couldn't save her. She forced air into her lungs. *We would all be dead if we'd tried. Juniper isn't going to die. She's alive.* She shook her head, as if that would help her raging distress. *She's alive. She's alive. Alive.*

Sweat trickled down the back of her neck. The room closed in. The tightness in her chest was familiar, one that she constantly battled—the first time being when her grandmother had disappeared and many times since then. *Out. Out. I need to get out. Breathe, Leo.*

Her chest felt as though someone was sitting on it. Her vision muddled, making it clear that the breathing techniques her therapist had taught her wouldn't do a damn thing to fight off this anxiety attack. One that had been impending since the relic had ripped them out of the Modern-Era.

Out. Get out. Air. I. Need. Air. She warped into the en suite bathroom. *Breathe. One. Two. Three.*

She turned the water on, the heat radiating from her palms warming the icy water. She focused on breathing as she cupped her hands, creating a small pool under the faucet. It boiled in seconds. She splashed the water on her face and dried it with a soft towel. She turned, meeting her own stale expression in the mirror, as the water on her hands evaporated to steam.

Fiery child. Her grandmother's voice playing in her mind was like a kick to her chest.

Her eyes widened, fearing what her power—what she'd do if provoked any further. *If I don't get some air, I'll burn this house down. No, no.*

Flames overtook her eyes. She threw water on her face once more, brushed her teeth, and warped into the hallway in record time.

She leaned against the dark wallpaper, clinging to the wall as she took deep breaths. The pounding between her temples matched the beat of her thundering heart; the lightness of her limbs clued her in to what she'd been denying—that she would pass out. Her eyes stayed closed as she inhaled, her gasps audible, trying to convince her mind that she was intaking oxygen and not breathing through a paper bag—though she wished she had one. It was her go-to strategy in moments as desperate as these.

Not today, demons, she thought as she continued to force rhythmic breaths. Today was simply *not* the day she could afford to have a panic attack. There was never a preferable time—but today, she didn't have the time for these kinds of emotional shenanigans. Her scalding palms trembled. She lost the battle, and fearing that she may burn down this exquisite house, she sank to the ground and put her head between her knees. At least, if she did lose consciousness, the fall to the ground would be short.

Not aware of how long she'd been there, or her surroundings, she jumped when a familiar Rosebayish accent muttered, "Someone's running hot this morning."

Her head snapped up. "Benn!"

"Who else?" He flashed a grin at her. "Are you planning on staying down there for a bit?"

Still short of breath, she shrugged. She shifted her hot palms under her knees so he wouldn't notice them shaking, resting her chin on her knee.

"Mind if I join you?"

She nodded her permission.

He sank down as she had, but he was slower to reach the ground. She couldn't decide if it was her mood making him proceed with caution or if it was the near-death experience he'd survived yesterday. She assumed the former, much to her chagrin.

They both stared at the wall in front of them until Benn broke the silence. "It is a great view, isn't it?"

A smile played on her lips as she pushed the dizziness out of her mind. "Sure beats the mud walls I've been staring at in Laviegata."

"You love to stare at walls. Tell me, what do you see in them?" He was looking at her, but she kept her eyes trained on the wallpaper in front of them, her vision still befogging from her disordered breathing.

She sighed. "Answers. I see answers in them. All the things that could go wrong. Or right. Mostly wrong though."

"Hmm." Benn looked at the wall like he was trying to see what she claimed the wall could provide. He turned back to her and smirked. "I have known you for a week now and you are just now telling me that you're a Seer?"

Laughter burst through her lips as she said, "Looks like the near-death dance has made you even *more* sarcastic. And here I was thinking that was impossible."

Benn snorted. "Not quite. I'm just trying to keep up with you, Leo."

Her heart fluttered at that comment—at the use of her treasured nickname. It sounded so *familiar.* Her eyes locked on his. "Keep up with me? I heard *you* were the most powerful time-wielder in history. It should be *me* trying to keep up with *you.*"

"You say that like you are not one of the legs of the legendary Prophesied Pair." He reached out and grazed his hand against hers, his smile fading. He gave her a once-over that was full of concern, his dark eyes sliding to hers. "Your mind is different this morning. I don't need the power to see when something is bothering you." He took her shaking hands from under her knees as he asked, "Will you tell me what you're thinking?"

"Don't you already know?"

"I'd prefer to hear it from you." His voice remained even.

Her response came out weak. "It's my anxiety; it's a daily struggle, but I can usually manage it." She cleared her throat, hoping to hear her voice come out stronger. It didn't. "But I tend to have panic attacks when I'm v-very stressed. You probably know that already... you know, with that emotion power of yours." She turned back toward the wall, ignoring the fact that his eyes still roamed her face. Her cheeks burned in embarrassment; her dreaded anxiety had interrupted the playful moment between them.

Because now is not the time for being playful, she scolded herself.

"You have endless things to be anxious about right now. We all do. Give yourself some grace."

Leo tightened her grip on her knees, wishing she could melt into a puddle and never reform. "You nearly died yesterday, yet you seem cool as a cucumber."

His laugh was hollow. "Oh, on the contrary. I couldn't be less *cool.*"

She leveled a doubtful stare at him. "*Really?*"

"Really," he responded. "Levi woke me up this morning to force me to eat. I promised him I would." He pushed his hand through his hair, his mouth tilted up toward the corner on one side. "But I left my plate to come find you. I was groggy before we even landed in Papaver yesterday. I knew my power reserve was low. If I'm being honest, I don't even remember landing in that alley. I was so terrified I'd lose my grip on your hand while we were warping through the eras. When I woke up, Levi reassured me multiple times you were here. Sleeping. Safe. But it wasn't enough. I needed to see you for myself. I was—" His voice dropped to a whisper. "Afraid that I'd lost you. I couldn't shake the feeling, despite his reassurance. It was like something was tugging me toward you."

"Levi's going to have your head for leaving your plate," she said as a new blush covered her cheeks—only this time, it was in response to his words.

He tilted her chin, his finger tracing the blush. "And I'll have his head for promising me you were safe, but not mentioning that you weren't... that you weren't okay. I should've come to find you sooner."

Their mouths were so close now that they were sharing the same breath. She knew he could sense the swirl of emotions racing through her mind, but for once,

261

she didn't mind if he picked up on the feelings she couldn't put into words. Warmth spread through her—it wasn't the fire she was so accustomed to, but warmth like the coveted sunshine on her skin in her favorite park.

She huffed a weak laugh. "Well, Benn, you found me. Here I am."

Not your best, Leo. She could almost hear Juniper making fun of her for that failure at flirtation.

His eyes didn't waver from hers. "Indeed I did, Leo." He leaned closer, stopping when he was just short of her lips, and whispered, "I can help with the panic spells. Just say the word."

"You would do that?" The question sounded silly, considering he had nearly died yesterday moving them through the eras. But that was for Levi's safety as well. It felt new—*different*—to ask him to use his power to help *her*.

"When are you going to accept that I'd do anything to help you?" His smile was soft, but his eyes remained serious. "You want me to beg; is that it?"

She leaned into his touch, feeling the warmth of his presence against her mind. Knowing how close he'd come to death, she couldn't ignore how protected and seen she felt with him—despite all her efforts to suppress their connection. At that moment, she vowed never to take it for granted again. His eyes moved to her lips, inching imperceptibly closer. Her heart fluttered; he was waiting for her to close the distance.

She flinched back, remembering the silk wrap that still held her curls. Instinctively, her hand moved to the wrap, and he blocked it with a chuckle, like he knew what she'd been reaching for.

"Benn! Are you serious right now?" Levi appeared next to them in the hallway. Leola jumped at his furious tone, ducking her head into the injunction where Benn's shoulder met his collarbone. "Boyd said you needed to eat to replenish your power reserve. I come back inside, your plate is untouched, and you're nowhere to be found. Sorry, Leo, he's grounded until that plate is clean."

At the reminder of his low power reserve, an embarrassing tremble ran through her limbs, the tightening in her chest squeezing to the point of pain.

Benn sent Levi a scathing look. "Give me two minutes and I'll be back in the kitchen."

"Benn—" Levi warned.

His eyes were back on hers as his words cut Levi's off. "*Two* minutes."

"I'm counting. Do not make me come back up here," Levi admonished before disappearing.

She held a hand up. "Don't."

His eyes widened. "Why the hell not? And do not tell me you're fine. You're shaking right in front of—"

"Levi's right. Your power reserve is the priority." She rolled her neck, attempting to look stronger than she felt. "You shouldn't use it on... this." She sighed as she gestured to herself.

"We talked about this before we left the Camp." His jaw hardened. "I can respect your boundaries, but you're obviously in pain and I wield emotions. Use me."

"Your power—"

"Stop," he released an aggravated sigh. "It's small magic to help you. I know I pushed my limits yesterday, but easing your pain won't affect my power."

"*You scared me yesterday,*" she whispered. The words were out now, and she couldn't get them back. Her trembling became more pronounced, the shaking traveling to her jaw. He watched her with an intensity that should have made her squirm, his eyes jumping from her hands to her jaw. "If you promise it won't affect you, then fine. Maybe you could help with the anxiety—just this once."

His calming power washed over her skin like a warmed blanket—the impending panic attack subsided—clearing her brain of the fog. She sagged against the wall, eyes remaining on his, placing a soft touch on his jaw as she breathed, "Thank you."

She leaned forward to brush a kiss on his cheek. It was an awkward angle from the way they were leaning against the wall.

"*Benn!*" Levi's command came from the nearest stairwell.

Benn shook his head, rising to his full height, as he rolled his eyes and said, "I'm being summoned."

He offered a hand to her; she took it, pulling herself up. His hands cradled her face as he pressed a soft kiss to her forehead.

"Until next time, Leo." He disappeared from the hallway before she could say anything.

— BENN —

He pushed his plate to the center of the table; after three helpings of leftover chili, he was uncomfortably full. Now that he'd slept and ate, his restless energy was unbearable. Levi had demanded that he remain at the kitchen table while the others trained; he absolutely despised that.

His mind wandered to his earlier conversation with his best friend.

"Truly foolish. Idiotic. Amateur behavior," Levi scolded him once he saw his power reserve had surpassed 50%. That meant he was on the path to recovery, so his friend must have deemed that as the perfect time to jump on him.

He tried to reason with Levi. "I hadn't eaten since before our visit to Daemon's prison, which was stupid, but I truly didn't have a chance. Yes, I warped us all 140 years in the future and 878 miles away from our enemies—which is a stretch—but look, we're all alive."

Levi scowled, hissing at him, "You almost left me—you're my best friend and you almost died. *Again.* I'd have rather been in danger than know you might die next to me in some rat-infested alley. Where we would have been stuck, by the way, if you'd died. I wouldn't have even been able to take you to Sena—or even to Asha. You're the only one who can time warp here, you know. You would have left me with your corpse." Levi crossed his arms, shaking his head in disbelief.

Benn felt a twinge of guilt. "The important thing is that we're all safe; Carole and Daemon and any other Ope twat won't know where to look for us."

"You're a real prick, you know that?" Levi scoffed. "No, the important thing is that *you* are alive. We can take any Ope twats that come our way *together*. I'm still mad at you. And no, I do not forgive you."

His eyes traveled out the window to where Leo was training with Gordon.

Levi followed his eyes as he said, "Would have been a damn shame if you'd died before that flower could blossom into anything."

He grimaced at the word choice but kept watching her. "What in the Ancestral hell do you mean by *flower*?"

"You know, your budding love story? *Situationship?*" Levi shrugged. "I don't know what to call it in wartime."

"Anything but *that* word, please. Spend two days with those Poppycallians and now you're using their cringey terms?" He laughed, earning him a smile from his friend.

Levi's eyes flashed and his smile dropped. "Still mad at you."

He was quiet for a moment, then he asked, "You saw something, didn't you?"

"Nothing you don't already know. She was terrified for you yesterday." He looked down at the plate in front of Benn, pushing it toward him. "Eat and hydrate. If you come outside before your power reserve is past 60%, I'll have Leola burn you to a crisp."

The others trained with Gordon and Boyd from a shaded spot in the garden. He was apprehensive to trust their hosts, but they were vetted Underground soldiers;

Levi had checked the surrounding areas for threats which offered Benn some peace. They wouldn't have ever come to this house if Levi didn't wholly trust that they were safe here. While he would *never* admit it, he was relieved to be able to rest; he was exhausted. Additionally, he was intrigued to see what kind of forces the sisters could become with mentorship.

Both Juniper and Levi trained with weapons. Predictably, Juniper was a strong fighter—light on her feet with impeccable balance and rhythm honed from years of fencing. Her sword movements were more fluid than professors he'd trained with at the Academy. Both Levi and Juniper had high levels of confidence, which promised to make their sparring sessions intense and entertaining.

"Don't go easy on me, Runes," Levi quipped as his wooden sword met hers with a crack.

Juniper chuckled. "Is that what's happening? Because it seems like I'm kicking your ass."

"You're smaller than him. Use it to your advantage," Boyd coached from the sideline.

Levi huffed. "Says the one with a *coach*." His skill with a sword was undeniable; he had an edge given that he'd begun weapon training in his foster home, but Juniper kept him on his toes, each movement of her feet making it clear she wouldn't be easily disarmed.

Good. A little humbling for those two, Benn thought.

His eyes drifted toward the mass of auburn curls, remembering their encounter in the hallway this morning.

He'd woken up in a sweat, not able to breathe or think; he assumed she'd been asleep still, her mind remaining restful. Because of that, he couldn't sense her mind fully like he'd gotten used to doing. He could track the emotions of a sleeping person, but it required more power; he'd resisted the urge to check on her, to let his power recharge.

Later, her sudden panic washed over him like a drugging haze with a bitter, tar-like taste, narrowing his senses to her. He recognized it, the same as the crushing fear he'd felt from her back in the barracks when it had overtaken him. He'd ditched his plate, the second Levi left him unattended, to find her. She spotted him and a wave of relief washed over her, surprising him. Then, she'd accepted his help—a seemingly impossible step for the firepoweress.

Just yesterday, he'd thought himself a dead man, but today, everything was different.

She pulled back from Gordon, wiping sweat off her forehead as she raised her hand to her hair and spun her wrist. The curls lifted into a bun of copper and henna—the shorter pieces framing her face as she remained laser-focused on the waterpower's instructions.

She's been practicing. To his delight, she'd gotten more skilled with the smaller magic he'd been teaching them. He'd been comatose for all of a day, and now, both the sisters had new talents to add to their arsenal.

He rose from the patio table so he could get a better look at her—her brows furrowed in concentration as she started to push streams of water into the air, flowing like streams in a fountain.

Holy demons, she wields two elements. He gasped. There she went, surprising him again.

Gordon was instructing her, but Benn couldn't make out the words from this far away. As Leola juggled the streams, they turned to steam. Leola huffed in frustration.

She tried again.

Again.

And again.

With each failed attempt, the water streams evaporated faster, signaling her exasperation. There was no way she was going to be able to summon the ice unless her mind was calm. He could help with that—from afar, of course—but he was itching to be near her. He chewed on his cheek, weighing the consequences.

He peeked into the area of his mind that showed his power reserve, seeing that his power was at 58%. Levi would riot.

Fuck it. He warped to Leola, startling her.

"*Gods!*" She jumped a foot backward and heat brushed his face. Not fire—this was heat that radiated from her body. Not only was she glaring at him for breaking her focus, but he could sense the anguish coming off her in tangible waves.

Levi started to protest, but he cut that off with a hand. The yard was wrapped in a rare, lovely silence—the kind Benn only experienced when he froze time. Time-freezing, a coveted power unique to his lineage, required immense energy and always stirred memories of his mother. These memories left him hollow, plaguing him with longing to ask her the questions that haunted his heart.

Despite that, it was power so many yearned for and today, he would exercise the power to show Leo what it was like to *freeze* something. More importantly, he'd give her a moment to fail without an audience. For all parts of her that were unyielding and tenacious, Benn saw deeper into her fierce mind. It was paramount for her to appear strong at all times; it seemed to be both the glue that fused her stubborn being together and the barrier that stood in her way. He was determined to create a safe space for her to be vulnerable in.

Another perk of this capability was that he could unfreeze beings around him— a skill he preferred to keep close to his chest, but he was breaking all of the rules today. He threaded his fingers through hers, unfreezing her.

She was already yelling, "I had it!"

He kept his voice gentle as he explained, "I thought I might show you something."

She hadn't noticed the time freeze.

"Well, I'm working with Gordon on—" Her eyes shifted from his to Gordon's, who Benn now stood in front of. Her head tilted to the side. "What in the Ancestral hell? Is he—"

"Frozen," he answered. "They all are."

Her mouth opened, shock widening her eyes to caramel moons.

"It won't hurt them. Listen, I know how you feel about failure," Benn said as he lifted his other hand to her face. "I told you before that you could be vulnerable with me—I meant it. Try to summon the ice. Fail and fail again. It's okay. No one will see. It's only us here now. The second you want me to resume time, I will."

She eyed him, then the others, as she asked, "You used your time magic... to give me privacy?"

"I thought it might help to have less eyes on you while you learn something new." The nervousness she elicited from him left him adding, "Or, if it doesn't help, I could soften your emotions and return back to my spot in the garden."

Her grip tightened on his hand. "No!" She lowered her voice, composing herself as she continued, "No, this is fine. You're fine here."

Uncertainty flickered in her brown eyes. She dropped his hand, but he kept his touch on her cheek. "Uh—once we stop touching, you'll freeze along with the time. A bit strange, I know."

"Keep your hand there then. I need both of my hands free."

His stomach tightened at the permission she granted him—at the uncharted waters they'd entered. A strange sensation of heat flooded his senses—different from her firepower. It was familiar but... also not. He racked his brain trying to determine what the feeling was until—

"In case you were wondering, your presence is *not* helping me cool down." Her cheeks reddened as she avoided his eyes.

Timidity blanketed her, and he wanted to smile as the soft emotion encased her. It was like a looming darkness in her mind, a lingering storm cloud.

"Summon the flames," he said.

A pleasant heat coursed through him—the same as what she felt as they moved through her; there was no *cooling* Leola. He had been able to sense fire running through her veins the minute the block was removed from her power. But he'd never observed her power when she was summoning the water.

"Maybe the key is not cooling you, but modifying the flame somehow—channeling the power in a different direction. Summon the water," he said, earning him a look of disbelief. "Baby steps."

He focused on the power that lived beneath her skin—it was as it usually was: hot, roaring, rushing. Then, something changed. The water didn't dim the heat, instead, it ran alongside it in a parallel fashion.

A flowing sphere of water hovered above her hand. With his hand still resting on her cheek, he focused on the path the power circulated through her body until he could imagine it.

"Turn it to steam," he said.

The parallel streams of power—fire and water—melded together. He opened his eyes and found hers. He shifted, not expecting her to be watching him. "You have dual-capabilities. It is rare for elementals. This is going to sound strange." He used one hand to hold up two fingers, keeping his hold on her chin with the other. "But your powers are running parallel. Mine do the same thing, though they aren't elemental. When you use the steam, they are connecting and working together. To separate them, you need to pull them apart. Envision them in your mind—like a river splitting into different streams, or like when you rip a paper towel on the pre-cut lines." He closed his eyes again so he could envision the path.

"I think I feel what you're talking about," she said, her uncertainty loud in his mind.

"You can do it, Leo." The ball of water she'd been holding boiled. He opened his eyes to look down as the sphere morphed until it was a swirling ball of flame and water—moving in parallel, never touching. They appeared to be fighting for control, a sign that she was taking his advice. Expecting ice, Benn jumped when the flame turned violet.

Leola gasped as she squealed, "I feel it! It is cold! Colder than *ice.*" Her eyes were closed, but the flame flared as it was tested by its maker.

"Incredible," he murmured.

Purple flames lined both of her hands. This was not ice—but a cold fire?

"Leo, it is—" He trailed off, the words dissolving into nothingness.

She opened her eyes but didn't react to what she looked at. He felt the defeat flood her as she commented, "It is not ice."

The flames dimmed. He reached out as she pulled her hands back.

"No." She held the flames to her chest, like they were kittens. "I don't know this flame. It might hurt you." Wonder twinkled in her mind.

"Flame is flame. I'll forgive you for any pain you cause me." His hand reached into the flame, and he fought the urge to recoil, but when his hands met the flame, he felt nothing. He sensed her apprehension, and understood. "You don't need to hold back."

"You sure about that, Wyndmere?"

"You think I'm that fragile? A little burn won't take me ou—*fucking hell.*" He pulled his hand back to see it blistering. "What in the demons was that? That is *not* fire."

"Of course it's not. It's more like ice. *Iceflame.*" He watched again as she pulled the flames up to her face and nuzzled them as if they were cuddling her right back. They slithered to her shoulders like snakes. He was both terrified and awe-struck. Once her hands were free, she took his withering hand in hers.

He winced and she mirrored the expression. "The flame only burns people if I want it to. I thought maybe the ice would do the same. You got all cocky, so I tested it out," she said as her eyes flicked to his. "I was right, as usual."

"As usual," he deadpanned. "*Iceflame?* Care to explain that word? They didn't teach us that at the Academy."

She shrugged, touching one of the flames that was curled around her neck. "I coined that name. An ice that *burns.*"

He was quiet, watching her again.

She gazed up at him. "Thank you for this moment."

"Thank *you* for the blisters."

To his surprise, she began laughing. Laughing so hard that he thought she might fall over. The sound was as lovely as it was contagious, and soon, he was joining her. In the frozen world was their laughter, an orchestra in the silence. Her eyes collided with his and her breath caught.

He framed her face with his hands, searching her eyes for the sign he needed. She closed the distance between them. Her lips grazed his before she pulled back to gauge his reaction. He pulled her to him, pressing their bodies together and kissed her full lips. She kissed him with the same desperation and ferocity that he met her with. All of the tension that had built around them—between them—channeled into this moment. Her hands fisted in his shirt, pulling their bodies flush. His head dizzied. Unfocused. Dazed. He held the kiss until he had to pull back, wishing so badly that they could stay in this moment forever. She tried to pull his mouth back to hers, but he simply placed a chaste kiss on her cheek. He trailed a finger down her cheek touching her swollen lips. Her brown eyes blinked at him, full of a new heat.

His power reserve had dwindled back to 50% and he couldn't risk losing more while he was recovering. He needed to release the time freeze. He flashed a grin, not wanting to show how much power he'd used to maintain the freeze.

"*Later,*" he whispered, stepping out of her arms as he dropped his hands. She froze, her hands still reaching toward him. He strode to where he'd previously been watching and released his hold on time. Time resumed as it had been before.

"*Benn!* We agreed, no bullshit before you were at 60%..." Levi had been looking in the direction where Benn had warped, so his eyes landed right on Leola. He whirled toward where Benn now stood. He tried to look innocent, but he knew he failed the moment he made eye contact with his friend. Levi looked at him and then back at Leo again, whose face was flushed.

Juniper's sing-song tease floated into the air. "If you wanted to make out, you could have just *told* us."

Boyd and Gordon laughed.

Levi smirked, crossing his arms over his chest. "I wouldn't even be mad if you weren't at... 49.5%? *Demons*, what were you two doing?"

Purple flames surrounded them all and everyone gasped. Even Benn jumped out of the way of the flames. "He was helping me find these," Leola said, a twinge of excitement lighting up her voice.

He looked toward her and saw that the flames had engulfed her body. She was covered in a magnificent glow of amaranthine.

"Don't worry, it'll only burn you if I want it to." She smirked.

Juniper crossed the yard to be by her side. "Shit, you're totally cooler than me now."

A crown of amethyst flame erupted on top of Juniper's head. "Impossible, Bug."

Gordon reached toward the flames, comparing it to the ice in his hand. "I have never seen anything like this. It's not ice—"

Boyd looked to Leola, like he was seeing a Goddess. His eyes shimmered as he examined the flames. "No, it causes blisters, frostbite, delirium. It's different from ice."

Leola flashed a bright smile as she said, "I call it Iceflame."

CHAPTER 25

— LEOLA —

TURNS OUT THE YEARS she spent fencing and practicing archery were proving to be quite useful. She found herself wondering if her grandparents' requirement that she participate in those sports had been intentional—if they'd been inadvertently trying to help her gain combative skills during her Mundane childhood. After a near perfect round of target practice, Benn had let out a low whistle.

She chuckled, remembering the mock bow she had given him. "Care to try, Wyndmere?"

He had leaned in so close that his lips glanced off of hers. "No, thank you. I'll beat you some other time." He had moved away as a blush sprinted to her cheeks, much to her embarrassment.

Juniper's voice shook her out of her thoughts. "Earth to Leo."

She blinked, looking up to find her sister smirking at her.

"Daydreaming again, are we?" Juniper used small magic to twist her braids into a bun on top of her head. "I'm going to shower. Need anything out of the bathroom?"

"I have everything I need; leave me here to rot." She yawned, collapsing into a heap on her bed.

———

A soft knock woke her.

Disoriented and unsure how long she'd been sleeping, she said, "Come in."

The door opened and Benn strode into her room the same moment she realized she was *still* in a towel. He paused his steps, his eyes catching on the towel for a heartbeat before he met her gaze. Standing across from him, her towel fell short over her lithe frame. She shifted, trying to conceal both her nervousness and anything the towel didn't cover.

"Um, *hi*," she said quietly.

"Um, hi back." His words adopted an uncharacteristic hoarseness, but he kept his eyes trained on hers as he shut the door behind him. He cleared his throat. "I came by to tell you that Levi is going to inspect the wards in here again. He's working on something with Boyd in the library. He didn't want you two to fall asleep before he had the chance to come in."

She nodded, wondering if that was his only reason for coming by.

Recovered now, he took a casual stance against the doorframe as he said, "My guess is Levi doesn't want to startle a sleeping Juniper. He's got trauma from the claws." He gestured to his face. "So, uh yeah—stay awake for a bit. He shouldn't be long."

"Noted. I'll be sure to pass the message to Juniper so there are *no* accidents tonight." A light smile played on her lips at his nervous energy. She had never seen him this *flustered*. She schooled her face into a cool mask as she asked, "Was there anything else, Wyndmere?"

A muscle in his jaw ticked, a small but telling crack in his cool composure. "Look, about earlier... I wasn't expecting that to happen at that moment. I don't

275

regret it, but I didn't cast the time freeze with that in mind. I need you to know that."
His gaze was so sincere that she couldn't fight the full smile that broke on her lips.

His eyes heated as she walked to him, kissing him the way he had kissed her earlier that day. It was slow and full and explorative. He shifted, deepening the kiss as his hands brushed against the curls framing her face—not pulling, but tugging like he couldn't resist testing the texture with his fingers. Kissing Benn like this dizzied her and she longed to stay in this moment—in his arms, where she was safe and understood and treasured. His grip in her hair tightened; what had started as a slow, explorative kiss blossomed into something much more passionate. His fingertips grazed her shoulder, moving lower and stilling once they met the fabric of her towel.

He pulled back, resting his forehead against hers; they were both breathless. "That towel is going to be the death of me," he quipped.

She had a fleeting thought that in another world, she would have taken the risqué move and dropped the towel, if not only to tease him, but this was not another world. In this world, their time was limited, their private moments rare... and her younger sister was sharing this room with her. So, she used one hand to keep the towel fastened and used the other to pull his face to hers, kissing him hard, reveling in the groan that rumbled in his throat.

The shower switched off. She pulled back, holding his dazed eyes in hers, and whispered, "Maybe when Levi comes back, you can come back with him." She sent a pointed look toward the bathroom door. Her sister would want details that required privacy, so she pushed him gently away from her and said, "Until next time."

Her sister's voice called from the bathroom, "Benn, I know you're out there. Don't let Leo kick you out on my behalf."

She rolled her eyes at her sister's keen instincts.

The door handle was already in his hand, but her heart warmed at the look in his eyes; he was asking for her permission without asking out loud.

She gestured to her bed and tossed a soft smile over her shoulder. "I guess you can stay a little longer. Make yourself comfortable." She was still in a towel, after all. It seemed off-putting to tell Benn to close his eyes after the intimate moment they shared only a few minutes ago, but he had never seen her naked... and this was not going to be the first time. Unfortunately. When she turned to tell him to shield his eyes, she smiled sheepishly, because he had, of course, done that without needing to be asked.

"Sena raised a gentleman," she commented, gathering the sleeping clothes she'd stolen from the thrift store—an oversized band t-shirt and boxer shorts.

Benn chuckled. "Her and Asha."

It wasn't a hair wash day, so she used small magic to unfurl the tangles in her curls and pinned them up in a clip.

Juniper walked out in a nearly identical outfit, already saying, "I'm so glad you guys finally went for it. Truthfully, Benn-ifer, I didn't think you had it in you to make the first move. Though I must say, Levi and I had a bet going and you severely messed that up for me with today's move." She plopped onto her bed with a dramatic sigh. "I had you pegged for a more *private* setting for the first kiss. But I didn't know you could *stop* time—and *what's* more private than that?"

Leola's cheeks reddened as she sent her sister a scalding, *stop-talking* look.

He snorted. "You made a bet with a *Seer*? And here I was, thinking you were smarter than that, Juniper."

Juniper gasped. "That lying snake. I should've known he knew something when he moved his bet up to today."

Leola's cheeks burned, needing this conversation to end. As soon as possible. She groaned, but even her grievances didn't dim her curiosity. "What did you even bet? A ration card?"

Juniper answered, more focused on securing her braids into a silk wrap than the conversation, "A sandwich from our favorite deli once we're back home."

Home. The word crashed through her. Juniper had said it so casually, like the thought was not so impossible—so unreachable. She'd kept any thought of going home in the mental box where she stored useless ideas. Her cruel mind projected an image of her grandparents. Her Papa. She was now grappling with the fact that *they* had seen their grandmother, and Papa probably had no clue where Grandmava had even been deployed.

Or does he? Does he... know where we are? Given that Benn had not even fully known where they would land, the answer was definitely no.

His squeeze on her hand freed her from her own mind as she took a deep breath. Calming magic tingled across her skin—there he was, studying her like she was the only thing of importance in all of Heri.

He kept her hand in his and leaned back against the wall. "Could I partake in any of the other bets you and Levi make? It's been a boring few days. I could use the distraction." His mouth lifted at the corner.

"Sure, but I'm not cluing you in to *any* that involve you or Leo," Juniper said as her eyebrow raised, waiting for him to challenge her.

Raising his free hand, Benn replied, "Of course not. I wouldn't dream of getting in between a Runes sister and a winning bet."

Juniper examined her red-tipped nails, her voice holding a note of teasing. "That's wise. I'd think you would have enough going on these days... you know, with Leo's flamin' hot attitude."

"*Okay,*" Leola cut in. "Let's all relax." She'd had enough of this banter. "Bug, we all know that you're just grouchy because Daemon still has that hold on your power. Leave my *attitude* out of it."

Juniper sat back against her pillow with an exasperated huff. "Ugh. You are so right, that has been chapping my ass all day. Sorry you had to see that, Benn." She fanned herself, her voice taking on a high-pitched tone full of mimicry. "I'm usually a much more pleasant lady."

"Let's hope the *pleasantry* is out the window the next time you see that silver-haired prick," Benn replied.

Juniper leaned forward, away from her pillows as her voice dropped an octave. "Benn, there was something I didn't get a chance to tell you before we left Roswell. Someone helped me get out of the prison." Her voice shook. "When Daemon caught me, I thought that I was absolutely done for. But then, this woman—a prisoner—caught my attention. She created a portal—at least that's what it looked like. After I hit Daemon, I dove into it and well, it took me to... wherever you found me."

His eyebrows furrowed in confusion as his voice came out raspy. "The time magic that I sensed in that portal seemed to find... me. I sensed the magic, but it was different from any other time magic I'd seen before. The source was really familiar." The wheels in his mind turned. "There are rumors that Josephine is in that prison. I have never let myself hope..."

Juniper's eyes were sad as she said, "I did not get a chance to talk to her or any of the prisoners, but the resemblance was uncanny."

Benn's hand tightened in Leola's, and she wasn't sure if he was aware of the movement. He only nodded then covered his eyes for a fleeting moment.

When he spoke again, his voice was thick with emotion. "You saw my mother. She must have known—somehow—that I'd be looking for you. But, how? I haven't seen her since I was in toddlerhood; she doesn't even know me now."

Juniper seemed to scan the room for information that was not there, her reply as thick as Benn's. "Daemon didn't say anything about you, but he mentioned mine and Leo's names several times."

His grip tightened on her hand even more.

Looking between them, Leola said, "Maybe he has talked to the prisoners about us? You said he was narcissistic and chatty—maybe he's getting worried, so he's giving them information unintentionally. Maybe the prisoners know we're coming for them. Maybe Benn's mother knew who you were, Bug."

His voice was quiet. "If Daemon knows she helped you, my mother surely paid the shining price for casting that time portal." A singular tear fell down his cheek. "We have been targeted, so I assume that if my mother survived the battle, Daemon executed her on the spot for that. All of these years, I did not hold out hope that she had survived, but Asha did. If she did, but is dead now... I don't have the heart to give that news to my sister." His voice dropped to a broken whisper. "She'll be devastated."

Leola used her free hand to press a light touch to his chin, attempting to comfort him as she said, "Gordon told us about Josephine while you were recovering last night. If anyone can survive that prison, it's her."

His eyes left to a far-away place, but, still, he traced circles on her hand.

Levi burst into the room, holding up the key Juniper had stolen from Daemon's prison like a lion presenting their cub. "I found it!"

"Levi Miravale, don't tell me that you *lost* the key I gave you?" Juniper snapped.

"Of course I didn't *lose* the key. I *found* the prison. Boyd and I spent the last hour searching for it. We found it—using this. I know exactly where it is now, and I know how to get there. The path is clear..." Levi trailed off and ran a hand through his hair. "The only snag is the *getting* there part."

"How bad is it?" A frown played across Benn's features.

"The good news is that it's in the Modern-Era. We could access it from any time period, but we need to rescue the prisoners in their current state," Levi explained.

Benn nodded as he said, "Tell me the *bad* news."

Levi rubbed his hands together, looking at each of them before speaking. "Well, it's not entirely bad. Daemon took extra precautions when building this prison. I was able to confirm, with Boyd's help, that the entrance is under a volcano."

Benn scoffed. "What part of that is not *entirely* bad?"

"Boyd and I looked at all possible options of getting inside; the only option is with this key. The wards around it are old and strong. I even tried to channel another vision to create a portal. No luck with that either, and since we no longer have a powerful illusionist with us, that wouldn't work if we tried it anyway." Levi sat at the foot of Juniper's bed and moved the key around in his fingers. "After we went in, he strengthened his wards against all portals and any kind of illusionist magic, so now the only way in... well, it's with this key."

"Through a volcano." Benn's doubt was obvious.

A cloth appeared out of thin air as Levi swiped it across his frames, answering, "The second part of the good news is that we have two of the most powerful poweresses in the room right now—"

A tremble ran through Benn's hand. "*No*."

"—and, Boyd thinks that Leo could get to the door."

"*Are they insane*?" Juniper's voice was incredulous.

"That's ridiculous," Benn snapped at the same time. "She is an elemental poweress, not an immortal."

Leola sucked on her cheek, stomach knotting in apprehension, but she would be the one to decide if she could or could not do something. "I'd be willing to hear why he thinks it could work."

She ignored the expressions of shock aimed her way.

The Seer, however, grinned. "Well, you have an extremely high tolerance for heat—in fact, you're likely immune to fire."

"I am. Boiling water doesn't affect me either," she said as she let out a nervous chuckle. "I hate the idea of testing if I'm lava-proof... only to find out I'm not."

"And I hate the idea of you *dying*, Leo," Juniper added.

Levi ignored her, explaining, "The library downstairs is vast, with years of knowledge and notes. Boyd and Gordon are down there searching for *anything* related to firepower." He sent a look toward Benn that she couldn't interpret. "You're the most powerful firepoweress in our history. We know you can wield different types of flames—who is to say you can't wield lava?" Levi's emerald eyes flashed.

"You know, in the comics, there's a God who walks on lava temporarily. Leo, what if you're a Lava-wielding God?" Juniper was noticeably calmer now.

She chuckled. "You mean, a Lava-wielding Goddess."

Juniper rolled her shoulders, rising off the bed. "I have some energy left; I could go check out the library for a bit. You know, see if I could help them in their research."

Levi stood to follow her as he said, "Wait for me. I need to inspect the wards first, but I'll come with you." He eyed Benn and Leola, like a father preparing to lecture his children. "You two need to *rest*. And like, actually rest, not whatever you were doing in the garden today. And don't think it's because I'm not rooting for this to happen." He pointed back and forth between the two of them. "You two will be solid together. Leo, your power reserve is lower than his now. If we want you to take a deep dive into a volcano, you need to be fully charged."

"Who said *we* wanted that?" Benn's tone was sharp as a dagger.

Levi ran his hands on the walls in the room in the same fashion as he had done the previous night. "Wards are looking pristine. Bravo to me. I see no threats on the horizon. I'll go research for the next few hours with Juniper and our hosts." He clapped his hands together. "Remember what I said. *Please* do not make me come back up here like a camp counselor."

Juniper shifted out of the doorway and back into the room with a conspiratorial grin. "You heard the Seer. If I hear any strange noises in here, it is a Nightshade facial for both of you."

"As fun as this has been—" Benn warped to the doorway, shuffling them out. "Juniper, I'll be in the room across the hall before you are back. No facials necessary."

"PG only, sis," she called with a laugh.

Benn shut the door and crossed the room to her immediately, holding her face in his hands as he searched her eyes like he was burning them to memory.

She spoke first. "You don't like this plan."

"I *loathe* this plan." He sighed, his thumbs stroking her cheeks. "I loathe any plan where you are in danger."

"You nearly *died* yesterday, so I think you owe me a main-character-moment." She pulled him down to the bed as she said, "I get to be the focus of the dangerous plan this time."

Benn muttered some unintelligible curses under his breath. "My plan was not to die. It was to keep you and Juniper safe. I serve the Underground, remember?"

"And what do you think I'm doing? Diving into a volcano for fun?" She leveled a look at him. "Besides, did you not hear Levi? I'm the *strongest* firepoweress in history."

"Why do I feel like you don't believe that?" His words were tender.

"I guess I'm still getting used to it all. Last week, everything I knew—the world I knew—it changed completely. You know, the day we got warped by that relic, I was shopping for my Papa in a Mundaner store. My biggest worries surrounded ration cards and the return of Libata laws. I was powerless. Today, I have a chance at saving so many people. Or possibly even *failing* them." She pulled away from him, resting her head on the pillows behind her. "Everything has changed. My life is unrecognizable. I have new memories and new *trauma* to sort through. For Gods' sake, I have *magical* powers. What will I tell Marilyn?"

His nose scrunched as he asked, "Who the hell is Marilyn?"

"My therapist," she said. "How am I ever going to enjoy a tea shop again? Life as a Mundaner was brutal before. Now I know there's another facet of the world, and it has more problems than I even thought. Who knew that was possible? I've seen what the new regime—Opasteg—is capable of. Poppycallians are being moved to offshore housing if they don't comply with Daemon's sanctions—whatever that means. And now I have the chance to save the entire world from the narcissistic, sadistic secret-society that I thought was a myth last week. The very society that most Mundaners write off as a myth." Her palms heated as she forced air into her lungs.

"Evil performs best when it is hidden in plain sight," Benn murmured, and a familiar sense of calm entered her mind. "All of that is correct... and infuriating. All we can do is take it one day at a time, Leo. You are still human. You are still you. You still have Juniper, and now you have me. As for tea shops, I'll go to tea with you."

"You don't seem like a tea guy," she remarked.

He rolled his eyes. "Obviously, I'm a *tea guy*. Rosebayers worship tea."

The idea of exploring a tea shop with Benn sounded so... domesticated and joyful when the dystopian state of their world haunted her every thought. She had no idea what to think of the longevity of their relationship. She wondered if it would fizzle out as quickly as it had started. So she kept her tone casual. "Maybe we could go to tea in Rosebay. I have always wanted to go there, actually. I can get travel documents now, if we make it out of this."

Benn pressed a kiss to her palm. "We will. And then we'll explore Rosebay— Asha will be dying to meet you."

"Meet me? That sounds..." She dropped the words, not wanting to say them.

His eyes twinkled. "Permanent?"

"Intimidating," she corrected as she sent a pointed glance his way. "Presumptuous."

"Sure, we'll go to my hometown and *not* visit my sister." Benn shrugged. "We can do it your way, Leo. Unless, of course, you wanted her to like you."

She smacked his arm, wondering silently about his powerful, affluent family. She figured she would like his grandmother, especially if she were anything like Grandmava. The thought of her grandmother bought her a one-way ticket straight to anxiety-attack territory.

He was watchful—calculating, as usual. "After tonight, I need one more full day and night to recover so I can warp us to the prison. In the meantime, can I trust you to go easy on yourself for the next few days?" His hand moved to her temples, light and affectionate. "*Emotionally?*"

His observation left her raw. She whispered, "I'm not sure what that is like."

Benn sent her a sad smile as he questioned, "How do you usually deal with panic spells?"

"Therapy. Exercise," she said, avoiding his eyes. "I read... *a lot*."

He murmured, "To escape, I presume?"

She dodged the question, asking one of her own. "What about your emotions? Does your power help you at all to manage them?"

He looked to the ceiling, exhaling. "You know, only Asha has ever asked me that. You remind me of her." She held out hope that Benn would answer her question. He sighed. "Yes and no. I showed signs of my power prior to being initiated—that's common in powerful Ancestral lines. I was not near as powerful as you and Juniper were but still there were *signs*." His eyes flitted to hers as he kept explaining, "When I was a youngling, I had heightened sensitivities to the emotions and moods around me—to the point where the line became blurry on what I was feeling and what others were feeling... what I absorbed versus what I actually felt. Sometimes, I worry that my personality doesn't exist and is just a collection of all of the people I have observed over the years. With training, I learned to tune it out and to categorize myself in one space and others in another. I can't read people's minds but reading emotions—it's *constant* noise. Sometimes, the emotion-bending feels like a curse. I prefer the timepower. It is more taxing on my body, but it is predictable. It is much less taxing on my mind."

"Sounds exhausting," she said simply.

He winced. "I should be grateful to have two great powers. I'm sorry. I shouldn't have ranted like that. I am grateful," he said, his tone robotic. She assumed that this was not the first time he had spoken those words aloud. "Once I learned to shield, things got better. It was like my mind was quiet for the first time. My mind was my *own*. There are some perks, though."

She raised an eyebrow in question. "Such as?"

"I can read people as soon as I meet them. Once I *connect* with the person, their emotions start to have familiar tastes or colors or scents. It makes it easier to find them in a crowd, but the range stops at about twenty miles." He shook his head. "And thank the Gods that it does. I'd need to shield a lot more if the range reached further."

"How does the *shield* work?"

"At the Academy, a professor taught me how to shield. He taught me to build a wall in my mind. It's a brick wall, and I remove bricks one-by-one to let people's emotions in. Same as what I taught you and Juniper in Laviegata... but on a much larger scale." Benn looked at the ceiling, like he was seeing the memory play out in front of him. "That professor changed my life. Prior to that, my mind was filled with noise all the time. Now, it is mostly quiet."

"Mostly?" she questioned.

Benn shifted away from her as his jaw ticked. "I can't shield from you." She flinched. His eyes were pleading on hers. "Believe me, I have tried. I know it's an invasion of privacy for you. For anyone. I wish I could give you that privacy. I have never had a problem shielding from someone before. I've never experienced this kind of break in my power."

Embarrassed heat flooded her cheeks. "Is it something I'm doing?"

"No. At least, I don't think so. I plan to ask Asha about it whenever I see her next." His words came out fast. "For whatever reason, your emotions call to me more *loudly* than others. They were distracting at first—it has gotten easier as I spend more time with you."

Benn was choosing his words with *extreme* caution. She had never seen him ramble.

"Gods, I'm sorry." She laughed, keeping her tone light. "My mind can be a bit hectic. That must be annoying."

"Don't." He held a hand up. "Your mind is not *annoying*." He looked away from her, but grinned before adding, "It is *nice*."

"Nice," she repeated.

She wondered, again, what his life was like prior to going on Assignment. He was the grandson of the Underground's elected leader, his mom was the most powerful time-wielder in history, and he had grown up in some form of a spotlight, though he never acknowledged it. *What is it like, to be under insurmountable pressure for the whole of your life?*

Leola and Juniper were the Prophesied Pair, but they had grown up with a Mundane upbringing—despite the mistreatment, she considered that a privilege. She wondered how different she or her sister would have been if circumstances had been different and they had found themselves at the Academy—if they had grown up knowing who they were.

Benn quirked a brow at her. "I sense wonder. What are you *wondering* about, Leo?"

"You. I'm wondering about you." His eyes flickered with delight, so she kept speaking. "I want to know about you—all of you. Not just what you show others. I like those parts, but I get the feeling that it is only the *tip* of the iceberg." She flicked his nose.

"The *iceberg?*" He laughed.

"The iceberg. The Bennjamin Wyndmere Iceberg."

He leaned closer to her as he said, "One day, I'll show you all of me. But only if you show me all of the Leola Runes Iceberg, too." His eyes shined.

She held out her pinky. "Swear it."

His jaw flexed as he eyed her hand. "In this world, a promise or a *swear* is binding. Are you certain you want that?"

She certainly did not know that detail, though she didn't hate the idea. "A promise to learn more about you? I'm all in."

His eyes seemed to savor hers as he said, "That and a promise to let me into the beautiful mind of yours—fully."

"I thought you said you couldn't shield from me," she questioned as pulled her hand back. "What about you? You have gotten a preview. Are *you* sure you want to keep watching?"

"Absolutely. You're becoming my favorite topic, Runes."

"Then, I swear." She held her pinky out once again.

He looped his finger around hers. A surge of electricity crackled between them.

Her lips parted as she asked, "I'm guessing I didn't imagine that, did I?"

"Nope. Now you're bound to learn about the Benn Wyndmere Iceberg." His mouth tilted into a side smirk. "You have nineteen seasons to catch up on."

She leaned into him, cuddling him closer to her. "Gods, I better start now then."

They spent the next hour talking about normal life—their friends, shows they had enjoyed, concerts they had seen and concerts they still wanted to go to. They talked about traveling—she was not surprised to learn that he was well traveled. She hadn't given much thought to how she'd never left Poppycal, especially since the Coup. There were also laws that prevented Mundaners from crossing regional lines. He vowed to show her all his favorite places and she had made him swear on that promise, too.

CHAPTER 26

— BENN —

Year: 1996
5 July
Papaver, Heri

H E WOKE WITH A FULL POWER RESERVE. He and Levi spent the morning sparring with Juniper and Leola. It was not surprising at all that the sisters were developing an expertise for swordsmanship. They were naturals, and he marveled at the way they intercepted their opponent's moves—it was almost as if it were innate. He had trained for years before he could hold his own with the pell, but here Juniper was, causing him to trip over his own feet.

Again.

She retreated a step, as if to leave time for him to regain his footing, so he used the millisecond pause to his advantage and swung, knocking the wooden sword out of her hand.

"Cheater! I stopped because I thought you'd given up." Her eyes narrowed to angry slits.

"The fight isn't over until the opponent is dying or dead. You would be wise to remember that." His mouth tilted up at the corner, but he was completely serious.

Normally, he would not use a cheap shot while teaching, but they were about to be fighting against real enemies—enemies who wouldn't hesitate. He swallowed the fears that had been building, haunting his private thoughts.

"Fair," Juniper said, as she rolled her shoulders before picking up the wooden sword. "Let's go again, Benny."

By the time he rested against a tree, it was late morning and he was watching Leo practice archery. She'd caught him and chuckled before she performed an aerial cartwheel prior to sinking an arrow right into the target. He'd clapped, offering her a tilt of his head.

She'd responded with, "Surprised I'm good at this, Wyndmere?"

"Not in the slightest, Runes," he'd answered.

They took their lunches into the library that'd been transformed into a war room overnight. Their hosts were well-trained Underground members, and the longer he spent with them, the more impressed he was.

They were from the Modern-Era but had been deployed to the 1996 Papaver Post a few years prior. Once here, they had built a life in Papaver undercover while they carried out missions for the Underground. They'd been soldiers in the past, but now they enjoyed intelligence work—work they had referred to as "leisurely." In their spare time, they invented and sold weapons.

To prevent nepotism, the elected officials of the Underground didn't share membership information—or any classified information—with their kin, so Benn soaked up any information they shared like a sponge.

Gordon tapped the table, now littered with documents, as he said, "I gathered everything I have on Daemon's Inner Circle. Memorize these faces." He laid out a map, smoothing the edges with his palms. "From the HQ library, we were able to pull the most recent map of the volcano—I'll warn you, it's only the surrounding areas. In this folder, you have case studies for different weaponry organized by terrain. You can borrow anything you need from us, so take a look at this before dinner. And finally—"

"A Darkbeing catalogue," Levi whispered. "I've never seen one in real life before."

Gordon's hardened eyes softened as he looked toward Levi. "Highly classified. Boyd thought you'd enjoy reading it."

The wealth of knowledge they had in this room was both inspiring and daunting. If it were not for Gordon placing all of the information into a folder for them to take to the Modern-Era, they would be screwed; Benn's head was throbbing just trying to keep up with all of these details.

Gordon sealed the folder with small magic as he explained, "This is enchanted. It will only open for each of your fingerprints. It cannot be damaged by fire, water, lava—anything. If anyone other than yourselves attempts to open it, it will appear as 'classified' papers, but will self-detonate within four minutes. If that happens, I suggest running like hell."

———

They spent the rest of the afternoon in the library while they planned their journey to the prison and determined their way *out*. A few hours of strategizing had gone by, yet they still hadn't figured out how to capture Daemon, get the prisoners out safely, and not end up dead themselves.

"Daemon chose a volcano in the Salemfir region. HQ reports beasts, monsters, wards, and Opasteg members guarding the area, so we need to warp as close as possible and move on foot from there. The closer we get before tipping off whatever wards Daemon has in place... the better." Benn flipped through a book, tossing comments into the air between Levi and Juniper's bickering.

Levi's eyes flashed. "The second that Juniper uses an *inkling* of power, Daemon will know we're there."

"Let Boyd worry about that piece," Gordon chirped from a large, wooden desk on the opposite side of the room.

"We should still go with my plan," Juniper pressed.

Levi shook his head, looking like he wanted to rip his blonde hair out, and jutted a finger toward the map. "Benn warps us to Modern-Era Papaver in one go. After a break, we warp to Salemfir, rent a car, and travel to the volcano. From there, we can go on foot. I'm telling you... this is the quickest way."

Juniper swatted Levi's hand away from the map. "And I'm telling *you* that if we do that, Benn's power will be depleted again. We will need a few days, at least, to recover. We need the dual-power at his *maximum* potential in case we need to move prisoners. He is no use to us dead—nor powerless."

Levi sent a pleading look toward Benn.

Benn chewed the inside of his bottom lip. "Juniper is right—"

"Ha!" she exclaimed, sticking her tongue out at the Seer.

Benn pushed off the wall as he continued, "As much as I may want to, I can't use all of my power reserve again." He leveled a look at Juniper. "*But* Levi is also correct. We're on borrowed time. We need to act quickly to save as many prisoners as possible. We have no idea what kind of evil shit Daemon is planning. He knows he needs to move quickly—at the very least, he knows that Juniper made it inside his prison. Every second that passes, he gets more desperate to use the stolen power, and we know that using that power is his only path to defeating the Prophesied Pair."

"Which cannot happen," Juniper added. "We could extend Levi's plan over the course of a few days. That still leaves our time-wielder with *limited* power, which is not ideal, but at least it means you're still breathing, Benn." She drummed her fingers on the floor.

Levi's eyes tightened as they darted along the map. "What if we send an Underground taskforce to clear the area for us before we send you two in? That would give us time to recover."

"Calling in help is the best idea I've heard today," said Leola, who was nose-deep in a copy of *Historic Gatherings of Mass Power*. "Daemon is watching our every move. We can't arrive at the prison with no power reserves left to execute the plan or fight—if we need to. What if you asked Asha to help? We could send the people Daemon *isn't* watching to do recon."

Benn blinked a few times, annoyed that he didn't consider that before. "We can ask my grandmother. Sena and Asha could gather forces to set up an Underground camp—a triage center of sorts—where they can plan to take the prisoners after they escape. We can meet with them beforehand. Another team can do recon and sweeps while we prepare. We need to be discreet; once we get the message to them, they'll find a place for a triage camp and give me the coordinates. No vellums or—"

Juniper's voice held a hint of humor. "What about a payphone? Once we land in the Modern-Era? You know, I have always wanted to use one."

"Gods, sometimes I forget how young y'all are." Gordon frowned into his open blueprints. "I'll look around and see if we have any prepaid phones to loan to you. They may not withstand a warp through time, but it's worth a try. Now, don't tell me you have always wanted to use one of *those*, Juniper. They are not so glamorous, girl." He evaporated from the room.

Boyd strode in and said to all of them, "Ah, the Ampules are ready—the Gods are blessing us today. It is an optimal time to test—now that you two are being tracked. Juniper and Levi, I'll need your blood."

He took Juniper's hand in a gentle hold. She jumped when Boyd pricked her finger, immediately taking a tissue from him as he used the Ampule to collect the droplets.

"Don't tell me you're scared of a little blood, Runes?" Levi teased as Boyd did the same to him.

293

"Shut up, Miravale." She squeezed her finger. "And it's only my *own* blood that I don't like seeing. Not the blood of my enemies."

Boyd stalked back to the large desk where Gordon had previously been sitting as he said, "I'll use your blood to create a similar magic trail that you can use to throw anyone hunting you off of your trail. Obviously, Seers can mask magic trails, but the power could not be used unless the Seer was present—until now. I invented these Ampules. They trap a magic trail and mimic it, so it can be used to deter a tracker. I'll prepare a few for you to take with you. When you're ready to use them, simply open the lid and dump the Ampule out. The wind will do the rest. Trackers move quickly." His amethyst eyes glowed as he ended his conversation with a warning: "You will need to warp immediately after opening them, so elect whoever is fastest."

"That would be me," Benn murmured with a raised hand.

"Wonderful. I'll make a few Ampules that Gordon and I can disperse as decoys. The Opes won't know where to look."

"Boyd, you *genius*." Levi smirked.

Levi and Juniper went back to debating the best route to take to the prison. Benn had resorted to letting them hash out the ideas before giving input—neither of them were too keen on listening to his opinions today. He stole a glance toward Leola, seeing without meaning to, into her peaceful mind. His headspace was the complete opposite, acting as his own stockade.

He was desperate to keep his mind occupied; he tried to think of what more he could do to contribute. He would contact his grandmother once they arrived in the Modern-Era, but he didn't have an immediate actionable task and sitting still was the bane of his existence. He trailed his fingers along the numerous jewel-toned spines of the books in front of him.

This had become Benn's favorite room in the home—the dark walls each their own wallpapered mural, the floors a rich oak, and the numerous shelves that showcased the vast collection of books lining every built-in that covered three of the four walls. On the fourth wall were floor-to-ceiling windows that offered a sweeping view of the backyard, Leola sat in a plush chair, her distant gaze lost somewhere beyond the glass. Wisps of her auburn curls escaped the loose bun atop her head, a style he'd come to recognize as a quiet signature style she favored when thoughts weighed on her mind. He was drawn to her, captivated by the small, unspoken details he noticed only because he'd studied her at length. He was bereft, yearning for her in a way that left his soul aching to be closer.

Her mind had called to his from the moment they'd met. Again, he tried to fortify his shields, the defenses he'd trained so carefully—but with her, they slipped away like mist. Others' thoughts intruded, muddling his own. But hers? Her presence embraced him, a spell that threaded throughout his mind, comforting and undeniable.

It was like their souls were bound by an invisible, ancient filament, an enchantment both natural and otherworldly. He often found himself wishing for Asha's insight, providing some answer as to why this auburn-haired sorceress could unravel his shields with little to no effort. He'd trained against every supernatural force he knew, yet nothing had prepared him for her arrival.

His shields, once able to block every stray emotion within twenty miles, vanished in her presence. In that undefended space lived a pull so deep, a longing so profound, a connection so vital that he wished this tether—or whatever it was— would remain unbreakable. Each touch and intimate moment they had shared in recent days only intensified the mystifying pull.

"Stop ogling my sister and start reading," Juniper cut into his thoughts, appearing next to him to grab a book off the shelf.

He didn't have a comeback, so he shook his head and returned his efforts to raising a shield impenetrable to her mind. Nothing worked. He didn't want this access; he wanted to learn more about her the normal way, not be privy to her emotions without her consent. Despite his unrelenting self-loathing at his ability to read her emotions, he could no longer deny that it was rather *nice* to be able to escape to the firepoweress' mind; it had become his unexpected place of reprieve. He recalled her mention of the fact that she read to tamper down her anxiety and he wondered if that was the reason for her calm state today.

Juniper shifted her eyes up from the book as she whispered, "You could sit by her, you know."

"Stop," he murmured. "I'm busy."

"You aren't." Levi was next to him now, taking another book off the shelf.

"Don't you two have a map to argue over?" he shot back.

"*We*"—Levi gestured to the whole of the room—"have a regime to defeat. A world to save. Juniper's right; if you're going to stare, at least do it with a book in hand. Start with this one."

His friend tossed him a thick book: *An Emotion-Wielder's Guide.* Haruki Ito, a professor from the Academy, was listed as the author.

"Now, go sit," Levi said as he waved him away.

He took the seat next to Leola's and opened the front cover, the tranquility of her mind wrapping around him like warmth from a hearth. He scanned the index for anything related to mental shields—or failing ones, for that matter—and flipped to that page.

```
There are a few circumstances in which shields
fail. Most commonly, this can be a result of
improper training or failure to master the
skill. In addition, shields will fail if the
wielder has diminished their power reserve.
(Refer to Chapter 12: Proper Use of Power, page
158, Section 1.2) Third, shields will fail in
the presence of their mate before and after a
mating bond has been identified or accepted.
```

Tension gripped his bones, and a tremor ran through his hand as his eyes locked on the word: *mate.* Mates were not uncommon, but he'd never expected to find his, especially not at the age of nineteen. It seemed so formal—so mature.

It's not possible. He kept his eyes on the text, lifting the book to hide his face behind the spine. All the while, her emotions played in his mind like a serene movie scene.

He continued reading:

> The reason for the lack of shielding between mates is to allow them to communicate across vast distances, playing into the telepathic channel of communication that accompanies mating bonds. The mental connection may be inhibited by ancient magic, curses, or time, but it can never be shielded against by the mates themselves. In the case of a strong pair, the mates will be able to sense each other's emotions, even if they are not emotion-wielding. However, this capability will not be accessible until both members of the pair have identified and accepted the mating bond.

He flexed his white-knuckle grip on the book as he tried to ignore the roaring in his ears and the distinct burn of emerald eyes examining him. He'd spent years educating himself on the power of Seers, and while he didn't know everything, he knew that his best friend could sense any change in him. Levi had a strong sense for wards and ancient magic. Mating bonds were ancient magic. If he knew anything about the Seer, he'd sensed Leola and Benn were mates—or had even guessed.

He unshielded, letting his friend's emotions speak to him. Smugness. Knowing. And another that did not surprise him: undiluted joy.

He turned to catch his eye, giving him an imperceptible shake of his head. Levi's quiet smirk confirmed that he would keep quiet about this. Levi returned to his conversation with Juniper like he had not just witnessed the life-altering revelation that Benn was currently enduring. He shifted his attention back to the book, shield risen.

Admiration flickered through Leola's mind as his gaze jumped up to meet hers. Faint pink blossomed underneath her freckles before she looked back down into her book.

What if her admiration is due to us being mates and not her true feelings? Is that even possible? His stomach twisted, recalling what he knew about mates. Levi's parents had been mates, but they had been executed. His grandparents were mates, but his grandfather was dead. His stomach twisted again at that thought—a *dead* mate. Something he'd never given thought to was suddenly his most dreaded fear—perhaps even his potential undoing.

Air. I need some air. He was furiously annoyed that he had discovered this *now*, in the days and hours that led up to the biggest moment of his—and her—life. He scarcely had a spare moment to think these days, let alone fortify a—

A gentle hand touched the side of his face, lifting his chin to look into familiar caramel eyes.

Curiosity. Concern. Her mind spoke to him as she raised a questioning brow that mirrored the emotions he read on her. He assumed he was staring at her like an idiot because she sent him a tentative smile. Her calmness washed over his mind in waves, opening his chest to breathe again.

She released her hold on his chin, blew him a kiss, and returned her eyes to the book she held. He was the warmest he had ever been; everything was bubbly and new—even in the face of this dystopia shrouding the world.

Maybe she is my mate. Meant for me. And I for her. It was a gratifying, terrifying, earth-shattering realization. One that he was in no way ready to confront, so he tore his eyes from her and landed them back on his book.

———

Leola cursed. "I found something." Her eyes flashed with trepidation as she looked toward him.

She masked her feelings, then read aloud:

> "Mass gatherings of power are prohibited and punishable by death. In the event of the law being broken, it takes great power to stop this. History shows us that there are a few ways it can be done.
>
> Option one: killing the power(ess/ex) who is responsible. This can offer success, but will not resolve the problem. Beware: when using the power of many beings, their power can manifest in unexpected ways. It is important to learn your opponent before confrontation.
>
> Option two: breaking the spell or wards used to gather this power. This is the safest way, but it is dangerous, as the person responsible for gathering the power will have a sense that it is being toyed with the moment the magic is interfered with. It takes great power to undo spellwork of this nature.
>
> Option three: absorbing the power into a different being. For one being, this is extremely dangerous, as it can impact the power(ess/ex)'s mind and soul. This sacrifice cannot be undone."

"So, all points lead to us being fucked." Juniper scowled.

Benn leaned forward, frowning at the options. "Daemon has to die. The prophecy mentions two powers going against Daemon—you two. Is there anything in the text about *two* poweresses trying to undo the mass gathering?"

Leola scanned, shaking her head. "What if we *can't* kill him? Daemon knows this information, too. How are we supposed to know if Daemon hasn't already taken precautions to keep himself safe?" Her eyes searched his like he had all of the answers—if only he did.

"Then we will need a Plan B," Benn muttered, staring out the windows.

Benn flinched at Leola's words. "Plan B, I absorb the power."

"*Are you mad?*" Levi screeched before he could respond.

She shrugged, avoiding his gaze, as she said, "That is our only option—unless someone has any other ideas."

"I've got one. How about anything other than an option that is complete dogshit?" Levi's words were firm. "*No.* Did you not process what you just read?" He loosely quoted the tome, "'*Impact the mind and soul. Sacrifice that cannot be undone.*' No. Absolutely not."

Juniper's eyes sharpened on her sister. "Yeah. Respectfully, fuck that, sis; I'm not down with that plan."

Her eyes hardened in response. "We aren't burning out Levi to undo the magic. Even if we do kill Daemon—which we don't know if *we* can—that leaves the mass power idle for the next evil asshole who tries to steal it. So either way, it has to go somewhere. And you aren't absorbing the power."

Juniper didn't hesitate in her response. "Neither are you."

"I don't remember saying it was up for debate," Leola snapped, before sighing. "Bug, if it meant you could see mom again, and Benn, you and Asha could see your mother again, I'd do it. Levi, if it meant avenging your family, I'd do it. I'd make that sacrifice." She looked at each of them, her eyes resting on his as her tone softened. "And I would do it happily."

Benn kept his voice quiet. "And what about the aftermath? Of you being impacted—in a way that is unknown—forever? My vote is no, too. *I'm* not willing to make that sacrifice, Leo. You can say I'm selfish, but I won't sacrifice *you*. We need to keep looking. There's always another way." She started to protest, but he pulled the book from her hand, opening the page to where the marker sat and scanned the text.

He read aloud:

```
"If the power has not been seized by the
power(ess/ex) who has collected it, it is
possible to return it to the power(ess/ex) it
was stolen from. To do this, simply locate the
power source and have the power(ess/ex) touch
the gathered magic. Their soul will call to
their power until it returns."
```

He looked up, his words steady and his eyes elsewhere. "This whole time, we have been thinking of how we will *save* the prisoners. We need to break the plan into pieces. We need to free them first, and show them how to regain their own power. We relocate them and *then* we kill Daemon. What if we could free them and return their power before he even knows we're there?"

Juniper agreed, small magic fashioning her braids into a low bun. "I like where you're going with this, Benny, but how do we free the prisoners? The key I found can't unlock the door *and* the shackles. I checked."

"I can melt the shackles." Benn flinched and felt the others mirror the reaction. Leola rolled her eyes, clarifying, "With my *hands*. Not my flames."

"The shackles are made with power-blocking metals," Juniper said, then called over her shoulder to Boyd, "Will it hurt her if she touches them?"

Boyd answered, not looking up from the desk, "I can prepare an antidote for you to take with dinner. It will protect you so long as your blood is not touched by the metal."

A twinge of relief warmed his heart. "Splendid. We can have the Underground ready the supplies we need for basic triage for the prisoners. The prisoners will be emaciated—especially after all this time." He cleared his throat to mask the quaking in his voice as he continued, "Once they have their power back, I can warp them back to the Underground camp. Levi will keep watch for Daemon or any Opasteg lurking in the area. Juniper can kill anything that gets close to us."

Juniper did her signature mock evil laugh.

Levi's voice was calm, but the frustration shone through his mignonette gaze. "I love it. It sounds foolproof, but you can't warp them all, brother. You know that."

He met his eyes. "I might have to."

Levi's eyebrows creased, his tone taking on an edge of exasperation. "Tell Asha we need one more strong power or poweress. There has to be someone who can warp multiple people as quickly as you can. Or maybe—Leader Wyndmere could make a suggestion? She must have someone in her inner circle who can assist. If you won't do that, then at least let me help. I'm not as quick as you, but I can take some of the load off."

"No, we need all of your focus on the wards, spells, and any threats that might attack. We know they will; you're our best chance at us *not* being taken by surprise." His words were detached; this was the voice of an Underground General he'd heard his grandmother use countless times.

The worry that flooded the auburn-tinged mind across from him gave him pause.

"Benn, this plan does not work if you do it all alone. Asha will help find someone if you let her know how dire the situation is, so you will tell her. You said that you won't sacrifice me? Well, I won't sacrifice you." Her voice was even, but when Benn met her gaze, flames had replaced her retinas. Her voice softened, but the flames didn't ebb. "Promise me you won't try to do your part alone."

He kept his tone neutral. "I can't promise that I won't do everything to save you. To save you all. To save Heri."

The soft tone dissipated as Leola said, "Fine, I guess we're going with Plan B of Leo taking all of the power and sacrificing her body and soul in the process. Sorry guys, we could have worked as a team, but Benn ruined it." She shrugged like that was a nonchalant admission.

He narrowed his eyes on hers, which were still masked in blaze.

Levi smirked. "Nice going, man. We almost had the Runes sisters agreeing to something we proposed."

The flames flared brighter in her eyes. "Promise me, Benn." Her eyebrows raised in challenge.

He groaned and grabbed her outstretched pinky. "I promise I'll get help from Asha."

She pulled it out of his reach before the promise could bind.

Clever, as always, he thought to himself.

She shook her head at him. "Promise you will *not* deplete your power reserve to save us."

His eyes flicked to Levi, whose knowing smirk was as aggravating as it was endearing. He could almost hear Levi saying, *"You've found yourself a mate who is a fair opponent in promise semantics."*

Because he was an honest male, he'd chosen to explain how promises functioned between magic-wielders to Leo the night prior; because he was selfish in any and all ways regarding the safety of the woman across from him, he, now, regretted that choice. Regardless, he took the opportunity to make a deal with her. "Only if *you* promise not to do the same for me and Levi."

He'd intentionally left Juniper's name out of the promise. Why? Because it wasn't a fair ask, and he wouldn't make the woman he loved choose between him and the *first* girl she loved. Her sister was her world; Benn had seen that from the first time he'd scanned Leola's mind in Laviegata.

She searched his eyes for three heartbeats, before she breathed, "Fine."

Lightning fast, his pinky wrapped around hers, as he said, "We have a deal, then." Electricity buzzed in his hand as he locked pinkies with her—with his mate.

———

While the dinner their hosts served them was delicious, the morose pit fueled by the war and his newfound discovery grated on him with every bite. They planned to leave before sunrise, promising Boyd and Gordon that they'd wake them to say a proper goodbye.

He walked with Leola to her and Juniper's room but didn't have the gall to tell her what he had learned—about their destiny to be mates. He debated the choice, but landed on saving the revelation for another moment, deferring to future Bennjamin to decide.

With Juniper reading in bed and Levi surveying the wards around the house, they had a brief moment of privacy. He wasted no time, pulling Leola to him and putting his mouth to hers. She wrapped her arms around his neck, pulling their bodies flush to each other, eliciting an involuntary groan from Benn. He deepened the kiss, their tongues met, and then, he was lost. Their connection made the fracturing world minute. Kissing her made it seem as if they had all the time in the world—like the dark eyes of their impending doom were not staring them in the face. This—her body curling around his—was all that mattered. This was where he hoped to exist—

Levi cleared his throat at the edge of the hallway as he forced himself to pull away, heat crossing his cheeks at breakneck pace.

He tucked a curl behind her ear as he said, "Sweet dreams, Leo." Putting his mouth close to her ear, he whispered, "My flame."

Delighted surprise flashed in her emotions, and she kissed him once more. "Blessed night, Levi." She called to his friend, then met his eyes and flashed a playful smirk at him. "Sweet dreams, Wyndmere. Dream of... me."

With a soft bat of her eyelashes, she closed the door behind her, leaving him behind to stare at the door. His limbs were so light that he wondered if he might faint.

The Seer chuckled behind him, cocking his head to the side. "Careful, man, you're not far off."

He nudged his shoulder and they walked down the hall together. "Chill with that Seeing business. I'm fine."

"Sure thing, captain. Or should I say *mate*," Levi said as he let out a full laugh. "That joke was terrible." A smile pulled at his lips regardless.

———

A tremor ran through the house. He rolled to the side to see Levi reaching for the nightstand, hand seeking his thick-framed glasses in the darkness. A jolt of energy shook the house again.

Levi groaned as his glasses fell off the nightstand. "*Fuck.*"

Another jolt hit, setting his magic ablaze. Light flashed outside the large arch-shaped window in their room, covering the space in blinding light. Benn's hands moved to shield his eyes.

Levi crawled to the window. "Someone is—" The room illuminated in white, followed by the unmistakable sound of glass shattering. "Fuck, I can't see anything!" He closed his eyes, his fingers moving to his temples, using his Seer power as his line of sight. "Something—a Darkbeing is—*shit!* Get to the sisters. NOW! I'll get Gordon and Boyd."

Levi was gone before he could process the words. His blood turned to ice as he warped into the room across the hall.

Both sisters appeared confused—half-sleeping—as if they'd been woken up the same way Benn had. The light burned his eyes, the house shaking with intense waves that had him stumbling.

He cursed, scrambling to the window to force the shutters closed. He had no clue who or *what* was waiting for them outside that window, but he could sense the oily malice pressing in on the glass.

He gave Juniper's shoulders a shake before crossing to Leola's bed, cradling her face. "Get up, Leo." Eyes wide with fear, she nodded, unwrapping her hair. "We have to move, *now*. Something is here."

Juniper now perched in front of the window, her fingers having opened the shutters a crack. "*Daemon.* That son of a bitch. I'd know that silver hair anywhere."

He grabbed her, tugging her back from the window as he slammed the shutters shut with his free hand. "Are you mad? *Don't* let him see you." He reached down, feeling for their enchanted pack. He threw it over his shoulder, motioning for them to follow. "Let's go."

He moved to grab both their hands to warp them, but Leola pulled away. "No. You need to conserve your power. I'll take us."

He loathed the idea of separating, but she was right. Leola and Juniper hadn't been warping long, but Leola had made vast improvements at the skill over the last week.

"Levi went to get Gordon and Boyd. Find them, then warp there. I need to get my things, but I'll catch up with you."

Another tremor ran through the house, causing all three of them to falter. Leola grabbed Juniper's hand, disappearing from the room. He did the same, landing back in his and Levi's room. The blinding light fought through the shuttered windows. He grimaced and grabbed their packs, doing a quick scan for anything they'd left behind, then he cast a spear of magic to Levi's location within the house and warped.

He landed in a room he hadn't seen yet. It was a wine cellar. Boyd carried a massive stack of books and papers, while Gordon appeared to be surveying the wine bottles. Levi flexed his fingers, replacing his sleeping clothes with street clothes as Benn did the same. The sisters looked completely different than when he'd seen them minutes ago—both in street wear, hair styled out of their silk wraps.

Another tremor. Dust rained down from the ceiling.

Gordon's hand landed on a bottle as he muttered a spell. In a blink, the room transformed.

The walls were now covered in weapons, supplies, and screens that showcased camera feeds in all areas of their house, both inside and outside. This was not a wine cellar at all.

His eyes were wide as saucers, as he asked, "You have an *armory*?"

Gordon shrugged. "Why wouldn't we? We designed half of these weapons ourselves." He snatched Benn's pack, striding toward a rack that held uniforms and armor, pulling four sets and dropping them in the pack. He pointed to the wall of weapons. "Arm yourselves. Take supplies—whatever you need. I'll get the weapons Boyd has been creating for you. Move quickly; *go*."

An animalistic screech sounded from the screen displaying the patio.

The sisters moved to the weapon wall; Juniper held the pack open as Leola grabbed one of everything—flares, swords, bows, knives, shooting stars. She was packing for all four of them, so he went to the supplies, stocking up on water and food. Levi sorted through books and folders from the pile Boyd had carried in.

Gordon hissed as the Darkbeings rushed inside their home. "*Beasts*. The floors are new." Ice crackled up the monsters' legs, undoubtedly sourced from his power.

"Shall I kill them? They know I'm here already!" Juniper yelled, hands flexing at her sides.

Screeching roared from the level above. His eyes tilted up, losing count of the many, *many* sets of footsteps upstairs.

"No. Conserve your energy." Gordon grabbed Juniper's face and kissed both her cheeks. "Never let them see how powerful you are until the *last* possible second."

He grabbed Leola and did the same. Her eyes glistened with tears.

The sadness filling the room was tangy and heavy on his tongue, but he kept his shield lowered in case his power picked up any useful information on their attackers. The emotions were suffocating—like forty-pound weights on his chest.

Gordon's voice was even but had an edge of distress that pained Benn's chest. "It's time, younglings. It was lovely to meet you all." A screech cut him off. Gordon reached toward him, kissing his cheeks. He grabbed Levi, straightening his jacket and did the same to him. "Y'all take care of yourselves. Save your parents. And Benn, tell your sweet mama, 'Gordo says hi.'" He stepped back, letting his husband take his place.

Tears pricked his eyes as he struggled to hide the emotion in his voice. "Come with us. I can take you and Boyd, too."

"No. We need to throw them off track," Boyd said as he shook his head, pulling them each into an embrace. "It was a pleasure. Make Daemon pay. And then make him pay again. You are all that stands in the way of his success."

Footsteps pounded down the stairs; they had seconds before the Darkbeings obliterated the cellar door. The screeching loudened and tears were flowing from everyone in the room as they bid goodbye to the males who had taken them in.

Juniper screamed as the monsters' nails scratched at the cellar door.

He secured the sisters' pack and his own around his shoulders. Leola tucked her sister into her arms as Benn wrapped an arm around her, securing her tight to his side. Levi tossed one last book into his pack, threw it over his shoulder, and looped his arm in Benn's free arm.

The impact of whatever dark power lurked broke the wards around the armory as Benn time warped them out, narrowly avoiding the blast that followed.

CHAPTER 27

— LEOLA —

Year: Modern-Era
6 July
Multiple Locations, Heri

THEY LANDED IN AN ALLEY IN PAPAVER—a block from where they had been staying with Gordon and Boyd. Benn glanced toward each of them, giving them each a once-over. She acknowledged his burning gaze with a shaky nod as he scanned her body for injuries.

"Modern-Era Papaver," Juniper said, her voice hollow and hushed—heartbreak evident. "I'd always wanted to visit Papaver, and we didn't even get to explore. Now I never want to come back."

Leola squeezed her hand, failing to keep her words even. "We will come back under different circumstances."

Juniper said nothing, but she noticed the thick tears her sister fought to contain.

Benn cast a brief look toward Juniper, his eyes teeming with devastation, before sliding his gaze to Levi. "How's my power reserve after that?"

Levi closed his eyes behind his thick frames, as if he could envision the power thrumming under Benn's skin, and answered, "87%. Better than I expected, honestly. Time warping is usually a draining power." Levi's pointed scowl tipped off Leo at what Benn had planned to do next.

She whirled to the dual-power with narrowed eyes. "Don't you dare. You aren't draining your power to move us, you—" Before she could finish her thought, a Benn-scented wind swept them up, landing them in a midnight-dark forest. "Promised," she muttered as she glowered at him.

Benn's eyes stayed on hers as he chuckled. She couldn't believe he had the nerve to *chuckle*. "What is it now, Levi?"

The Seer laughed, letting out a whistle. "79%. You are one powerful son of a bitch."

He fist bumped Benn while Leola scoffed, pushing her hair over her shoulder as she pulled out of Benn's embrace. He stopped her, placing a soft kiss on her mouth before freeing her. "And I kept that promise. My reserve is not drained. Plus, it sped up our timeline and put more space between us and our enemies."

She shook her head at him, turning away to survey the forest.

"See, Leo? Everyone's happy," Juniper quipped. "But, seriously Benny, don't die on our account, I've never seen my sister so... enamored."

Heat rushed up her cheeks. "Gods, spare me."

Juniper winked at her, before wagging a manicured finger at Benn. "You use that power wisely."

Levi and Benn chuckled. She blinked away the flames that had taken over her eyes, avoiding Benn's gaze.

"I will." Benn's voice matched the quiet of the forest, though a hint of the laughter remained in his words. "What can I say? They don't call me the 'most powerful time-wielder' for nothing." His palms shook in a jazz-hand motion. "I might as well use the power to keep my people safe." His face darkened, eyes focusing hard on the trees around him. He pulled out the glowing sage-colored Ampules, rolling them between his fingers. "Enough chit chat. We need to move. You guys start walking, and I'll drop these in a few different eras and catch up with you."

Leola turned toward him, a brow lifted in challenge. "I'm not a fan of that option. No one should be going off on their own."

"It is *the* option. We know they are tracking Juniper. Right now, we have nightcover on our side. It's best if we use it. Plus, I move faster and burn less of my reserve when I travel alone." His tone remained firm, leaving no room for argument. "We landed somewhere outside Salemfir, but I'm not sure where exactly. There are maps in the pack. Levi, figure out where we are. We need to find a payphone, so I can call Sena. I'll catch up with you all in a few minutes." Benn vanished without sparing them another glance.

Her eyes heated, confirming that her temper had set her eyes ablaze again. She rolled her neck, striding toward Juniper and Levi who were huddled over a map.

Juniper fished into the pack to pull out a phone that would now work in the Modern-Era. "GPS will be faster."

"*Absolutely not,*" Levi snapped, snatching the phone from her hand. "They are tracking your magic, which means they are undoubtedly tracking our phones, too. We already have a target on our backs—using this would just show them where to aim." He turned the phone off and dropped it into his pack.

"You mean we need to do all of this the old-fashioned way?" Juniper asked, her exasperation obvious.

"If we want to keep our heads, we do. Don't tell me you didn't take Topography." Levi's voice was clipped, as if every school offered that course.

She chuckled. "Topography at Poppycal Academy of the Arts? No way."

"Well, lucky for us all, I was the top of my class." Levi's less-than-humble brag earned him an eye roll from Juniper.

"Of course you were," Juniper muttered. "I'm sure Seers *really* struggle with reading maps as it is."

"I can't speak for other Seers, but *I* struggle with nothing," Levi replied wryly as he used small magic to summon a compass to his palm.

"How?" was all Juniper asked.

"Retrieval spell," Levi said without looking up. "Save us from this mess and I'll teach you how."

Leola loaded her quiver and tossed a dagger toward Juniper, who still bickered with the Seer. Needing to clear her mind, her eyes rose to the night sky—clear with visible clouds and a bright waning moon. They'd planned to leave the 1996 Papaver Post at sunrise, but with the Darkbeing attack, those plans had been thwarted.

She hummed, pacing ten yards away from the others.

Movement in the trees caught her attention, halting her feet. The voices bickering behind her faded into silence as her focus sharpened, locking onto the spot where she could have sworn something had *shifted*. Heart pounding, she squinted, leaning onto the balls of her feet, every muscle tense. A blur of black fur emerged from the shadows, crashing into her with the force of a bus.

The world tilted and the impact hit her like a thunderclap, rotting sticks and mud squelching against her back told her where she'd landed. Black filled her vision as long teeth gnashed in her face. The beast pinned her arms, knocking her bow and leaving no room to grab her dagger. She strained her neck, putting desperate centimeters between her throat and its mouth.

Heat sparked from her fingertips, incinerating the animal. Its heavy body leaned into hers, filling her nose with the stench of burning, furry flesh. She shoved it off of her, rolling onto her knees. With barely a thought, flames engulfed the beasts attacking Juniper and Levi as well. Levi pushed the beast off of him and Juniper did the same; she extinguished her flames, allowing the darkness to swallow them up again.

A few beats of silence passed before Juniper's grunt sounded behind her. "What in the Ancestral f—"

"*Quiet*," Leo cut her off, letting her eyes adjust to the blackness.

Leola's fingernails dug into the wet dirt as she scanned for movement. Though the forest was silent, she couldn't ignore the distinct prickle of something *near* them. She caught sight of one that was impeccably camouflaged against the inky trees. Her stomach pitched in fear as her eyes outlined its shape; they were a hybrid between a bear and a wolf and, worst of all, the beasts had them surrounded.

They were still—as if waiting for a command—but kept their beady eyes trained on the trio. The robotic stillness in which they sat made her wonder if they were exactly that—*robots*. She kept her eyes on the one she had seen initially, monitoring its non-movements; she was afraid that the second that she broke eye contact, it would attack. She did not move—did not breathe—as she tried to figure out how many lurked beyond.

As if hearing her thoughts, Levi whispered, "Twenty-eight. Standing in a Fibonacci sequence."

The beasts suddenly swarmed them as her magic erupted, burning each one like a torch in the dark. She shoved to her feet, using her sleeve to block the unbearable smell their death brought on. Her fingers rested at her sides, waiting for a third wave of hybrids to move in on them.

Levi whistled behind her and said, "You just took out twenty-eight Lykosos and *still* have a full power reserve. Remind me never to get on your bad side."

But she was not impressed or relieved. In fact, she was fighting the rising nausea.

She leaned down to get a closer look, tears stinging her eyes. "I—I have never killed an animal."

Levi patted her shoulder, voice softening. "You did the right thing. If you hadn't killed them, they would have certainly killed us. Lykosos are vicious and bloodthirsty. You wouldn't think so, but they are actually herbivores. They just like to kill for sport." A dagger materialized in Levi's hand. He sliced deep into the charred fur, voice hitching as he continued, "Excellent hunters—designed to kill. Their master gives them a scent to track and the pack will begin hunting; they won't stop until they've found their target. Someone sent them here... to hunt us."

She watched in horror as his arms went elbow-deep into the insides of the Lykoso. He pulled gore out of the animal and held it out to them.

Juniper audibly gagged, choking out the words, "*What're you doing?*"

"This is the best way to get the Lykosos' scent on us. It will mask our scents and—hopefully—" He paused, rubbing the blood on his face, neck and clothes. "Dissuade any of those fuckers—or something worse—from following us. Daemon surely has monsters ready to hunt us, and even the baddest of monsters fear Lykosos."

Juniper cursed fluidly and Leola swallowed her bile, but they both began to do the same as Levi. She held her breath as the coppery scent filled her nose. She kept her eyes trained on the sky, ignoring Juniper's gags, as she reached into the still-warm body of the animal again and again until Levi determined they were no longer trackable.

Benn landed next to them, remarking in a flat tone, "You haven't even moved." They all glowered at him, as he took in the surroundings and sniffed. "Gods. Are these—?"

"Lykosos," Levi answered. "Daemon must've sent them. Leo took them out for us and we masked our scents with their blood. You should do the same."

Benn flinched but went to his knees before reaching into the carcass. "Levi, did we pack syringes in that pack? Toss me a few." He covered his body and face in blood and caught what looked like a pack of 100 syringes. He pulled a few out of the case, withdrawing blood from the carcass he'd just been elbow-deep inside. She didn't need to look at Juniper to know they shared a mirrored expression of disgust on their faces. Benn looked at Juniper and then her, putting a lid on one of the syringes, as he said simply, "Their blood has healing properties."

Juniper picked up the case, tossing several syringes to Leola and Levi. "Let's fill them all then. I mean, we are attempting to rescue hundreds of people who have been imprisoned for over a decade. Might as well come prepared."

She scanned the dark trees again, keeping her voice low. "Good call. Let's do it fast. I don't want to run into whatever Daemon is sending our way."

Levi collected the syringes from each of them and secured them in the syringe case, which he put back into the pack. "From the map, it looks like Benn landed us in Brooks Park," he said, folding the map, while holding out his fingers in a counting fashion. "Downtown Salemfir is roughly three miles to the east. We can get a car and find a payphone there."

"And a bathroom to wash our hands," Juniper retorted as they all joined hands—still caked in blood—as Benn warped them to Salemfir.

While Benn used a payphone across the street, the other three hid in the shadows in an alley on the outskirts of downtown Salemfir.

"You know, I've always wanted to come here, too. Is this what traveling for work is like? You go to all these places, but never get the time to do anything fun," Juniper said in a low voice, flicking her dagger between her fingers.

Leola kept her eyes on Benn. "Papaver. Salemfir. Keep adding to the list; we'll visit them all. We aren't Mundaners, so we can travel." The admission felt weird as she said it, like a piece of her that had always existed was just... gone.

"Sure, take advantage of the privilege not offered to all," Juniper said, emotion leaking into her tone. "We need to survive first before we can cross regional lines."

"We will," Leola replied.

She couldn't bring herself to think of this plan going any way except perfect. Her stomach sank at the thought of all that rested on the line if it didn't. She pushed the emotions into the imaginary box she kept them in, stashing them away for later examination.

Juniper's hand squeezed hers and she whispered, "I love you, Leo."

"I love you, sis," she replied, tears stinging her eyes.

Levi rounded the corner. "No beasts in the area that I can see. No one is tracking us either—yet. Benn must have done his job well."

She nodded, eyes traveling back toward Benn, who remained at the payphone. "How is his power reserve?"

Levi's answer was quick, as he'd probably already checked. "79% still. Warping short distances won't impact his power reserve too much."

"What will—aside from using his power?" Juniper's voice held a note of curiosity.

Levi seemed to consider before answering, "Poor nutrition. Exhaustion." He shrugged. "Poison."

Benn warped into the shadowy alley, his shoulder brushing Leo's. His hands stayed in his pockets. "Sena will gather forces. We will meet them near the prison this afternoon."

Leola brushed her hand against his, trying to catch his gaze. He looked back in the direction of the payphone as his jaw flexed; he was tense.

Lifting a finger in the air, Levi said, "Step one is complete. There's an unlocked car about a half mile from here. We'll go get it and pick you guys up." Levi tugged Juniper's arm and started walking.

She was both shocked and thrilled that the two seemed to be getting along at the moment, though she was reluctant to let Juniper out of her sight. She figured the two of them had left to give her and Benn a moment of privacy. She watched them walk further down the street, forcing herself to remember that her little sister didn't need constant protection anymore.

Her eyes trailed to Benn, whose spine was taut.

"You spoke to your sister," she remarked; she phrased it as a statement and not a question, hoping it would encourage him to talk about it.

He nodded, still avoiding her gaze.

She tilted his chin so that his espresso-toned eyes met hers. "Are you okay?"

His jaw flexed, his voice quiet as he answered, "Yes. No. I mean—it was nice to hear her voice, but I'm terrified to involve her in this." He touched her cheek and sighed. "But we need to. We have no other options. If we don't ask for help, we will lose the opportunity to kill Daemon. We wouldn't be able to rescue prisoners. We would jeopardize all of Heri—and things are already in shambles as it is." His eyes captured hers. "But what worries me most, is the fact that without their help, we won't survive this." His voice dropped to a whisper. "And I—I can't lose you."

Her chest squeezed at the pain in his voice. "You won't." She kissed him. Again, she buried the thought of something happening to Benn—or Juniper—deep into the imaginary box that was becoming more capacious with each passing second.

His eyes hardened as he said, "You're more afraid of losing us than losing your own life." His hands dropped to her waist, shoulders deflating. His voice was even despite the edge that lingered. "I can't be mad at you for that, but don't think for a second that it is reassuring to me. I can read your emotions, Leo; your intentions are visible to me. You promised you wouldn't sacrifice yourself for me."

"Only because you made me the same promise in exchange." She smirked at him, pressing her mouth to his. Arguing would get them nowhere, and she had no plans to compromise here.

He pressed her against the wall of the alley, caging her into his embrace as his mouth glanced off of hers. "If something happens to you, your sister will be *livid*."

"And what will your best friend think if something happens to *you*?" A fleeting thought crossed her mind that this was their roundabout way of communicating their worry for one another—like the idea of their new connection breaking was as unfathomable to him as it was to her. The thought was equal parts reassuring and agonizing.

His mouth took hers instantly. Hungry. Desperate. She pulled him closer. For one stolen, blissful moment, it was only them in the world. The world started and stopped with the feeling of his mouth. Her skin warmed and her mind went to that fuzzy place that it loved to go to when she was with him like this.

317

"I need to tell you something," he breathed against her lips.

She pulled back, searching his face. Unsettling, uncharacteristic fear had taken over his features.

She mimicked the emotion and heat traveled to her palms in response. "What is it?"

He sighed. "Remember how I mentioned that I can't shield from you? That your emotions are *distracting* to me, at times. And that this is the first time I haven't been able to shield from someone—" He cleared his throat. "Or anyone for that matter."

He let out a breath as he pulled away from her; she hated the distance as much as she hated the apprehension that ruled his usually nonchalant expression. She let her hands drop to her sides, fighting the instinct to reach for him.

"Yesterday, in the library, I read something." Wariness flickered in his dark eyes.

Worry tingled down her spine. She wondered if he was permanently injured after the Soulsiphon attacked him in the cavern or his near-death experience in Papaver—or was her *presence* here having a negative impact on his power?

Heat traveled to her eyes and she inhaled, hoping to quell the flames, as she said, "Tell me what you read."

"Please know that I'm as shocked as you are—"

Cue the molten of the flames of her eyes.

"Shit." He looked like he might vomit, but his delivery was detached, taking on the same tone he used to discuss war. "Well it seems that emotion-benders cannot shield from their mates."

She blinked at him, the words not registering.

"Leo?" His voice sounded like it'd been raked over gravel.

"Benn."

"We're mates, Leo," he said as he reached to touch her face, stopping when let his hand drop short. "Fated or destined to be. Not confirmed yet, of course."

The flames in her eyes extinguished. She stared at nothing beyond his shoulder. Mates were not uncommon, but she was new to this world. Over the last few days, she'd read a few excerpts that discussed mates, but she'd skimmed over any passages—

"*Leola*." His rasp shook her out of her thoughts. "Did you hear me? Say something other than my name. *Please*."

She was shocked; she needed more information.

Her tone robotic, she said, "Mates. Okay." She met his intense stare, trying to discern what this news meant.

"By the Gods." He let out a string of curses. "You are—feeling *a lot*. Scared. Bewildered. Uncertain."

"Happy?" she cut in, but her nervous tone betrayed her true feelings. She cleared her throat and tried again, "Scared. Bewildered. *Shocked*. Safe. And... *happy* with you."

His eyes were inquisitive as a slow smile spread over his face, repeating her words, "*Happy* with me?"

She held his gaze and grinned shyly. "Happy with you, Bennjamin."

He crossed the alley again, closing her in against the wall. "I'm *happy* with you, too, Leo." His hand moved up through her hair as their mouths met. He pulled back, touching his forehead to hers, murmuring, "You are scared. I'm scared, too. You are shocked; believe me, I'm as shocked as you are. I was not expecting this."

She let her lips linger on his, barely pulling back to whisper, "The timing is interesting. We have not even been on a date yet. I mean, I *just* met you. And we're about to embark on an impossible mission."

He rested his cheek into her hair as he said, "The timing is that of a demon's creation."

A note of interest slipped through into her voice. "Are you happy it's me?"

His arms tightened around her as he answered. "How could I not be? It's not a secret that I care for you, Leola. In a different world, I'd play the long game—you know, *woo* you—before admitting that. It feels silly not to admit that now..." He swallowed. "Given the circumstances."

"Given the circumstances," she echoed, pulling back to straighten his crewneck. "Your mate. I'm not sure I know what that means. I got my power and my memories back, but I didn't grow up in this world like you did. You know *everything* while I know nothing."

Her giddiness dissolved, her self-consciousness about her own shortcomings taking over. *Does he want a mate he has to teach?*

She'd grown up in the Mundaner world and the Wyndmeres were royalty, as far as the magic world was concerned.

His arms rested above her hips, his eyes softening as he whispered, "*Stop*. You are worried about what comes next; don't. We have some big tasks ahead of us. We can just—be. As we have been."

She considered that, putting the pieces together that she did know. "Mates usually figure the connection out pretty quick, right? It is where the idea of *love at first sight* originates from?"

"Yes—and we have only just met. So, that tracks," he said, his voice even, but his clenched jaw indicated otherwise.

"That tracks," she repeated the unique phrase, continuing her questions. "But the 'mating bond' is not automatically accepted? For it to become official, mates need to—well, uh, *mate*? Or is that only a theme in fables?"

His words came out slowly, laced with a gentleness that had her heart warming. "That is true, but do not feel pressured. All of the people who met their mates while we were at the Academy continued to date for a while—before taking the next step—before they mated, officially."

She smiled at the nervous energy seeping off of him. It was endearing.

"Oh my." She mocked a gasp, her melodic giggle echoing in the alley as she teased, "Are we *dating*, Benn?"

His gaze turned sheepish as he said, "Well, I did tell Asha she would be meeting my girlfriend this afternoon."

She tapped her chin with a manicured finger. "Hmm, I don't remember you asking me to be your girlfriend."

He tilted her chin up with his other hand and said, "I didn't. I was banking on you agreeing to the term, though it doesn't sound permanent enough for us. It will have to work until we have a break from wartime." He sent her a sideways glance. "If you don't, that will be terribly embarrassing. Asha will never let me hear the end of that. Or Levi. Or Juniper." He winced and she thought he might really be afraid.

She put him out of his misery. "Girlfriend it is." She stretched onto her toes to kiss his cheek. "As for the *mates,* you need to take me to dinner first. At least."

He laughed fully. "Of course. I'm a gentleman, and it is improper to call someone your mate before—" He cleared his throat, as his breath caught on the term. "*Mating.*"

"We wouldn't want to be *improper*, now would we?" she teased, really enjoying watching this never ruffled—sometimes bossy—man squirm.

"Never," he answered as he held her gaze so she could see when his eyes heated. "We'll get to that part when the time is right. There is no rush at all; I'd wait however long you need me to—we will wait until you are ready for that kind of commitment."

Her lips brushed his and she inhaled his scent. She teased him again, hoping to coax out the relaxed man she'd grown so accustomed to. "Of course. When the time is right." She wrapped her arms around his neck, whispering, "And in a pinch, I'm sure there's a cheap inn we could run to nearby."

His eyes went so wide that she wondered if they might fall out of their sockets. She giggled and he recovered, tossing back, "Who needs an inn when we have this luxurious and private alley?"

She swatted him away from her, throwing back her head in laughter. His laugh was baritone and rich, and she touched his throat in response, wishing she could bottle the sound.

A black sedan stopped in front of the alley as Juniper called out, "Come on, lovebirds, we're losing nightcover."

Benn tugged her hand, pulling her to his side as they ran to the car, sliding into the backseat.

Levi turned back to them, fist-bumping Benn as he said, "Looks like Juniper owes me another sandwich."

Juniper gasped. "You told her already? *Dammit.* I thought you would wait until post volcano-dive."

"*Benn,*" Leola scolded, nudging his shoulder. "How did they know before I did?"

His hands were raised in innocence as he replied, "I said nothing. Levi figured it out the minute I did. It is hard to keep secrets from a Seer."

"It is impossible," Levi corrected, but his face turned bashful. "I told Juniper."

Her sister shrugged. "He told me last night, so we could bet on when Benn would tell you."

She frowned and responded, "Lovely."

Juniper smirked. "In case anyone cares, I have lost all bets with Levi. I'm going to go into sandwich debt."

"Actually, not all bets, it seems," Levi mused, polishing his thick-framed glasses in the driver seat. "You guessed that Benn would tell Asha that Leo was his *girlfriend* when he called her. I guessed that he would tell Asha that she was his *mate*. Point for you, J."

She clapped in the front seat, laughing. "*Yes!* Victory is sweet. Let's get this show on the road, Blondie. I'm ready to take on Daemon so I can use my powers again. And use it to beat his dictator ass."

Levi shifted the stolen car into gear as he quipped, "Time to un-coup the Red Coup."

CHAPTER 28

— BENN —

Year: Modern-Era
6 July
Salemfîr, Heri

U NEASINESS WASHED OVER him as he scanned the forest, bouncing on the balls of his feet at the exact coordinates his grandmother had told him on the phone. His calmness was feigned as his nerves ran amok. He hadn't seen his grandmother since initiation and, as much as he hated to acknowledge it, he was not the same man he'd been that night. His Assignment exposed him to unimaginable trauma and brutality, but that was to be expected. He was confident that he could heal from that and move on to become a stronger man. He had killed for the Underground, completed his Assignment, and followed every instruction on the vellums he'd received. He hadn't abandoned his post, though he'd dreamed of doing so every single day. No one knew that, of course. So much had changed—his love life, his priorities, himself. And simultaneously, so many things around him remained stagnant—the fractured world, his need to prove himself worthy of his power, the difficult relationship with his grandmother.

So why was he surprised to be battling such immense dread as he awaited her arrival? A strange, blurred line had always existed between who Sena was to him and Asha versus who she was to the Underground. He preferred to be around her behind closed doors, where she was free to be her nurturing self and not the calculating leader that he equally revered and feared. In all of his intellectual training, there was no guidance for navigating this relationship; in fact, there'd never been a space to ask, and because of that, he found himself wishing that their reunion would have been under different circumstances.

His jaw clenched and unclenched. Contrary to the nervousness, he buzzed with excitement at the thought of seeing his sister again. When he'd received his assignment for the 1855 Roswell Post, he had assumed he'd die before seeing her again. He paced around the clearing for the hundredth time, thankful for this brief reprieve of privacy, where no one would witness his restless fidgeting. Leola would have noticed his energy was off had she been here with him.

Leola. His mind sang her name. Among the swarm of emotions that accompanied his position in this war, there she was: a beacon in the darkness. Soon, he would introduce her to the two other most important women in his life. Shortly after, they'd all put on their warrior hats to determine how to defeat the regime and save Heri from mass imprisonment. Oh, and in addition, they'd need to free multiple hundreds of magic-wielding prisoners from the regime leader himself. And, right at the center of this bleak situation was the only girl he'd ever loved, along with her sister.

What could go wrong? His thoughts pricked at his skin, sharp as shattered glass.

He scanned the forest yet again, as if he would blink and miss their arrival. The morning sun warmed his cheeks. The sky was lovely, complete with an array of milky pinks and warm yellows; he would have marveled at this sunrise in a different world, but today, he found himself scoffing at the irony of the beautiful sunrise starting off the day that may end with his downfall.

He shifted against the tree, feeling the tight Underground leathers, courtesy of Boyd, stretch against his skin. It was protective armor, but the material was like any athleisure clothing he would wear for a workout. The material was impenetrable and reactionary to their power. Leola's was fireproof and Juniper's could reinforce itself when she tore through it with vines—or at least that's what Boyd had said.

The sisters were off changing into their leathers while Levi put cloaking spells in place around the camp. Levi excelled at this kind of practice; he assured them that it would be enough to hide the triage camp and the soldiers from the enemies that lurked, waiting to pounce. Levi's goal was to have the cloak in place before Sena and Asha arrived with Underground forces, so Benn was to keep watch in the area.

He flexed his fingers around his dagger. Strapped to his back were dual Katanas—another gift from Boyd and Gordon. With the exception of movies and video games, he had only seen these weapons one time during a special presentation at the Academy; needless to say, the soldier inside him was giddily excited to use the weapons. Leo had gathered enough weapons from the armory to last a lifetime. The sisters could rely on the power of their magic, but he and Levi fought with weapons *and* magic. Well, at least they had at the Academy. Their school had been attacked one time, but other than that, he'd never seen battle.

"Weapons are what a skilled warrior relies on when their power reserve is failing them." His weaponry professor's voice played in his mind.

The days that followed would bring times where he would be relying on both his power reserve *and* his combat training. He had foolishly promised Leo that he wouldn't sacrifice himself for her, so he was magically bound to oblige. That meant he needed his power reserve to last longer than even he thought it should, and he really didn't plan on watching her die.

He was no stranger to death; he had seen it many times, but the thought of Leola's limp body in his arms almost brought him to his knees. He blinked the image away and listened for her mind instead. She was out of his range, but he could still *sense* her as if she were standing a few feet from him. The connection was muffled, but undeniably present.

A perk of their destiny to be mates. The moment he met her, he'd been captivated; her beauty alone was striking, yes, but there was something else—something bewildering that drew him to her like a whispered promise. The connection was bottomless, laced with wonder, like their souls had recognized each other across lifetimes. He now knew *that* to be the ever growing mating bond living between them.

It was the fierceness that lived behind her golden-bronze eyes—eyes that swallowed him whole every time their gazes collided. It was her unwillingness to show vulnerability to anyone but him. It was her reserved nature that accompanied her quick, wicked humor. The way she seemed to exist in this world to protect Juniper, but upon looking deeper, she had made it her purpose to protect anyone left vulnerable. She was a warrior, a queen, one of the two Prophesied Pair, and most paramount of all, his girlfriend. He thanked the Gods for offering him the opportunity to serve as her mate because this was definitely a love match—they'd never spoken the words, but he was foolishly, irrevocably, joyfully, in love with her. And she actually *liked* him—horror stories had been told of mates despising one another. Their connection was chemical and they weren't even mated yet.

She was everything to him; a week ago, he hadn't even known of her existence, and now, his heart was owned by the magnificent firepoweress. She dominated his thoughts, his mind, his reason. She could set him aflame and he would let her, especially if it meant that he could look at her while she did it.

Prior to Assignment, he had only heard whispers of the Prophesied Pair that would defeat Daemon. It seemed to be a myth that magic beings had stopped paying attention to, or so he had thought. Grandmava had done her job so well that only the Runeses and his grandmother had known where they were hidden. It was genius: hide them, let the Underground and Opasteg dismiss it to myth and doubt their existence, then reveal them when the time was right, when no one would expect it.

His heart pained at the thought of his lost friend. Whatever death had met her, he prayed it was swift and painless—

Earth magic scented the air, yanking him from his thoughts. He tensed, rolling his neck as he dropped his arms to his sides. The magic trail floated in the air around him, though he couldn't see the person wielding it.

"Show yourself," he commanded. His voice dripped with lethal calm.

A mature voice—male—drawled, "Don't move, boy. I mean no harm, unless you do something stupid."

He whirled toward where the voice was coming from but saw no one. A whistle sounded from above, drawing his eyes skyward. A man sat in the treetops, watching him. He looked to be in his 70s, his magic an unyielding force under his deep-caramel complexion.

Earthpower. Strong shield. He couldn't be sure if the man was Underground or Opasteg, and while he could break the shield surrounding his mind, he waited in efforts to preserve his power.

"Tell me who you are," Benn hissed through gritted teeth.

"I could request the same of you." The man was angry; Benn didn't need his power to determine that. "I'm looking for someone. There's a cloaking spell in place that is hindering my search. I won't hurt you if you tell me where they are," the Earthpower said as he jumped out of the tree, landing with graceful ease.

He raised an eyebrow, letting his temper leak into his words. "I *will* hurt you if you don't tell me who you are." He was relieved to know that the cloaking wards Levi had constructed were in place. They were working well if the man had to talk to him to locate whoever he was looking for. The man could have chosen to remain hidden, though Benn would have likely sensed his presence anyway.

He's motivated enough to ask for my *help.* He kept his eyes on the man—he was bald, with freshly-trimmed, silver facial hair and thick eyebrows to match. He had a similar build to his own—muscles threaded throughout his lean frame, and he stood the same height as Benn. Powers grew stronger with age, so Benn was prepared to fight. The man floated toward him, hands in his pockets as he gave him a scrutinizing once-over. He returned the look, holding his dagger in his hand.

The man sniffed the air. His tone was gruff when he said, "Sena's lineage."

Benn debated throwing the dagger straight into his socket. Thick vines erupted from the ground, courtesy of the man, restraining his wrists and ankles as they worked to hinder him.

"Like I said, I mean you no harm." The man's tone was flat, bored.

He scoffed, seriously doubting that, as he moved to yank his ankle free. The vines stretched further over his thighs until they covered his midsection, anchoring him to the ground. The man reached into his pocket and revealed an old photograph—two younglings smiling in the arms of the same Earthpower who currently held him captive. One girl had bouncing auburn curls, while the other girl was toothless with raven-dark curls. The photo was worn, like it had been in his wallet for a decade. "Now, take me to my granddaughters."

Another twist of unexpected fate. Benn pulled against the vines, still on guard. He had heard the girls speak fondly of their Papa, but knew glamours could be used to disguise oneself. He didn't trust this man, but he had a friend who possessed an uncanny ability to read people, glamoured or not.

"Levi," he called, keeping his voice low but knowing that the Seer would be listening. His best friend landed soundlessly next to him.

"Ah, Mr. Runes. I knew you'd be joining us," Levi said, his voice cheery as Benn resisted the urge to roll his eyes, not surprised that his friend knew exactly who this gentleman was. Though, he would have appreciated a warning to expect his arrival.

"Call me Booker." The man approached Levi, gruff face transforming into a smile. The vines released Benn, slithering back into the ground. "That's one hell of a cloaking spell. This is your work? I was searching the area for a long time."

Levi beamed at the compliment. "Yes, sir. Benn is watching the area, but I'll take you to your granddaughters. The wards will open to anyone who is

Underground, but there is only one entrance. You will have no problem getting inside, sir."

"Again, call me Booker. Sorry about the vines, kid." Booker clapped his shoulder before warping away with Levi.

———

"Brother!" Asha landed next to him an hour later, pulling him into an iron-tight hug. He returned the embrace with fervor. He opened his shield briefly to feel closer to her—closer to *home*. Her mind was airy, bubbly, and loving. For as long as he could remember, his sister had been his favorite person on the planet; his eyes stung as they both held onto the embrace. Her whisper was thick with emotion. "I didn't think I'd see you again."

He had no words to respond, so he said nothing as he let go of her before turning toward his grandmother. He moved to hug her but paused and bowed. "Leader Wyndmere."

Sena's response was fierce, as he'd expected. "Oh for Gods' sake, I know you're on duty, boy. But you'd better hug me. At ease."

"Oma," he replaced the formal term for his grandmother's nickname. He hugged her tight, his nervousness washing away as he inhaled her scent. Roses. She also smelled like home.

Both of the women were dressed in armor similar to his. He assumed Asha carried weapons that were expertly concealed, while his grandmother's wooden walking stick was enchanted to morph into any weapon she needed, only to be wielded by her. Asha's blonde curls were bound into chest-length twists and his grandmother had pulled her silver braids into a bun. On the top of her head rested a petite sun-burst crown. He'd never seen it in real life, but he knew it as the iconic crown she wore to battle. "I have missed you both," he said as he glanced between them. "Every moment."

His grandmother cupped his face and beamed at him. "As we have missed you." She examined him from head-to-toe. "I am so proud of you, Bennjamin." She was as intense as she was loving and hearing these words leave her mouth thrilled him. They healed him.

"You look slim, brother," Asha remarked, the concern in her voice evident.

"Yeah, they don't feed the Chattels well," he responded curtly.

Both of the women flinched, but he merely shrugged.

Having not expected them to arrive alone, he asked, "Where are the others?"

Sena grinned. "We shall get them later. I wanted to meet the Prophesied Pair before I had to put my leader hat on. And, of course, get a look at this *Leola*."

He sent a glare toward Asha, who sent an apologetic glance in return, explaining, "What did you expect? Oma knew right away. You emotion-benders are impossible to keep secrets from."

"There are no *secrets* between family," his grandmother said, shaking her head at Asha as her smiling eyes returned to his. Her tone became giddy. "Take me to her, please. I'm eager to meet your mate."

He groaned. "Oma, we're dating. *Please* don't call her my mate."

Sena tapped the top of her wooden walking stick, smirking sidelong at Asha. "Oh, Benn, she will join the family soon enough. I'm not sure what you two are waiting for."

He gawked at her, gesturing to the surrounding wooded area. "*Waiting for*? Have you forgotten we're at war? Or that Leo needs to defeat the leader of the enemy? That the fate of Heri rests in *her* hands?"

Asha giggled and his grandmother winked at him, remarking, "I'm sure there will be an opportunity. We can arrange for you two to have your own tent tonight." Both of the women started laughing; clearly, they were enjoying this conversation more than he was.

"I won't be *mating* with Leo in a *tent*." His voice was incredulous, fully in disbelief that this conversation was even happening. He inhaled a breath, heat rushing to his cheeks in embarrassment as his accent thickened.

"I'm surprised you waited this long." His grandmother flicked his nose, adopting a sing-song voice.

He threw his hands in the air, mouth agape, as he said, "It—the moment is important. Worth waiting for. Special. Not to be shared or *tainted* with this war or the impending doom. Not to occur in a Gods damned tent with an *audience*. I deserve more than that. *Leo* deserves more than that. And might I add, Oma, we have been incredibly *busy* preparing for this day." The ladies were in hysterics, not even sparing him a glance as he ranted. He resisted the urge to laugh with them, adding, "You have no class. *Pigs*, the both of you. Absolute *prying* pigs."

"Benn, you're such a gentleman. We are only teasing you." Asha's calm voice still held remnants of laughter.

"Did I say I missed you? On second thought, maybe I need to retract that statement." He grabbed both their hands. "Now get a grip on yourselves before you scare her away."

"You love her," Asha said quietly, a sad smile in her voice.

He didn't answer. Of course he did. He loved her with his entire soul, but she might die fighting Opasteg. Or he might even die in the same fashion, so what was the point of discussing it?

He met her gaze, her eyes staring into his soul, as if she were reading him like a book. "You need to tell her."

He frowned at the finality of her tone. "I will."

"*Before*, Bennjamin," Asha murmured.

He did not like that, the way his sister said so much with so little.

"I will, in my own time."

His grandmother tapped her walking stick on the ground, urging them forward as she said, "Let's go, kids. We don't have all day."

331

They warped into the only entrance to the camp where they found the sisters. He sensed the rawness of her emotions instantly—the sisters had finally reunited with their grandfather.

"Leola. Juniper," he called. Both sisters turned toward him, Leola's caramel gaze stealing his breath. He cleared his throat. "Meet my grandmother, Sena, and my sister, Asha."

A full smile crossed Juniper's face as she extended a hand toward both of them, introducing herself, "Juniper Runes, it is a pleasure to meet you both."

Leola introduced herself and bowed. "Ladies."

Juniper watched her, then mimicked the motion.

"Ah, the Prophesied Pair. How lovely it is to finally meet you." He watched with trepidation as his grandmother approached the sisters. "Rise." Sena scanned them both, stopping in front of Juniper, placing a hand on her chin.

"Juniper. *Blessed* by Mother Gaia. Earthpoweress. Power roars within you, child." Sena moved to Leola, placing a gentle finger under her chin that forced her to look up. "Leola. Child of fire. An elemental poweress—so *strong*. I can sense your power crackling in your veins like a mighty hearth. Both of you are as magnificent and radiant as your grandmother said you would be."

Sena glanced over her shoulder at him, before returning her eyes to Leola. "Not to boil your worth down to something so inconsequential as *looks*, but you are stunning. I assumed as much, but I can see why my Bennjamin is so smitten with you. He should be. Your beauty is alluring—it's like staring at the sun."

Pink colored her cheeks as she tossed a shy smile toward Benn before responding to his grandmother, "Thank you, Leader Wyndmere. I'm just as smitten with your grandson."

Asha clapped her hands in delight, pushing their grandmother out of the way to get to Leola and Juniper. "A reunion with my sweet brother, a meeting with the Prophesied Pair, *and* getting to know Benn's *girlfriend*, all in one day? What an absolutely splendid morning." She looked toward him, tossing her twists over shoulder. "The war is putting a bit of a damper on the mood, isn't it? Pesky Opes— always ruining *everything*," Asha prattled along happily, though her words dripped with sarcasm.

Juniper snorted. "The worst. You know, Daemon is not even interesting in person. He's putting us through all of this, and for *what*? I doubt the asshole even knows."

His sister and grandmother audibly gasped, Asha murmuring, "You've met the beast?"

Juniper nodded, pointing to the silver markings on her neck. "Oh yes, Mother Gaia gave me an all-access pass to his prison. He even offered me a job, then gifted me this lovely *tracker* when I refused to join him." She rolled her eyes.

Her rage palpable, yet her words calm, his grandmother asked, "Daemon has a *tracker* on you and has not found you yet?"

He leaned forward, explaining, "She hasn't used any magic since it was placed."

"Well, that has got to go," she replied, putting her fingers on both sides of Juniper's neck. She chanted a quiet spell and peeled the silver markings away. Juniper tensed, and Benn knew it took every bit of willpower available for Leola to stay where she was and trust his grandmother. He slipped his hand around her waist—just in case. Finally, the tension left Juniper's shoulders, and Leola deflated.

His grandmother smirked as she said, "Being the elected leader comes with great gifts. I can remove tracker marks with a simple spell. You may use your power freely now, Earthpoweress."

Juniper's claws extended out of her fingers like a descendant of the blade-handed hero from his comics.

She flexed a bladed hand and said, "Thank the Gods. I have missed these babies."

His grandmother reached out to touch the space above the sisters, her voice detached. "This cloaking spell is near impossible to detect. Levi masked this place well. Opasteg won't be able to see the troops once we move them in." He was not surprised by the shift in her mood as she turned to address him. "It's time, Bennjamin. We need to move them." So quickly, Leader Wyndmere had arrived and his Oma was nowhere to be found.

Asha stepped forward, placing a protective arm in front of his chest. "Oma, he can't move them all by himself. He will drain his power reserve." She eyed the sisters as though she were unsure if she wanted to challenge Sena with an audience. She made her decision as her pleading eyes shifted back to Sena's, but her voice remained firm. "We talked about this."

Sena, the leader, answered, "Yes, granddaughter, I remember. It is more complicated with this one entrance. It will take someone with great skill to move them, and Bennjamin is the only one who can. Daemon may not know where we are, but he certainly knows we're coming. They are practically sitting ducks there. We will not have a repeat of our last failure. I won't leave them there."

Asha was unrelenting as she pushed back, "You won't sacrifice Benn's safety either, Oma."

"Teach me." Leola's voice cut into the tense conversation like a knife. She stepped out of his arms, closer to his grandmother and sister. "Teach me how to move them through the entrance. I'll help Benn. We can move quicker together. It'll be safer for him."

Sena sent an assessing look over Leola that Benn despised, asking, "Has warping been a draining power for you? We need the Pair at full power tomorrow."

"I'll rest for the remainder of the day." Her eyes returned to his—her emotions falling over him like a gust of warm wind.

She was *scared*. There was something else; that familiar defensive instinct was rearing its head—again, for *him*. Taking on the role that Asha had fiercely tried to step into but somehow slipping under the ice that lived within his grandmother's calculative mind.

He moved to object, but she shook her head at him. "We do it together or we find another way. Benn promised to be *conservative* with his power reserve." His jaw tensed at Leola's ratting him out. She raised an eyebrow at him, announcing, "He almost died a few days ago. Did he tell you that? His power reserve dropped to 1.5%."

Relentless woman, he thought, though he couldn't shake the warmth that gathered in his chest at her courage. *Well played.*

"*Bennjamin.*" Fury—and a tinge of fear—flashed in his grandmother's gaze.

Asha smacked him on the arm. "You idiot."

He shot a flat stare at Leo that shouted *thanks-a-lot.* She smiled sweetly, and he knew the smile was everything but that.

Sena snapped, and a table of food and water appeared.

Her words were concise and serious. "Eat and hydrate, and Benn, give her a quick lesson on how to find entrances in cloaking spells." She did a quick glance around the area and said, "I'm off to find my friend, Booker."

Juniper and Asha filled plates and walked out of earshot to the other side of the meadow. Leola and Benn found seats on the soft forest ground.

"You thought you'd break our promise that easily, Wyndmere," Leo said as she popped a piece of fruit into her mouth. It was a short statement, but the anger and hurt flashing in her emotions might as well have been a red strobe light. He could taste the emotions, metallic and sticky in his throat, souring his food. He put another forkful of food in his mouth, weighing how best to respond. He'd sensed these emotions on her before, but this was the first time her anger had ever been directed toward him, and admittedly, he didn't love it. In fact, he loathed it.

"You thought me moving a few troops would break our promise?" He tried to diffuse her anger, keeping his tone playful. "You underestimate my power, Leo."

The emotions only strengthened. She looked at him, her hard gaze unflinching on his, as she explained, "*Two thousand* troops, Benn. That is how many Levi said to expect Leader Wyndmere to bring."

Flames replaced the browns of her eyes.

He let his smile drop, but didn't break eye contact as he said, "I volunteered because we didn't have another option."

"I don't believe that," she snapped, shoving a bite of food into her mouth. Distrust flared and, unfortunately, this emotion caused him physical pain. He was used to shielding from this but, of course, was unable to with her. Doubt fleeted through her mind, which he also hated; however, at least it was alleviating the pain of the distrust pulsating through his girlfriend and now through him.

He watched her swallow, waiting for her to elaborate. "Or, did you volunteer because you cannot bear to appear weak in front of your grandmother—in front of me?"

He stilled, hating to hear the words leave her mouth, hating that the words held so much truth. Her inferno gaze burnt as much as her words did, leaving him raw.

"It is not about appearing weak in front of you; it is that I cannot bear to lose *you*. The promise was I would not *sacrifice* myself for you... but I didn't say anything about not pushing the boundaries." He was quiet for a moment and exhaled, wanting to end this conversation, but she spoke before he could.

"Fine. I'd be lying if I said I wasn't planning to do the same." Understanding ran through her mind—a cool puff of air amongst the heat. A few moments passed before she said, "I see how much you want her approval. She loves you. She is proud of you. She was angry when I mentioned the stunt you pulled the other day. I did that, you know, to get a read on Leader Wyndmere. She *loves* you."

It was healing to hear, though he didn't care to examine that. His grandmother had shown him love all his life—she had raised him. But maybe a piece of him distrusted her love after she had sent him to Roswell with no contact, especially when he knew full well she had the means to check in.

And she hadn't.

He'd been miserable. Treated as a slave for months—and today, she had embraced him like it was any normal day. It wasn't. A piece of his soul had died at Roswell; nothing was normal for him now. The version of himself that had landed at the 1855 Roswell Post had not walked out.

He went to speak, but the firepoweress put her hands on his face in the same manner as he'd done to her many times before. She leaned in, pressing her forehead to his. "Leader Wyndmere. Asha. Juniper. Levi. *Me*. You dying hurts all of us, Benn. Remember that." She kissed him, pulling back to whisper, "Besides, Levi really needs you."

He recognized what she was saying as something else entirely; she needed him. She crossed her arms and lifted her gaze to the treetops.

"I'm a powerful being," he said, stacking his discarded bowl on top of hers before sending them to the mess station with a small magic bind. He wrapped his arms around her, kissing her hair. "Do not underestimate me, Runes."

"Never." She pulled out of his embrace, jumping to her feet. "Now, teach me."

He got up and they walked the perimeter of the cloak. He explained how to warp to an entrance with a cloaking spell in place, amazed at how fast she understood. He taught her how to identify a cloaking spell and its entrances.

"It's simple, really. You reach for Point A and Point B. The same as you do when you warp, every time. You lock hands with the people you're moving. Before you warp, you visualize the cloak. You may see a few clues—a blurry section of air or an obscure shape. That is where you will find an entrance. Most cloaking spells have a few holes, but Levi is skilled. His will only have one. Today, you're looking for a small star-shape in the cloak. Once you see it, you cast your magic to that opening, in a similar motion to how you warp, and warp the people—and yourself—to it. Carrying additional weight will feel like a parachute pulling you back. You've warped Juniper, and given your extensive power reserve, this shouldn't be a weight you cannot bear. The people will land at the entrance. Levi will pull them in from there. We will need to move fast; do not linger." He ran his finger through his hair, debating the amount of people that would be safe for her to warp. "Any questions?"

"Why a star?" Her brows furrowed in question. "It seems easy to spot."

"It's an old joke of ours. Any time he wanted to leave space for me in a cloaking spell, he used a star," he answered with a soft chuckle.

"A star, huh? Won't it be easy for Daemon or any Opes to see?"

"No, they may see the perimeter itself, but they would need an equally powerful Seer to see the entrance. To enter, the Seer would need to break the cloak. HQ reports that they don't have one. But Seers are rare and they like to remain hidden, so it's best to always stay prepared." He placed her hand on the perimeter of the cloaking spell as he continued, "It will feel like you're pressing into latex. It's not a wall by any means, but it takes powerful magic to break through."

She nodded. "So anyone could use the entrance?"

"No, this entrance is enchanted, which means it's to be used only by myself or Levi, but either of us could pull people in. However, with... your proximity to me... his cloaking spell will grant you access."

She cocked her head, her curiosity bubbling to the surface, as she asked, "But— we have not mated yet. How will the spell know?"

"Magic knows. Plus, my scent is all over you. It'll let you in." He chewed his lip, ignoring the heat rushing to his cheeks.

"*Oh.* Thank the Gods you don't smell." She nudged his shoulder. "We have been spending a lot of time together, huh?"

They reached a secluded area of the perimeter as he smirked. "Indeed, we have."

He pulled her to him, pressed his mouth to hers, and pressed kisses along her jaw and behind her ear. She melted like butter against his touch, and her involuntary sounds made his head swim. He was breathless by the time he moved back to her mouth, but he broke the kiss. He kept her body close to his, not ready to release her yet. He tried and miserably failed to keep his breathless voice even as he said, "Wouldn't want the cloaking spell to reject you. Now we know my scent is fresh on you. Just in case."

While that was true, there were a few methods he could have used to make sure his scent was present, although none would have been as fun as his hands on her.

She shot him a censorious look, echoing, "Just in case."

He brushed her hair out of her face, trying to memorize the way her caramel irises held his. They drank him in like he was the only male she'd ever looked at or would ever look at again.

He yearned to stay here—in this hidden place at the perimeter of the cloaking spell. He didn't give himself a moment to consider how many more times he'd see her look at him in this way. In a way that was reserved for him and him only.

He rasped, "Are you ready?" He wasn't.

She kissed him one last time before saying, "Let's go, *mate.*"

He beamed at the words and nipped at her neck, delighting at her surprised gasp. "Keep making noises like that and you'll give our hiding place away."

"I seem to remember you saying that to me in a different forest," she said with a smirk.

He pulled away from her, letting his fingers linger on her lips for one quiet moment as he groaned, "Stop distracting me, Leo."

"Is that what's happening?" she shot back.

He dropped his hand, taking hers in his as he cast his magic to his grandmother. The mist cleared and he said, "Grandmother, I need the coordinates of the troops' locations. We're ready."

CHAPTER 29

— LEOLA —

EYES, SO MANY EYES WERE ON HER. Benn warped them to the coordinates where the Underground forces were waiting, where they stood front and center as the dual-power gave announcements.

She'd known how many people would be here, yet somehow, she was surprised. She'd never struggled with confidence, but as she looked around at all of these magical beings, some of which were armed to the teeth, her stomach roiled.

They stood on a rock formation, which elevated them above the troops so everyone could see and hear them. She looked to Benn, who was explaining to the troops how the next couple of hours were going to go. They had landed here and he immediately went to work. When she'd tried to stand in the shadows behind him, he'd pulled her by his side. The crowd soaked in his eloquent words like a sponge. He was destined to lead.

He was made for this, she thought, but couldn't help but wonder, *how the hell did I get chosen as one of the Prophesied Pair, when the Gods had him as an option?*

He sent a quizzical glance toward her, and she tensed. *Shit, shit. What did I miss? Something about moving them.* He must have addressed her and she hadn't been paying attention.

He gestured to her, introducing her to everyone in front of them. "Fellow members, thank you for being here—for trusting us. Let me introduce Leola Runes, one of the poweresses of the Prophesied Pair." Gasps sounded in the crowd. She contemplated waving but bowed instead; it seemed more appropriate for this occasion. He continued, "Leola and I will be moving you into the camp. Please separate into two lines. She will move twenty soldiers at a time. I'll move fifty. As you all know, it is essential you stay connected to the person next to you at all times— holding hands or looping arms will work splendidly. If you break the connection, we won't be using the resources to find you. Once we warp, we'll reach a drop point, just outside the camp." Levi appeared next to him on the rock.

The Seer had left after they landed to put another cloaking spell around the area where the troops currently stood—it would protect them from human passersby or any of Daemon's ilk. Leader Wyndmere was hoping to catch Daemon by surprise— they might do it, if this went smoothly.

"Conscript Miravale will grant you passage into the camp entrance in segments of fifty." Levi gave a soft tilt of his head to the troops.

Levi took over the communication to the troops. "At this time, there is a cloaking spell in place here. I built one surrounding the camp as well. Once you leave here, and until you are inside the camp, it is essential that you stay silent." He glanced around. Leola wondered if he was intentionally trying to keep his words vague. "We know Daemon is watching us, but he has not discovered where we are—yet. That could change. You will all be exposed at the drop location. Stay alert. Stay silent. Move quickly and be ready to defend at all times." She mentally noted he had not made mention of the attack from the Lykosos earlier today. He clasped his hands together, continuing, "This is the first step to taking out Opasteg. We have long awaited this opportunity. Let's not waste it." He raised his fist in the air and the crowd mimicked the motion.

Cheers erupted, weapons raised, and streams of magic shot into the air.

And with that, they began their mission.

It ended up being easier than she'd expected. It was exhausting, but not difficult. Benn had explained the process to her and that was exactly how it went. She locked hands with the person next to her, which then connected her to every person that she was warping as long as they had a hold on one another. Once they were connected, she envisioned where they currently stood and where they were attempting to go. The cloaking spell appeared as a blurry fog. It was impossible to see with the naked eye, until Benn had shown her what to look for. Once she was looking at the perimeter of the cloaking spell, she searched for the star-shaped entrance and cast her power toward it. Then, they moved.

The landing was rough, and she apologized, pulling the person next to her off the ground. It was an older, fair-skinned man. His blonde hair was disheveled, but Leola was relieved to see he was otherwise unharmed.

He grinned, dusting his leathers off, as he complimented her, "Well done, kid."

She checked on each of the people she had warped with to ensure they were all accounted for. Thankfully, each of them was unfazed by the hard landing. By the time she reached Levi, the tension had left her shoulders. She watched him work in pure awe as he began pulling people through the quarter-sized, star shaped entrance. Each person stepped forward, touched the entrance, and then they were whisked away—like they had never been standing there at all. Poof. Gone. Made invisible by Levi's cloaking spell.

Levi winked at her, his emerald eyes much more hazel today. She did a double take as he waved her away. She warped back to the site, latching onto more troops, repeating the process again and again.

Six hours later, she was sitting back at the Underground site, exhausted. It was the kind of exhaustion that was uncomfortable, but not detrimental. She lay on the ground, sensing the dual-power before he appeared beside her.

"I'm giving myself five minutes to sit here," she said, not bothering to open her eyes. "Then, I'm off to find Juniper. I haven't seen her all day."

"She's with Asha. I saw her on my way in. They were helping troops get settled with their supplies." Benn caressed her cheek, murmuring, "You deserve to sit here. You were a marvel today."

She kept her eyes closed. Even if she wanted to, she would need to physically pry her eyelids open at this point, and she was not going to do that. Her arms were leaden at her sides. "It was kind of weird to have all those people watching me. That's more of Juniper's thing. I guess it comes with the territory of being..." She'd never referred to her or her sister as the term, but she whispered it anyway, "*The Prophesied Pair.*"

"Hmm," he mused. "I suppose it does come with the territory. But, if it makes you feel better, you shine wonderfully in the spotlight."

She huffed in annoyance. "I'd prefer to avoid the spotlight at all costs."

He chuckled as Levi landed next to him. The Seer eyed them both warily, muttering, "Well, that was even more tedious and awful than I expected. How are you two doing?"

Benn's tone was flat. "I'm dragging. My guess is that our power reserves are below 40%."

"Precisely." He crossed his arms over his chest. "It was necessary, but we need you both at 100% tomorrow."

She cast a sideways glance at Levi. "So *bossy*. You need to be mindful, too, Seer."

"Always am." He smirked. "Dying young is overrated. Don't drain yourselves."

She sat up with a start, plagued with a sudden need to warn her sister as Levi had warned her. "Juniper—"

He waved a reassuring hand, his tone remaining cool as he said, "She has actually been modest with her power use today. She said she's saving it for Daemon." He looked to the sky through his thick frames. She assumed he was seeing something, something somewhere else. "There's more planning to be done, but it sounds like we'll send you and Juniper to the volcano entrance at sunrise."

She nodded. "I want to spend some time with her and Papa." She looked toward Benn, who was relaxing next to her. She touched his chest and said, "You guys stay here. Levi, please watch Benn and make sure he doesn't get any stupid ideas."

"You're my girlfriend, not my keeper," he noted.

"Ha-ha," she sarcastically said as she walked away from them, crossing the camp toward her family.

She watched her Papa from the shadowy forest, admiring the efficient and skillful way he fashioned weapons using his Earthpower and the materials offered by the forest. Despite the shift of her newfound life, it would take her time to get used to seeing *him* as a magical being. He was as threatening as a teddy bear in her eyes, yet here he was, creating weapons faster than any Modern-Era technology could.

She'd been worrying for him daily, assuming he would be lost without her and her sister. When he'd shown up today, it was clear that that was not the case. Now was the time to get answers to the questions muddling her mind.

"Come on out, Leo. I know you're there," he called without turning to look at her.

She straightened, clearing her throat in greeting. "Papa." She walked to the table he leaned over. Bowls holding powders of various colors covered the table; arrows and spears were arranged by size in neat piles. She ran her finger over an arrow, avoiding the sharp point on the end. Her antagonizing mind had plagued her during the entire walk over here, but somehow, she arrived here utterly speechless. Minutes passed before his eyes met hers; she warmed at his familiar gaze, one that was intent but kind.

"I—we didn't mean to leave you," she said, starting small. "I heard you and Juniper got to talk earlier."

"Yes, we talked." She swore she saw his hands tremble. "I know you saw your grandmother at the 1855 Roswell Post. I'm glad you got to spend some time with her." His voice caught on the last sentence.

"You knew she was there all along?"

Booker sighed, running his hands over his head. "Sena came to me a few weeks ago. She told me that Ava was doing well. I was thrilled; I had a hard time when your grandmother was called to that post. I wanted to be the one to go, but my calling was to remain in the Modern-Era with you girls and protect you until the time came. I possess strong defensive magic. It would have been useful if Daemon did learn where you two were—my role was to do what was needed to protect you." Tears glistened in his maple-toned eyes. "I knew from Sena's arrival that her intentions weren't to tell me of my wife's endeavors. I knew that once she showed up at our house, she would have news for me regarding you and your sister. Selfishly, I tried to deny it. I prayed to the Gods that somehow, some way, you two wouldn't be the true Pair. But we had known for a while, since you were young girls—it was *you*. Still, the news brought me to my knees. You and Juniper would be called to serve. I pushed back. I told Sena, 'They know nothing of the Underground! Who will teach them? How will they receive a vellum? How will they access their power?' The powers that Ava and I had chosen to take from you girls so long ago." He sighed and continued, "Sena handed me a vellum, one that warned of a relic that would cross your paths and transport you both. I read it—I read it one hundred times. It was true; the plan was in place. You and Juniper would be transported to the 1855 Roswell Post, where you would meet your grandmother—and Bennjamin."

Her mouth parted. "You knew he would be there?"

"Oh, yes, I have known him for years, albeit from afar, but he is no stranger to me. I was a professor at the Academy when your mother attended." This was news to Leola. "I retired after your mother was captured. I walked the halls that he grew up in and I knew the professors who taught him. I even crossed paths with Bennjamin when he was a young boy, before we had to go into hiding. I knew he was a brilliant power—just like his mother, sweet Josephine. Any Assignment in the 1800s would be an unpleasant one, so I was relieved to know that he and Ava would get to spend time together at their post. When we were forced into hiding—into hiding you girls—Ava and I mourned the fact that Sena's family had to cut contact with us. The Wyndmeres were our best friends. Your mother and Josephine were *so* close. It was for the best, but we always found ourselves wondering about Josephine's children. The night we lost your mother... It felt like we were losing another daughter. When we learned that Josephine had been imprisoned as well, that was even worse. But Daemon repeatedly attacked the powerful families—our choice to hide gave you and Juniper a safe upbringing. Despite how painful it was—how wrong it seemed—it's what your mother would have wanted for you.

"I knew you and Junebug would be in good, capable hands with Sena's grandson." He paused and the next words came out as an emotional whisper. "But despite everything I knew, it still—it *broke* me—to send you away with no warning. I wanted so badly to explain to you what was happening, but there was no time. The Underground let me know that Daemon had gotten word that you were in Poppycal. To ensure you were protected, I followed you and Juniper while you shopped that day. I disposed of a few Opes hanging around. You two were so vulnerable—so *exposed*. You were oblivious to the magic and power around you—the magic within you. You knew nothing of the evil that was threatening you. I knew I had no other option but to follow through with the plan and send you away. I promised myself that if you two and I crossed paths that day, I'd come clean about everything. Every last thing. But then, you two disappeared from that deli; I sensed time magic all around the street, as if an explosion of the power had occurred. Then, I saw a man—an Ope Corruptor—run out of the deli. He was irate. I followed him. He was careless—unsuspecting of any Underground in the area. He met with another Ope, claiming he'd seen the Prophesied Pair. He explained that he had an inkling of where you went—he had put tracking magic on the '*girl with the braids.*' I knew he was talking about my Bug. I contemplated killing him on the spot. I resisted and went to

Sena instead, telling her everything I heard and saw. In exchange, she comforted me by letting me know that you two had made it safely to your grandmother and the time-wielder."

She reached out and caught a tear that had spilled out onto his cheek. Her heart cracked as his words broke him. She hadn't seen her Papa cry since her mother had disappeared.

"I forgive you, Papa." Her own tears warmed her face. "Everything you did—Grandmava did. I understand and I forgive you. We forgive you." He scooped her up in a tight embrace. She leaned in and inhaled his familiar scent—balsam—the scent transporting her to their living room in Poppycal.

Juniper appeared beside them and joined in on the hug.

It felt right to be in his arms. Safe.

He pulled back and looked into each of their eyes, kissing their foreheads.

His voice shook with the emotion that he was fighting. "I never thought I could know a love like this—especially after losing my children. But I was wrong. I'm so incredibly proud of you both. No matter what happens tomorrow, you two are the *best* things that have ever happened to me. You are my greatest prize. It was worth all of the pain I have endured to have you two girls. You are *everything*."

They embraced again, standing in the shadows of the forest for long minutes.

Later, Leo sat idly by her sister and Papa, admiring them as they gushed over poison formulas. At one point, Juniper looked so thrilled that Leola swore she saw stars in her eyes.

Earthpowers. She couldn't help but grin.

They were both magnificent. Their Papa excelled at building weapons out of wood and infusing them with poison, while Juniper used her innate power to comprise her thorned claws, her own version of noxious blades. She thought her Papa might fall over in awe when Juniper flexed her fingers to summon the Nightshade claws. They even fist-bumped. She absorbed the moment, committing the image of Juniper's and Papa's twin smiles as they connected about their similar power to her memory.

"I hate to break this up." Benn appeared next to her, lacing his finger in hers. "I saved you from the boring diplomacy parts, but we need to start planning. I figured you'd want to be present for that."

She nodded, warping with Benn, while the Earthpowers warped together.

Leader Wyndmere's tent was large enough to accommodate twenty people. She studied the map sprawled across the table, a barrier between Sena's inner circle and the 'younglings,' as the generals had begun to call them. Juniper, Leola, Booker, Levi, and Benn stood to the left of Sena. On the right stood members of Sena's inner circle and Asha. The map showcased the surrounding area, red dots marking the movements of enemy forces.

"Levi enchanted the map to refresh with the movements of the enemies every four minutes," Sena said as she pointed. "Here, we can see troops—magic-wielders and creatures."

Leola squinted in the candlelight, resisting the urge to fidget. She moved her hands to her hips, crossed them over her chest, and then moved them back to her hips again.

Juniper cast a sideways glance at her, mouthing, "You okay?"

She straightened as she mouthed back, "Never better."

Juniper smirked, returning her eyes back to the enchanted map.

"We need to decide how the Pair is entering the volcano. Too many troops will announce their arrival," a man whose name she'd forgotten explained.

"Not enough troops leaves them vulnerable," Benn said over her shoulder, shooting a look of daggers at the man across from her.

ECHOES OF HOLLOW AND EMBER

"If they are the Prophesied Pair, do they need defense?" another power scoffed. "The Gods said *they* would defeat Daemon, not our entire army. We haven't seen their power."

"Leola assisted me in moving you all here today. A feat I couldn't have done without her help," Benn interjected. "Juniper spent the day using her power to create weapons. Raja, you can't mean to doubt them, to doubt the Gods, when the resource they chose has finally arrived to save us?"

Raja. Right, that was the name she'd been looking for.

"You're biased." Raja looked to both of them with the same affection someone would have for a squashed insect as he said, "We're aware of your affections for *this* one."

"Leola," she said, standing taller. She was close to Raja's height anyway but wanted to stand up for herself. "That is my name. You may use it."

"You won't disrespect her when she and her sister are what is standing in between us and our ruin, Raja," Sena snarled. "Now be helpful or you will leave my tent."

He shrunk but didn't speak again.

Sena pointed to the base of the mountain and sent a pointed look toward the dark-haired power in her inner circle. "Let's stay focused. We place troops here. The pair will hike up to the volcano, make their way inside, and signal once they've made it."

"We could use a flare?" Leola suggested.

"Too obvious," Benn muttered.

Fair, she thought, pursing her lips.

"Bennjamin, *mates* are able to communicate through a mental bond," Leader Wyndmere noted. "It would be helpful—"

"Enough, Grandmother." Benn's voice was as firm as a fist.

She was not seriously suggesting in front of all these people that they mate—be intimate—for the first time.

In front of Papa? Disbelieving, Leola's eyes flitted between the dual-power and his grandmother, who looked to be in a silent war taking place in the form of eye communication.

He broke the contact, his apologetic eyes searching hers as a soothing wave caressed her arms.

Leola suggested, "Can we use a burner phone? Or a real phone as a signal? I mean this may sound dumb, but can't I just *text* Benn once I'm in there?"

Looks were exchanged across the room.

Leader Wyndmere hummed. "That might work."

Leo almost smirked at the irony that the eldest generation hadn't considered using Modern-era technology to win a war in the Modern-Era. Nevertheless, she was pleased that one of her ideas had made it into the plan.

Still put off by the strategic discussion about her and Benn's sex life in front of everyone, she spoke again. "So, we will land inside the volcano, then I'll open the entrance. Once we're inside, we will free the prisoners so they can gain back their stolen powers. When they are freed and ready to move, we will call in Benn to start warping them out to safety," Leola said as she looked toward Benn. His jaw was ticking, as it did when his thoughts turned to a chasm. She waited for him to say something, but when he didn't, she continued, "Once the prisoners are out, we'll take on Daemon. I imagine he will notice the disturbance in his prison and show up there on his own accord, though."

"Sounds easy enough," Juniper chimed in over her shoulder, pointing a resolute chin toward Raja. "Care to comment?"

He crossed his arms in defiance, avoiding her gaze.

Levi's face twisted into a grimace, his fingers gracing a few points on the map. "Something is lingering here. I can't see it. It's like it is hidden. I'd bet that means that Daemon does not want *me* to see it. It could be a trap—maybe hidden forces." He scrubbed his face with his hand, which had a pearlescent bronze, sun-kissed hue to it from the day they had. "I think we need to be prepared for a counterattack."

"We are supposed to have the element of surprise on our hands," Leader Wyndmere commented, eyebrows raised.

Papa cut in, "It is better to cover all of our bases. Last time, we underestimated Opasteg. They bested us—at a great cost."

Benn sighed. "We bring troops in to support a counterattack. They secure the perimeter, while Leola and Juniper hike. I go in once I get the signal and move the prisoners. The troops remain there for any counterattack or added protection. Asha stays on guard for messages that come through—just in case they can be useful."

"Phone or no phone, Benn can call me for back-up. I can plan to stand by to help move the prisoners while I keep watch for threats. You'll need me to break the wards and spells put on that place anyway," Levi said.

Leola raised her eyebrows in question. Up until this point, she hadn't known Benn and Levi could communicate telepathically.

Levi noticed her silent question—in that unnerving way that she'd still not gotten used to. "Seers can hear messages from people they are deeply connected to—signals of distress or excitement. Benn and I are practically brothers, so I can *see* him most of the time." He laughed at his own pun. "I'll keep my eyes open for any signals from Benn. Asha—you can listen for any Ancestral guidance."

Asha nodded. "I think we should consider sending protective forces with the Pair as they hike and enter the volcano. We may surprise Daemon, but he will appear there as soon as he feels their presence. The prison is expertly warded. There is no way he will let them just... waltz inside. Daemon may be a pompous asshole, but he is not *stupid*. If it is too easy to walk in, that's because Daemon made it that way."

Benn leaned heavily over the table as he sighed. "Asha is right. A trap—of some kind, I'm sure—is waiting for you two." His contemplative gaze swept over Leo's face, so swift that she couldn't read it fully. "I can guard them as they enter the volcano."

"No." Juniper shook her head.

"So he can catch *all* of us in the trap? No," Leola cut him off with harsh finality. "We go in and we send a signal to *you*—just as we discussed. If we don't send word, you know something went wrong. You make a plan with the others, and you come in to rescue us."

"I won't send you into a trap," he pressed, low enough so only she could hear.

"It's not up to you," she said in the same volume, before turning to speak to the group. "We will move faster, just us two. This is all assuming I can wield the lava apart enough to go into it. We'd be fools to assume I can make space for an army."

"She's right," Sena said. "We send them, wait for the signal, and have rescue troops on standby."

"How will we get into the volcano if Leola—our strongest firepoweress—is trapped inside?" Benn asked.

The validity of his question chilled Leola to the core—the thought of Juniper trapped in a volcano if *she* failed solidified in her mind like lead. Her eyes heated as her panic rose; suddenly, the tent was crowded. The voices around her reverberated into an anxiety-heightening mush.

"You'll have to leave it up to me," Levi said as he pulled his frames off to clean them. "We'll get to them. I like this. With multiple plans in play, any Ope Seers will have a hell of a time intercepting us."

Juniper flexed her claws. "Daemon and the other Opes have not seen our power. To them, we might still seem like a myth. Let's hope they underestimate us, we get inside easy-peasy, the prisoners are freed, and Daemon's head is on a stake by dinner time." She shrugged.

She latched onto her sister's words, needing a way to get out of the tent fast. "Easy-peasy. Nothing we can't handle."

She patted Benn's arm, and he met her eyes with a frown. He looked less than pleased, but the options were too limited for him to be picky. The sooner they agreed to a plan, the sooner she could leave this tent—the frenzied thoughts were prevailing, and she needed out. A look of understanding softened his features.

His tone was clipped as he asked, "Are we finished for tonight?"

Leader Wyndmere tapped her walking stick. "We will stay and iron out the details. You younglings get some rest. We'll meet just before dawn to begin." With a graceful wave, they were dismissed.

She was first out of the tent, hands on her head as she looked up toward the sky.

Strong arms surrounded her. "Breathe. Let me help," Benn murmured as he rested his head on hers, his power blanketing her panic. "Sena is wanting me to return. I need to spend a few more minutes in the war tent. Will you wait up for me?"

She nodded, taking in her first full breath since walking outside.

"That's better." She could hear the relief in his voice, as he said, "I won't be long. I'll find you when I'm done talking to Sena." He warped into the tent before she could respond.

———

It was a warm, cloudless night. Moonlight and starlight shone exquisitely, and she found herself admiring the sky for long minutes. She wondered what awaited her tomorrow—what awaited all of them. She wondered who she would be after tomorrow; would she even recognize herself? Is this the last night sky she would get to enjoy?

"Leola," a soft voice interrupted her thoughts.

She looked up to meet the blonde's eyes—having only just realized that she and Asha were the only ones who stood near Leader Sena's tent. She'd gotten so lost in the darkness—of the night sky and her thoughts—that she'd been oblivious to her surroundings.

Asha's smile was warm and inviting—like a bright light you wanted to lean into, as Benn had described it. She returned it with a genuine smile of her own.

"I wanted to talk to you before tomorrow."

She straightened. "Of course."

"I need to say... I have never seen Bennjamin so happy. Life has forced him to be wary, determined, calculating—he's always under her microscope. But on the inside, I knew my carefree, joyful brother still lived in the tough shell he has been forced to build." She looked toward the war tent. "I see pieces of him returning— parts of him I thought had been lost at the Academy."

Leola's gaze followed hers as she asked, "What happened there?"

Asha sighed, pulling her blonde twists over her shoulder. "You'll have to let my brother tell you. One day, when the enemy is defeated. When he feels ready to share."

Leola wondered if they would actually get that time—time beyond tonight. She never considered her life ending early, but with tomorrow's events approaching, she was painfully aware of her mortality. Her palms heated in response. She pushed the thought away and said, "He deserves to be happy. He's lovely."

That was the understatement of the century; he was everything.

Asha watched her with a knowing smile. "So do you. So are you."

She didn't acknowledge that; tonight wasn't the night to prioritize *her* happiness. "I'm glad I got to meet you, Asha. Benn adores you. I hope we get more time to spend more time together... after this."

The warmth in her eyes had Leola's throat tightening. Unexpectedly, Asha wrapped strong arms around her; she stiffened for one heartbeat before returning the embrace, relishing in the safeness of the hug. They'd only met this morning, but it felt as though she'd known Asha for years. Perhaps this was a quality both of the Wyndemere siblings possessed—the ability to foster a safe place for anyone they met, even strangers.

Asha whispered, "We will, if the Ancestors are as kind as I know them to be."

"Blessed night, Asha." Papa appeared next to her, already speaking. "May I borrow my granddaughter?"

"Gods, I'm popular tonight," Leola said.

Asha chuckled, releasing her. "She's all yours."

She gave a nod to Asha, who sent a wave back, walking shoulder-to-shoulder with Papa.

"I wanted to test something. I tried with Juniper earlier today—to teach her how to wield windpower. I taught Power Access at the Academy, preparing students to wield before their magic manifested." He let out a wry chuckle. "Your father was an absolute scumbag. However, he was a powerful windpower. I'm hoping one of you can wield his power. Juniper seemed to be close to accessing it, but she mentioned you couldn't use ice. Maybe you can try the wind instead."

She raised her brows at the mention of the man—her father—her grandparents never acknowledged. Of course, she hadn't known he'd been a windpower, but it made sense. She summoned the purple iceflame to her palm, and her grandfather's jaw dropped.

"*Wow.* What is that?"

"Fire that acts like ice—it causes blisters and frostbite," she said as she ignored the twinge of annoyance resulting from not being able to wield true ice. "Most of the water I wield turns to steam. This flame is the closest thing to ice in my arsenal."

"You are magnificent." Her grandfather patted her head. "Don't be too hard on yourself, Leo. You wield fire, water.... and whatever this is. Many would kill for those powers. Being critical of yourself will only get in your way." He took her hands. "Now, close your eyes. Imagine a breeze. A living breeze surrounding you and pulling at your skin. It is easiest to draw power out of yourself when you're comfortable with it."

She did as he said, remnants of a breeze tickling her arms. It was soft—nearly unnoticeable.

"Open your eyes." His smooth voice filled the air.

She did. Fallen leaves floated around them; her mouth fell open.

"Am I doing that?" The leaves fell to the ground, and she deflated a bit.

Her grandfather's grin wrinkled the skin around his brown eyes, and he clapped. "Yes! Of course you did. I'll tell you the same as I told your sister: use the wind to fuel your innate power. Use it as a shield to protect you or to disorient your enemy. Wind is a great power." He shrugged. "And if that son of a bitch didn't give you anything other than life, at least he gave you that."

She snorted at her grandfather's words. He laughed with her. She leaned in and hugged him. "Thank you, Papa. For being here and for teaching me that."

"Oh, Leo. Don't thank me. I'll protect you until my last breath." His voice was thick, and she forced herself to ignore the sadness in his words.

She stood in the embrace, wanting to savor the feelings it elicited: secure, tranquil, formidable. All of these were sentiments she would need to rely on tomorrow as she somehow did what was expected of her.

He pulled back. "You need to rest now. Go find Juniper; make sure she plans to do the same. You were always a bit more cautious. At this moment, I imagine your sister is a bit more excited than you are." He winked at her. "I love you, firesprite."

"Love you, Papa," she said, sending a pulse of power to Juniper's location, and warping.

She found Juniper and Asha huddled together, chatting about a reality show.

She plopped down next to them, muttering, "Hate to be the fun buster, but we should go to bed soon."

"Ugh, but Asha has the season finale downloaded to her tableau. I *really* want to watch it!" Juniper's voice came out as a whine.

She sucked her cheek, truthfully, she wanted to watch it, too, though she knew they should retire for the night. She debated, shooting her sister a censorious look. Juniper returned it with an insistent glare.

"Leo." Benn's voice interrupted their brief staredown.

She looked over her shoulder, catching his intense eyes locked on her own. Her stomach fluttered.

She turned toward Juniper as she offered, "30 minutes? You can watch half of it and we'll watch the second half tomorrow night."

Something to look forward to, she thought but didn't dare say aloud.

"Yesyesyes!" Juniper clapped her hands, leaning into Asha's tableau. "Take your time, Benny. I bet we get a whole hour if we're lucky." She winked at Asha.

She shook her head in Juniper's direction, but didn't acknowledge the quip. Benn held out a hand and she used it to pull herself up. He kept his hold on her hand; they walked in easy silence until they reached a far part of the camp—away from the nervous chatter.

His eyes searched her face. "How are you feeling about tomorrow?"

She sent him an arched look. "You can't tell?"

He bit his inner lip. "You know I can. But your emotions are changing fast. It's always better if you tell me yourself, always. It's better than cheating and... well, taking a look for myself."

"It is not cheating if it is your power, Benn."

He waited. She dropped his hand and wrapped her arms around her own body in a tight hug. She didn't want to discuss this—admitting her feelings to him would be the first admission of the lurking thought that they might not succeed. A thought that, as much as she had tried to ignore it, had been pestering her all day. It was a betrayal to herself—to the Underground. It was a betrayal to her mother, his mother, and all the parents and loved ones trapped in Daemon's cavern. She hugged herself tighter, staring deeper into the dark meadow where they stood.

Her response came out in a whisper. "I'm hoping I'm enough. I'm hoping that I'm strong enough—that I'm *brave* enough to succeed tomorrow."

His touch was light on her cheek as his thick brows drew together. "What about this *entire* experience has made you think you won't be?"

"I don't know," she answered honestly.

She could trace it back to every moment of self-doubt that had made her question her place in the so-called "Prophesied Pair." Confident by nature, she was still so *new* to this world—and this role.

"I see it; sometimes emotions are hard to decipher, even in our own minds. I can explain what I'm seeing, if you would like me to. Then we can talk through it."

His voice was gentle, yet the taut line of his jaw betrayed him; he was doing this solely out of love, out of a fierce, unyielding need to help her. Even as every fiber of his being resisted it, his quiet words told her he would rather not use his emotion-wielding power on her, but his devotion kept him rooted there, doing it anyway.

She nodded her consent, and he took her hand back in his, rubbing idle circles, as he said, "It's the pressure. The pressure of others, though it is likely amplified by your own emotions. The pressure to be great is... making you doubtful. You're uncertain. Not of your power, but of something else?" Benn mused as she listened.

He released her hand as he spread a blanket on the grass that she hadn't noticed he was holding. He sat down gracefully and pulled her onto his lap. "I know that feeling. I'm quite familiar with it, actually. I think they call it Imposter Syndrome."

He chuckled, and she scowled in response.

"You are *everything*, Leo." He pressed his lips to her temple, pulling her tighter to his chest. "And it's not all on *you*, by the way. Juniper will be by your side, and she is a *force*. In addition to her, you'll have me and Levi and the entire Underground on your side. We're not going to let you take *all* the credit in defeating Daemon and his Opasteg filth." His straight, white teeth shone bright in the moonlit meadow.

She settled her head against his chest, tilting her face up so she could see the stars. Distantly, she wished that there would be answers written in the constellations. There weren't, so she tried to find solace in his warm embrace instead.

They fell into a comfortable silence again as his fingers trailed circles across her arms. He placed delicate kisses across her jaw. Her mind drifted back to Leader Wyndmere's earlier comment—about their mating. The question she was about to ask had butterflies fluttering under her skin—dizzied and excitable. He stiffened, no doubt, reading the anticipation in her emotions.

"Should we—would it be better if we could communicate telepathically tomorrow?" Her question interrupted the silence.

He stilled, pausing his circles; his quiet response tickled her cheek. "Why do you say that?"

She was having a hell of a time getting the words out, thankfully, the darkness masked the flaring heat in her cheeks. "The—what Leader Wyndmere said in the tent. Your grandmother... might have a point."

He turned her to face him, his eyes canvassing hers. Annoyance flickered there as he said, "She does *not* make decisions for us." His voice was hard, authoritative, not directed at her but at the suggestion of acting on something out of mere suggestion; Leola could have guessed he'd react this way. Her chivalric defender.

She swallowed, reiterating, "I would do—that—tonight. If it puts us in a better position tomorrow."

She bit her cheek, wishing to the Gods that they'd mask her emotions from this male for once. She'd had intimate relationships before—but, with the added aspect of *mating*, the commitment was otherworldly and consuming. She was more than willing—eagerly excited to reach that point with him—but she'd only learned they were mates this morning. She'd only learned what mates *were* a few days ago. She wanted more time to spend with Benn, to get to know him, before diving into that. However, in regard to the prospect of succeeding tomorrow, she was prepared to do whatever was needed... even if that meant forfeiting her own life.

Maybe we should do it. Or is it wrong for us to mate just to be a stronger threat to Daemon? Maybe— The thoughts raged in her head until his voice interrupted them.

"*Stop. I sense your apprehension, Leo.*" He straightened, his hand pushing her hair over her shoulder. "*Stop, please. I don't want that moment between us to feel desperate—frantic. I want it to be memorable. I want it to be on our own terms. I want you—not in a desperate way—*"

She pulled back. "I didn't say I wasn't desperate for you."

"I *am* desperate for you." His eyes heated. "However, our first time... I am going to cherish you. Just as I intend to every time that follows—" His voice took on the hoarseness that she'd only heard when they were alone. "So, I'd like to wait... wait for something more romantic—a bit more private—than a war camp."

Relief flooded her; she knew that he could sense that shift. For those words and the boyish expression on his face, she kissed him fully.

She broke the kiss. "Are you sure? I want this, too. I want you—but tonight, the fear is weighing on me."

He held her chin between his thumb and forefinger, murmuring, "Then tonight is not the night for this. For us. We'll save it. It will be something for us to look forward to after this is all over." She leaned into his words, kissing him again, letting her hands explore his muscled arms and the sharp panes of his face, their mouths fused together, only parting to come up for air.

Their passion deepened, each teasing caress melting into urgent, breathless touches—fingers tracing, grasping, holding on as if they could freeze time, each touch a silent plea, a promise for a moment in the future.

She was lost in the haze that was being with Benn when she whispered, "I love you." The haze cleared. She panicked, trying to backtrack as she stuttered out, "I—I think."

He smiled against her mouth, tangling his fingers in her curls as he spoke against her lips. "I can say, with certainty, that I am completely, inescapably in love with you." His fingers traced her jawline with aching tenderness, lifting her face to his as if drawn by gravity itself. His espresso-hued eyes locked onto hers, intertwining their souls and syncing their heartbeats. "You consume me, Leo. I want you for eternity. Until I meet the Gods and beyond that."

Tears burned her eyes, her voice barely a whisper. "That sounds suspiciously like a goodbye, Bennjamin."

He kissed the tear that spilled onto her cheek. "It is not a goodbye. It's a promise, my flame."

CHAPTER 30

— BENN —

Year: Modern-Era
7 July
Salemfir, Heri

DAWN ARRIVED, KICKSTARTING THE MORNING with the camp already abuzz with activity. He stood near the weapons caches so he could observe each soldier as they collected what they needed for the day. He'd selected and packed his weapons last night—as well as any spares he might need. He pasted a permanent scowl on his face that he hoped was giving the essence of steadfast, focused leadership—hopefully not indicative of the swirling tension in his gut.

His failure to hide his nervousness was evident by the eyebrow Asha tilted toward him as she approached. He couldn't force a smile, so he merely nodded at her. They observed the movement of the camp, not speaking, while he picked at his nails with his dagger. They were clean, but the act was giving him something to do—something to focus on. His sister placed a gentle touch to his free hand, pulling it away from the dagger.

She spoke in a volume only he would hear. "Relax, brother. The sisters are strong." She sheathed her sword. "The Ancestors are... hopeful. Perhaps we'll see mother again today."

His ears perked up; Fas weren't permitted to reveal the moods or messages of the Ancestors or Gods, yet Asha was doing just that—sharing the insight that had been gifted to her. With a wink, she strode off. As he stared at her retreating back, the flash of hope melded into pure dread. She was hopeful that their mother was alive, but he didn't share that sentiment—especially after Josephine had helped Juniper escape through that time portal a few days ago. Daemon would have been a fool to keep the legendary time-wielder alive after that kind of betrayal.

Tears pricked in his eyes as a familiar firepoweress appeared next to him, pressing her lips to his cheek. He pulled her into his arms, reveling in her scent as he said, "Happy Morning, Leo."

"Today's the day." Her voice was cheery as she ducked out of his arms to grab throwing stars and a dagger.

"Today's the day," he echoed, attempting to disguise the stress in his voice. "You have your climbing gear?" He asked a question he already knew the answer to, mostly to fill the silence and to drown out the roar of panic building between his temples.

Juniper scoffed; he'd been so focused on Leola that he hadn't noticed the other sister appear. "*You have your climbing gear?*" She mocked his accent that sounded a bit more Salemfirite than Rosebayish, but Benn chuckled as he turned toward her. Her voice returned to normal as she asked, "Are you seriously asking that, Benny? You think we're going to arrive at the volcano without it?"

He rolled his eyes, shaking his head. "Happy Morning to you, Juniper. You are *just* the person I've been wanting to see." The time relic hummed in his pocket; he pulled it out and dropped it into her waiting palm. "I believe this belongs to you. He's glamoured, so Daemon won't sense its presence. He knows his orders—to help you and Leo. He will even self-destruct if needed."

Juniper beamed at the pocket watch, stroking the face with both admiration and skepticism.

He tapped the face of the pocket watch. "He owes me. Simply rub the face, whisper what you need, and he will deliver. Powerful relic, that one. Good find," he remarked, knowing the watch would relish in the compliment.

It hummed in thanks.

Protect them, my friend. Benn spoke to the pocket watch wordlessly, letting his appreciation leak into his words. This was the relic that had brought the sisters to him, tipped off Levi that Benn was at Roswell, and helped catalyze the moment that changed his entire life. *Return them to me, safely. Once again.*

I will protect them with my being. Until we meet again, my time friend. The scratchy voice had once sent chills down his spine, but today, he found himself comforted by its response.

Levi landed next to Benn, wincing at the relic. "I *hate* when they speak."

A questioning look passed between the sisters.

Levi tilted his head, indicating for Benn to follow. He kissed Leola's forehead and fell into step with the Seer.

"Don't tell me—you've made friends with the relic?" Levi shivered.

Once they were out of earshot of the sisters *and* the relic, Benn replied, "I'll do pretty much anything to save my mate."

They walked east, following the path to the volcano. Levi led at the front, advising the troops to be on their guard to defend; they were the first line of defense for whatever awaited them. Benn moved along the rear, keeping a close watch on the surrounding forest. Members of the Order, including Asha and Raja, were scattered throughout to relay orders from Leader Wyndmere, who rode in the middle. Above, Booker led a group of Earthpowers through the trees to provide aerial cover.

He'd lowered his shield to get an overall sense of what was happening around him—utilizing the emotions of the troops to give him a full scope. *Alertness. Determination. Fear. Adrenaline. Rage. Fear. Fear. Fear.* The general mood of the group was consistent. Consistency was easy—predictable.

The sisters walked near Levi so they were protected in case of any ambush. In their private discussion, the Seer had explained that while the shifting plans would allow them to surprise Opasteg, some threat loomed that Levi couldn't see—could only sense.

"Station the Pair close to me. Once the threat is concrete, I'll have a minute's notice. I'll make it count." Benn scowled as his closest friend's words played in his mind.

In the sea of minds, Leola's was the most prominent. It hummed in *anticipation*—buzzing like a bee in a spring breeze, fast and fleeting. The anticipation turned to resignation. Not fearful, but he hadn't expected fear to be the theme of his mate today. The crunching sounds of the dead leaves under his boots were distant in his mind as he contemplated how he should feel about her feeling *resigned*.

Resigned about what? Dying? His stomach lurched.

He sent a wave of calming magic her way; gratitude flickered through her auburn-tinted mind, soon followed by adoration—as though she'd recognized it was him.

He relished in the emotion; he would hold onto that thought for later—later, after they'd survived this dreadful day. From toddlerhood, he'd been trained to be a weapon, so going out in battle seemed like a fitting, honorable way to meet the Gods. However, that all changed with the arrival of the firepoweress who was as vital to this war as she was to his existence. Now a death brought on by battle seemed like *theft*. Of his time and of his purpose. And if she died—

He cut the thought off, though it opened the floodgates to a rabbit hole of deaths he would not—could not—accept today. Asha. Levi. His grandmother. Juniper. *Josephine*. So many hopes and wishes, each its own plaguing thought that swallowed the space in the forefront of his mind. Guilt settled into his gut like a lead weight; he knew he was asking the Gods for too much today, when he should be prioritizing the prosperity of the mission, not his own life being spared—of all things. As much as he despised the thought of his own untimely meeting with Mors, he didn't dare ask the Gods to consider his survival.

His anxiety was a cursed, overactive troll this morning.

He looked toward where Booker led the Earthpowers through the treetops.

Their minds were serene. Quiet. Content.

Benn longed to share the tranquility that hummed in their minds. He may be confident in his abilities, but peace had been a stranger to him for a long while. He inhaled the dewy, morning air. Faint sunlight crested the mountain peaks, but Benn guessed it would melt into watercolors any minute. Already, soft waves of lilac painted the sky.

The forest around them held the type of quietude that put a soldier on edge. Typically, he found solace in the quiet, but this morning... it roared at him. Noise was obvious—telling. Silence was pin-pricking torture. As they walked, the agitation of the troops heightened. Something was amiss, yet the forest maintained a pristine stillness. An otherworldly noiselessness. They continued on, reaching their destination without any disturbance.

Benn rolled his shoulders, needing to appear as the unruffled dual-powered, former Conscript, now General, Grandson of the Leader Wyndmere, he was expected to be. Everyone around him believed the facade, looking to him for strength—everyone except one pair of caramel eyes that saw right through it, lingering on him from afar as he stood listening to reports. He didn't dare look toward her while he was listening to the battle plans. Why? Because her eyes would leave him raw. They saw too much—a personal window into his soul.

Levi landed soundlessly on his right. Asha followed. He couldn't resist; his eyes caught a familiar caramel gaze, and his breathing hitched.

"No messages," Asha answered the question before he could ask. Her voice had barely breached a whisper.

Benn nodded his acknowledgement, though his eyes never left his mate. Levi confirmed the same.

He pulled off his thick glasses to clean the frames, peering at the amaranthine-hued sky as he said, "I'm going to send forces in groups to various spots on the mountain. It is far too quiet in this forest."

He sensed Levi's distrust in the quiet. It was both affirming and terrifying to learn that the Seer felt the same discomfort he'd been trying to ignore. The longer they stood here, the longer they were exposed. It was time to move.

He kept his responses curt, needing to savor his last few moments with Leola.

When he spoke, the voice of a commander came out. "Asha, let Booker know to continue aerial coverage with the Earthpowers. It's time." His voice was unrecognizable; it sounded foreign to him, but his best friend and sister nodded, disappearing without a word of protest. Troops began to disperse around him as Benn strode to the area where the sisters sat with his grandmother. He catalogued Juniper's casual stance against the tree and Leader Wyndmere's tapping of her staff into the mossy earth, but his eyes were on *hers*. They'd never left, the intensity of their gazes growing stronger as he closed the distance between them.

"Juniper, Grandmother. A moment, please." His words were quick; he wasn't sure when people started taking orders from him, but it was working in his favor today.

A heartbeat passed and they were alone.

His mouth took hers, not waiting for her to speak. It was different from previous kisses, passionate and desperate and over too soon. He pulled back, gripping her face in his hands—not hard enough to hurt, but enough to keep her eyes level with his. Her stare was intent, like she was trying to memorize his face. Or assess him.

Or both. He hated that. He detested that their time together had always been limited—perpetually borrowed and never on their own clock.

A sheen of tears glistened in her honeyed gaze. His throat burned as he fought his own tears that rose in response. Tears would only complicate their last moment together. He pressed his forehead to hers, stroking her cheeks with his thumbs.

"Leo. You are meant for this. You are stronger than *you* even know," he said, breaking the silence as he regurgitated the words he'd been preparing since he'd seen her this morning. "The Ancestors and the Gods *chose* you and Juniper. For this. For today. You will prevail. You will come out of that cavern. Alive." His throat tightened around the doubt-filled lump there. He didn't doubt her, but he sure as Mors doubted the enemy. "You will come back to me. Our story does not end today."

Her eyes flickered, her hand stroking his cheek. "I'll send word when it is time for you to join us via burner phone." Humor flashed into her mind—he assumed it was at the absurdity of using the outdated phone to communicate. Then, her eyes turned sad. "You're not allowed to worry about me. Stay focused. You will come out, too. You will survive—or else the deal is off." He shuddered as she pressed a soft kiss to the base of his throat.

As much as he longed to get lost in this moment, the promise they'd made rang clear in his thoughts. They'd promised not to sacrifice themselves for one another, but the fierceness in her eyes confirmed what he both feared and admired in her— she would do whatever was necessary to beat Daemon and save the people she loved.

"The deal is *on*. You've got a Benn-sized iceberg to explore," he reminded her, placing a kiss on her lips. A tremor ran through his hands, at the dreaded farewell. "I love you."

"I'll see you soon. I'll come back to you, or you will come find me—whichever happens first." She straightened his leathers out of habit because Benn knew they had been impeccable when he'd first approached her. "I love you, too."

The words came out in a broken whisper that hit his heart like a well-placed spear.

Fuck. He let his hands drop, catching one of her hands on the way; their linked pinky fingers were their only remaining connection.

She took a decisive step away from him, pulling her hair into a magicked bun as she called out into the dewy air. "Bug."

Juniper and Leader Wyndmere appeared. Benn was surprised when Juniper tackled him into a hug. "Goodbye for now, Benny! It's been a pleasure—really, it has been." A playful smile crossed her face that didn't match the mood of the morning at all, but was unsurprising for her.

Levi landed next to her and Juniper hugged him in the same fashion. He staggered backwards, nearly losing his balance. "Thanks for everything, Blondie. Even though your know-it-all vibe *is* the bane of my existence," Juniper said.

Levi's smile reached his eyes, his words thick with emotion. "It's not over, Earthpoweress. The battle of the brains will continue. No mercy, today, Runeses; give Daemon what he asked for. I'll see you both soon."

He went to ruffle Juniper's braids, and she smacked his hand away with a snarl. "Do *not* touch."

Leader Wyndmere cleared her throat. "Stay focused. Protect each other. Signal when it's time to move in."

Leola nodded at her. "We will see you *all* soon."

The troops who had been sent ahead to clear the path signaled in Benn's mind. *Safe.*

They were good to move.

He squeezed her hand once more, then released it as he gestured toward the volcano.

She sent one last wry smile in his direction before she looped an arm in her sister's and started up the path. Her heart filled with a yearning that tugged at his mind. He kept his feet planted, but his soul tore in half as his mate walked in the direction of the prison.

Of their enemy. Of impending doom or of certain death.

Or perhaps, all three.

CHAPTER 31

— LEOLA —

"**F**UCK THIS HIKE," Leola grumbled. Her legs and muscles screamed. The hike appeared short, but it was deceivingly steep.

Juniper's sing-song laughter danced close behind her. "You hate hiking."

"Even more so today," she mumbled, letting her sister pass her.

Her winded breathing was too loud in her ears. The air was warm and dense—she wasn't totally convinced she was getting oxygen at all.

The usual light mood between the sisters was different... it felt altered.

Restless. Strained.

She spoke first. "I'd be lying if I said I was not terrified."

Her sister's answer was full of sarcasm. "Well, of course. This man has been wanting to kill us since before we even knew how to count. We'd be stupid not to be terrified."

She raised an eyebrow to the watercolor sky above them, agreeing, "That's true."

A moment passed before Juniper said, "Daemon's a loser." Then, she turned, calling louder, "Hey Herians, Daemon is a loser!" Her words echoed through the canyon.

Leo chuckled at the insult. "I hope he heard you."

"Me too." Juniper's tone was quiet and laced with defiance. "Pompous asshole."

Leola huffed. "I mean, why wage a whole-ass war? We can't fight it out in small groups? Or maybe—crowdfund his therapy sessions? Can't we talk it out?" She waved to the valley beyond. "We have so many magic-wielders risking their lives—to either defeat or fight for him—yet he's still adamant about keeping up this war. He is willing to lose his own people for *this*? How is this despotic lunatic the same man who helped form the Underground? How is it possible that he has strayed so far from the visions of the Gods? Leader Wyndmere offers peace, yet Daemon imprisons a majority of the Underground. Leader Wyndmere puts forces on the ground to retaliate; he sends Opasteg to inflict terror on Mundaners. Daemon will literally die on this hill—the hill to bring back Labor Camps—all so he can make himself all-powerful and ruin Heri at the same time. He could have put his immortal energy into anything else, but *no,* now we have to dive into a volcano today." She took a breath after her rant, willing coolness into her palm.

She didn't need to start a wildfire before they had even made it halfway to their destination.

"Today ends with us sending his ass to Mors, wrapped in pretty Solstice gift paper," Juniper said. She made a motion similar to bow-tying with her hands.

Leola let out a breathy laugh.

Juniper changed the subject, asking, "So if you're Benn's mate, does that mean that you could lead the Underground one day? Is it like a royal family?"

She snorted. "I have no idea, but if I know Benn and Asha at all, they do not want to be considered royalty. Leader Wyndmere was *elected*. I'm not sure who the leader was prior to her." She sucked on her cheek, debating the information she knew, and deciding that if she did survive today, that would be one of her first questions for Benn.

"Hmm. So more of a dynasty then. Fun." Juniper smirked conspiratorially. "*Spooky.*"

"My being *mates* with Benn loops you in, too, sis." She emphasized the peculiar word—though she was fully in love with Benn, the word *mates* sounded otherworldly to her.

So permanent. The thought filled her with a thrill and a quiet fear—she was only nineteen, after all, and the idea of something lasting forever was as comforting as it was daunting. Her love life up to now had been a scattered collection of flings and fleeting moments, but what her and Benn shared was different. When she thought of him, it was not only a spark or a passing passion; it was a connection, steady and profound, that seemed capable of withstanding time itself. Being near him made her feel whole, like he was the missing piece she hadn't known she was searching for. She could not imagine a life where he wasn't beside her anymore, and for the first time, she dared to hope that maybe—just maybe—what they shared could last.

But this was a war. With the life she'd lived in a Mundane world, under the thumb of a corrupt regime, nothing could be trusted to last forever.

After today, when we survive, we can think of forever. She shook her head and kept moving, widening her stride.

They neared the top of the mountain; the ground trembled beneath her feet.

"You feel that?" Juniper's voice was tinged with fear.

"Yes," Leo answered quickly, gaining steps so she was in front of her sister.

Juniper's voice came out breathless—uncharacteristically nervous. "Okay, cool, just checking."

She ran a scrutinizing look across the volcano, noting the skyrocketing temperature around them. Being fireproof, she wanted to be the first one to look inside it.

"Stay here, Bug." She ran up the last few yards to the mouth of the volcano.

She threw a glance over her shoulder, shocked to see that her sister had actually listened. Juniper was not one to back down from any challenge, so this was a sign that she, too, dreaded whatever awaited them.

She wasn't entirely sure what she'd been hoping for once she reached the mouth of the volcano, but she scowled when it turned out to be exactly as they'd expected. No hidden path, no clever shortcut—just the entrance with molten lava bubbling ominously beneath the surface. The smoke was thick, obscuring her view.

She shifted down onto her knees. She opened her pack to pull out binoculars, fixing them over her eyes. She scanned the wide opening. At first glance, it was a beautiful, horrifying, majestic sight—too magnificent to behold and proof of the existence of divinity. But, as her eyes lingered, she couldn't ignore the irony of the Gods sending her and her sister on this doomed mission to save the world they'd both created and allowed to spiral into cruelty. When she met Mors, she'd be inquiring why he'd chosen *this* option—why he'd chosen them.

Juniper appeared, her laugh riddled with anxiety. "I don't know why I assumed it would be full."

"I did, too." She squinted into the binoculars, looking—praying that there would be a clue or a path or—

"Am I crazy, or is that a staircase?"

Leola yanked the binoculars from her cheeks to look at where her sister was pointing. Her eyes followed Juniper's black-tipped finger toward an object in the distance. She rose off the ground to get a better look.

"Yes!" On the east side of the volcano was the top of a staircase—dark as obsidian and nearly impossible to see unless you were searching for it. She wanted to jump for joy.

Juniper sent her a sideways glance. "Uh—there is lava on all sides of the stairs. We will never make it."

Leo dared to step closer to the edge of the volcano. Her hands stayed at her side as she contemplated the possibility of drawing power from the volcano. Her body was buzzing with energy, but she had no way to discern if that was power or mere anticipation, or maybe a mixture of both. The buzzing was familiar yet entirely different, as if her firepower were an old acquaintance rather than a trusted friend. Whatever was calling to her from within the volcano was not that. It was vibrant and new. The fire had thrummed under her skin. *This* power writhed at her fingertips— she needed to figure out how to harness it. As if it called to her, her fingers splayed toward the molten entrance.

A *zapping* sensation rocked her fingers, cracking up through the sinew of her shoulder—almost as if she'd gripped a lightning bolt.

"*Ow!*" she screeched as stars blurred her vision. She staggered back a step, gritting her teeth so hard, she was sure her jaw would snap under the pressure.

Another *zap* hit her hand. Every nerve ending stood at attention. The zapping reverberated with a force so hard that she could not think past it—could not *breathe* past it. It roared, filling her ears like jackhammer on concrete. A world away, her feet lifted off of the ground, but she was beyond focusing on that. The pain of the shockwaves ripping through her absorbed her focus. A scream tore through her throat before she consented to the sound—its echo bouncing off the surrounding canyon as it shredded her vocal cords.

And then, it was over. The shockwaves. The pain. The noise. She landed on the ground, doubled over and gasping for air.

"Gods above," Juniper murmured. "*Leo.*"

Her head snapped up, blinking away the tears wetting her eyes. Molten lava swirled in the air.

She didn't balk, for now this unfamiliar force had become *familiar*. It was a part of her. She rose to her feet. With a twitch of her fingers, the lava became *malleable*. It moved slowly and gingerly, like soft taffy or glass being blown—it reminded her of the orange lava lamp she'd had in her room all her life.

Moving the lava was different than moving the flame; it required more effort. She felt herself straining to control the mass, but she willed heat into her veins until the lava became easier to manipulate. Sweat beaded against her eyebrow and trickled down her cheeks. She blinked the salty drops away and kept pushing. Minutes later, the lava began to move at her command—obeying her at will. It was different from her flames, but it was *controllable*.

She crossed the distance to where the obsidian staircase began, eyeing the path, careful to never break her connection with the lava. The black staircase went down inside the volcano until it submerged and disappeared. It looked like stairs leading into a pool—except these stairs led a path into bubbling magma and not cool water.

She inhaled, raised both hands, and the lava mirrored her movements. It was an orchestra, Leola its conductor. She left her forefinger and middle fingers out, curling her thumbs, ring, and pinky fingers into her fist. With that, she flicked her wrists in an outward motion and the powerful, orange liquid *moved*. It parted around the stairs, opening a path and exposing a walkway that led down, down, down into the abyss of the volcano.

Her jaw dropped. "Holy demons, it worked."

"Holy Ancestor shit," Juniper said, her mouth agape. She pulled her phone out of the pack and snapped a photo. "I'm going to need this evidence later to convince myself that I didn't hallucinate the entire thing."

Both sisters peered down the staircase. Not being able to see the bottom only heightened the anxiety that fisted Leola's stomach.

"It would have been too easy if we could see the bottom of the steps, huh? That's where the Gods' blessings ran out." Her quiet observation was heavy with sarcasm.

"It was simply too much to ask. I mean, come on Leo, you were gifted with volcanic power today, after all." Juniper stretched to her tip-toes to take another picture, smirking. "We have to work for something—right?"

"Do you think I'm the first poweress to do that?" she asked baldly, still in shock that she could yield *lava*.

"Pretty sure, sis. We'd need to check with Levi, of course, since he seems to know everything," Juniper said as she rolled her eyes, giving Leola a cursory once-over. "Is the lava putting a strain on your power reserve?"

She sucked on her cheek; she'd been ignoring the pressure on her power. "I mean—I definitely feel it. But, without Levi, I can't be sure how quickly it's draining."

"Enough standing around then. Let's go." Juniper hesitated, her foot pausing before it hit the first step. She looked back at Leo, declaring, "I'll go first. Whatever is waiting for us, I can kill. *Do not* let this lava close in on me."

She shot her a deadpan look that shouted *obviously.* "Send Benn a text that we're going in. I think I can leave a small space open for them to enter down these stairs."

Juniper's brows pinched with doubt.

"Send it now. Who knows if the phone will work down there."

Juniper shrugged and sent a text using the burner phone. "Okay, here we go. Don't follow until you hear the signal."

She disappeared down the stairs as Leola kept the lava parted, holding her breath while she waited; her arms shook with the effort. One minute passed. Then two.

Juniper snapped twice, signaling it was safe. Levi had taught them it was the Underground's universal signal for safety. She followed the snaps down the steps.

Catching up to her sister, they descended together, hand-in-hand. Juniper in front, Leo behind her. The air warmed like a sauna around them. It wasn't long before the sky was swallowed up with darkness, the only light was the orange hue that was being cast by the inferno. Her power flexed and writhed; she wondered idly if the volcanic energy was feeding her power reserve. She didn't want to use all of her power on this endeavor when they still needed to face off with Daemon, his Opasteg cronies, and rescue the prisoners. She inhaled, steeling her focus.

Just a bit further, she hoped.

They rounded the last of the long steps, remaining silent. The lava that had surrounded them was not flowing through this part of the volcano and, in the absence of the light provided by the magma, unyielding darkness surrounded them. They were now at the base of the volcano.

She blinked a few times, testing her vision. Her eyes did not adjust; she closed them and continued to walk, reinforcing her grip on Juniper's hand. She focused her power on keeping the stairs into the volcano clear so they could be used by the Underground troops. She maintained that tether to the opening, while Juniper led them down the path. Eventually, the use of the power grew easy—tedious. Her mouth tilted into a slight smile at the realization.

They continued walking, slowing when their shoes began sticking to the ground. Still hand in hand, Juniper paused. Thick mucus dripped along the walls. It stank of rotting fruit or... flesh.

The loud drip of mucus echoing off the cavern floor was joined by a low growl in the darkness. Juniper's tight squeeze on her hand had her half-thinking she would break it; however, her attention was split between holding her tether on the lava and on whatever was responsible for the growl. It loudened, but the creature didn't reveal itself. That was until glowing, red eyes opened at the end of the dark path. Many eyes blinking in disordered patterns.

The beast slithered toward them, its long, thick body sticking to the wetness caused by its own gooey secretions. A powerful roar erupted from the beast causing them both to rear back. Leola's back hit the wall. Fight or retreat—those were the only options.

Juniper grunted, attacking it and impaling it, but it continued advancing. Slithering closer to them as if poisonous vines were not puncturing its body from all directions. She yanked Juniper closer to her as the beast's body filled the space in front of them, the roars reverberating off the walls. Juniper struck repeatedly—it was centimeters from eating Juniper's face when it finally slowed. The roaring stopped. The beast took its last wet breath before collapsing onto its side. Even sideways, it was still as tall as Leo herself. Eyes covered its entire face, its mouth hanging open to showcase serpentine fangs.

Juniper stuttered, "What—in the Ancestral hell was *that*?" She panted, resting her hands on her knees. "I—I thought it was going to eat us."

"It definitely would have eaten us." Heart racing, she dropped her voice to a whisper. "What else is down here?"

"No idea, but I doubt that was the last of the beasts." Her whisper was barely audible, like she was trying not to disturb the darkness that lurked beyond. "The Lykosos were the appetizers. The *many-eyed-beast* was the first course."

Leo scanned the tunnel, still too dark for her to see anything ahead. "Many-eyed-beast? Is that what we're calling *it*?"

Juniper shuddered against her arm. "Yep. I need Levi's know-it-all self to give us the official name."

She grimaced at the long tongue that hung out of the dead beast's mouth. A shiver skittered down her spine. It seemed like something was still there—watching them.

"Get your blades out, Bug," she whispered.

Juniper released her hand and unsheathed her twin blades. "Keep that tunnel open and stay behind me."

She shot a spear of her power toward the tunnel that surrounded the staircase to test it. *Still open.*

She pooled the iceflame in her hands, letting it drop to the ground to send it along their walkway. Purple iceflame spread for miles in front of them.

Her eyes went wide as she whispered, "*Shit.* This path is longer than I thought."

Juniper picked up her pace. "At least we can see now. Let's move."

The only way Leola could orient herself in this tunnel was by the temperature fluctuations. As they walked further from the heat, she knew they were approaching... *something*. She prayed to the Gods that they were getting closer—that this walk would end soon.

She kept her focus trained on the tunnel around the stairs. Blessedly, the iceflame was an extension of her typical power, so it was small magic to keep it glowing ahead of them. She was so focused on the tunnel that she missed Juniper's signal to stop walking, crashing right into her rigid back.

Rabid, winged animals whipped past their faces. Before she could register what was happening, Juniper hurled throwing stars at each beast. Each one landed on the ground with a splashing thud.

Juniper huffed a sigh of relief. "Dead." She nudged one with her shoe, crinkling her nose. "It looks like a bat and a stingray had a baby. An ugly baby."

She leaned down to get a closer look. "The fangs are concerning."

"You know, Benn had us take all of that blood from the Lykosos. He said it had healing properties—I wonder if any of these beasts have that same ability." Juniper reached out to touch the dead animal, but paused her hand, yanking the throwing star out of its eye instead.

Leo grimaced as she said, "Let's hope they collect anything useful on their way in." There was no way that she was touching one of these winged beasts if she could help it.

Juniper started walking, twin blades ready at her sides. "I hope this cave walk is a *cakewalk* for them." She tossed a wink over her shoulder, clearly finding humor in her joke. "By the time they get down here, I'll have killed every threat."

And she did.

They encountered beast after beast—even a few demons—and Juniper killed each one with smooth efficiency. It was like Juniper had been doing this kind of killing their entire lives instead of attending a Mundaner art school, spending hours in thrift stores, and tending to her beloved garden.

Leo kept her voice quiet, reflecting on how she was managing the weight of the lava without exhausting her power reserve. "Grandmava was right. Our powers do thrive together."

The sadness was evident in Juniper's words as she whispered, "I miss her."

Leola's voice turned to venom. "One day, we will go back to Roswell and slaughter all of the Overseers and the Master. All of them who—" She choked on the words. "—who hunted her down."

Juniper put out her hand, stopping Leola mid-stride. Before them was a red, ancient door—rectangular, with a tiny keyhole at waist level. Silently, Juniper reached for the chain around her neck. The key. She undid the chain; her hand trembled as she slid it into the lock. Magic flared. The door *popped* open. The sisters exchanged a glance before She tugged on the handle. It was heavy, but she pulled it open far enough for them to squeeze through. She left it ajar, ensuring Benn, Levi, and the others could follow them in.

The smell hit her first. Decay. Feces. Death. She covered her face and scanned the area, hand brushing the dagger sheathed on her hip. At last, they had finally arrived—they were officially inside Daemon's prison.

CHAPTER 32

— BENN —

LEVI'S ARMS WERE AROUND HIM before her scream reached his ears. It was the type of blood-curdling scream that would serve as nightmare fuel for the rest of his days.

Pain was the only emotion he could read on her. The pain was as severe as it was blinding. It was going to swallow him—like her panic at Roswell had done. He couldn't think past it. He stopped breathing, but didn't have the mind to acknowledge that. He contemplated pausing time so he could warp to her—block whatever it was causing that pain.

"*Don't.*" the Seer's yell was frantic—far away, like he knew what Benn was debating. His iron grip restraining Benn's arms could definitely be attributed to his precognitive abilities. "*Wait!* You need to wait." His words were pained and blurry, distant like Benn was underwater.

Regardless, he wasn't listening; all that mattered to him was seeing Leola and protecting her from the pain that held her in its unyielding grasp. The pain he was now experiencing alongside her. He yanked at Levi's hands, but he managed to hold him long enough for her screaming to stop.

Silence swallowed her scream. His mind cleared, the burn in his—*her*—body subsided, and he cast his power into her mind. Seconds ago, it was reeling, but now it was... subdued.

He pressed, searching for any indication that she was unharmed. But then, roseate awe swirled among her thoughts.

Benn glanced skyward; molten lava hovered above the valley like thousands of twinkling stars—the orange orbs so bright that his eyes burned.

"What in the Ancestral hell?" he murmured.

"She's done it!" Levi whispered, shaking his shoulders from behind. "She's fucking done it!"

Benn absorbed variations of excitement, astonishment, and hopefulness bubble into the minds of the troops around him, as they realized what Leola had accomplished. He knew they would be cheering if they hadn't been forced into silence so as not to give themselves away to anything lurking in the wooded area.

Pride swirled in his chest. His girlfriend—*mate*—could harness flame and volcanic energy. She was a marvel, and she loved *him*.

He beamed at the pride flickering throughout her mind. This was the first time that he'd sensed this emotion on her. And today, Leola, a truly wondrous poweress, was feeling proud of herself.

A poweress chosen by the Gods, themselves. Finally, you see yourself as I see you. He cheered her on, wishing he could say the words to her—yearning to see the expression on her face as she became empowered by her own accomplishment. *You deserve all the praise, Leo.*

The burner phone buzzed in his pocket. He pulled it out to see a message notification blinking on the pixelated screen:

> We're going in. Use the stairs on the NE side.
> Leo will leave a space open for you to move through.
> 20 minutes.
> -J

Phase one of the plan they'd worked out last night was complete. This plan would only work if *everything* played out precisely; they were operating on borrowed time, so that meant the plan was tight, leaving purposeful, limited space for improvising and holes to mask their intentions from Ope Seers or Fas.

After hours of deliberation the previous night, they were still uncertain about how the sisters and the Underground forces would enter the volcano. It was an assumption, not a guarantee—as Benn had reminded his grandmother of repeatedly—that Leola was lava-proof. In his mind, it had been a complete stretch, and he hated the idea of her testing it in this mission full of unknowns. So here he sat, assuming that when she was screaming, he was hearing her being burned alive. But he was wrong. She'd found a way in, and now he would lead forces in through the same path.

This was ideal.

This is what they hoped would happen.

Why, then, was his anxiety barreling through him like a freight train?

He unclenched his jaw that had been locked since moonrise. He flashed the message to the others and Leader Wyndmere sent a silent signal to the troops. He and Levi would take a portion of elite forces into the volcano, where they would assist in the rescuing of the prisoners and the obliteration of Daemon. The remainder of the soldiers would accompany Leader Wyndmere and the Order—some taking defensive posts to confront threats while others escorted the freed magic-wielders to safety.

Asha looked at Benn with shining and determined eyes—a look that he knew well. *Hope.* She had so much hope that Josephine was alive; he had none. He nodded to his sister, praying that maybe—*just maybe*—he could get their mother out. For Asha. Selfishly, his near-mated instincts grated on him to prioritize Leo above all, even his mother, but contrarily, he was more than willing to sacrifice himself if it meant his sister, his mate, *and* his mother made it out alive. That, he would die for.

For his sister.

For his best friend.

For his mate.

For *her* sister.

For his mother.

Save them, not me. He straightened, still refusing to ask greedily of the Gods today to spare his own life. *Save them, not me. Save them, not me. Save them, not me.*

They needed to get to that entrance before it was discovered by the enemy. The walk up the mountain was steep and spelled against warping.

The elite group, constructed by the Order, consisted of members chosen for their extensive power reserves, training, and skill. Using Juniper's vague directions, Benn guided the group toward the entrance.

Levi walked to his side, muttering, "Damn. What are the odds this doesn't swallow us up the moment we step in?"

Benn frowned at the tunnel, watching his friend crouch down to touch the sides of the stairs, careful to avoid the molten magma. He was grateful Levi was here to inspect Leola's barrier around the tunnel because burning alive wasn't the way he planned to go and if it failed—

Fear flashed into the minds around him, its tight grip squeezing his lungs until he raised his shield to subdue it.

Levi rose, addressing them all. "At ease, soldiers." He crossed his arms. "Time is limited. The tunnel is open, safe, and shielded—for now. I can feel the hold of magic keeping it open, but in the event that Leola Runes encounters something that removes her focus or interrupts her power, it will close."

Shit. Benn didn't like the sound of that.

He schooled his face into the militant mask as he turned toward the group. "If you are not up for this task, I won't make you go, nor will I judge you for not going through with it. You are free to join Leader Wyndmere and General Asha in their endeavors." Benn surveyed the tunnel. "But for those who wish to stay, we need to move. Make peace with your decision, but make it now. Remember who you're doing this for, and we might just prevail today."

A poweress with copper, curly hair and porcelain skin stepped forward. "Daemon imprisoned my mother and uncle. I'll go into that tunnel with you."

His chest tightened at the words.

An olive-skinned male with long hair tied back into a bun did the same, his voice thick with emotion. "Daemon orphaned me. Opasteg—his vision for Heri—ends *today*."

"My power is water. I can hold the back line and try to keep us cool, if need be," said a blonde poweress.

A shorter ebony-skinned power with locs echoed her sentiment, "I'm a waterpower as well. We will hold the back line."

More magic-wielders stepped up, agreeing to venture into the tunnel. Tears stung his eyes as he took in the emotions radiating from the group. Salutes were exchanged as Benn identified each of the strengths in the group; simultaneously, the Seer organized the walking order until it was most advantageous to them.

With one last look at those behind him, he said, "Remember the Underground."

Levi went first to anticipate any beasts or traps. Benn followed behind him. The Illusionists came next, then the other elementals—earth and wind. Waterpowers were the last to enter.

Levi turned toward him, walking backwards, as he said, "From the looks of it, they descended for forty-five minutes. We need to do it in half that time. The tunnel will begin to close in twenty-five minutes—ish. Leo will be too far in or too preoccupied for it to hold."

Benn watched him, relaying the message as he picked up his pace. "Twenty minutes, soldiers. In twenty-five minutes, the tunnel closes."

They cleared the tunnel in 19 minutes. Levi cloaked the entrance so that if anyone followed them in, they would be met with a block and sent to Mors' palace.

Benn kept his orders concise, his voice low. "Spread out amongst your power. Alternate. Stay vigilant—keep your power and weapons ready."

Levi and Benn walked at the front. Small bursts of purple flame lit the path. Their steps were light, yet hurried.

Some kind of thick liquid leaked down onto the ground. Levi tensed and Benn paused, raising a fist in the air. The troops behind him paused. The Seer knelt down as Benn craned his neck to see the beast that blocked their path. It was dead, having been slain by large thorns that punctured its entire body.

"Sloppy work. She must have been desperate," Levi whispered as his eyes traveled along the cavern walls. "An Argos. Faster than lightning. Carnivorous. Nasty beast. Rarely encountered by someone who lives to tell the tale." He hopped up, stepping around it. "Don't touch it. Their skin carries disease."

Levi held a hand up as they encountered more dead beasts. This time, they were fanged bats.

He chuckled. "Nightlings." He pulled the throwing stars out of the dead animals, wiping them on his leathers. "She grabbed some of the stars, but not all. She'll want these back."

Over and over, they encountered slaughtered beasts. Each time, Benn was shocked. He knew the sisters were powerful, but these beasts were demons, some of which were notoriously impossible to kill.

"There are no burn marks on any of these," he remarked.

"It looks like Juniper walked first and defended while Leo held the tunnel open and lit the path," Levi said.

Benn scanned the violet flames. "You taught Juniper well."

"Of course I did," he said. "She is the key. She's a quick study, too."

"Can you sense their power reserves?" he asked.

The Seer frowned as he answered, "Not from here. Whatever wards are guarding this place are messing with my range."

———

Nothing had survived Juniper, so they cleared the path fast, hopping over each dead beast as they moved through the tunnel with ease. The prison door was in sight when they heard screams begin to echo through the cavern from the direction in which they came. Screams of terror, pleading, and denial. Benn closed his eyes, shielding against the emotions clawing through his mind. He breathed a sigh of relief when they fell away. He had no intention of experiencing the emotions of the dying.

"It sounds like my barrier spell did well." Levi's smile didn't reach his eyes and he shifted on his heels. Benn clapped him on the shoulder, knowing that his friend did not enjoy killing—even when it was the enemy. Levi looked past him, no doubt seeing something Benn could not. His voice was grim. "Opasteg knows we're here. That *was* the only entrance. Daemon will be creating another one—and fast."

They broke into a sprint toward the door.

Benn huffed, "Where's our way out?"

Levi cut him off. "I'll build one."

Benn pulled the syringes of Lykoso blood from his pack. He kept a few for himself and passed the rest to the russet-haired power next to him. That man passed them to the person next to him, and that continued until they each held several syringes of the healing blood.

"Soldiers. We have no idea what we're walking into. As it stands, current orders are: split up and administer this blood to the prisoners. It will heal them enough so they can walk. Then, lead the prisoners to the mass power source gathered in the center of the prison. It is bright and it is massive; you can't miss it. Once they touch it, their power should return to them. As you know, we can't warp out of here, so Levi will be working on ways to get us out. Once you have a way out, take as many prisoners as possible. Get back to the triage camp; find a member of the Order. Take care of yourselves. Be mindful of your power reserves. Remember the Underground."

A slow smile spread across Levi's face as he spoke the next instructions. "Illusionists in the group—stick with me. Let's kill this son of a bitch once and for all. Remember the Underground."

They'd reached the door, and Benn used his strength to pull it open.

"Remember the Underground," was echoed by the soldiers as they entered the prison.

CHAPTER 33

— LEOLA —

"HOW FAST CAN YOU KILL THE GUARDS?"

Juniper craned her neck, listening. "Five minutes?"

"Three would be better." She set her pack on the ground and sent another beat of power toward the tether holding the lava open, before smirking at her sister. "I'll time you."

"We haven't played that game in a decade." Juniper rolled her eyes, taking a few steps toward the middle of the prison, before shooting a rope of vines out of her wrist, and hoisting herself up to the top levels. She whispered, "I'll see you in two."

Chuckling under her breath, Leo reached into the pack, appreciating for the first time in her life that her sister was somewhat of a collector. This pack had weapons, poisons, blankets, and about a hundred other things she didn't recognize but knew would be useful today. She stacked everything into neat piles near the entrance where Benn would come in, knowing he or Levi would decide what they needed.

Juniper skidded around the corner; she was winded, and her words came out in a rush. "I killed the Soulsiphons on the upper levels easily, but the ones on the lower levels knew I was coming. Or rather, that *something* was. I killed them all, though.

More guards than last time. All Soulsiphons." She stood, wiping off her daggers. "No Opes. No Corruptors. No Daemon. If he hadn't sensed my magic before, he definitely knows we're here now. Hopefully your tunnel will only hold for our troops."

Her heart jumped at that thought—she hadn't set any traps in the tunnel for any Opasteg that happened to travel through. She had not known how to do so.

She shook her head, clearing it. *No time to worry now.*

She counted the vials in her shaking hands. They had ten vials of Lykoso blood; the rest would come with Benn, Levi, and the troops. They were to prioritize the most emaciated of the prisoners because their healing would take the longest.

"I know which prisoners to start with," Juniper said, keeping her voice low.

"You inject while I melt the shackles," Leola said as she handed the vials to her and stood eye-level with her sister.

"Got it."

She forced all of the strength she could muster into her words. "We both make it out alive today." She was still trying to convince herself, but was satisfied that her words carried the essence of ferocity that her heart was missing. She kissed Juniper's cheeks, pulling her into a tight hug, murmuring, "No tears, sis. Not until the sadist is dead."

"No tears," Juniper echoed.

"You can do *anything*," Leola whispered the words that she'd been telling her sister since she could utter them. "*You* are magic."

"So can you." Juniper's arms tightened around her. "*We* are magic."

She pulled back to look at her sister, who'd matured eons since they'd left their Mundane life behind, but she still saw the toothless, bright-eyed youngling staring back at her.

Juniper whispered, "Love you, Leo."

"Love you, Junebug."

She held her sister for one more second, memorizing the feeling of her embrace and then she released her. Without a look back, Juniper cast her power, using a vine to pull herself up in the same fashion she'd done before. She willed heat into her palms as she ran toward the prisoner lying closest to her with silent feet. She stepped over an empty pair of chains that had been discarded in a heap. As she approached the first prisoner, her steps were quick, but intentional, making enough noise so her presence would be known. She had no intention of scaring any of the prisoners, lest she cause them to expend energy they couldn't spare.

Her knees hit the icy ground, and her breath clouded in the air in small puffs.

"Hello there," she said as she sucked on her cheek, not knowing what to say while feeling compelled to say something—*anything*—to this person before she removed their shackles. Her voice stayed soft as she continued, "This will be painless. I'm here to help you. Stay calm. "

The magic-wielder's milky eyes opened into small slits, drifting closed after a few seconds.

 She tried to avoid the gaze as she gently lifted their wrists. The hair on the person was too thin and the facial features too emaciated to indicate their true appearance.

Each of their bones and tendons were showing through translucent skin, but the shackles were spelled to hold firm. She ignored the bile rising in her throat as she felt their papery skin against her own. She inhaled, touching the power-blocking metal with one finger, waiting for pain that never came.

It worked. The tonic had worked, just as Boyd had explained; her power wouldn't be impacted by the metals as long as the material didn't touch her blood. *Here we go.*

Holding the shackles in her hands, she willed fire to heat her palms. Her rumbling temper made it easy to summon the innate inferno; the shackles melted like butter. She moved to the prisoner's ankles and did the same. She let the shackles fall to the ground, gritting her teeth as she pushed them to the side.

She did this repeatedly, over and over again, her fire raging like the magma that guarded this wretched prison. Each of these prisoners were eye-to-eye with Mors; their skin was peeling off with the shackles, like it had grown to be part of the shackles over time. Horror and heartbreak ran through her congruently as she freed each magic-wielder.

Daemon will pay. She envisioned *him* in these chains; a wicked grin spread across her face.

This dungeon was threatening her grip on sanity. The trauma was too much; she needed to get out. The prisoners needed to get out. They needed the other vials of Lykoso blood—*now*.

She melted another pair of shackles. *Come on, Benn. Come on. Come on.*

She moved from prisoner to prisoner, freeing the powers and poweresses on the lowest level in a blink. With each time she freed someone, a tiny crack in her heart healed. She wouldn't feel better until these prisoners had reclaimed their power—walking free, breathing clean air, and seeing sunshine.

And Daemon's head is on a spike. First Heri, now this. Her insatiable bloodlust to destroy the immortal burned within her, fierce and unrelenting.

She cleared the next level, running up the path to the upper levels. Immediately, she saw why Juniper had focused her efforts here first. This level held moisture, allowing for fungus to grow on the walls.

She crouched in front of the first prisoner and, to her horror, saw that the fungus had grown into their skin. She melted the shackles as wetness began to hit her face.

Shit, is this moldy water? No, no, no, no. She wiped her face with the back of her hand, only to realize the wetness on her face was from her own tears. She refused to slow her pace, but by the time she reached the end of this level, her sobs were echoing through the cavern. So many people were trapped here—for over a decade—torn from their lives, their families, their children, all in the name of greed and power. Her own mother was here—somewhere—and she wouldn't even recognize her. For all she knew, she'd already unshackled her. She swallowed the turmoil of emotions as she reached the final level, her eyes scanning the prisoners as she knelt down to continue her work on the shackles.

A quiet cough sounded next to her. She jumped. All of the prisoners she'd helped so far had been silent, but not this one. She leaned forward to peer down the twist of the path. There was a prisoner—still shackled—moving. *Stretching.* Her mouth parted in awe as the poweress rolled her neck and examined her restricted wrists.

"Hello, poweress." Juniper's voice floated through the wet air. "Welcome back. My name is Juniper Runes and my sister, Leo, and I are here to save you."

She worked faster, wanting to get closer to the poweress who was moving and free her so she could reclaim her power from the gathered orb of magic. The shackles that held the prisoner next to the poweress dropped to the ground. Finally, Leola knelt in front of her, listening to her sister speak to the other prisoners who were rising from their healing injections. The poweress was dazed, blinking slowly, but her features were starting to take shape. She reached for her shackles and the poweress flinched, pulling her hands out of her grip.

She flinched, too, regretting the motion, as she tried to explain, "I am sorry I startled you. I'm here to free you. I'll remove these shackles. Don't worry, I won't hurt you."

She didn't speak, but shifted her wrists closer; Leo took them into her hands. She melted them and they clattered to the ground.

Juniper appeared at her side, reaching for the poweress, pulling her to her feet. Leola moved to the next prisoner as Juniper guided the poweress to the sparkling orb.

"Daemon took your power when you were imprisoned here. Reach out and take it back. We have friends on the way to move you after that," Juniper said, her voice informative, yet tender.

The poweress followed the instructions. Bright sparks flew and the poweress hovered off the ground as her power found its way back into her body. She landed in a crouched position on the ground next to Juniper.

"I feel it. For the first time since... we got here." She rose. "Thank you."

Juniper released a celebratory chirp. "It worked!"

Leola did the same, throwing a fist into the air because... she was right. Their plan that'd been a quagmire of outlandish concepts had actually worked.

She made quick work of the rest of the chains and watched in awe as more and more prisoners walked toward the orb to regain their powers. At least twenty of them now stood away from their chains, even though Juniper had only used ten vials.

"How?" she asked as her sister strode toward her.

"Well, I figured they didn't need to be completely healed since the others are bringing more vials. I wanted to save as many as I could. I wanted to limit Daemon's power as much as possible," Juniper said as she picked her claws. "So, I spread out the blood to more magic-wielders."

"Genius."

Juniper shrugged.

"How many?"

"I spread out ten vials to heal thirty prisoners. So, Daemon will lose the magic of thirty beings, at least. Thank the Gods," Juniper replied.

"Thank the Gods? Thank *you*!" Leola hugged her.

Around them, prisoners started to stretch and rise, stunned by their surroundings—by their own appearances. By... them.

"It's the Pair," someone murmured as a magic-wielder approached them in awe. "You've come for us."

Leola met her sister's eyes. "Yes... we did. You can call us Leola and Juniper."

"The Runes sisters at your service." Juniper bowed.

Footsteps rounded the corner and Leola turned in defense, only to be swept up into strong arms, and greeted by a familiar voice. "Leo."

"Told you we'd see each other again," she whispered close to his ear.

Benn set her back on her feet, placing a soft kiss on her forehead. He pulled back, examining her for injuries. Levi appeared next to Juniper, handing her a pack of syringes while surveying the orb.

"Thanks to Juniper, we'll have leftover Lykoso blood," he said as he cleaned his glasses and sent Juniper a nod of approval. "Nice work, poweress."

Juniper grinned, turning to Benn. "I sent the magic-wielders up to the path to be moved. There are many others who still need blood. I only used a third of a vial on each one that is standing so we could spread it out if needed."

Benn nodded at Levi, who bounded up the path. At this point, she'd gotten used to their wordless communication.

Benn called, "Yorkmere. Pearsongal." Two soldiers stepped forward. "Follow Miravale up the path and begin moving magic-wielders. He's constructing an exit. Take as many as you can straight to the Underground camp. Leader Wyndmere is waiting for you there. Don't return back here. We can't risk magic trails being picked up by the Opes."

Juniper handed Leola a few more vials, saying, "Take these."

Leola turned to walk away; Benn pulled her back.

She looked at him in question. "I melted all of the shackles. The prisoners should be relatively easy to move. We need to get them the blood."

"I know. I needed one more second to tell you how extraordinary you are." He lowered his voice so only she could hear. "Stay alert. We aren't in the clear yet. Now you can go, Runes."

"Yes, General Wyndmere," she quipped, bringing her lips close to his. "I'll see you on the outside; we have an inn to get to." With a wink and a few decisive steps back, she grabbed Juniper. "Let's move, Bug."

Juniper's face held a familiar scrunch that Leola recognized as inner strife. The prisoners were out; they'd moved them all to the Underground triage site. Benn, Asha, and Levi were sorting through the freed magic-wielders and, strangely, Juniper sat alone toward the perimeter of the camp, staring in the direction of the prison.

"Bug," she called as she approached her.

She sat catatonic, leaning against a boulder. She was unnaturally still, debating—*calculating*—something.

Leola followed her gaze, not seeing whatever her sister saw there, and turned her eyes back to Juniper. "Hey." She waved a gentle hand in front of her frozen gaze.

She jumped as if just noticing her presence. Juniper mumbled, "We didn't get everyone."

Leola's blood chilled.

"I checked each prisoner's face." She had tears in her eyes. "Josephine was not with them. She was not in the groups of wounded or the dead. I checked three times."

An icy shock straightened her spine. In the midst of the rushed work, she hadn't thought of Josephine Wyndmere.

She cursed herself for not realizing and muttered, "But Benn didn't say any—"

"Of course he didn't!" Juniper snapped, throwing her hands up. "He has been worried that Daemon hurt her—or worse—for helping *me*. He probably assumed we wouldn't find her there; he didn't say anything so we could move faster and save more people."

She scowled at the fact that Benn chose to say nothing about his mother because he was not willing to risk the success of the Underground, risk her safety. She knew the Wyndmeres wanted Josephine safe, so why had none of them said anything? Unless—

"Maybe..." Her voice trailed off as she peered back toward the camp for any sign of the dual-power. "Maybe they haven't realized she was not among the rescued. I mean—Benn and Asha hardly remember what she looks like, and Sena is in the war tent."

The prisoners were atrophied. Even with the Lykoso blood, they would need time for recovery and rehabilitation. She'd overheard Levi strategizing how they would begin to identify the people who were too impacted to know their own identity. Her heart was a sinking stone at the thought of the Wyndmere siblings looking for their mother and hoping. Her own mother was amongst the rescued— she had not yet awoken, but Papa was waiting by her side. In the coming days or months, the sisters would get to know their mother and she them. Benn and Asha would not get that chance. If there was any possibility that they missed Josephine or another wing of prisoners entirely—

She gripped Juniper's hand as she said, "We need to go back."

Juniper nodded. "I'll tell Papa. You get—"

"No." Her grip tightened. She knew Benn would want to go with her; he and Levi were needed here to protect the freed prisoners and fight any ambush from Daemon. "We need to act fast. We can go and be back before they even know we've left. I can get in and out of the prison again; Levi showed me how."

Wariness flashed in her eyes. "We can't just go without telling anyone."

"You're right." Flustered at the thought of losing even a *single* second of time they may have to rescue Josephine, she weighed the options. Benn would drop everything to help them, but taking him from his post would jeopardize the magic-wielders they'd already rescued, and his calming power was keeping them comfortable. She wouldn't be the reason they lost the comfort they needed—they *deserved*—as they began their healing. "Fine, but not Benn or Papa. We're strong enough to go alone. I don't want Mother waking up without Papa, and I don't want Benn to neglect his work with the magic-wielders." She grabbed the sleeve of a passerby soldier. He looked to be about the same age as her. "Hey, what's your name?"

His mouth gaped as he looked at her hand on his sleeve as his eyes flicked back up to look at her. "Harmos," he coughed. "Trevor Harmos."

She raised a brow at his reaction to her. "Nice to meet you, Trevor. I'm Leo."

"I know," he interrupted, now gawking between her and Juniper.

She grimaced; she would never get used to the way magic-wielders looked at her.

She cleared her throat. "Please send word to General Wyndemere that Juniper and I are headed back to the prison."

He shook his head. "I don't think that is a good idea."

"Appreciate the sentiment, but no one is asking you." Her snap was more aggressive than she meant it to be, but they were running out of time. *Josephine* was running out of time.

Juniper chirped behind her, "Wait 15 minutes to tell General Wyndmere." Her claws were out, but her voice was sweet. "And, Trevor, give us your weapons and pack, please."

His cheeks were ruddy, but he pulled his pack off and handed his weapons over. Voice quivering, he said, "Is that an order?"

"Uh—sure, thank you," she said as she buckled the pack around her shoulders. Next to her, Juniper had their enchanted pack around her shoulders and Trevor's weapons in her hands.

"Fame is weird," Juniper remarked.

Trevor took off in a sprint toward the war tent, likely running to find Benn.

"So much for following orders," Juniper called to his retreating back.

"Whatever. They'll catch up and help, if we need it." She shrugged.

"We won't need it." Juniper rolled her eyes and grabbed Leola's hand.

"Let's go," Leo said as she warped them to the new entrance of the cavern.

CHAPTER 34

— BENN —

BENN WAS FOCUSED, MOVING QUICKLY while taking in reports, maintaining his hold on the magic-wielders' emotions. Quelling the pain of others was draining, but with the help from his grandmother, they'd managed to keep the freed prisoners comfortable. Now it was time to assist the Fas and Seers in identifying the magic-wielders and get vellums to their families. From there, Healers would examine each prisoner and categorize them into either A, B or C—A represented the group that was ready to be discharged, B symbolized anyone who would need more care, and C represented people who needed critical care.

They could start reuniting families as soon as tonight and that was what mattered.

Right? His thoughts were conflicted.

He swallowed, hearing most of what the soldier next to him reported. He needed to find Asha and break the news. He needed to tell her so he could be there for her when her hope shattered; while they would be reuniting families all night long, his family would not be getting that gift.

He kept walking, aiming for the Fa tent, where he knew he'd find Asha, fighting the burning in his chest.

I wanted to see Mother. Just one time. Juniper said she looked *like* me. He shut down the thoughts; the thoughts were as useless as they were intrusive. An enemy that had exclusive access to his mind. He didn't have time to feel the weight of losing his mother again today. He walked faster, knowing and not caring that he was fully ignoring the soldier who was reporting. He paused and turned toward the kid. He looked to be a year younger than Benn. He had brown hair and flushed cheeks.

Benn's voice was gruff as he addressed him. "I need to see to something urgent. Take the report to Conscript Miravale."

"Yes, General Wyndmere," the soldier said as he saluted and strode away in the opposite direction.

He sighed in relief and started back on his walk toward the Fa tent.

He was thankful that they'd found Leola and Juniper's mother; maybe that could be enough for him. It would have to be. Deep down, though, he knew that it would not be enough for Asha. His pulse quickened and he needed a moment.

To panic.

To breathe.

To panic more.

He was roughly fifty yards away when he ducked into a nearby tent to take a few breaths. At the mercy of the Gods, it was empty.

His mind drifted to happier moments, trying to keep his raging grief at arm's length. He breathed deeply before returning his mind to the night prior, when he'd spent time with Leola in the meadow. Her soft murmur of the words that made his stomach clench.

She got out, he reminded himself, for the hundredth time. *She got out.*

He would get to sleep tonight with her in his arms. She was safe. It was a privilege he had not expected to get. He needed to consider himself lucky and be grateful, not ask the Gods for even more blessings.

Maybe that is Grandmother talking. The thought was distant.

He had been raised to maintain low expectations—especially in wartime. He knew that Leola would hate that he'd reiterated that teaching. He almost chuckled at the idea of her caramel-like scowl.

He yearned to see into her mind—just for a moment. She was never hard for him to find. He could always feel her; besides that, he loved her mind—it was free. It was safe. He sent out a pulse to search for her and was met with silence.

Strange. He sent out a seeking sweep that easily would have picked her mind up. Or rather, it *should* have.

He tried again. Nothing.

He cast the power further.

Nothing.

His brow furrowed as he lowered his shield, reaching for Juniper's mind, knowing they were together.

Nothing.

Something was off. He threw open the entrance to the tent he was hiding in and came face to face with a mess of blonde hair and emerald eyes.

Levi held onto a frightened-looking soldier, a glower ruling his features, as he said, "They went back. No support."

"How long ago?"

"I came as fast as I could—" The soldier tripped over his words; Levi released his collar.

Benn put up a hand, and his voice came out in a lethal quietness. *"How long?"*

"Fifteen minutes."

Benn's protective instincts flared, and he grabbed the Seer's hand, warping them to the opening Levi had built to free the prisoners.

———

"What in the Ancestral hell?" Levi grimaced, lifting his hands to the entrance. He pressed. "It is covered by some... some kind of shield. I can't get in. *Fuck*."

Benn wrung his hands together, trying not to pace. Levi excelled in opening wards and spellwork, but he was struggling. Sweat dripped off of his blonde curls as he willed his power over and over into the entrance to the tunnel.

"What is the problem?" Benn asked, fearing the answer.

"Someone interfered with my spellwork," Levi grunted, his fingers working. "These spells—they aren't mine. I don't know them." He took a few steps back, peering around the cavern entrance. "I see them, but I can't undo them. It's like... like someone knew I'd come. It's like they are spelled against me. And you."

Benn leaned into the shield, searching for any sort of indication that Leola or Juniper were inside.

Nothing.

He had no sense of their minds, but he knew they were in there.

Of course they were.

"Benn, someone knows we're coming in. They are expecting us to undo these spells. Whatever this is—it knows our magic." Levi's eyes turned to his, horrorstruck. "They're magic-siphoning wards. If we go in there, we'll be powerless. Once the wards know our magic, it'll be gone. I'm guessing it is similar to the spells that trapped the prisoners. Someone did this on purpose." He huffed a sigh in frustration and pressed on the entrance again as he explained, "This was the trap I couldn't see."

His stomach bottomed out. Somewhere, a crack reverberated in the spell that was blocking them from entering.

"It's breaking," Benn said as he chewed the inside of his cheek, moving on to his thumb. "I'm going inside. They went back for Josephine; this was the reason we didn't find her... it's all a trap... You're staying. Wait for me here."

"You're kidding." Levi laughed, but it was hollow, a bright burst of power flowing from his palm and into the shield. "I'm not *staying* for shit. I'll be right there with you, brother, and you know it." He pressed again as another crack sounded. He stepped back and sent a surge of magic into the shield, bringing it down in a large crash. "There," he said as he flexed his hand. "Wards are down, but now my power's gone."

Without another breath, Benn took off in a sprint to enter the cavern, his power draining with every step along the way.

CHAPTER 35

— LEOLA —

"**S**PLIT UP. SEARCH EACH LEVEL until we find her. Snap twice if you do," she whispered. "Save your power."

This time around, they dove into the cavern at breakneck speed; even with the scarce light, the route was burned into their minds. With each stride into the chilling, suffocating darkness, they sharpened their plan, bracing for what lay ahead.

Armed with a vial of Lykoso blood and a weapon, they discarded their packs on the path. Levi's entrance spit them right back at the entrance where they would split up to begin their search as Leola skidded to a halt. "Bug," she said, her voice barely audible as she pointed.

Josephine lay motionless and shackled in front of them—not to a wall, but to a wooden table.

"Gods, where'd that come from?" Juniper asked.

She was motionless, bound and in a thin, white sheet that was not suitable for clothing. Her dark curls were matted against the side of her head. Each pane of her face was swollen, bruised, and caked in blood. Leola's chest clenched at the sight of her. Josephine let out a strangled whimper.

"She's alive," Juniper said as she lunged, injecting an entire vial of Lykoso blood into Josephine's leg.

She inspected her head wounds and prayed to the Gods that the healing properties in the Lykoso blood would be successful on someone who had been beaten beyond recognition. She didn't need to wonder who would do this. She already knew the answer.

She rose and scanned the main room of the cavern. Something was different than before, but she didn't know what had changed. The sooner they could carry Josephine out of here, the better. She went to her knees beside Josephine and Juniper. Juniper's hands cradled Josephine's cheeks, holding her face upright. With one last scan of the dark cavern, Leola moved to grab the shackles so she could melt them—as she'd done countless times today. Her hands grazed the metal, slicing into her palm, and she was met with debilitating pain. Teeth gritted, she tried to let go of the shackles, but it was impossible. She was being electrocuted, bound by a magnetic force to the iron and she couldn't fight it. All feeling left her body as she sank to the ground in a heap next to Josephine. All the movement in her limbs stopped; her body was no longer convulsing from the pain because she could no longer feel her hands. Every muscle in her body gave out; she released the shackles just as her cheek hit the cold ground.

"LEO!" Juniper screamed, flipping her onto her back. "What's wrong?"

"The—shackles," she uttered; even the shortest sentence was a challenge. Tears slid down Juniper's cheeks, shattering her heart. She tried again to form words, but all she could manage to choke out was, "*My hands.*"

"But the tonic... oh Gods, the shackles cut you." Juniper flinched away from the shackles that held Josephine and dragged Leola away from them, not stopping until she had propped her shoulders and head up against a nearby wall. "Stay," was the only word she said to Leola.

Not that she could move if she wanted to.

Juniper stood, unsheathing her dual swords.

From where Juniper had left her, she could see Josephine, Juniper, and the strange table. Out of place.

Someone was setting up for a meeting or... a party. Her mind started to swim.

A wet gasp yanked her from her thoughts, and she dragged her eyes toward Josephine's, whose hands pulled back, bringing the shackles to her too-thin chest.

"Not just the metals. Poison," she wheezed. "Juniper, you must go. He knew you'd come back. He put some kind of poison on the shackles—" Her dark eyes, swollen and bruised, but glaringly similar to Benn's, landed on Leola. "*No. You weren't supposed to come back.*"

The crack in her voice made Leola's pulse spike, and she shoved her remaining energy into the command. "Bug, *go. Leave now.* Find Benn."

Her eyes burned. *It was a trap; we should have known.*

Juniper still had a chance to get out of this cavern—to save herself. Juniper's eyes flitted between Leola and Josephine, and Leola knew exactly why; her sister was debating her options—weighing her chances of getting them *all* to safety. That opportunity was long gone.

"You have a chance. *Leave.* He wins if you don't," she said, her slurred words hoarse as she gritted her teeth. "*GO!*"

"No!" Juniper's voice was hushed, but the fire in it roared. "He expects us both to have been affected by the poison. Now, hush, Leo. Josephine, play dead."

She had no choice but to obey the command of her sister; her eyes were closing without her consent anyway. Around her, the cavern darkened until it was pure blackness.

———

Footsteps sounded, and a menacing whisper filled the air. "The fools have returned."

Her eyes blinked open to see Juniper and Josephine laying on the ground to her left. She, herself, had not moved, and both Juniper and Josephine looked convincingly dead.

Her brain fog prevented her from moving. She couldn't figure out how much— or how little—time had passed. Her eyes were weighted and it was a constant battle to keep them open and focused on the evil immortal advancing toward them.

Daemon was in leathers that looked similar to theirs—sleek and impenetrable, but they were blood-red instead of the familiar green that the Underground wore. He was not alone; in fact, he had an army of Opasteg behind him. Cloaked figures stood all around the room and—judging by the elevated noise in the cavern—filled all of the levels.

"Fools." Daemon gestured to the crowd. "Come on, say it with me."

"Fools!" the crowd echoed.

She would've been trembling if she had the power in her limbs. Daemon crept toward Josephine and Juniper, hardly sparing a glance at Leola's limp body along the wall.

He brushed a spiny finger across Juniper's cheek as he said, "You walked into my trap. I knew all I needed to do was *wait* and you would return on your own. That Seer knew immediately that Josephine was not present here during your *rescue* mission. Bennjamin knew, too. They moved on and continued with their mission. Always putting the Underground first." Daemon scoffed, picking up Josephine's chin. "Such a pity that your son cared more about success than his own mother. *Selfish swine.* Just like this Wyndmere here." His silver-tipped boot kicked Josephine in the ribs. She didn't move.

"Of course, I knew Juniper had seen *you* here during her last visit. I knew you had *helped* Juniper escape. Only Josephine Wyndmere would have the power reserve to free herself from my magic—albeit briefly. Nevertheless, it was as impactful as it was aggravating. From the start, I'd planned to capture the sisters. The Fa spoke of the Prophesied Pair. I figured I'd break up the pair, lure one of the sisters into my cavern, entrap her, and wait for the other to come to the rescue. Then, I would have a hold on both of you." He flashed a frown toward Juniper. "Did I expect you all to waltz in here with a *Seer's* help? No. I'll admit, that was unexpected. But I swore that the next time the Runes sisters entered this cavern, they would not leave. Juniper Runes would have been *mine* if not for you, Josephine Wyndmere, and I will not forget that. Ever." He sneered at Josephine, turned on his heel, and strode toward where Leola lay.

Daemon crouched down so that he was eye level with her, and he gripped her chin; she had no choice but to look directly into his cold, black eyes. A straight-white smile stretched across his brown skin. The maniacal gleam shining in his eyes left her wishing she could rip it off.

Get your fucking hands off me. She wanted to scream... but she was frozen. Limp.

He appeared happy, but his tone contradicted the emotion. "You see, I was devising ingenious methods of trapping one of the Prophesied Pair, and yes, each would've been successful. However, when you used the Seer's vision to *trespass* into my cavern, I used it to learn." His grip tightened, though all she was able to feel was light pressure. "I'm *everyone's* villain. I helped found the Underground. I was dedicated, I was loyal, I was intelligent, and I was kind. I fought for a better world alongside my brothers and sisters. But when we were awarded power by the Gods, I was not awarded anything *close* to what the others were. I was given crumbs, especially when compared to the powers gifted to my peers," his voice boomed.

"I politely asked to put in a request to the Gods for more power and was denied by the other Founders. I was cheated. I was played. After being told I had 'limited' power, that I needed to accept that fate and the gift I had been given, I decided that I'd get the power that I was owed. And not just that, I'd become more powerful than the other Founders could have ever dreamed. I would become the strongest magic-wielder in all of history, and I would not stop until I was successful. From there, I left that corrupt organization to build something new. A place where you wouldn't be considered selfish for wanting more—wanting what you deserved. When I went after the Underground years ago, I was able to gain some recruits. Some had to be killed in the process, but when I knew I had a Wyndmere in my possession and would eventually harvest her power, I knew I'd won. Happily, I waited in my home as the scholars of Opasteg cataloged and examined the magic-wielders we had captured. I wondered who the Prophesied Pair was. I'll be honest, I assumed it was a mated couple I had captured or perhaps a mated pair of elder members that was still out there. But... I was wrong.

"My scholars returned to tell me they hadn't been captured and they were *not* elder members of the Underground; in fact, they were *younglings*. It was ridiculous that two small children would be my demise. I could not accept that," he said, laughing. "I was on the precipice of success." His voice roared in Leola's ears as he spat the words, his breath hot against her face. "Alas, the Gods had cursed me yet again. I demanded my scholars tell me who these children were so that I could capture them and harness their power at once. The best they could do for me was provide a list of all of the living lineage of magic-wielders. I tortured every prisoner tenfold for information regarding who these children were. I even *kidnapped* younglings to test their power. Still, I could not locate them. In the darkest of hours, I contemplated exterminating the younglings I held captive, but I'm no fool; we know the cost of killing an innocent magical being, and I could not risk losing my soul. So, I knew I must find the children, capture them, drain their power, and take it as my own—after all, there are no laws against that."

Tears streamed down her cheeks, her face never shifting out of the stoic expression she wore.

His look of disgust was etched into her memory before he dropped her chin, causing her head to bob forward so she stared down at her own legs.

He kept talking while Leola focused her dwindling energy on processing his words. "So, I made a new plan. I'd wait for the Prophesied Pair to show themselves to *me*. I waited. I schemed. I placed scouts in the Academy, who observed Bennjamin

Wyndmere, Josephine's all-powerful, prodigal son. I kept my eyes on him, watching him ally himself with the powerful Miravale Seer. I thought I'd ended the Miravale line; I was disappointed to see that I failed, and one had befriended the Wyndmere boy. Overrun with glee, I thought, *'This must be the Prophesied Pair!'* I sent my scholars to retrieve them so I could carry out my plans. But, upon investigation, we'd been fooled once again."

Daemon continued on like everyone was agreeing with him; he rarely paused in his storytelling. He told the story of his reign of terror like he was forced to do it, even though he had done it all on his own accord. Her thoughts were slow-moving, molasses flowing through her mind. To her horror, Daemon began to remove her leathers. She found herself struggling to focus as he continued his rambling tirade.

"I was angry, but I knew I was getting close. I held onto the faith in my own self—I knew I was destined to do this and I knew I'd prevail. Then, a spike of power tipped off my scouts. They headed to Poppycal, where two young girls were using magic outside of their home. I then paused everything I was doing to go get them myself, but my idiot scouts were somehow bested by these *girls.* In disbelief, I went to the house. I arrived to find my men slaughtered and burned. To my absolute horror, the girls were *gone.* Any and all traces of their magic had been masked and were no longer traceable. I tried everything—*everything*—to get to them and I just could not. Until, over a decade later, another spike in magic appeared near the place we had last spotted the Prophesied Pair. I sent my best Corruptor to retrieve them and they escaped again, but this time, I had an idea of where they had gone. At last, I'd finally located them!" His delusional laugh echoed off the walls. "I sent scouts to Laviegata. Do I admit that I had gotten a bit lackadaisical in my Opasteg involvement? Yes, because the Miravale boy was initiated—under a false name, I might add—and entered into my army as a Seer. Then, he helped the Pair *escape* from me. A mistake on my part. Sure, Sena won that round, but I've always known the Miravale lineage would be a pain. He'll pay for that. Sena will pay, too. Bennjamin and Josephine will pay. Juniper Runes will pay. And you will pay, as well, *Leola*

Runes." His dead eyes were locked on hers again. "I'm sure you are wondering how you will pay; go on, ask me." He chuckled. "Oh wait, you can't ask me. I'd think you were dead if it weren't for the tears. Not to worry, I'll tell you."

Daemon shimmied her out of the armored breastplate she wore, her vambrace, gauntlets, and neck guard all tossed aside like trash into a pile that held all of the armor from her lower body as well. She wanted to kick him straight in the chest or burn him to ash, but the poison rendered her helpless.

Why? Why? Why, why, why? She lay motionless as he removed the rest of her armor, praying desperately that Juniper would continue to appear incapacitated.

Daemon was talking only to her, so she had to assume that he believed Juniper's act. She couldn't be sure if Josephine was acting, too, or if she'd passed on. Her stomach roiled as the cold air hit her skin; Leola was now free of all armor and leathers, wearing only her undergarments. Daemon propped her head up once more so she could see him, the table, and her sister.

An Opasteg soldier lit candles in various areas around the room. Daemon crossed the room to trail his fingers over the strange table that was in the center of the dark cavern and sighed. "Too bad that tonic didn't protect your blood, huh? The poison on the shackles did marvelously on blocking your powers... better than I'd expected. I knew I could trap the Runes sisters—that this would work. But I had never imagined their proximity to the other great pair I had come to know over the years. Granted, I hadn't thought much of Bennjamin Wyndmere or Levi Miravale— especially once I knew they were no use to me. No, I hadn't thought of them until their trespassing occurred last week. When I arrived back at my cavern, I sensed the magic trail of a great time-wielder lingering—Josephine's boy has more power than even she has. His power has tripled the amount that his mother possesses. Now, you tell me what's better: harvesting the power of a time-wielder or harvesting that power from *two* of them?" he said to no one in particular. "In addition, I sensed a magic trail that only potential mates can leave. My emotion-benders scented Bennjamin's innate instinct to protect *Leola* and they knew immediately: Josephine's son had found his mate." He gave her an empathetic frown that was not convincing. "My plan began to morph. Yes, I already had the legendary Josephine Wyndmere. I would still *trap* the Pair. Using the girls, I'd then trap the most powerful time-wielder in history, Bennjamin. With him, I might get the most powerful Seer in history—an added bonus. Then, I'd harvest each of their magic to wield as my own. The first step went well, as the Pair is trapped." He gestured to Juniper and herself; Leola's mouth went dry as the desert. "We needn't wait long, though; Bennjamin and Levi are already undoing the tedious wards I put in place to keep them out of here. What they will fail to realize is that once the wards learn their magic and they are permitted to enter, they will be sealed inside with their powers nullified." Daemon made a sweeping motion with his hand as cheers echoed throughout the cavern.

She wondered if she would vomit. Inside, she was screaming and thrashing—trying to free herself from this poison.

Nothing.

No movement.

She had freed so many others today, only to have Daemon make her a prisoner in her own body.

"Now, let us get ready for the first harvest," Daemon said as he scooped her from the floor into his arms and carried her to the long table in the center of the room.

As he walked with her, she counted the Opasteg soldiers standing around them. They were outnumbered a hundred to one at least, and the poison did not seem to be wearing off in the slightest. Each of their hungry eyes raked over her; she wondered what he had promised them in exchange for their loyalty, or if he had not promised them anything and their hearts were just as greedy, cruel, and dead as his. He laid her down with the delicateness of someone who was preparing to slaughter an animal, while hoping to keep them calm. Dazedly, she wondered if that was his intention all along.

Something bound her arms and legs.

413

"Oh, yes, I forgot that Leola cannot move. Silly me. These will not be needed today," Daemon said as he let out a laugh that echoed. The Opasteg soldiers began laughing in response, too. The restraints disappeared. His laughter died as he said, "Send for me when you have prepared the subject."

She tried but failed to pull away when a woman stepped forward to undress her completely. She covered her in a sheet similar to what Josephine had been wearing when they had found her shackled to the very table Leola now lay on. The fingers on her left hand twitched, but otherwise, she was utterly powerless.

Cold. Powerless. Nearly naked. Surrounded by enemies. The words repeated over and over again. *Run, Bug. Run. Please run, Juniper. Find Benn—tell him not to come for me. Run. Run. Run.*

With her head tilted toward the ceiling of the cavern, all she could see was the dark walls and the soft flicker of the flames from the candles surrounding her. Another Opasteg appeared in her vision—a man this time. He did not look into her eyes as he sliced into her arm. While she didn't feel the pain, she could feel the wetness of her blood seeping into the sheet that covered her. He walked to the other side of the table and did the same to her other arm.

Drip. Drip. Drip.

No, no, no, no. The sound of her blood dropping to the floor was enough to indicate how rapidly it was leaving her body. She forced herself to be calm so that her heart rate would slow, as if she had a chance at making it off this table alive.

She was bleeding—her vision swimming again—the puddle surrounding her arm growing larger with each breath. She wanted to yell for her sister to run and hide, but words were impossible. She knew Juniper must be staying on the ground for a reason; she wouldn't move until the most opportune time.

Laying in her own blood, teetering on the line of consciousness, her eyes drifted closed.

Her eyes opened to muffled voices. The usual calm in his gaze was replaced by pure desperation—his eyes flitting between her and someone else she couldn't see. At the sight of Benn, at that face she loved, immense relief flooded her. A gift to see him one last time before the Gods swept her into oblivion.

Daemon's snarl came back to her in a rush. "*Now, what's better: harvesting the power of a time-wielder or harvesting that power from two time-wielders?*"

No, no, no, you shouldn't be here, Benn. She let out a choked whimper, though she wished it were the words she was screaming in her mind instead. She coughed and his eyes snapped to hers. She mouthed words but produced nothing intelligible. He pressed a soft finger to her mouth.

Don't you see them? The realization hit her like a freight train, fast and hard; somehow, he didn't know Opasteg was here. An illusion was at play.

"Shh, *please*, Leo. Please stay quiet. We'll find a way out of this."

They wouldn't; he might. This Benn was frantic. She forced another sound out. He *needed* to know what was happening, even if these were the last words she would ever say to him. If she could save him, she needed to try.

She coughed again, and whispered, "*Go.*"

He shook his head, cradling her face, turning to the person next to him. "Stay with me, Leo. Don't talk. You need to conserve your energy."

She squirmed, catching his attention as she whispered her final word, "*Trap.*"

His eyes met hers again, as a blast of power knocked him out of her sight.

CHAPTER 36

— BENN —

H IS HEAD MET THE CAVERN WALL with a sudden crunch, his body slumping down to the ground as stars blotted his vision. His first response was to reach for his cheekbone—well, where his cheekbone should have been—but his fingertips were met with swollen, destroyed flesh.

"*Fuck*," he said aloud to no one in particular. His cheekbone was either broken or disintegrated. He checked his extremities to see a bone from his right leg protruding through his leathers and armor.

A cough next to him caught his attention. He turned to see a mass of blonde curls, matted with blood.

Levi.

He groaned, rolling to face Benn as he said, "Found him."

Benn tried to move but was stopped by the searing pain in his leg. He sagged and inhaled; the last thing he needed right now was to pass out.

His friend's question was quiet. "You see my glasses?"

Benn used his hands to find what his eyes couldn't see; his hands met the icy ground until a wrangled bunch of metal was within his reach. The glasses were in the same condition as his cheekbone, but they were better than nothing. He leaned forward and placed them into Levi's waiting hand.

416

"Mors' hell," was his response.

Awareness that could only be attributed to lingering, unwanted eyes heightened his senses. His hand caught Levi's shoulder, hoping to lead his friend to the same realization. Opasteg soldiers surrounded them.

Dozens.

Hundreds.

Where were they before? Benn forced his groggy mind to think back. The cavern had been cleared of any enemies when they entered. Levi confirmed that there was no threat present. It wouldn't have stopped Benn from entering, but his friend had still had the wherewithal to check the surroundings anyway so they could prepare.

"A cloaking spell," Levi coughed, his eyes flickering. "How—? I'm *so* sorry. I didn't see it, Benn."

"Don't be." *Trap* was her last word to him before the impact. Her hoarse voice was like acid in his ears. She'd known. He'd known. "He brought all of his forces. We didn't stand a chance."

It was not surprising that the immortal had used Josephine as bait for the sisters—hell, even for himself. But getting ambushed by the entire Opasteg army wasn't something even the best of warriors could have trained for.

Levi motioned to Benn with a slight nod. He followed his gaze to the immortal. Daemon was talking to someone, gesturing toward Leola from across the cavern, completely unaware that Juniper was now standing. His heart pounded as he watched Juniper caress Leola's face as she lay still on the table.

When they'd found the sisters, Juniper had been so still that he'd assumed she was dead, though his focus had been occupied by Leo. Beside her had been a woman, beaten to a pulp. With one stricken glance from Levi, however, Benn had known exactly who she was.

His mother.

He'd sensed the *relief* that soaked into Levi as he discovered one of them—or perhaps—both of them to be alive. However, Benn couldn't think past the emotions that flooded him at the sight of Leo's bleeding body.

So much blood. Covering his hands. Seeping into his leathers. The only warm thing in this wretched place had been her blood.

His instinct to protect her had flared as he'd tried to remove her body from the dais, but she was stuck.

"Paralytic poison," Levi had murmured.

"Trap."

Then, the blow of power hit.

In awe, he watched as Juniper readied her twin swords. Surprise sparked in the Seer's mind. Juniper glanced around at the enemy magic-wielders and demons, as if cataloguing how many there were.

She is going for his army. Benn leaned forward as she raised her swords into the air, bringing them down hard into the ground. The cavern shook as she released her power in the form of hundreds of scythe-like blades, decapitating hundreds of soldiers on the ground level, including the ones standing closest to Benn and Levi. Their bodies thudded to the ground in unison, falling in droves onto the main level, raining down on the dais. She threw out a hand to shield herself and Leola; the falling body parts bounced off the barrier Benn couldn't see.

"By the Gods," Levi murmured, a rush of air blowing his hair back. "*Wind.*"

She raised her arms; thorns erupted from the ground, ripping through the spiraling levels of the prison, seeking out the flesh of the remaining soldiers and beasts. The horrifying, yet cathartic, wet sound of puncturing flesh echoed off the cavern walls until it was replaced with charged silence.

Benn's mouth parted as he whispered, "She leveled his troops."

Levi huffed, clutching at his ribs. "She's the key."

"You fiend." Juniper's voice was hollow as she fell forward, using her blades to keep herself upright. "You keep your filthy, ancient, parasitic hands off of her."

"You think you are in the place to give me orders, child? You may have taken out some of my soldiers, but you thought you could beat *me*?" Rage pulsed in waves off Daemon, but it was his laugh that chilled Benn's blood.

"I know I can," Juniper said, her limbs shaking as she spoke.

"Your sister sits on *my* dais, her power ready to be harvested. A legendary time-wielder lies here, next in line for the same fate. Your friends are injured—close to death. Your power reserve is under ten percent," he said, his tone incredulous as he stared at Juniper. "Oh my, you *stupid, little girl*. Some poweress was sent to kill me—by the Gods—blessed by Gaia. Oh no, I'm so scared. I'll save you for last, Juniper Runes, so you know what is coming for you. Now—" The cracking of his knuckles was the only sound. "Time for a lesson on what real power looks like."

Benn gasped in agony as Leola's body rose off the dais; her eyes were closed. She looked restful... almost like she was dreaming. For one fleeting moment, he admired her perfect face, until her body went careening through the air to the opposite side of the cavern. Despite his low power reserve, he attempted to stop time, but his power was nullified.

"*No.*" Benn's voice cracked, along with his soul.

Levi's hand blocked his eyes before he could see how she landed. A stake wedged itself through his chest as he tried to reach for her—to get closer to her—but he could not. His injuries were too severe, his low power reserve preventing his quick healing, so every movement was accompanied with excruciating pain.

Juniper's screams raged throughout the cavern. Benn was screaming, too. Distantly, Levi was yelling—*begging*—her to move.

To run.

She didn't. Through the crack in Levi's fingers, Benn watched Juniper sink to the ground.

His mind searched for Leola's—for any kind of emotion to confirm that she was still breathing.

There was only silence.

Slow as molasses, Daemon turned toward Juniper as he released another surge of power that had dust raining from the upper levels, sending her hurtling into stone. The crunch of her body was deafening. Levi curled into a ball on the cold stone ground.

Benn wished for death in this moment. There would be nothing more painful than what he'd just witnessed. Every second he spent in this life without her would be desolate and colorless. He blinked at the dais as a familiar figure came into his vision again. Daemon had never left, but now, once again, Leola's body hovered over the dais.

He's brought her back. His drooping mouth fell open.

Benn cast his magic—wishing that he might sense Leola.

Nothing.

On instinct, he reached for his hold on time, but he was still met with a gaping void.

Daemon's outstretched palms had her mangled body floating, until he laid her on the dais once more.

Although he knew it was futile, he threw out the last pulse of his emotion-bending magic to hear inside her mind... If these were her last moments, he needed to be there with her.

Horror. Shock. Panic. Desperation. But no pain, which was only slightly relieving to him. No pain meant that she was even closer to death than he'd realized. His hands trembled as he watched.

Daemon chanted an ancient spell in a language he'd never heard. Darkness swirled out of his hands.

"What is he *doing*?" Benn croaked.

Levi shuddered. "I—I can't see it."

The chanting rang through the cavern, reverberating off the walls. Leola's stagnant blood began to bubble and peel off the dais as it swirled into the air, mixing with the blackness seeping from his hands, until it traveled into Daemon's waiting grasp. The chanting stopped abruptly.

Silence swirled around them until Levi spoke three words that stole his breath: "He drained her."

He watched in frozen horror as the immortal approached the battered Leola, drew a long blade out of a sheath at his hip, and decapitated her.

Benn croaked, his arms giving out as he fell flat to the ground.

He couldn't look away, but wished he'd been able to, as Daemon held the head of his mate—the love of his life—in the air like a trophy. "Just as you did to my army, Juniper Runes... I've now done to your sister. You chose her fate. She'll never have peace; she'll reach Mors in pieces. You did this, Juniper. The Pair was a farce, meant to give hope to the weak minded. And to you, Bennjamin Wyndmere, my troops may be dead, but enjoy this last view of your mate, who you couldn't save. Just like your mother. Just like your Miravale friend. Just like... Heri."

His sobs were uncontrollable—guttural and animalistic. Bitter tears trailed sideways down his face, wetting the cavern floor below him where he rested his broken cheek. In this state of grief, time did not exist. Benn had—not that it mattered to him—no sense of how long he'd spent on the ground. It was only the sensation of Levi's white-knuckled grip on his arm that returned him to his body.

He squinted at Levi through his tears and saw that the Seer's eyes were as wide as saucers. He didn't want to, but despite his better judgment, he turned his eyes back to where her headless body lay. Fearing the gruesome image, he winced, only to find that what he was seeing now looked wholly... different.

CHAPTER 37

— LEOLA —

*G*ODS, *THAT WAS PAINFUL.* Leola listened to her self-narration, hating it immediately. She was dead already, so why did this voice need to accompany her?

She was floating, or at least she thought she was.

No, I'm not floating; I'm dead. The impact of the collision that brought her here was loud enough to split her eardrums.

Benn is here. She blinked as the events played out in front of her blurred eyes, her head still swimming from the poison and the impact of the blast. *No, no, not Benn.*

She coughed, and her ribs cursed her as she filled her lungs with what had to be the heaviest oxygen she'd ever encountered.

Daemon lifted me. I was floating. Floating above that table. She had tried to open her eyes, to grasp a glimpse of anything to orient herself, before she was met with the weightless sensation as she tumbled through the air. Dimly, she remembered the crack of her jaw against the rock and she tried to grimace in response, but she couldn't. *That's definitely broken.*

She landed behind a group of boulders, where she now lay. It was cold, numbingly so, but she didn't mind at all. The surface of the rock was icy against her broken jaw; if anything, it offered temporary relief. Something wet dribbled out of her nose and mouth. The sickening, coppery liquid was hot in her throat. Blood was overflowing from some internal damage.

Not good. Her voice sounded in her mind again. *Now would be a great time to spit, Leo.*

But she didn't. She didn't have the energy to spit. She didn't have the energy to move at all.

Not dead yet, just dying. Got it. Only the imaginary voice remained, and even that was fading.

The pain was so prevalent that her life ending seemed like a small mercy from the Gods, so she tried to murmur, "I love you, Bug. I love you, Benn."

But the words did not reach anyone.

They were trapped, blocked by her unmoving mouth—forever. She thought maybe the acceptance of that thought would kill her.

Except, it didn't.

Her body was frozen in this dark corner of the cave.

Reflecting. Eyes scanning the darkness. Playing the words she'd wished she'd been able to say.

Mom's somewhere—she's safe with Papa. We came for Josephine. I wanted to save Josephine so bad. Bug, you knew she would be here. Her slowing heart clenched. *We didn't save her, Benn. It was a trap. I don't even think he left enough of your mother to save.* She choked on the blood dribbling out of her mouth. *Benn, did you survive that hit? This is my fault; it was my decision to come back to the cavern without reinforcements. I'm so sorry, sis. It was supposed to be fast. And now, Daemon will harvest my power—maybe others—and destroy Heri. I handed his success to him on a Solstice platter. A beautiful, dusty antique platter that you'd have thrifted in a musty*

*store if we'd been in a different life. If we had not been here, in this reeking, fucking
cave. Oh Gods, Bug. I don't even know where you are—*

She coughed, swallowing the blood filling her mouth. She had no choice now
but to let some of it out. It was a sickening combination of blood and drool, but she
was too exhausted to care. She just wanted a little bit of air. Then, she would close
her eyes and rest.

One, ragged breath.

Another.

Another.

Her eyes drooped.

Familiar, tight hands gripped her face as a voice said, "It is not your time, Leo."
Lavender filled the air. Her eyes cracked open.

Oh no. She was hallucinating now; topaz eyes peered into her own. Juniper's
eyes. But they weren't Juniper's at all. They were familiar, though. Warm. Crinkled
at the edges.

She frowned, but couldn't gather the energy to speak the name. *Grandmava?*

"Gods, look at what he has done. To you. To Junebug." Grandmava's voice was
hushed, and Leola yearned to lean into her embrace and close her eyes again, but her
soft hands released her face. Leo caught herself just before her neck flopped
backwards. "You'll stay. This will have to be enough."

A painful sensation danced up her leg, seeping deep into her muscle. She moved
to close her eyes, and the hands were on her face again; this time, Leola released a
choked sob.

Grandmava kissed both of her cheeks, smoothing the mess of her hair. She
leaned into it and inhaled, the pain in her lungs finally relenting.

"*Grandmava,*" she breathed her name.

Her grandmother sighed. "Yes, child?"

"*Stay*," she rasped. Wherever they were going from here, she thought dazedly that it would be better—easier—if they went together. "Don't leave me here."

"Oh, Leo, I have one more thing to do. Thank you for getting my baby—your mama—out of here." Grandmava's strong arms surrounded her, releasing her too soon. "You have done well—*so well*—my girl. Do not worry for me. From here, I'm off to the next phase."

New tears cascaded down her cheeks.

"No, no. Don't you cry for me, Leo. Look for me in the trees. You'll always find me there." She sent Leola a familiar wink. The calming magic filled the air again and Leola watched in confusion as Grandmava's face and body transformed into something that mirrored... her. Her brows furrowed as she saw *herself* turn and rise into the air, floating straight to Daemon's hand.

The cracked blood left her mouth drier than a parched earth, but there was no new blood. She could breathe again. Feeling was returning to her limbs.

Watching Daemon toy with her body was maddening, but being outside of her body, she felt nothing. She saw everything, though, grateful for whatever block was preventing her from the pain she should be experiencing.

If Grandmava can place a magic block, maybe this is a pain block. Gods, now I have to watch myself die? No... I'm already dead. The stupid voice was back. Her eyes drifted close again.

Not today, demons. Her eyes flew open, sensing her own demise. As she had guessed, there *she* was, thirty yards away, floating above Daemon. She squinted at the strangeness. She rolled onto her stomach as her hands moved along the ground, attempting to push herself up.

She forced herself up until she was on her knees. The cold sensation cleared her mind. Far away, she saw her body move. It landed on the dais as Daemon was chanting a spell—her blood was flowing toward him. He was harvesting her magic, as the bastard had promised he would.

Leola squinted, gasping in horror as Daemon reached for a blade she hadn't noticed on his person. She needed to get there, and fast. Every attempt to stand was unsuccesful as she fought with her fatigued body. Her limbs were no longer answering her commands and each one was caked in dust and blood and grime. She was *slow*, but if she could only reach her body—maybe she could stop him. She was tempted to call out in warning, but the blood that had flowed through her mouth had left it barren, preventing her voice from projecting. Black tinted her limited vision. She was exhausted, but her grip on the boulder tightened as she hoisted herself onto her feet.

She glanced at her bare toes, now discolored from the blood loss and the cold of the cavern. She inhaled, steadying herself and looked up again.

To her horror, Daemon now held her own *head* in his hands. She wanted to close her eyes, but couldn't, so she braced herself to witness her severed head being flashed around the cavern.

Am I dead? Some kind of ghost? She stepped forward, the confusion deepening her frown. *Was Grandmava a near-death hallucination?*

A scream yanked her out of her thoughts. A scream so dire that it could only be the scream of someone who loved another for the duration of their entire lifespan. Someone who loved someone from their first breath—someone who would love that someone for their entire being.

She—not just her body, but her spirit—recoiled at the sound.

Bug.

Juniper was screaming—no, wailing—for her. Dying had never scared Leo, but the thought of dying and *listening* while her sister witnessed her death was not something she could endure.

No. No. No. She felt her knees sink back to the ground and when she landed, the confusion dissipated. The pain as her knees collided into the stone was too great.

She was *alive*, somehow.

Grandmava had done something, formed some illusion and Leola was still here, *alive* in this cavern. She needed to move. She pressed her palms into the stone, failing to rise over and over again. She was so *weak*.

So she waited, hearing Juniper's screams of terror and watching Daemon shake her severed head.

Tears flowed down her face and she thought it might be a mercy if they had drowned her—if only to save her from hearing her sister's screams any longer.

As if Juniper's wails were not enough, Benn's screams followed, shattering her already-broken soul into pieces. She, again, tried to hoist herself up as she listened to Benn mourn what they could have had.

As friends.

As lovers.

As *mates*.

His roaring scream echoed through the prison in tandem with her sister's sounds.

She wanted to tell him that she was here, that she was still alive. She was moving, but she had to focus. Finally, finally, *finally*, she rose onto shaking legs. Her fear was embodied and thrown into her face as she watched her own severed head transform into her grandmother's.

Not a hallucination. Rage propelled her forward as she limped toward the immortal. Without command, flames erupted into the cave, lighting it and heating it all at once. She felt the flames seek out Juniper, Benn, Josephine, and Levi to protect them. As for Daemon's army, their bodies were burned to a crisp.

Leola bared her teeth as she stepped through the flames, sending a white-hot stream of fire toward Daemon. "You cruel, disgusting *beast*."

Daemon sneered, dropping her grandmother's head, but she didn't stop.

This will end now.

Hands still at her sides, repeated streams of fire from all directions sought out Daemon, trying to exhaust him. He had caused so much pain and fear. She was chosen to serve up his last moments, and she aimed to deliver a fraction of what he'd inflicted on others. She would wait to kill him until the last possible moment. The fool was taunting her, but she couldn't hear his words over the raging flames that invigorated the cavern. He sent a surge of magic toward her, of which she blocked with a wall of flames.

Again, he tried to hit Leola, but she dodged it.

He tried to ambush her from behind and the magic rolled off of her shield like it was nothing.

She fired a purple stream of iceflame to his boots. It cracked up his legs, anchoring him to the ground. He roared in pain; she relished in the sound.

"Enough is enough. You meet Mors today, Daemon. I hope the Darkbeings you employ tear you limb from limb, eat you alive, revive you, and then repeat the process." Her voice was hoarse, throat still caked in old blood, but she didn't care as she lifted her palms and aimed them at the monster.

In one hand, she channeled her flame; in the other, she channeled iceflame. For the first time, she combined both of her versions of her power. The fear flickering in Daemon's eyes was the first welcome sight in the cavern as she released her power.

Her palms heated and cooled.

Her power flowed.

Molten orange and lavender eddies spiraled, combining in the air, hitting Daemon with a burst of flame that shook the cavern to its core. She poured the last amount of her power reserve into the surge of magic, sending the stream in his direction for several minutes. He collapsed into a charred mess. All that was left was ash.

Even then, she didn't stop the stream of fire. She burned for the years and memories that Grandmava had been forced to remove from her and Juniper's minds, to keep them hidden from this evil immortal. She burned for the males in Papaver that had offered them sanctuary only to be ambushed by a horde of his demons. She burned for Benn and Asha growing up motherless. She burned for Levi being raised in an orphanage along with many other children whose parents had suffered a terrible fate at Daemon's evil hands. She burned for everyone that Daemon had ever imprisoned, tortured, or killed. She burned for her mother being *robbed* of her life with her children. She burned for every prisoner she was able to free from this vile place. She burned for Grandmava, whose remains lay discarded too close to her feet.

Gentle hands came over hers as the flames extinguished, absorbing into her hands. She leaned into her sister's touch, abundant tears warming her face. She was not sure if they were her own, Juniper's, or a combination of the two. They sank to the cold ground together. She shifted Juniper's face into her own shoulder to prevent her from seeing what was left of Grandmava. She squeezed her own eyes shut, trying to avoid the same harrowing sight.

She trembled, slipping in and out of consciousness, but she was not ready to let go of her sister—whose cries she could still hear, though they'd stopped.

"We need to go. You need rest, Leo," she said, her voice sad but firm. "Can you lift her?"

Familiar arms scooped Leola up and her palms warmed, nearly exploding in defense.

"*Easy*, my flame. I'm here. Your power reserve is too low. Your job is done."

Benn. Her eyes were too heavy to open as she leaned into his touch.

She murmured, "You're alive."

His arms wrapped around her, and they were moving before he answered, "Juniper had an extra vial of Lykoso blood on her. Don't worry about me. About any of us. We're okay. Thanks to you and Juniper... and Grandmava. Rest, my love. Please."

"Bug." Her whisper was meant to be a question, but it sounded more like a slurred statement.

"I'm here, sis," Juniper said, her voice quiet, but close enough that Leola let her hand hang out of his embrace, reaching toward the sound. Worlds away, she felt the familiar grip of Juniper's palm on her own. Her vision faded as the world around them went silent.

CHAPTER 38

— BENN —

Year: Modern-Era
22 July
Poppycal, Heri

H E OPENED THE DOOR FOR ASHA, swiping the coffee out of her hand. She walked toward Leola to smooth the blankets tucked around her.

"Eat and rest. She'll wake soon." Asha gave him a cursory once-over as she continued, "You know, she's not going to want to wake up to a smelly brute. Swap out with someone. Clean yourself up—in a shower that isn't in this place. Clear your mind. You know she's safe here. Go outside for a few minutes, brother."

He groaned. "Has anyone ever told you you're bossy?"

She didn't look at him. "Of course, you don't get in my position without getting things done."

"I'll consider it." He frowned, sniffing his clothes. "And I don't smell."

She wrinkled her nose, before pulling him into a tight hug. "I need to work. I'm serious, Benn. Chat later, then."

She disappeared. Though he typically enjoyed her company, he was glad for the silence. After all, he preferred to brood in peace.

Two weeks, nine hours, and forty-eight minutes.

Two weeks that he'd been in the infirmary enduring this torture. Counting the rhythmic rise and fall of her chest, only filling his lungs when her sternum rose. He released the tension in his clenched fists, flexing his fingers. Even with the knowledge that the room was well-guarded, his mind wouldn't rest.

His feet tapped, restless on the porcelain tiles. For the third time in minutes, he brushed clammy palms across his joggers. Drumming his fingers on the side table, he glanced down at the book, missives, and lunch that Asha dropped off for him. He'd opened the missives—even the near-death of his love couldn't keep the war at bay. The food and book remained untouched.

They weren't needed when his mind was consumed by the war and the caramel-hued eyes he couldn't meet. He wanted to leave to shower or exercise or even sit outside somewhere. While there were a few people he could rely on to sit by her side, his mind couldn't fathom leaving her again. The last time he had, she'd snuck away to rescue his mother and he had watched—

He cut the thought off. With a heaving sigh, and a rub of his temples, he tried to take in even breaths, as Levi had reminded him to do.

My mind is not my own today. Shifting around, he crossed his arms over his chest before he stole one look at her; instantly, he regretted it. *Get a grip, Benn.*

He was well-known, if not praised, for his calm and controlled nature. Even for an emotion-bender, his own emotional control was a coveted skill. He forced his lungs to expand, which did nothing to calm his nerves. His thoughts could only be compared to a wrathful void, torturing him every time his eyes closed, plagued with an onslaught of images.

Images of her limp body in his arms.

Of the flood of blood pouring out of her wounds that he couldn't stop.

Of her severed head.

I've lost it. His head fell forward into his hands and he pressed his shoes into the floor, trying to ground himself. *This bond is going to kill me. Calm down, Benn. You need to—*

A quick knock on the door interrupted his thoughts. He lowered his shield before moving to open it, leaving his dagger sheathed.

"And I thought Levi was exaggerating." Juniper's eyebrows raised as she stepped around Benn. Levi leaned against the frame with his arms crossed.

"You don't have to say it; Asha already told me that I need a shower," he said with a clipped tone as his hand scrubbed down his unshaven face.

"I'm trading you places. The Seer said you could use some fresh air." He waited for her teasing response, but her eyes turned solemn. "Leo will be fine. The healers said so. We have nothing to worry about, or else I'd be here day and night, right next to you."

Benn looked toward Levi in question, needing the otherworldly confirmation that only a Seer could provide. Even though he had been told the same by the healing staff.

Numerous times, at that.

Levi answered his silent question, "She will be fine, I've seen that since we left the cavern and I see it now. *You*, on the other hand, need to leave this room."

"Any sign of when she will wake up?" Benn asked, not that he was hopeful. His fists curled as he glanced toward Leola again.

He shrugged as he answered, "You know I don't usually get a timeline."

"It has been *two* weeks." His eyes raked over her too-still body, tucked tight into the infirmary linens.

Despite himself, his mind flashed back to the condition he'd found her in. The bloody sheet that hardly covered her. The stickiness of her blood coating his hands constantly haunted his thoughts.

He blinked the memories away, his jaw ticking in response. "A change of scenery would probably be good."

Juniper was the preferred person to leave his mate with for a couple reasons, the first being she would stop at nothing to protect Leola. The second was Juniper was a proven assassin—quick on her feet and effective with magic or weapons. With one last glance at Leola and a resigned sigh, he looked at Juniper.

Before he could speak, she cut him off with a clawed hand. "I hope you aren't about to tell *me* to make sure to protect *my* sister. You'll only insult me." She moved to the bed, squeezing Leola's hand.

"Call me if *anything* changes. I won't go far."

"Oh, I know you won't, Benny. You couldn't leave my sister for long even if you wanted to." She didn't look up, now holding the book that Asha had dropped off for him. She sunk into the chair that was in the corner of Leola's room, waving them away. "I'll see you guys soon, I'm sure."

"Let's go then." Levi grabbed his hand, and they landed in an unfamiliar hotel. "Sena set up a room for us. I've been staying here. Asha and Sena have, too. Juniper's been staying at Booker's."

"Figures." Benn didn't need to reflect on the poshness of this hotel. His grandmother's proclivity to the finer things was a mystery to him. He followed Levi into their shared room, where he was grateful to find some of his clothes. "My clothes are here?"

"Asha brought them," Levi answered, kicking off his shoes.

Benn smiled at the familiarity of his own clothes, running his fingers over the fabric. "Splendid."

He reached for a clean pair of joggers and a quarter-zip, his eyes roaming lower into the hotel closet and catching on a shoebox. Inside was a pair of his favorite sneakers, and he nearly fell over with happiness. "Never thought I'd see these again."

Levi's chuckle was warm as he fell onto one of the beds behind Benn. "Tell me about it. You know how happy I am to not have to wear Ope clothes anymore? I swear, all they wear is leather—*leather*—in the Laviegata heat. I mean, be serious, no one can be comfortable in that. I think my toes have permanent nerve damage from being pinched in those boots."

Benn shot him a sideways glance and returned the laugh. "I wore Chattel rags for months."

Levi sat up, clutching his healed ribs that shook with laughter. "Okay, you win. I couldn't believe the sight of you when I saw you. I have never seen my friend so... so *unkempt*."

"Well, it's not like they have a barber for the Chattels." He gave him an incredulous look as he continued, "I had to glamour twists to keep my hair down."

Levi mirrored the look with mock-horror. "For demons' sake, I thought I taught you to glamour better than that."

Benn laughed his first real laugh in weeks, falling onto the other bed.

Levi pulled his frames off to wipe a tear that was falling down his cheek. "That Assignment was shit. Absolutely shit. And the amount of Ope twats I had to spend time with? It was enough to last a lifetime. More than that, actually."

"If it wasn't a violation of my Oath, I would go back and wipe Roswell off the face of the planet." They continued laughing until they fell into a comfortable silence.

Benn couldn't fight his curiosity as he asked, "How's Josephine?"

He could not bring himself to refer to her as his mother; the term held a relevance he wasn't ready to trust. He'd grown up reading about her success at the Academy, but he'd never associated Josephine Wyndmere with the mother that had been taken from him. Since toddlerhood, he'd been parentless. It was one of the many things that he and Levi bonded over when they'd met. He had never dreamed of meeting the legendary time-wielder. She had always been somewhat of a myth to him. Even now, he still couldn't believe that he might get the chance to. It didn't seem real; it seemed like, in a blink, the opportunity to know her would be rescinded.

"Josephine is... magnificent," the Seer said, his words holding notes of admiration. "She is just how people have described her—and so much more. She reminds me of you."

He nodded through the tightness in his throat. "I'll meet her after Leo has recovered. I'm sure my grandmother sent her back to Rosebay already anyway."

"Yes, she is in Rosebay," Levi mused. "It's not like you could warp there in mere seconds or anything."

Benn sent him an arched look and Levi put his hands up.

"I know, I know. You have *priorities* here." Levi winked at him and said, "I'm sure it's hard to trust it, Benn, that Leo and Josephine are alive. Just try."

"You know that's impossible for me." He rose from the bed to go to the en suite bathroom.

———

After a shower and fresh clothes, Benn felt like a new man. The walk back to the infirmary was short, and Levi had insisted that he get some fresh air before returning to "brood at her bedside."

Benn shivered, blowing on his hands. "How is it that Poppycal is nearly as cold as Rosebay?"

Levi scoffed, "I'm not sure. I thought this was supposed to be sunny Poppycal. This weather is shit, but the food isn't half-bad."

"Really? Maybe I'll stay a while." He smirked.

Shock had Levi's mouth gaping until they both started laughing.

"No. Never. I'm headed back to Rosebay the second Leo is up for it. I've got to show her around my city."

"Among other things," Levi quipped, hiding the grin on his face. "Speaking of the poweress..."

Juniper's name flashed on his phone and Benn put it to his ear. "Hey, Juniper."

A familiar voice had his pulse skyrocketing.

"Actually, it's Leo."

His heart somersaulted and, with barely a thought, he warped right into her room, pulling his best friend along with him.

Exhausted, honeyed eyes stopped him in his tracks. His knees gave out at the sight of her.

Smiling. Healthy. *Whole.*

Her smile softened, no doubt noting the desperation that was written across his face as she said, "Walking out on me already, Wyndmere?"

He took in his first full inhale since realizing she'd left the camp to track down Josephine.

He schooled his face into a teasing smile, crossed the room toward her and lifted her chin until their gazes met. "As if I ever could, Runes."

CHAPTER 39

— BENN —

Year: Modern-Era
2 September
Poppycal, Heri

BENN STRAIGHTENED HIS SPORT COAT for the third time, running a self-assessing gaze over his outfit. He tilted his wrist to check the time—though he already knew the time. Not because of his timepower, but because he had his first, official date with Leola tonight. The non-traditional start of their relationship—one that involved Soulsiphon demons, a vicious battle, a volcano, a divisive war, two near death experiences and even brief time spent together at a Labor Camp. Their past had not left much opportunity for romance.

Beyond the dangers, they'd taken advantage of countless treasured moments—stolen glances, playful smiles, and intimate, shared nights filled with quiet passion. Since the day he'd been sent to find her and her sister in the woods, each passing day had deepened the bond they shared. It was as if fate had drawn them together for more than just the mission. To be partners as they saved Heri.

Leola.

His girlfriend.

His lover.

His mate—officially, perhaps—after tonight.

"You are shaking in your boots, Brother-In-Law."

He whirled to see Juniper standing behind him as he snapped, "What are you *doing* in here?"

"Guess Levi's wards are faulty." She shrugged and fell back onto his neat bed.

"Impossible." The Seer strode in, dressed far more casual than Benn. "I gave the Runeses access to this room—obviously. What if they'd needed help from us?"

"Oh, I think we have more than proven we can handle ourselves, but I do appreciate the sentiment, Miravale." Juniper examined her red-tipped nails. She stood from the bed, brushing her twists over her shoulder as she said, "Leo's going to be a minute. Her hair is not cooperating. I was sent to deliver the message."

Benn let out a sigh of relief that he hoped would go unnoticed.

It didn't.

Levi's mouth fell open. "You are... you really are *shaking in your boots*." His words caught on the last of the sentence in a laugh, as he repeated Juniper's Poppycallian phrase.

He grimaced at both of them as he said, "Tonight is important. Lay off."

"Woah. Is the *ever* calm dual-power feeling *testy*?" Juniper smirked while Levi coughed in his hand to stifle a laugh.

Benn returned the smirk, but held his laughter in. "Remind me again why you're still here. Both of you." He walked to the armchair in the corner of the suite and sat. "I'm not nervous. Just ready to go."

They exchanged a look that had Benn's eyes narrowing.

"I bet you're ready for a lot of things, Benny," Juniper murmured.

Levi couldn't hold in his laugh this time.

His cheeks flooded with heat and he rolled his eyes, as if she was not precisely on the mark. "For demons' sake, Juniper."

She gasped in mock-horror. "Don't tell me you're a virgin."

"Far from it." Levi fell backwards onto the bed, laughing harder at his own admission.

He didn't prefer to go down that path with anyone, let alone his girlfriend's sister, but he did have to fight the urge to laugh along with them.

"Enough. We can draw the line there, Runes," he said, shaking his head for emphasis.

The thought of being with Leola in that way was detrimental to his self-control to say the least. And they hadn't even decided if that was actually the plan for tonight; he would wait as long as she needed or wanted to. Eternity, if that's what she wished.

There was no sense in using his imagination to torture himself.

Or was there?

"You have nothing to be nervous about." Levi cleared his throat, getting Benn's attention, and sent a reassuring smile toward him, likely sensing where his thoughts had gone. "You and Leo are *made* for each other. I have seen it all along."

"Levi's right. Tonight will be perfect, obviously. You both deserve the most exquisite night. And whether you end up as mates or end the night as *dates,* it will still be lovely." Juniper beamed at him, and he lowered his shields so he could let some of their emotions into his mind.

Excitement. Pride. Joy. These were all emotions that he loved to experience in others. Such a change from the Underground camp, the infirmary, and the war rooms he'd spent most of his time in the last six weeks. He returned the giddy smiles that Levi and Juniper were shooting his way.

Rose-tinted nervousness caressed his mind. He stood from the chair to move toward the door, scooping up the bouquet he had stashed on the way. He swiftly opened it.

Her fist was still raised and prepared to knock. The air left the room as his focus narrowed to the woman in front of him. Her face left him speechless—as usual. Today, she had left her hair down, pulling half of it back, leaving curled pieces down to frame her face, which highlighted her freckles and full lips that he adored. She wore a strapless, pearlescent dress that had a unique waistline he'd spend the next decade dreaming about. His eyes were drawn to the curves that enamored him, and he scolded himself for ogling her in the hallway, shifting his eyes back to her shimmering gaze.

She let out a laugh and gestured to the dress. "I thought it might be fitting." Her eyes rose to his as her hand smoothed the skirt of the dress. "You know, to wear white, tonight."

Mundaners wear white for their marriage day, that's right. He felt himself nod like an idiot.

He could almost hear Levi saying, *Say something, man. Anything.*

"The white is lovely. Magnificent." He cleared his throat, trying again, "Though you look exquisite in anything."

Her relief brushed against his senses, warming him from head to toe, followed by a wave of familiar confidence that he was used to sensing from her.

"Well, I can do a lot better than what you have seen in the last two months, I assure you."

"I fell for you in Chattel clothing." He slid his hand to the back of her neck, not able to resist touching her. "You'll have my full attention no matter what you wear— but, if you want to take me out at the knee, this dress is an excellent strategy."

"Good to know." She laughed again, leaning up to place a soft kiss on his lips. "Are those for me?"

He looked down at the forgotten bouquet in his hands and raised it to her waiting arms. "Yes."

He read the humor on his friends and answered it with a withering glare toward Juniper and Levi, who were peeking around the wall behind him.

She pulled him through the door with a roll of her eyes as she said, "We'll see you guys later."

"Oh, I highly doubt *that*," Juniper chirped through the closing door.

Nervousness—or maybe tension—flickered in her mind as Benn led them to the doors of the elevator.

He nudged her shoulder, even though his hand held hers. "Aren't you going to ask me where we're headed tonight?"

"Nope. I like surprises." Pink flooded the skin under her freckles as she looked up to his face. "No one has ever planned a date for me before. This is a first."

"First of many, my love," he murmured before he wrapped his arm around her shoulders and kissed her temple. "Romance is possible, even in wartime."

"With all of the leaflets and vellums coming your way these days, I'm surprised you could find the time, General Wyndmere."

"For you?" He pushed the button on the elevator and her eyebrows raised. "I'll always make time."

"*Up?*"

"To the roof." Benn kept his answer short, waiting for her curious mind to show itself.

She sucked on her cheek as she muttered, "I assume there's food up there."

He sent a censorious grimace her way. "Are you implying that I would ask you on a date tonight and *not* feed you? You'd become a beast."

"Always the quick learner." She chuckled. "I just didn't know there was a restaurant up there."

There wasn't, but there was a terrace as well as a chef commissioned for the night.

"You checked?"

She shrugged. "Potentially."

He raised a brow at her. "Doubting my date planning skills, Runes?"

The other Runes sister had spent the day transforming the mediocre terrace into a lush, garden-like space. She promised to leave room for the chef to prepare dinner but had refused to let Benn come up to see her work, so he hoped it would be as beautiful as she'd described.

The metal doors opened to an enchanting scene—hundreds of candles twinkled around the terrace, each vase surrounded by endless fresh blooms and luscious greenery. Soft string instruments played in the background—from a speaker or enchantment, Benn wasn't sure.

"It's stunning," she whispered when she stepped out of the elevator. She did a slow turn, admiring the scene before her.

"I might have called in some help."

"I know my sister's work when I see it." Her mouth parted. "But this... this is ethereal, Benn."

He took her hand and pulled her to the candle-lit table that was set up in the middle, where a spread of cheeses, varying fruits, meats, and breads awaited them.

She pointed to the appetizer. "Now, *this* is *not* Juniper."

"There's a chef nearby." He chuckled.

She scanned the area and pulled him into her arms. "No one has ever made me feel this special."

He shifted her in his arms, swaying to the music playing. "Tonight is a *special* night. Our first official date." He kissed her, using his arm to guide her into a twirl, which she matched with ease.

"He can dance, too?"

The warm smoldering of her eyes left his heart fluttering like a hummingbird. Her smile drew him in like a moth to a flame. The emotion swimming in her eyes and her mind were like a confession, whispering her affection for him to his heart whilst caressing his soul at the same movement.

He pulled her close, stopping only when he was a breath away from kissing her, smirking instead as he said, "*He* can do anything."

She laughed and Benn let her fall into a small dip.

The night sped by—their laughs and crackling energy paired with champagne and ending with a view of the sunset over the Poppycal skyline. Even the weather was pleasant, and Leola had insisted that was a rare treat in the summer.

When it was time to leave, Benn thanked the chef and placed his coat around her shoulders. The sight of her in his clothing made his stomach flutter.

Gods forsaken mating bond, he chided himself.

His self-control was laughable. He took a deep breath to calm himself, but all it did was flood his brain with her scent, which was absolutely no help at all.

"Did you enjoy dinner?" He pushed the button on the elevator and took a small, yet decisive step away from her. He kept his hand a respectful distance away from any of her curves as he placed it on the small of her back.

Relax. Straight to her door and then back to yours. Levi would commend him and Juniper would tease him for being a gentleman, but he didn't care. He couldn't possibly care when he needed to get into a cold shower as soon as possible without defiling the honor of the woman he adored, embarrassing himself in the process.

The elevator opened and he guided her inside, pushing the button for their floor.

"Dinner was perfect."

Desire flooded his senses... but it wasn't his. It was auburn-tinged and floating off of the woman whose shoulder brushed his. "Wrong floor," she remarked.

He peeked under his lashes to see her watching him. "Benn, please don't tell me that after all of that, you're not planning to share a room with me tonight?"

His mouth dried; in her hand was her key.

Confused, he added with sarcasm, "I can only guess how pleased Juniper would be to find me in the room you two are *sharing*." She and Juniper had been sharing a room here, since Booker had left for HQ.

Leola tilted her head to the side as she said, "As funny as that would be, you're off the mark. They didn't tell you?"

He shook his head.

With a smirk, and a sing-song tone that he loved to hear her use, she said, "This key is to *our* room. A gift from Sena. That is, if you'd like to join me, of course."

He nearly choked as the realization hit, followed by loving pride that his grandmother had given Leo the choice to invite him to their room. He had gone into this night with no expectations, and he loved the idea that his grandmother had left it up to his mate, just as he had.

His response was one thousand times smoother than he felt. "I'll join you anywhere, if you will have me."

She smirked, hitting the button for a different floor, as she said, "I'd *have* you in this elevator if you'd let me."

Benn clenched his fist so he wouldn't hit the STOP button and poured his power into calming his senses. He was seconds away from giving into his hormone-induced instincts, and her desire filling his mind was going to drive him to madness.

He leveled a stare at her that was full of heat, saying, "We'll save the elevator for the next round."

Her eyes returned the heat and he planted his feet to keep his distance.

Thirty of the longest seconds of his life passed as the elevator traveled to their floor. He didn't care what floor they ended up on—as long as it meant they would meet a door that *locked*. And fast, especially before he did take her up on the elevator idea. The last thing he needed was camera footage of them—

The door dinged open, and he held a hand out, signaling for her to step through first; she tugged him through the elevator with strength that had him stumbling.

Halfway down the hallway, she released his hand, kicked off her heels, warped ten yards away from him, and turned toward him as she taunted, "Think you can catch me, Wyndmere?"

A flicker of bravery flashed into her mind followed by mischievousness. A smirk danced across her face that made him slow as he leaned down to pick up her discarded shoes.

With a graceful tug, her dress was unzipped and floating down to the floor, leaving only his jacket covering her. His mouth fell agape, every thought floating out of his mind as he watched her. He warped to her with every intention of scooping into his arms, but when he landed, she was over the threshold, holding it open for him while she laughed.

He stepped through the warded door, noting for one second that those wards were his friend's creation, soundproofing it and protecting them from threats, to which he was grateful for. One less thing for him to consider.

Her mouth was on his instantly. He caught her in his arms and moved until they reached a bed covered in rose petals. Leola landed on the bed and a blush danced over her cheeks.

Embarrassment flooded her mind.

He tilted a curious brow at her as he asked, "You just told me you would have me in an elevator and stripped to nothing in the hallway, but the rose petals are making you feel... embarrassed?"

She laughed and pulled his mouth to meet hers as she said, "I was serious about the elevator. You owe me."

Desire flooded her mind until he could no longer think straight. They had been tiptoeing around their connection for the sake of the war and what remained of his self-control was threadbare.

He pulled his mouth from hers and kept his voice at a whisper. "Are you sure you're ready for this... tonight? I would wait for you, for eternity, Leo."

— LEOLA —

If there was even a chance that her heart did not belong fully to Benn, those words alone would have ensured it did. Her core heated and she slipped out of his jacket, watching in gratification as his jaw slackened at the sight of her.

She willed her palms to cool as she helped him undress, but the anticipation and excitement nearly made that feat impossible. Heat radiated off of her palms, but it was an afterthought for her. Judging by the hungry look in his eyes, he wasn't thinking of her fire-bearing palms either.

She'd expected to be pleased when they eventually took this step. But being with Benn in this way was… well, it was mind blowing. He was generous and moved with a confidence and gracefulness that she'd never experienced before. As he brought her to repeated moments of ecstasy, she wondered if it was their love for each other deepening the connection or the fact that they were mated by the Gods—chosen by the Gods to belong to one another.

Every movement was better than the one prior and she swore that she could feel their mating connection binding. The bond was a magnet, looping their souls together in an unbreakable chain.

Twice, she almost lost control of her flames as they rode the throws of passion together. Each time, he smirked at her, knowing he caused her near loss of control, before losing himself in her body.

She stroked his back as they lay tangled together. "I hope I didn't burn you."

"If you had, it would have been worth it." He smirked, kissing her hair.

"Is it normally like this? For mates?" She stared at the ceiling and felt her cheeks heat.

His voice held a smile. "Mind blowing chemistry? No, Leo, I think you got lucky."

She landed a playful smack on his arm, and he rolled her body so that her legs caged his.

He kissed her, pulling back to say, "I'm not sure I'll get used to this. Having you—here—like this."

She rolled her hips. "With all of this mind-blowing chemistry, you mean?" She pushed his earlier words back at him with a smile.

"No. Here in my arms. Safe. Alive. The memories of that day in the cavern..." His eyes searched her face as though he was trying to memorize it. "They still haunt me."

They haunted her, too. The smells, the sights, the terror. All of it. Every second—every moment of every day—the cavern haunted her. As much as she fought it, she was still there, hearing Juniper and Benn scream for her as she lay in the frigid darkness.

She did not have the words to show she was okay, so she kissed him instead. The kiss turned heated and soon, they were going for another round. He groaned as she placed hungry kisses down his neck.

A crisp knock sounded on the door.

"No. Not now," he said as his arms tightened on her body. She was content to ignore whoever was on the other side, so she went back to kissing him, daring to venture lower.

Asha's voice sounded through the closed door with a twinge of embarrassment. "I hate to do this to new mates, but your presence is requested at Headquarters."

His hands stilled, and Leola chuckled at the frustration in his clenched jaw.

She rose from Benn and tossed him a robe, while sliding into her own. She opened the door to Asha and Leader Wyndmere, regretting that she didn't check the peephole first.

"Happy Mating! Welcome to the family!" Asha's hug around her was iron tight.

Distantly, Leo wondered if she'd ever felt this exposed or embarrassed in her entire life.

"You even smell like Bennjamin!"

Nope, this was the most exposed and embarrassed she had *ever* felt. She might as well melt into a puddle right here on this hotel floor.

Demons, everyone knows. How does she already know? She went stiff as a board in the embrace. Her smile was small as her eyes traveled to Leader Wyndmere.

"*Impeccable timing.*" His answer was calm, but it was in *her* mind. "*What are the odds of them noticing a time freeze?*"

She let go of Asha and whirled to her mate, whose shock matched hers.

"*Was that—? How?*" Her eyes were wide.

He jumped before steeling himself. "*The mating bond. My grandmother said we'd be able to communicate this way. It's—unsettling. New, I mean.*"

"*I don't hate it.*" She sent a knowing smirk toward him. "*It is kind of sneaky. We could totally gossip in here.*"

His laughter tickled her spine. "*Should I tell them to piss off so we can continue where we left off?*"

She bit her lip, considering the idea as her eyes heated.

"*Careful, Runes, keep looking at me with those eyes and I'll stop time for the next hour.*"

<hr />

— BENN —

His grandmother's throat cleared, effectively tearing them out of their mental conversation. Her tone was matter-of-fact as she said, "Opasteg's forces are rebuilding."

He tensed, saying aloud, "Even with the numbers they lost in the cavern?"

She nodded. "Even with the blow delivered by Ms. Runes, yes. Spies are reporting they've elected a new leader—someone who presumably will lead the regime."

"Someone we know?" His tone was emotionless, though his mind was raging.

Leader Wyndmere's eyes flickered in Leola's direction; he despised the look, because, with his grandmother's shields raised, he couldn't read it. "Somewhat. Heri needs us. Time to go to work." She eyed both of them. "Your things are packed.

Juniper, Levi, and Josephine are already at Headquarters. We gave you as much time as we could—"

"*I highly doubt that,*" Benn said to only Leola.

She stifled a giggle as he reached around her body to grab the duffel bag Asha held out.

"I expect your arrival in the next hour. Asha packed proper attire for you both. Bennjamin, if you wouldn't mind bringing your mate along once you're ready to go? Show her the way. Oh, and Happy Mating. We're thrilled to have another poweress in the family." With a curt nod, the women were gone.

Leola let the door close behind her and shivered. "Sena is all business tonight."

He answered the words with a scowl, unzipping the bag. "Leader Wyndmere in all of her glory."

The bag held two Underground green uniforms and sneakers that matched.

She held up one of the sneakers and asked, "Are these custom?"

"There's a branding team at Headquarters," he said in disbelief that he was about to land at the main site of the Underground. He'd started the year as a Conscript that was heading to Laviegata with hardly any security clearance. Now, having completed Assignment and survived battle, he was a General. Tonight, he and his *mate* would land at HQ.

She buttoned her canvas polo, before magicking her hair into a bun. Her question was soft and her mind read as quiet. Comfortable. Safe. Enamored. "So, where are we going?"

He pulled out the leaflet that listed the coordinates of the location and their official Report Summon. He tossed it in the fireplace. He should have known this was where headquarters was located. They were fully dressed now, so he folded their discarded clothes into the duffel and slung it over his shoulder. The question was still in her eyes as she watched him with laser-focus.

"Rosebay," he said. He kissed her fully, cherishing their last moment of privacy together before taking her hand in his, warping them right to the entrance of the buzzing Underground Headquarters. "Ready, my flame?"

Her tone was calm, but the dazed look in her eyes said otherwise. "Let's go to work, mate."

— END OF BOOK ONE —

LOOK FOR THE NEXT NOVEL IN THE SCORCHED DIVIDE SERIES
FLIP TO THE BACK FOR AN EXCLUSIVE SNEAK PEEK
HITTING THE SHELVES IN EARLY 2026

ACKNOWLEDGMENTS

To my husband: thank you for helping research, listening to me rant about the ideas surrounding this series for hours, throwing in vocabulary suggestions, reading scenes and chapters to tell me if they made sense, and cheering me on when my Imposter Syndrome tried to hold me back. There's not enough words for how much joy you bring me. <3 I love you forever and ever.

To my sister: thank you for organizing the pages and printing all 5 of my drafts. You are the ultimate blueprint for what a 5-star sister should be. Hehe.

To my mom, thank you for supporting my bookworm habits from the minute I could read. Thank you for reading the advanced copy I sent. Thank you for hyping me up at every opportunity and in every journey life brings.

To my mother-in-law, thank you for reading the advanced copy early, being excited for me each step of the way, and telling all your friends about it!

To my family and friends who supported me from every moment: from when this was just an idea I was terrified to talk about all the way until we hit publication date... THANK YOU! I couldn't be more blessed to have the best community of people in my corner. If I named each one of you, we'd need one hundred more pages.

To my cover designer, thank you for making all of my dreams come true. I gave you the roughest idea and you delivered the most beautiful cover, making my dreams and characters come to life!

To Sara, my editor, thank you for building up my confidence and helping me improve my writing. You helped me perfect my manuscript and never made me feel like you were taking my voice out of the writing.

To Tranisse, my proofreader, thank you so much for the work you did, time you spent, and feedback you gave. I am so appreciative.

To my formatter, I mean... look at this thing! You killed it. Thank you.

To the beta readers, thank you for the time spent and devotion to my unedited novel. I cried (happy tears) reading the feedback I received from each of you.

To the ARC readers, you know how much I love you all. Thank you for hyping me up and loving this story. Thank you thank you thank you and please be on my ARC team forever and ever!!

To the readers, THANK YOU for reading my debut. Keep your eye out for my next project via my newsletter and my socials! Please consider leaving me a review on Goodreads, Fable, Amazon, Barnes and Noble, etc. I would love to hear your thoughts on my work!

Endless thank yous to you **ALL** for being here,
TC Jenson

MEET TC JENSON

TC Jenson crafts tales that are fast-paced and immersive with themes of magic-wielding, rebellions, secret-societies, and romance. She brings richly-built worlds to life through complex characters who are just like you... but living in a Dystopian Fantasy world.

When she's not exploring a thrift store or traveling, you'll find her diving into tales of fantasy, romance, true crime, or historical fiction. Whatever it is, she's either within an arm's reach of a book, glued to her Kindle, or browsing a local bookstore.

As a lifelong bookworm turned author, she's thrilled to release her debut title, Echoes of Hollow and Ember, in 2025. EHAE follows two sisters who hold the key to ending the decades-long war that has plagued their people and divided their world... if they can survive the evil forces standing between them and success.

Visit her at www.tcjenson.com or connect with her on socials.

Scan to leave a review!

CHAPTER 1

— JUNIPER —

Rosebay, Heri
Modern-Era
Winter

"YOU DON'T NEED TO FOLLOW MY every step, Miravale," Juniper quipped, already over this conversation. She sent him a pointed look for emphasis as she quickened her stride.

"Ah, but I do, Earthpoweress," Levi chided, quickening his steps to match hers. "I'll leave you alone when you take my advice."

Being left alone was not what she wanted. Not really.

"And since when do you think I'm going to listen to a word you say?" she sent back, dodging a Conscript who shoved past her.

"You're not," he said, nodding his head as someone addressed him. Juniper didn't care to look at who it was. The hallway was too crowded already and she was running behind. "But I was hoping—"

A person ran into him with force; Levi grunted in response.

The Conscript bent down to pick up their scattered reports, mumbling, "Sorry, General Miravale."

"Ooh, he's a General now," Juniper commented, flickering her fingers.

With a twist of her wrist, she used a magic bind to gather the papers, suspending them into the air. Then, using the spell Levi had taught her, she returned them to their previous organized state, before sending them back into the arms of the Conscript.

"Thank you, Miss Runes." The kid watched her, seeming no older than she, though he definitely was, given his status as a Conscript.

She nodded at him. He took her in, the same way everyone did here, with an awe-struck look that made her squirm. He knew her, but she didn't know him.

"No problem," she said.

"At ease. Carry on, Conscript." Levi stepped between them, cutting off her view of the kid.

Juniper turned on her heel and started walking again, hoping to put as much space between her and the topic she'd been avoiding at all costs.

Levi caught up to her in seconds. "You've been practicing."

"Perfecting," she corrected with a slight smile.

He scoffed. "Work can always be done, Runes. But, I am impressed."

"Well thank the Gods. That's why I helped the poor guy... to impress you, Seer." Her sarcasm was thick as the honey in her voice.

"It was a compliment. Seeing as that didn't thaw you out—" He sighed, stopping her with a gentle tug on her arm. "I'll be more direct. Since you've shut down every method I've suggested so far, I was hoping you would consider talking to *me* about them."

"Consider this." She shook out of his grasp and flipped him off. "Not happening."

"Nice." He leveled a glare at her. "You know we're friends, right? Have you considered that maybe I want to help you?"

"Of course I have," she said. "I've also *considered* that you're Benn's spy and he's a direct line to my sister."

She hadn't told Leo. It was the first time in her entire existence that she'd kept something from her sister. Not out of spite... more out of dread. Leo had enough to worry about and enough healing to do herself. Leave it to the damn Seer to figure out her secret. Or, was it more of a nuisance than a secret? She couldn't be sure.

His jaw ticked as he pressed, "If you don't talk to someone, they'll be your ruin. Trust me... I can—"

"See it?" she cut him off with a wry smile and a wave of her hand. "I know. Stop invading my privacy and quit watching me. Ever heard of boundaries, Miravale?"

"Juniper." He tugged her into a private hallway. He blinked as his eyes flashed emerald. "Friends help each other. That's what we do. I know you haven't told—"

"Don't." She stopped him, pulling her braids over her shoulder. "If you're my friend, you'll stop watching me. Let me sort it out. I can seek help from the therapists here if needed."

He looked bored, though she knew he was laser focused. On her. Seemed to be the theme these days.

"Don't lie to me," he said, straightening his leathers. "There's no way in the Ancestral hells that you're going to do that. Though I would encourage it if you were truly considering it, which you're not."

"Ugh. Stay out of my head, Miravale."

"You know it doesn't work like that, Runes." The look of annoyance that typically ruled his features returned, masking the hint of worry she'd seen there. "You got out. Daemon is defeated. And now, we work. You succeeded. We're actively at war. Every time we step out of these wards, we're at risk of being attacked. Don't let the past—*him*—steal these moments from you. In the moments of peace we do get, *you* deserve to rest. To heal. Just like everyone else does. Talk to me."

Her throat tightened at the emotion in his eyes, but the thought was interrupted by her beeping watch. "Great, now you've made me late."

He reached for her hand, gripping it in his, and warped. The feeling of the wind whipping across her face caught her by surprise. She jumped slightly and sent him a look of question.

"You think Sena's wards are powerful enough to restrict me?" He chuckled, shoving his hands into his pockets. "Maybe you haven't spent enough time with me yet."

He walked to his seat, leaving her with her mouth agape. No one could warp in HQ, not even Leader Sena Wyndmere.

He glanced up at the analog clock mounted to the wall, before saying, "Oh look, we're early. Keep that trick to yourself, will you? Sena probably knows I can do it... but, I'd hate to have to reexamine the wards again. Took me all of a day to untangle them."

Juniper snapped her jaw shut. Now, she was keeping two secrets from Leo.

www.ingramcontent.com/pod-product-compliance
Lightning Source LLC
Chambersburg PA
CBHW020811020726
47495CB00008B/2681